Twice Dead

A Caper

William Jordan

To order additional copies of this book, contact:
Xlibris Corporation
1-888-795-4274
www.Xlibris.com
Orders@Xlibris.com
48265

Contents

For

Meg Hellyer

and

all my classmates, past and present,
in the creative writing class
of the
Women's University Club, Seattle, Washington

1

Trouble in the Locker Room

1948

Trouble has a way of being patient like the trapdoor spider. It doesn't always stalk its prey. It lies in wait knowing that both the unsuspecting and the wary are equal opportunities. Everyone is vulnerable, but none more so than Sydney and Toby. As susceptible as they were to trouble, miraculous good fortune kept them from stumbling through the spider's door. Until now.

At twilight on a muggy August evening, Toby trudged up to the clubhouse from the eighteenth green. "Sydney, is that you on the porch?"

"Of course it is, Toby. You, if anyone, ought to know," he snapped. Customarily after a light supper in the Brookside Country Club dining room, Sydney would park himself in a wicker rocking chair on the broad veranda overlooking the finishing holes, waiting for the cool evening air. "Little late for you, isn't it? Practicing up for a match this week? If you're on your game, I pity your opponent."

"Decent of you to say so, Sydney. I'll take that as a compliment." Looking to visit, he dropped his golf bag at the foot of the stairs leading up to the veranda. Toby, in his seventies, stopped every couple of steps to catch his breath, often to look over his shoulder toward the course and mutter one of his profound thoughts. "You know, Sydney, this club is going to hell in a hand basket, and you don't look that far behind. Have you seen yourself lately? I've never seen you look so peaked. I think I'm a couple of years older than you, and I don't look half your age."

"At least I agree with you the club's been going to hell, especially since they put in those two tennis courts. Next thing you know, it'll be a goddamned swimming pool." His face grimaced with the thought of such a possibility. Eager to chat, he gestured for Toby to pull up a chair. "By the way, I'm not going to hell just yet. But I must tell you, Toby, I'm not feeling all that well. My blood isn't going anywhere. It just seems to sit around in quiet pools, if you take my meaning. Perhaps I need a good tonic."

Toby leaned back in his chair and looked sympathetically at his old friend. "Sorry if I came down on you a little hard." He winked and produced a credible grin. "Maybe if you rock that chair you're sitting in, you'll get your blood flowing again."

"You don't seem to understand, Toby. You're a friend as good as any man could have. But I can't tell if I'm in the early or final stages of senility."

"Now that's a lot of horse pucky, Sydney! You're as sharp as you ever were. I recall some bigwig doctor saying, 'If you think you're losing your mind, you haven't.' Anyway, it was something like that—read it myself—good enough to hang your hat on. Don't think for a minute you'll garner one drop of sympathy from me. Somehow, Sydney, you've decided to let yourself turn into an old fart like damn near everyone else around here. What you need is a change of pace, an adventure to get your juices flowing again. Then you'll be right as rain!"

Sydney rocked his chair. "Toby, you might be right, but I don't think I'm up to it any more. Haven't the moxie for it. Spent a good deal of my life enjoying the kind of peace and quiet I have at Brookside. Since I founded this place in '21, I've been quite content to hang up my traveling shoes."

"On reflection, I guess that goes for me too." Toby pulled his chair closer. "Remember when I joined in '23? Jones won the Open that year." Looking out over the course, he continued to reminisce. "The clubhouse was just bubbling out of the ground—you were the president, of course. Pals before then and chums ever since."

"Toby, I'm beginning to worry about the club. You must. There's a whole new crowd coming in here since the war. Socialists, mostly. Quite disturbing, and I'm uncomfortable about some of the changes I've seen around here, especially since we're no longer on the board. The old boys are dropping like flies. And women, did you ever see so many women?"

Imitating his idol Churchill, Sydney took out a cigar and waved it about like a tutorial pointer. "Brookside used to be a comfortable little sanctuary for the likes of us, Toby. But I've got this gnawing feeling the future of Brookside could be in jeopardy. The only thing you can be certain of these days is that Dewey's going to be in the White House."

Toby rocked forward, inwardly disturbed by these observations. "Sydney, just light that cigar you're fumbling with and stop all this palaver."

Members had long since finished their afternoon rounds and left the club. A golf shop attendant picked up Toby's bag and dashed back to the club storeroom with it. The pro shop locked up at six, and Alex, the locker room attendant, had already tidied up and left for the night. After Sydney's departure from the dining room, it also had closed down. Only these two old comrades were left on the veranda to contemplate tomorrow's activities and see themselves home.

Sydney leaned forward in his rocker, stood up and announced with authority, "Toby, it's getting late, my watch makes it thirty-two minutes past seven. I'm going back to the locker room and squeeze the sponge."

Toby laughed. "I wish you'd stop that idiotic sailor slang. Good idea though. I'll go with you since I have to lock the place up anyway. You know Sandy Cummings, the new club manager?"

"Yes, of course I do. He's young but still a nice-enough chap. Good manners, but sometimes he tends to get a little too familiar."

"Right, well he gave me the clubhouse keys and asked me to check things out, douse the lights, and close up shop for him. Sandy wanted to get home early tonight—didn't want to wait up for us to leave." He looked for Sydney's implicit approval. "You don't mind if we take a stroll around the outside of the club before we go to the locker room?"

"Not at all, Toby. I can certainly hold back my reservoir as long as you can hold yours." He was not impressed with Toby's newfound responsibility, but in deference to an old friend he accepted it grudgingly.

Slowly winding their way around and through the grounds of the club, they completed their journey and entered the club through the locker room door. Passing by rows of wood lockers, the pair of old-timers breathed in the familiar scents of drying towels, socks, open shoes, and forgotten underwear left in the shower room. From the dimly lit locker room they marched lockstep into the brightly lit toilet room with its new fluorescent lighting. Instantly, it turned their normally pale complexions into a putrid shade of yellow. Shoulder to shoulder, Sydney and Toby stood in front of the urinal staring politely at the ceiling while they relieved themselves.

Finishing first, Sydney turned away and said, "I hate to bring this to your attention, Toby, but it seems we're not alone in here."

"Nonsense, I didn't see or hear anyone!"

"Just look down the toilet room aisle and observe the second stall from the end, and tell me what you see."

Toby bent from the waist to peer below the compartment wall doors. "You're quite right. There's a pile of trousers on top of a pair of golf shoes! Obviously, there's a fellow in there taking a dump. We'll have to put a rush on him." Leaning back to zip up his pants he said, "Well, don't just stand around, Sydney, go knock on the door and tell him his time's up."

Sydney nodded and reluctantly walked down the short aisle and rapped politely on the slightly ajar door. There was no reply or response. A cold clammy feeling came over him. Something was amiss. With some trepidation he bucked up his courage and pushed the door open. Gasping, he stumbled back against the wall. His eyes bulged for a moment, and his chin dropped to the top of his meticulously tied bow tie. His cigar tumbled to the floor. He pulled himself together and straightened his attire with a downward tug on his vest. "Toby, we're not going to be locking up right away. You know Jeffrey Bartholomew, don't you?" he said picking up his cigar. "I think it's him in the stall, and I believe he could be dead!"

Exasperated that his plan to attend the movies that night might have to be postponed, Toby shouted, "Of course I know him. Don't just think, man—find out!"

"Find out if it's him—or find out if he's dead?" Sydney snapped back, annoyed with his friend's biting remark. "You could give me a hand over here."

"All right, all right, no need to panic. You'd better not be having me on! Hang tight, I'll have a look-see!"

Seated on the stool, the motionless body slumped forward, the head evenly spaced between the knees, the right arm draped over the toilet paper dispenser while the other hung limply with the fingers dangling only few inches from the floor. Next to the hand laid an open book of matches and the sports section of yesterday's *New York Daily News*.

"Yes, that's Jeffrey all right," Toby said staring down at the floor. "I'd recognize those god-awful trousers anywhere." He poked and jabbed his fingers into the torso several times. "No sign of life here. I'm no doctor, but I'd say poor Jeffrey has crossed the bar."

Sydney crouched over the body and grabbed both ears to raise the head. As he suspected, it was the ashen expressionless face of Jeffrey.

"There's no sign of breathing. He's quite limp and colder than a woman left at the altar."

"So what do you think we ought to do? We've got to inform the authorities."

"You're such a pragmatist, Toby. Can't you see, there are a lot of other problems we have to deal with? We just can't leave him on the toilet. Think of the club's reputation. Consider this. There's bound to be some sort of inquiry. All the sordid details will hit the papers, and I just don't mean the local rag. Imagine the ghastly headlines."

"You're quite right, old friend. We need to put the good of the club first. After all there doesn't appear to be any foul play. Damn shame really. Too bad it had to happen on our watch. Probably a stroke or heart attack, wouldn't you say?"

"Regardless of how he died, Toby, if Jeffrey's found here, you and I will be right in the middle of this mess." He stepped back to take in the full impact of the scene. "Damn! So much for you being a good sport to lock up tonight. On the other hand, it's a good thing we discovered him and not one of the staff. No telling what they'd have done under the circumstances."

"Just a bit of odd luck we're involved at all," said Toby. "Now, for the good of the club, 'Mr. Brains,' what in God's name do you think we should do?"

Sydney straightened himself up. "I think we should clean him up, get him dressed and lay him out on the course."

Toby cleared his throat and raised his voice in protest. "The devil you say!"

"Really, Toby, regardless of how much you may have disliked Jeffrey, a member of this club still deserves to die with his shoes on and trousers up. I remember hearing from Jeffrey's very own lips on a number of occasions, that if he had his choice of where to die, he would like to perish on the course. Leaving him out on a fairway is the least we can do for him. To have him found like this is so undignified, don't you know." Pausing to relight his cigar he added, "Consider his wife's feelings too. Having him found like this."

"That old trout!" Recalling gossip from another old-timer, he sputtered, "She wouldn't care where he died as long as he did. Married him for his money I'm told. Harriet's already planted two other husbands, and I have reason to believe she did them in. Both with a stomach condition, would you believe!"

"Well then, if not for Brookside or his wife Harriet, why don't we just do it for our own sake? Putting Jeffrey out on the course puts us out of the picture. We'll just clean things up and call the police. Anonymously of course."

"Now that sounds more like it. Seems like a simple-enough plan to me. Lots of merit actually. This obviously isn't a crime scene, so we wouldn't be interfering with the law." Toby fumbled for his pipe and said, "Be a good fellow and hand me those matches on the floor."

"Here you are, Toby," handing up the matchbook. "We're agreed then. Now my suggestion is that one of us tidies up Jeffrey, and the other tidies up the stall. That way when Alex comes in the morning, he won't suspect that Jeffrey or anyone else has been in here tonight." He rubbed his chin, "most importantly, the two of us." Raising his right hand toward Toby and appearing as if he were about to administer an oath, he said, "Just to be fair about this, I'll flip a coin for who gets what. Heads you clean up the stall, tails you clean up, Jeffrey." Sydney dropped the coin on the tile floor. It rolled to a stop against the end wall of the toilet room. Toby got Jeffrey.

*   *   *

Even working together, it was difficult for the pair to extricate Jeffrey from the toilet stall. Jeffrey was as limp as an octopus out of water and just as unmanageable, especially with his trousers down and his suspenders snagged over the toilet seat. Rivulets of sweat flowed across their furrowed brows, down their noses, and over puffing pink cheeks. Wheezing and grunting, they mumbled to each other that perhaps their plan to relocate Jeffrey was overly ambitious. However, they realized that they had progressed too far to either leave him stretched out on the floor or to put him back on the toilet seat in the stall.

For Toby to complete his duties, he had to enlist Sydney's help to roll Jeffrey over onto his chest. Unable to budge him on the slick tile floor, they decided that they needed some tools to deal with Jeffrey's two-hundred-pound-plus frame. After a short discussion, each went back to the locker room to retrieve a golf club. Returning, Toby put the grip handle of his 3-iron under Jeffrey's back and pried up with it. Sydney, on the opposite side wedged the head of his 8-iron under Jeffrey's arm and pulled on it like a rake. To their surprise and delight, it proved quite successful, and they congratulated each other on their perseverance and ingenuity.

By the time Jeffrey was scrubbed up and the toilet stall wiped down, the shower room towel basket overflowed. Sydney finished his task first and exclaimed, "On to the next operation, Toby! I've an idea how to get the old boy out to the course."

"You don't say. This better be good," said Toby glancing up from where he knelt on the floor. Observing Sydney flitting about, he raised his voice. "Your blood seems to be flowing all right now!"

Without replying, Sydney stepped over Jeffrey, scooted past Toby and made his way from the toilet room to the club's service entrance where several handcarts were kept to manage deliveries. Returning with a big flat bed two-wheeler he exclaimed, "We're on our way now, Toby." He panted heavily as he chocked the wheels and tilted the open end of the cart down toward Jeffrey's head. "Let's just roll him over one more time and slide him up on the bed. Come on, Toby, put your shoulder to it."

After considerable tugging, Jeffrey lay prone on the cart, nicely positioned between the two wheels and equally spaced from each end. Sydney busily straightened out Jeffrey's ruffled clothing, and out of a sense of decency and respect for the dead, Toby got his Brookside Club windbreaker from the locker room and placed it over Jeffrey's gray expressionless face.

"Before we go anywhere, Sydney, have you given any thought to exactly where we're going to put him? I certainly haven't. And if you can't tell, I'm getting pretty weary of this exercise."

"Be a little patient, I'll tell you as we go. I'll pull, you push." Sydney ordered. "Oh, and make sure he doesn't rock off the cart when we go down steps. First of all, we're going out of here the back way through the service entrance." He turned off the back porch light and peered outside to see if anyone was still around. "All clear." he whispered. "Here we go Toby, we're not taking him far from here. Just up on the seventeenth dogleg."

"Damn it, Sydney, isn't the sixteenth fairway closer? Seventeen is all uphill from here!"

"Yes, but Jeffrey also hoped he wouldn't die on the same hole that some other member had. Must have been an ego thing with him. Doc Featherstone dropped dead on the sixteenth green three years ago. Remember? So that's out. Besides Jeffrey and Doc never really got along."

"You're so damned sensitive about everything. It's going to land us in trouble one of these days."

Sydney did not reply. The sun had set, and dew was forming on the fairways as the evening temperature dropped. The wheels of Jeffrey's funereal cart sank into the soft fairways leaving a trail etched in the grass. As the two pallbearers struggled and weaved their way up the steep seventeenth fairway, a rising moon revealed the impressions made by their footprints and heavily laden cart.

"You know, Sydney, you're putting me and yourself to a lot of trouble for a fellow that rubbed a lot of the members the wrong way—including me."

"Oh, come to it, Toby. Think of the consequences to the club, and show the flag! Look up ahead. We're already at the turn of the dogleg." They stopped to rest for a moment. "Come to think of it, this was one of Jeffrey's favorite spots on the course. What say we lay him out here?"

Toby, between puffs replied, "Perfect!" Exhausted, he thought any place would be suitable. Looking around, he said, "You know, I think we've stumbled on the ideal spot for Jeffrey. He can be seen from the clubhouse bad light and all. More importantly, come to think of it, he can be seen from the road hole. I figure when we call the police, we can say we saw someone stretched out on the course and stopped at the clubhouse to report it."

"Good thinking, Toby! I believe you're getting into the spirit of this little misadventure. Then we're agreed. Now, when we drop him here in the fairway, let's turn his head toward the pond. It was his favorite view of the course. Talked about how beautiful it was on several occasions when we played seventeen." The lads positioned themselves on either side of the cart, and together they slowly tipped the open end. Like a burial at sea, Jeffrey slipped out of the cart feet first onto the waiting turf.

Sydney looked over at Toby. "Shouldn't we say a few words? I think we have time before the light goes really bad."

"All right, but let's make it short. And try not to get maudlin!"

The two stood erect facing the pond next to the crumpled body of Jeffrey. "Lord," Sydney began doffing his hat, "take Jeffrey Bartholomew, your humble servant, into your loving arms, we pray. Place him where the fairways are even greener than the one he now lies upon—give him the solace of—"

"Sorry to interrupt, but haven't we forgotten something? Don't we have to show what Jeffrey's been doing out here by himself? Besides staring at the pond that is."

"Amen, Toby! And amen to you too, Jeffrey. How stupid of me. We should have brought his clubs out here with him."

Almost twenty minutes passed before they arrived back at Jeffrey's resting place. Toby carefully placed the golf bag next to Jeffrey's body that was folded up in a semifetal position. He turned the open end of the bag to face the seventeenth green. Meanwhile, Sydney took a ball from the side pocket of the bag and rolled it a few feet up the fairway.

"Sydney, I think we should take a club from his bag and lay it alongside Jeffrey as if he were about to use it. From here he'd have an open shot to the green. I'd say it's a 4-iron. What do you think?"

"On reflection, I'd take a 5, but knowing Jeffrey's handicap I'd say a 3-iron would be more appropriate for him. He always was a bit too optimistic. Never took enough club to reach a green."

"Sydney, just lay down a 4-iron and be done with it! Let's make for the club and call the police before this whole damned thing gets out of hand."

Tired, but quite satisfied with their accomplishment, they walked head down, retracing their footsteps back to the clubhouse. There are only four telephones at Brookside—the pro shop, the men's locker room, the roof top turret, and the front desk, which they opted to use. "All right, Sydney, I did most of the dirty work in the locker room. You can call the police. Use a handkerchief to disguise your voice. You might even try a foreign accent to throw the cops off."

"Really, if you're so damned experienced at this sort of subterfuge, I think you should do it!"

"All right I will! No sense arguing about it at a time like this. Give me your handkerchief. Mine's pressed." Toby reached over the reception counter, slid the phone toward him, and dialed the local operator.

When asked what number he was calling, Toby lowered his voice an octave and said, "Operator, get me the poll-eece."

"Certainly, sir," came a polite reply. "I'll direct you to the town police right away, unless you require the state police." Toby grunted that the local police would do.

"This is Chief Bebee, what's the problem?"

"Bebce, is it? My little missus. and I were driving past a golf course when we noticed a man lying out there on the grass. It seemed an odd time and place for someone taking a nap. He wasn't moving. Anyway, we thought you poll-eece people ought to have a look-see."

Chief Bebee dropped both feet off his desk and cut in. "Sir, could you please give me your name and where you're calling from?" "I'm calling from—let me see—the Brookside Country Club, or so it says on the front door. Strange, the place is open, but there's no one around here, 'cept us of course."

Damn, Bebee said to himself, for some reason this telephone connection stinks. "I'd like you to wait there until I arrive." He plunged his cigarette into an ashtray and fumbled for his car keys. "You can take me where you saw this person lying on the ground. Now, what did you say your name was?"

"Hardly necessary for anyone to know, I think. Jus' doing me duty to report it. Like I said, my wife and I are jus' passing through town. Probably nothing to it, so to speak. Good night officer." Toby quickly hung up before Bebee could deliver a single word.

"Well done, Toby. Couldn't do better myself! We'd better close up shop and hightail it out of here before that cop Bebee shows up."

After closing the remaining windows and locking the rest of the outside doors, they walked across the road hole and headed back to the village along an adjacent path. Because the road hole skirted number 10 at Brookside, every year numerous golf shots from the tenth tee landed on passing vehicles. The official name of the road hole was Valley View Drive, but villagers had rechristened it Lookout Drive.

*   *   *

The pair strode in single file along the path to the village. As was their custom, they each carried a golf club with them that served a multitude of purposes. These midiron clubs were not only handy walking sticks but useful tools to find and rake out golf balls hit from the course across the road hole. On rare occasions, their clubs were used to fend off an aggressive dog that preferred golfers to mailmen. To villagers, always carrying a club in hand was much like wearing a class tie. It easily singled them out as uppity summer snobs instead of the polished gentlemen they imagined themselves to be.

Toby broke the silence, "Sydney, do you really think we did the right thing by Jeffrey?"

"Of course we did, Toby. No harm will come of it. Any of the members, at least the ones we know, would do the same thing for either of us. What we did will have to be our little secret. It's a shame that no one's around to give us a medal for it!" Reaching inside his coat pocket, he pulled out a silver cigar case. "You know, Toby, a lot of fine fellows have met their demise out on the course, just as I would wish for myself." When they both stopped to rest, he snipped off the end of his cigar. "I did feel a little sorry for Angus Whipple though. Must be a good twelve years ago now. Remember? He stood out there in one hell of a thunderstorm in the middle of the twelfth hole yelling at the caddies, 'Get out from under the trees unless you want to get hit by lightning.'"

Engaged in repacking his pipe, Toby responded," Of course I remember. Angus ran inside the shelter on the thirteenth when a bolt hit it. Burned it to the ground and fried Angus to a crisp along with it. Very tragic. Rotten shame. There's not so much as a plaque to mark the spot."

"Quite right," said Sydney. "Ironically, I happened to be talking to his widow just the other day about it. I told her it was damned fortunate the lightning hit the shelter and not the clubhouse. I was only trying to make light of what happened. Melissa, for whatever reason, didn't find the humor in it."

Toby was more comfortable now about having laid Jeffrey out on the course, but he still had a nagging concern about having moved the body. He relit his pipe and continued to press Sydney on the subject. "I don't remember that we've actually moved bodies around though, have we?"

"Oh, yes. Quite some years ago. As a matter of fact it resulted in a new club rule, one that I drafted. It's in the bylaws but not well circulated so to speak. Too macabre for the new members, I suppose. I'll never forget the day that Cedric "Bird Brain" Burdette died on the fifteenth green. A classic golf-course fatality. He dropped a decent downhill putt, picked his ball out of the hole, and keeled over from a fatal heart attack. Obviously, he couldn't be left on the green. I was in a foursome on the fourteenth, and unless Cedric was moved from the green, he would be holding up play. Stone dead as he was, he still wouldn't want to be remembered for that, don't you know?" Sydney let out a long sigh. "There wasn't much left to be done for him. Bill Ashley, his partner, closed Cedric's eyes. Then he sent Cedric's caddy back to the pro shop with a message to call the county coroner to come pick up Bird Brain."

Meanwhile, Toby had stopped to turn his back against the breeze in a futile effort to relight his pipe. Sydney slowed his pace to wait for him to catch up. Although a little irritated with Toby's preoccupation about moving a body, he resumed his recollection. "We saw Bill and his partner, Phil Broadhurst, drag Cedric behind the sand trap on the upland side of the green. They covered Cedric with their rain gear, returned to the green, putted out and waved us to play on up. So there you are. Not to put too fine a point on it, Toby, but it's a perfect paradigm for what we did with Jeffrey."

In his attempt to further settle Toby's nerves, Sydney was quite full of himself to the point of outright boastfulness. "As I was saying, that incident with Cedric resulted in a new club rule that says, 'In the event a ball comes to rest on or against an unconscious or deceased player, the body is construed to be a movable obstruction, and the player shall have the option to move the body for an unobstructed swing on line with the hole, or the ball shall be deemed to be unplayable, and the player shall have the option to take a two-club-length drop no nearer the hole without penalty.' The rule is quite clear. Thoughtful on my part, wouldn't you say?"

"Well, well, well!" said Toby. "I'm sure Cedric would be pleased to know that he didn't die in vain. He had the distinct honor of having a local club rule named after him just because of his untimely demise. Humph—using your logic, moving Jeffrey's body would be justified on the basis of freeing up a toilet stall! And tell me, does this club rule of yours trump state law?" A long silence fell on the pair.

It was Toby, as usual, who finally broke the ice. "Sorry, Sydney. Let's just leave it that we did the best thing we could for Jeffrey and the club too."

"You're quite right, Toby. No need to rationalize what we did or didn't do. We'd better be moving on, don't you think? With all our chitchat we haven't put much ground between us and the club."

"Come to think of it, where the devil are the police? They should have been whizzing past here a good twenty minutes ago."

"The Livermore Falls Police Department isn't exactly Scotland Yard. I needn't tell you that." He cupped a hand to his ear. "Speak of the devil. Listen up, I think I hear a car coming our way."

Straightening up, Toby squinted up the road hole where he could see the flashing lights of a squad car. "We shouldn't be spotted. Just to be on the safe side, let's get off the path and take cover."

They squatted behind a hedgerow of bushes as they watched Bebee whiz by headed for the clubhouse in a new black Chevy sedan, kicking up a cloud of dust and loose gravel as it passed the crouching pair. The minute the car lights disappeared over a rise in the road, they emerged from the bushes to resume their walk. Noting their disheveled appearance, without a word they proceeded to brush the dust and brambles off each other's pants and club blazers.

Sydney said triumphantly, "Well, there you have it, Toby. End of story. We should both be feeling rather proud of ourselves tonight, don't you think?"

Toby grinned. "Yes, I suppose you could say that. I'm pleased but tired."

Returning to the path, their steps took on a jauntier pace. Now, Toby was up ahead of Sydney. He poked at the path in front of him with his club, just to be sure of his footing in the dusk. Hiding behind a shroud of clouds, the moon was little help. Sydney stopped to put out his spent cigar.

"For me, old dear, I'm going to have a good stiff scotch before I slip into the hammock tonight!"

"Likewise!" said Toby. "Maybe even two. I'm glad we talked this whole thing out. I feel a damn sight the better for it. Clear conscience and all that, so to speak." A wry smile spread over Toby's face. "By the way, now that your blood isn't sitting around in pools, are you up for a game tomorrow?"

"Wouldn't think of disappointing you. Bring your old family money!"

"Done," said Toby. "How's about I pick you up in front of your place—say eight-thirtyish?"

Sydney nodded his approval. The pair had reached the juncture of the road hole with Main Street and Cemetery Drive. Exchanging farewell gestures, Sydney turned right for his hotel on the village green while Toby turned left to stroll to the comfort of his rooms at the Maple Leaf Inn on the Old West Road.

Tired from the evening's strenuous activity, Sydney still felt a certain exhilaration and sense of accomplishment that comes from the doing of great deeds. Toby may not hold Jeffrey in high esteem, but they had labored hard this evening to preserve the dignity of one of Brookside's members. More importantly they believed they had defended the club's once impeccable, but now fading, reputation by sheltering it from the appearance of an unseemly death. In their world, it was just as important for a golfer to die on the field of play as it was for a soldier to die on a battlefield.

2

Remembering Brookside 1921

Sydney, exhausted, collapsed in bed. He was tired but couldn't sleep. Forcing his eyes shut and wrestling with his covers, his mind flashed back to the beginnings of Brookside hoping that a pleasant memory would help him drift off to sleep. He tried counting the years backwards from 1948 to twenty-seven years earlier when he first gazed on the site of what was to become the Brookside Country Club. Then, just as now, he delighted in evening strolls through the village streets of Livermore Falls. The cool night air brought him back year after year, staying longer with each visit. He took every opportunity to leave the sweltering heat of summers in New York City. Unfortunately, it also took him away from his buddies and his treasured game of golf.

In July of '21 he was making a long trip up to Albany on business. Again, he made a stopover in Livermore Falls at one of the many lodgings along the main drag. Checking into his room, he picked up the newspaper on the dressing table and began perusing the local news. In retrospect, he felt a hidden hand was turning the pages when he arrived at an advertisement for the sale of the Benson Farm. In the back of his mind, he always wanted to create the perfect country club. He asked himself if this was the opportunity he'd been dreaming about. Now that it was staring him in the face, he had to ask another question. Was he bold enough to see it through?

He could tell from the ad that the dairy farm was very close to town, and its three hundred acres of cleared land was ripe for a golf course. As well off as Sydney was financially, he realized that a project this ambitious would be too big a burden to carry by himself, especially since he was still very involved as a partner in a growing law firm. He would need the capital and long-term financial backing of others to pull it off, not to mention engineers and designers willing to accede to his idiosyncratic wishes. He promised himself that if this project came to pass, there would be little or no compromise about the design of the clubhouse. Sydney had griped at length to his golfing pals Eric "Pinky" Robbins and Rodney Templeton that what Livermore Falls needed was a first-class golf course to compliment its other amenities.

Although the town was barely noticeable on a map, this handsome pastoral village of rolling hills and competing church spires already had a following that attracted a number of summer visitors who, between taking meals, mostly chose to read novels and chat away the time of day. Sydney visualized capitalizing on the town's attractions by introducing a more active and sporting crowd.

Sydney left his room to chat with the owner of the inn about the advertisement. He quickly learned that as a business the Benson farm was in decline. The Benson sons had left and had no interest in returning to work the farm. Like many other small dairy farms it was not profitable enough to hire, house, and feed the necessary help. He determined to his own satisfaction the property was being offered at a dirt-cheap price. Since dirt was the only thing he was interested in, he called the Benson's real estate agent.

* * *

By the end of the following day, the negotiations for the sale of the Benson farm had concluded. And now that the table was set, he phoned the Highlands City Club, knowing that on Friday evenings Rodney and Pinky would be there, fully engaged in their usual struggle-to-the-death chess match. He asked for Rodney, who became extremely agitated at being summoned to the phone, especially since it was his move. Marching from the library to phone in the lobby, Rodney asked the desk clerk who the idiot was on the other end.

"Wadsworth, sir," replied the desk clerk. "Long distance."

Rodney snapped up the phone, "Sydney, is this really you? What in the devil are you calling about at this hour?"

"It has to do with a piece of real estate, Rodney. I could use your advice. Pinky's too. I'd like both of you to drive up to Livermore Falls tomorrow. It's damn important, and you might find the trip worth your while."

"Really, Sydney. Pinky and I have a nine o'clock tee time tomorrow. Can't it wait?"

"I'm afraid not." A long silence followed before their conversation continued. It took some bullying to tear Eric and Rodney away from their golf match, but he successfully managed to tease his old golfing chums up to Livermore Falls.

Rodney had just left his position as CEO of the Republic National Bank to become its chairman of the board. Financially he had a conservative bent and was an influential charter member of several political think tanks that mostly ran on empty. Conservative as he was, however, he did have an Achilles heel that fit snugly into a golf shoe.

Pinky, on the other hand, was a successfully retired entrepreneur, which meant that he sold out his soft drink business just before it hit the skids. His impeccable timing elevated him to genius status, and several large companies in the region sought him to serve on their boards of directors. Typically he found the "business of business" boring compared to winning two bucks from Rodney in a round of golf.

The next morning, Sydney met his two pigeons on the porch of his lodgings. They were glad to see him, but their friendly, feigned smiles quickly changed to the appearance of two connoisseurs sipping a wine that had turned to vinegar. Pinky piped up, "Well, well, well, what's this all about, not a get-rich scheme, eh? That would be out of character."

"Indeed it would be." Sydney managed to work up a smile. "You know the Wadsworths always achieved their wealth the slow, tedious way. I wouldn't dream of asking you up here to bore you with some fast-buck scheme." Sydney knew this twosome already had all the money they would ever need for two lifetimes. And he suspected that these middle-aged bachelors desired a little more adventure than their Friday evening chess matches or the occasional disappointing tryst with the opposite sex.

Rodney was a tall slender man with wispy red hair. He was seen by his peers as a fashion plate known for his affected Harvard accent. Sydney knew him best for his fingernail fetish. A smoker at one time, Rodney probably didn't know what to do with his hands and fingers any more. But what he did with them now was a dead giveaway as to what he was thinking. In conversation, if he were disinterested or wanted to stall for time, he would hold up his fingernails for close inspection and begin a round of filing them with an emery board. He could register his impatience by rapping out "Yankee Doodle" with his honed nails on any hard surface. With his hands folded in front of him, whether standing or sitting, it generally meant he was in agreement with you. With his hands in his pockets, he was either playing it conservative or hanging onto his money.

Pinky, however, was inclined to communicate with the involuntary movement of his eyes and nose. If he didn't clearly understand what was being said, he would squint, which in turn rolled up his chubby nose. He registered his enthusiasm and excitement by popping his eyes and twitching his nostrils, fatal flaws in playing poker or chess.

In terms of negotiating skills, Sydney used his legal background and his ability to read what his pals were thinking. He forged a strategy that couched his pitch in the guise of seeking advice. Time was not his ally, and he had to press his proposition succinctly before they became impatient and returned to the city. Breaking a short silence, Sydney said, "Let's not stand around here. Why don't you pop back in your car and follow me? The property I want to show you isn't far from here, and there's nothing like seeing the goods."

They followed him south of town, and after a few blocks they turned east on Valley View Drive. As Sydney turned up the rutty driveway to the Benson farmhouse, he checked the rearview mirror to be sure that his pigeons hadn't flown the coup and headed back to New York.

At the top of the drive, the three men left their cars and stood silently to take in the lay of the land. Sydney opened the conversation exuding enthusiasm, "Well, gents, what do you think? If this isn't the most beautiful site for a country club you've ever seen, I don't know what is."

Sydney searched for facial expressions, their body language, anything that would express a positive response. None of the usual signs. Pinky, whose thick arms and legs restricted his movements, looked back and forth over the property as if he were watching a tennis match. Rodney stretched his neck, swiveled his hips, and viewed the landscape like a prairie dog on lookout pointing his index finger at salient points of interest.

Rodney looked at Pinky and said, "Well, what do you think?"

"I don't know. What do you think, Rodney?"

Sydney interrupted, "Perhaps it would help if I told you I took an option on this property yesterday. I could use your opinion."

"I suspected as much," Rodney nodded and folded his hands. "I don't doubt your vision or your ability, but please understand, I do have serious reservations that you can handle this project by yourself."

Pinky, evidently deciding to remain silent on the subject, squinted at Sydney, then at Rodney, then back at Sydney.

"To move on, gentlemen," said Sydney. "I have doubts too. That's why I intend to incorporate this venture and sell two hundred memberships to our friends and acquaintances. I think there should be two directors beside myself. Of course, they should be of impeccable character and substance. It goes without saying that these gentlemen must be golfers who adhere to golf's highest standard of conduct." He paused before continuing, "I thought if you two looked over the property, you might tell me whether this project has merit or not. You know how much I value your advice."

"Sydney, you're so transparent," said Pinky smiling and twitching his nose. "We'd be delighted to serve on your board. Just tell us how much of the ready you need." He squealed with laughter. "Rodney and I decided to back you before we drove up here."

"Steady, Pinky," Rodney added, "The caveat was that Sydney wasn't proposing something totally loopy."

Pinky opened his checkbook and spread it out on the hood of Sydney's car. Rodney did the same.

"Give us a figure, Sydney," said Pinky, "and we'll be on our way. Sorry we can't stay for lunch."

*   *   *

And so began a three-year sometimes-bumpy journey to the fruition of the golf course and clubhouse. For better or worse, Pinky and Rodney left Sydney to his own devices and sensibilities whenever the project required decisions involving design and construction. They just kept subscribing new members and sending fresh money to Sydney.

The village was delighted with the coming of Brookside because Sydney wisely employed every contractor he could from the locality. The local limestone quarry reopened. Every spare farm implement in town worked overtime grading and shaping the topography of the land into a golf course. Local interest sprouted in raising a crop of golfers instead of vegetables, and the pay was good. The groundbreaking ceremony for the clubhouse took place one year into the project. The town photographer was there to mark the event for posterity along with the high school band, which played several patriotic marches. A priest and three pastors blessed the occasion, after which the mayor hailed it as the beginning of a new era for Livermore Falls. Even Pinky and Rodney tore themselves away from New York to show up for the well-planned event. Along with Sydney, they were given a ceremonial shovel. All three proved much better at holding shovels than using them.

The rolling countryside provided a gentle foreground for the clubhouse, which was built in two years and boasted a buffet of architectural styles. The clubhouse obviously drew its inspiration from its exuberant creator, whose fault was not that he didn't love architecture but that he loved it too much. The exterior was a layer cake of architectural styles and historical periods starting with its Romanesque limestone arches on the first floor. The second floor, reminiscent of the Greek Revival period, was crowned by a steep-pitched slate roof interrupted by a series of dormers punctuated by gargoyles. Soaring above this cake was an imposing medieval turret anchoring the south end of the clubhouse. Along the ridge of the roof, a widow's walk led from the turret to an open terrace terminating the far end of the clubhouse. There, Sydney often took refuge to relish his masterpiece and take pleasure in what he had spawned. Brookside, in a sense, had become his surrogate child filling a much-needed void in his life. No less than five prominent and enthusiastic architects were engaged in the project. In the end, all had fled, except one, who refused to be named as the architect of record.

If the new Brookside clubhouse was a layer cake, so was Sydney, who successfully cloned all his idiosyncrasies in the final product. The clubhouse took on his persona and mirrored the complexities of his value system, tailored by his sense of propriety and polite manners. It revealed his attitudes about relationships with others, especially the female gender, his affinity for exclusivity, affection for the arts, and love of all things golf.

Once completed, the clubhouse assumed a life of its own, a living, breathing character on the landscape with a name of its very own, Brookside. No longer a skeleton of wood and stone, a shelter from the elements and the outside world, the clubhouse, for those who listened, often spoke softly to them. At the grand opening, a couple told Sydney that when they came through the front door, they thought they heard a whisper coming from out of nowhere, "Show your respect and remove your hat."

While it was the fond memories of Brookside's beginnings that helped Sydney drift off to sleep, it was a disturbing dream of last evening's activities that woke him hours before his appointment with Toby.

3

Missing

Sydney stood waiting outside the 1876 House, an old colonial-style inn with white wooden pillars, which fronted the Livermore Falls village green. The inn had served as his summer residence for over two decades. Built in the year of its name, it had suffered many indignities in the form of additions and remodels. Still it managed to maintain much of its original character. Not all the walls were plumb nor the wood floors level, but they went unnoticed by their repeat clientele who grew old along with the inn and over the years bore many of the same indignities and infirmities. Even though Sydney could have used an extra hour of rest on this particular morning, he was his usual punctual self and arrived at curbside by the appointed time of eight-fifteen.

Toby drove up in his green '40 Oldsmobile coupe. It was hardly an ostentatious car for his station, but handsome and quite suitable for a bachelor with a conservative taste quotient. He kept his Olds parked in the barn behind the Maple Leaf Inn. In the winter it was left there, up on blocks, with its radiator drained and battery disconnected until he returned the following year. Oliver, son of the inn's owner, earned a few extra dollars in the summer by keeping the car looking as if it just drove off the show room floor. This day was no exception. It sparkled in the early morning sun.

"All aboard, Sydney," said Toby, anticipating a good match.

As he swung the door shut behind him, Sydney replied cheerfully, "Top of the morning, Toby." Sitting back he felt something small and round wedged in the crease of the seat. He reached behind his back with some difficulty and pulled out a tube of lipstick. "This wouldn't be yours would it Toby, or have you taken up with someone I don't know?"

"Don't be ridiculous, Sydney! It probably belongs to Oliver's girlfriend, Amy. He's too young to drive. One evening when I went out to the barn, I caught the two of them sitting in my car. Oliver said they were just pretending to be at the drive-in theater." Toby shifted the Olds into second gear. "Well I tell you, at first, I was really surprised—shocked even. But honestly, I saw no real harm in it. I did put my foot down though and told them in no uncertain terms that if they wanted to sit in my car again, they needed my permission."

Sydney stared at Toby for several minutes in disbelief. Taking dead aim and speaking deliberately, "If you hold Oliver in high regard, and I know you do—he's your favorite caddy after all—I think you should warn him about the wiles of young girls and especially those wearing lipstick! I'll say no more about it."

"Thank you, Sydney, enough said. I'll take it up with Oliver." He turned the Olds down the road hole toward the clubhouse. For a brief moment, his mood changed as last evening's harrowing events flashed to mind. His bushy white mustache twitched nervously. The thought passed as quickly as it came when the Brookside clubhouse came into view.

An innocent sun-filled morning greeted Sydney and Toby as they drove into the grass carpeted parking lot. Birds sang their familiar melodies. The pungent smell of new mown grass filled the fresh morning air, while a chorus of sprinklers watered the course with the sound of their customary rat-a-tat-tat. Terry, the golf shop attendant, was raising the colors as they converged on the clubhouse. It was the sights and sounds of a scene that befit the arrival of royalty. They chatted enthusiastically about today's game, the wager, the effects of wind and weather, and of course, the nuances of golf.

How surprised they were when they suddenly came upon a disturbance at the main entrance. A small boisterous group had gathered under the portico, and they were having a very animated discussion amongst themselves, all of which proved most disconcerting to Sydney and Toby.

Chief Bebee was standing on the steps flapping his arms like a wild goose about to take off. The more he gestured for folks to calm down, the more talkative they became. Sydney and Toby believed that the police would have finished its work the night before. It crossed their minds that perhaps this was not the case.

"Good grief, Toby, there's old Two Bullets holding court in our portico." They both stopped dead in their tracks. Two Bullets, a decent respectable police officer, was either quiet and laconic or highly excitable. It all depended on whether he was in or out of his depth. His depth included parking tickets and resolving the occasional family dispute. Today, he was highly excitable.

"What in heaven's name are the police doing here this morning?" said Toby. "Couldn't Two Bullets finish up here last night? Humph. How did he get that idiotic nickname anyway?"

"First of all, Chief Robert 'Two Bullets' Bebee is the town cop, as you ought to know from your collection of parking tickets. It's a position I think he's been elected to for at least the last sixteen years."

"Could you please get on with it, Sydney, we have a nine-fifteen tee time."

"All right, Toby, you don't have to get in a snit. The story goes that he got his nickname from the town's only armed robbery, in 1939 I believe. A brazen daytime holdup. The robbers came running out of the Cornerstone National Bank shooting wildly at everyone in sight. Bebee rushed out of the coffee shop next door and became an immediate target. He turned tail to get out of the line of fire and took two shots in the buttocks. I think he may still be carrying them around."

"So why don't they call him Lead Ass?" laughed Toby.

"Because they just don't. You must remember the robbers got away. Paper claimed they made off with half a million in cash. Ridiculous, I say. Why would the bank have that much of the ready lying around? Never caught the bastards, and the worst of it is there's no trace of the money. Obviously, that holdup was not Bebee's finest hour, but at least the village didn't lose its chief. So there you have it, Toby, the origin of the name Two Bullets."

"Sounds perfectly logical to me." Toby smiles. "Actually it was fortunate Two Bullets got shot in the backside rather than in front—could've been rather disastrous to his plumbing!"

Wincing, Sydney asked, "Don't you think we're acting a little suspicious just standing here? Let's skip going through the lobby and head for the locker room door."

"Good thinking. We don't need to be late, and besides, I don't know that either of us has the foggiest notion of what's really going on anyway."

"Wouldn't you just know it?" Sydney's earlier pleasant mood had turned sour and irritable. "Look over there, the press is here too. Probably some cub reporter not even out of high school."

"I can't quite tell from this distance," said Toby, "but I think that cub reporter is Amy."

Sydney bit his lip. Like twins joined at the hip, Sydney and Toby slowly turned away from their original path. Toby mumbled, "The county coroner must have picked up Jeffrey last night. Maybe Bebee's here trying to tidy up a few details. Anyway, we're not involved. Hell's bells, all this fuss may not have anything to do with Jeffrey."

Glancing around, Sydney suddenly put a hand up to his throat as if he had swallowed a peach stone. "Oh god, I think it does. Would you look over there in the driveway, behind the police car. Isn't that Harriet Bartholomew's Lincoln Zephyr?"

"It sure is, and she usually spells trouble."

Before they could reach their destination, Chief Bebee bellowed in their direction, "You two, stop!" Waving at them to come over to the portico, he said, "If you fellows are who I think you are, I'd like to have a little talk with you." Obediently, they turned around, walked toward Chief Bebee, and while working their way through the dozen or so curious employees and club members, they were suddenly confronted by Amy, flashing her press card excitedly.

"Why, Toby—I mean, Mr. Worthington—what are you doing here?" Working summers for the *Livermore Falls Journal*, she hoped to get a big scoop. "Can I get an interview?"

"Never you mind, Amy. Later perhaps," said Toby with a quavering voice and a trembling lower lip. As a man who revered anonymity, he found all the attention suddenly thrust upon him most disturbing. However, he must not allow a temporary step out of character, and he reverted to his usual persona of an unflappable, self-disciplined gentleman.

Leading the way for Toby, Sydney finally brushed his way through the gathering and came to a stop in front of Chief Bebee. "What's all the commotion, Chief?" Working up a weak smile, "Did somebody die?"

"I'll ask the questions," said Bebee, who by his retort and demeanor tried to show his full command of the situation. "Funny you should ask that question though. In case you've forgotten or don't know, I'm Chief Robert Bebee. You wouldn't be Sydney Wadsworth and Tobias Worthington by any remote chance?"

Toby, who had regained most of his composure, replied smartly, "Of course we are!"

"Good. Well, I have a little mystery I need to solve, and I think you two may be able to help me out. So, why don't you follow me inside, and we'll go into the boardroom."

"Really, Chief," said Sydney indignantly, "glad to be of help and all that, but this must be pretty damned important to use the boardroom!"

Bebee didn't answer but turned to swagger, hands on hips, through the lobby and down a long gallery to the double doors of the boardroom. Like two beached seals, Sydney and Toby reluctantly waddled behind him. Under the archway of the boardroom doors, they both stopped to survey the room. On their left, Alex Wiley, the locker room attendant, and Sandy Cummings, the club manager, sat with their hands folded on top of the long boat shaped conference table. To the right, a young female officer sat stiffly in her neatly pressed uniform. Her hands were clasped around an open spiral note pad. At the far end of the table, Mrs. Bartholomew occupied and overflowed the high back executive chair directly under an imposing portrait inscribed "Sydney P. Wadsworth, Founder and Charter Member, 1921." Flanked on either side were smaller portraits of Eric Robbins and Rodney Templeton.

Sydney, infuriated by her audacity in assuming a place at the table that he felt was rightfully his, whispered angrily under his breath to Toby, "She's certainly got a lot of cheek."

Cupping his hand to Sydney's ear, Toby whispered, "I warned you about that old trout. Better watch your step."

Not in her usual golfing attire, Harriet wore a loose-fitting white blouse with a purple scarf and riding britches. Aloof to the others present, she opened her compact and caked on yet another layer of bright red lipstick. This was not acceptable behavior in polite company, and especially at Brookside. Sydney gaped and muttered to Toby, "I wouldn't be surprised if there are spurs on those boots of hers. I have a great deal of sympathy for any horse she straddles or any saddle she sits on for that matter."

"Ease off, Sydney, and lower your voice." murmured Toby. "I know why you're out of sorts. Try to remember how charitable you were towards her last night. Don't forget she did manage to snag three husbands. I understand Harriet used to cut quite a figure in her hay day."

"Well then, you've got quite an imagination, Toby."

Bebee turned to Sydney and Toby, "Why don't the both of you take a seat?" Standing alongside his chair, Bebee cleared his throat and said, "All right folks, let's get settled in. I'd like to introduce everyone to my personal aide. This is Officer Nancy Sullivan. She'll be taking notes, just for the record. Oh, and she'll be needing your full names and particulars before you leave. I believe the rest of you know each other."

Toby and Sydney took two empty seats down from Harriet's left but still in range of her heavily scented toilet water wafting over them. Sydney fidgeted with his tie, twiddling it between his thumbs. Toby asked Bebee, "Do you mind telling us what the deuce this is all about?"

"Soon enough, Mr. Worthington. You two were the last to arrive, so we can get down to business now. I called you and Mr. Wadsworth this morning, but I was informed that you both had already left for the club." Bebee sat down at the open end of the conference table and poured himself a cup of coffee from the club's silver service. He nodded for the others to help themselves.

Toby took out his pipe and began to pack it with a fresh supply of tobacco from his handsomely monogrammed brown leather pouch. Before he could put a match to it, Mrs. Bartholomew blurted out, "Don't you dare smoke that chimney in my presence!"

"My dear Harriet," said Toby staring up at the ceiling, "In this room, you shouldn't even be in my presence!" With a defiant glare back at her, he lit his pipe.

Bebee reclined in his chair swiveling from side to side. "Let's cut the gab and get started, if it's all right with everyone. Please start taking notes, Nancy." Leaning back he took off his cap, dropped it on the floor and folded both hands behind his neck. After a prolonged silence, evidently to collect his thoughts, Bebee bent forward and placed his forearms on the table. "Last evening, I received an anonymous call at the station. The caller said there was a body lying out on the golf course. Naturally, I went to investigate. It was getting quite dark when I arrived, but I did manage a good look around. Anybody know what I found?" Bebee glanced at the stoic faces around the room. Then he shattered the silence with a sharp, high pitched rhetorical answer, "Nobody!"

Sydney swallowed hard, trying not to divulge surprise on his part. Toby burst out coughing, "I need to be excused to attend to a personal matter in the men's room." Bebee nodded his approval.

Sydney suddenly blurted out, "Well then, chief, what seems to be the problem?" A tightlipped Harriet glared icy daggers at Sydney.

Bebee, irritated, rapped on the table, "I said I'd ask the questions, if you don't mind." He whispered to Nancy, "Make a note of Toby's unusual behavior when I said I hadn't found a body." Toby reentered the room and slid back into his chair. Bebee cleared his throat and began again, "Now that we're all in attendance, I'll tell you what I did find. A golf ball, a club, and a set of clubs in a bag belonging to Jeffrey Bartholomew."

Easing back in his chair, Bebee referred to his file notes. Peering above his reading glasses, his eyes narrowed to focus on the assemblage. "Now, I had no reason to be alarmed at what I found out on the seventeenth hole. I don't play golf myself, but some people I know can easily lose their temper during a game, even get out of control, throw things like their clubs. I reckon Jeffrey was out there by himself practicing and wasn't having a very good day. Maybe he whiffed, and in a fit of temper threw his club, then he threw his ball up the fairway, threw his bag down and threw himself on the ground in a tantrum. Just maybe he worked himself up into a seizure. Later, just lying there, this couple must have seen him, after which he must have come to his senses. I figure that he got up, left his stuff and walked on home. I certainly had no reason to expect foul play—just poor play."

Before Bebee could continue any further, Sydney interrupted. "I want you to know, Chief Bebee, that the scenario you just described is totally out of character for a member of this club." Sydney clenched his fists together on the table. "If any member of this club engaged in a display of bad temper like you just described, and it was witnessed—well, that member would be reported to the membership committee for immediate disciplinary action. There isn't a member here who'd dare risk being caught displaying the kind of bad temper you just described."

"He's right you know," said Toby.

"OK, so what if you two and Emily Post are right? I still need some explanation of what happened last evening. My theory holds water with the anonymous call. I have to admit though, it seemed awfully suspicious. The caller sounded like some idiotic baboon. Strange accent. Said he was passing through town with his wife." Bebee then said jokingly, "I hope they kept on going." Toby squirmed in his seat with Bebee's characterization of the call. "Lookout Drive," snickered Bebee, "isn't the way to pass through town unless you've got a whole lot of time on your hands."

Nancy snapped her pencil, turned to Bebee and asked, "Could I take a short break?"

"Certainly, Officer Sullivan," he replied getting up from his chair. "Need one myself. Think I'll step outside and have a cigarette. Clears the air for me. The rest of you can take five, but be back on time. I've got some important business to cover."

*   *   *

Brandishing a fresh pencil from the front desk, Nancy was ready to resume her note taking. Bebee glanced around taking attendance. Everyone had resumed their original places, except that Sydney and Toby had moved one more chair further away from Harriet.

"Now comes the interesting part," Bebee began, leaning over the conference table. "I had another call last night just after 2:00 a.m. at my home. It was from Harriet Bartholomew." All heads turned in her direction. "She was quite distressed that her husband had not returned home from the club yet."

"I'm a lot more than distressed, Chief Bebee!" said Harriet. "It's not like Jeffrey to go wondering off. We've been married eight years now, and nothing like this has ever happened to me before. Jeffrey has always been dependable." She wagged her finger at Bebee, "I've held my tongue all morning listening to this tripe. Now, you listen to me Two Bullets, I want to know what you're going to do about finding my husband?"

"Easy now, Mrs. Bartholomew." Bebee blinked at her show of anger. "We'll find Jeffrey," he said confidently. "I've already found his car in the parking lot this morning, and that's a good start, means he's on foot. Remember what I told you this morning, Mrs. Bartholomew? He isn't officially missing yet, so we don't want to be getting overheated."

"*Overheated* isn't the word! Do you know how embarrassing this whole mess is for me?"

Nancy raised her hand and said, "Chief, do you still want me to be taking all this down?"

"Yes, Nancy. We can do some editing later before you get it typed up. I still have a few questions I'd like answered if Mrs. Bartholomew is quite finished," he snapped. Bebee swung his chair around to look at Alex. "You're here, Alex, because I understand you may have been one of the last persons to see Mr. Bartholomew yesterday." Alex looked petrified. "Don't be nervous, Alex, just tell me the truth. Here, have a glass of ice water." Alex took a quick gulp. "Now describe to me the events of last night when you were with Jeffrey."

"Chief Bebee, sir. Jeffrey, that is Mr. Bartholomew, was alone with me in the bar around closing time. I served him three double dry martinis. He tossed them down like they were lemonade. No disrespect, Mrs. Bartholomew. Something bad was really bothering him. Oh, and I'm sure he'd been drinking before he came in. He kept mumbling to himself, over and over. I couldn't make out what he was trying to say. It isn't my business. Banged his fist on the bar too. He shoved his glass at me to get him another martini, but I told him I had to close up, and I wouldn't serve him any more liquor. I even had to put out a cigarette he dropped on the bar. After that, I took his car keys off the bar and put them in the cash register—told him he shouldn't be driving. He just grumbled at me. I remember helping him off the barstool. He staggered over to the locker room door, and that was the last I saw of him. He gets snockered in here every so often, but so help me I've never seen him that polluted. Sorry, Mrs. Bartholomew."

"Jeffrey's the one that's going to be sorry when I get my hands on him!" shot Harriet. "I picked up his new heart medicine just two days ago, and he's not to take it with alcohol under any circumstances. It could be fatal. I told him that. I can't believe he could be such a fool."

Harriet's outburst didn't go unnoticed by Bebee. This time neither Sydney nor Toby rushed to Jeffrey's defense. Harriet regained her composure and did a quick about face, realizing that she was not enlisting any sympathy. She sighed, "After all I do for that precious husband of mine, and now I have to deal with this too."

"Please, Mrs. B., Would you stop interrupting?" exclaimed Bebee. You're beginning to rankle me, and nobody likes me when I get that way. Now Alex, is there anything else? Did you notice anything different here when you came in this morning?"

Alex paused to wipe his sweaty forehead with a well-used handkerchief. "Only one thing. When I opened up this morning and went into the locker room, the towel basket in the shower room was full. I thought I emptied it last night before I closed up. It was all soggy and soiled. So, I took it down to the laundry room and stuck it in the wash. Should be done by now. Oh, somebody left a pair of socks and boxer shorts last night, but I usually leave that stuff where it is until late the next morning. After that it goes in the lost and found."

"Thank you, Alex. I think I got the picture. Now, I'd like to ask Mr. Cummings a question or two."

"Call me Sandy, Officer Bebee, I'm more comfortable with that. How can Brookside help you with your investigation?"

"First, Sandy, how is it that you asked Mr. Worthington to close up last night?"

"Well, Bob, may I call you Bob? Thursday was a special night out with my family. A dinner for my wife's birthday. I saw no harm in asking Mr. Worthington to close up the club for me. He and Mr. Wadsworth are usually the last to leave, and I didn't think the two of them would mind—as a favor." Sandy adjusted the knot in his club tie. "I understand they've been here forever. If I may say so, I can't imagine they would ever be careless or the least bit derelict when asked to do a simple chore for the club."

Sydney and Toby glanced at each other with smiles of conceit and self-satisfaction. "Thank you, Sandy. Seems a reasonable enough explanation." Although Chief Bebee was uncomfortable with Sandy's familiarity, it was certainly preferable to being called Two Bullets. "Now, we come to perhaps the last two people who might have seen Jeffrey Bartholomew last night. That is, after Alex saw him leave the bar."

"You must mean Toby and me, of course," said Sydney who suspected since the beginning of this inquiry that they would come under some sort of scrutiny. "Fire at will."

"Let's begin with your closing-up activities." Bebee was hopeful of getting at least a clue or two about Jeffrey's disappearance. "Tell me everything you saw, and did—front to back—and take your time. You first, Mr. Wadsworth."

"Certainly you don't expect me to remember every detail, but I'll give it a go." Sydney looked over at Toby and then back at Bebee. "Well, we were both on the veranda about seven thirty having our usual flap about things in general. Toby said he was closing the club last evening. First, we had a little outside walkabout. We took in the evening air, had a smoke, saw to it that the clubs and bags had been put to bed. Toby checked the pro shop door to be sure it was secure. A handful of cars were left in the parking lot, but we didn't see any enter or leave there on our watch. In our reconnoitering we didn't observe anyone either on the grounds or out on the course." Sydney digressed. "By the way, Sandy, make a note that the shutters on the east side dormers need a coat of paint before winter sets in."

Toby interrupted, "Excuse me, Sydney, but Sandy should have that sticky window in the scullery fixed. Difficult to shut. The screen's shot too. Can't have that."

Nancy raised her hand and asked, "Mr. Wadsworth, could you please spell that word you used that begins with an *r*? Recon—something."

"Stop, stop, stop!" exclaimed a flustered Bebee. This interview isn't getting us anywhere. I've got other fish to fry on this case, and I'm going to need everyone's help and cooperation. This is a high profile case surrounding the disappearance of a prominent citizen in this community and . . ."

"Save the speech, Bebee," said Harriet reverting to her previous demeanor, "and you might save your job! Just tell me what you're going to do."

"There's no call to threaten me, Mrs. B. For all I know your husband woke up on the seventeenth hole last night, left on foot, and went to a friend's house to sleep over. But like I said, I'm taking this seriously. The state police and hospitals have already been checked out. You know my hands are tied by the law. I can't declare Mr. Bartholomew a missing person yet. So there's no help from the county or state. But that doesn't mean I can't take a few steps of my own!"

Bebee got up from his chair and locked his thumbs in his gun belt. "In a small town like this, it's pretty hard to disappear." He turned to Sandy and said, "I want you to get going on a phone chain. Take charge. Call all the members and keep me informed. Find out if they've either seen or know anything at all about Jeffrey. I'm counting on the cooperation of Brookside members to assist my investigation, but not so's to interfere with police work. Next, I'm calling out the Boy Scout troop. I'm going to muster every organization I can drum up from the village to find our Mr. Bartholomew. Veterans' groups, legionnaires, volunteer firemen, the whole damn lot of them. Then I'm going to organize a sweep of the golf course fanning out from the seventeenth hole. If we don't find him or any clues as to his whereabouts by tomorrow, Saturday noon, I'm going to have Brookside's pond drained!"

Toby, mouth agape, sat in stunned silence. Sydney struggled to his feet, steadying himself on the edge of the conference table. His voice crackled, "Are you out of your mind, Bebee? The course could be shut down for at least a couple of days!"

"That's a real pity, Mr. Wadsworth. I guess you'll just have to find Jeffrey or go somewhere else to play golf. As for the pond, I don't have a diver. And if I did, it would be useless to send him into that muck hole you call a pond."

"That muck hole happens to be the reservoir for our irrigation system!" Sydney was inflamed. Toby watched Sydney's temperature rise to the boiling point. Like mercury in a thermometer, his pale complexion turned pink rising from his neck up to his forehead. "Furthermore, that muck hole is our fire protection! That's why it's dug deep. Drain it, and I'll see to it the town's held responsible if we have a fire!"

"OK, Wadsworth, calm down," said Bebee. "Don't go blowing a gasket on me." His attention turned again to Sandy. "Can you put one of your grounds people at my disposal? In case Mr. Bartholomew doesn't show up by noon Saturday, I'll need one of your people to operate the drain valve on your pond." Sandy could only manage a nod in the affirmative.

Bebee glared at Harriet and stormed out of the room saying, "Meetin's over! Satisfied, Mrs. Bartholomew?"

4

A Comeuppance

Bebee was first out the club's front door with Nancy trailing close behind. The portico was unoccupied except for Amy. Ignoring her presence at first, Bebee brushed aside her pleas for an interview and said to Nancy, "We're going to completely shut Brookside down by one o'clock today. Inside and out. I don't mind telling you, that I'm going to get a little pleasure out of making this Brookside crowd squirm."

Amy was walking toward her bike when she heard Bebee shout for her to come back. "I've got a story for you. You might just as well get it from me so you'll get it right."

"Coming! Is it about Mr. Bartholomew?"

"Yeah—but how did you know? Never mind, don't tell me. So you got yourself a summer job with the *Journal.* I know your dad, Amy. Good friend of mine. What I'd like you to do Amy, is get a public service piece in the morning paper. Think you can do that?"

"I'll give it my best shot, Chief. Fire away! This could be front page stuff."

Bebee said, "Use your own words. The headline should read something like this: 'Jeffrey Bartholomew Missing.' Then quote me. 'Chief Robert Bebee says that Mr. Bartholomew has been missing since last night and that he was last seen at Brookside Country Club wearing golf attire. Anyone having information or knowing of his whereabouts should contact the police station house immediately.' Got that? Give the phone number. Put in a brief biography if you can come up with one. You'll need his description, so if I were you, I'd go in the club and ask Sandy Cummings to give you his photograph. They have all their members' pictures hung up in the front lobby."

"I'm on my way, Chief," Amy jogged to the front door of the clubhouse, "and thanks for the scoop!"

Heading for his car, Bebee stopped abruptly and turned to Nancy, "I've got a chore for you that might earn you a promotion." She skipped up along side of him. He said, "It's an undercover job." I think this Wadsworth and Worthington know a lot more than they're telling us. Nancy, I want you to keep an eye on Sydney and Toby. Follow their movements. If Jeffrey's alive, this pair probably knows where he is. You'll have to dress in your street clothes. Muss up your hair, and skip the makeup. I can get you a car tomorrow, and keep your distance behind them." He paused to decide if he had forgotten anything. "I don't think those two old buffoons would recognize a tail anyway. So, are you up for it?"

"I think I can handle it," said Nancy. She relished the chance to do real police work rather than being confined to mundane steno duties. At her first post fresh out of the police academy, she was eager to please her new boss. She thought, *If they split up, I guess I'll have to decide which one to keep and eye on,* and to her own surprise she blurted out, "Oh, Chief, may I assume this duty is on overtime."

"Yes, yes. Keep your hours and expenses. I'll authorize it. You'll be expected to perform your usual duties as well, and I want you to report to me every day, understood?"

Nancy smiled and saluted. "Understood, Chief."

Seeing the chief and Nancy conversing, Harriet Bartholomew left the clubhouse through the ladies locker room door and traipsed to her car unnoticed. In a huff, she revved the powerful V12 engine, slipped it into forward gear, and banged into the back of Bebee's new squad car. Startled, Bebee signaled her to stop. Harriet backed her Lincoln up and gave it the gas again. Missing Bebee's car this time, she gunned it once more and drove over a corner of the traffic island, leaving the clubhouse, Bebee, and Nancy in a cloud of exhaust fumes and dust.

"That witch is in for it now! I warned her not to rankle me!" shouted Bebee. "Get Judge Gillespie to swear out a warrant for her arrest. I want her in court for hit and run, failure to obey a police officer, damages to public property, and anything else you can think of! Got that, Nancy?"

*   *   *

Everyone had left the boardroom, except Sydney and Toby who were glued to their chairs. They stared out at the golf course through the bay window opposite them. "Should have been a grand day, Toby," said Sydney. His words came slowly and softly reflecting his deep disappointment in the meeting that just ended. "Now that we've missed our tee time, I suppose there's nothing more to be done."

"Buck up, Sydney. This'll all blow over eventually. We ought to feel damned lucky we didn't get ourselves involved in this mess anymore than we already are. By the way, when were you going to tell Bebee what we did closing up last night, were you going to say what we did with Jeffrey?"

"Of all the questions, after all the years we've known each other. You ask?" Still staring out at the course, he replied, "Toby, I always tell the truth, you know that. Bebee never let me get to it."

"I know you're a truthful person, Sydney." Toby fondled his pipe. "It's just when you come to adding up your score, the truth suffers a little. Perhaps it's your lack of ability with ciphers."

"I'll admit I'm weak in math, but one thing I'm quite certain of is that whatever we did for Jeffrey has nothing to do with this debacle. Wasn't it only yesterday I mentioned that the existence of Brookside might be in jeopardy? Well, here it is today, right on our doorstep. Tomorrow, townspeople by the dozens will be trampling all over the course like shoppers at a yard sale. I'm afraid our dear old Brookside will be nothing more than a sieve in their path!"

"You've got that right, Sydney." Toby got up and walked over to the bay window. In the glass he could see his reflection and used it to straighten his tie. He spoke with his pipe firmly clenched in his teeth. "I pray we won't be put upon in our clubhouse, or there won't be an ashtray or piece of silver left. At best, we'll be ravaged by souvenir hunters or their ilk. I think I'll advise Sandy to lock things up for the onslaught tomorrow."

"Toby, I wish you wouldn't speak with that pipe in your mouth. It's bad form."

"I'm sorry, Sydney, but I didn't have any other place to put it when I had something important to say. And its not 'that pipe.' It happens to be a Dunhill. It has an oval shaped bowl and a distinctive burl to compliment my facial features." Fluffing his never-to-be-used-handkerchief in his breast pocket, he puffed on his pipe and turned to Sydney. "I don't think you should be admonishing me when you smoke those things that look like they've been retrieved from the floor of some dog kennel. Just because your cigars have a fancy paper ring on them and you keep them in a silver case, doesn't mean they're any better than old dog links!"

"Toby, why are we having a spat like some married couple? We must be overly taxed I guess. There's no point of us sniping at each other." Sydney put his unlit cigar back in its case. He went over to Toby and put a hand on his shoulder. "I like the analogy you just made, though, about my cigars. It made me think about how a cheap cigar can be all dressed up in a fancy wrapper. I suppose people like Jeffrey could be like that too. Not what they seem to be. Toby, what do we really know about him? You had your doubts. I always took him on face value."

"Other than he's married to Harriet and has a 26 handicap, not much," replied Toby. "I think it might be useful though to find out more about him. Whatever we learn can't hurt. It might even help us find him before Bebee and everyone else gets in a lather. If we could just turn up a clue or two about where he is, we might end up doing the club a good turn."

"All right, Toby, let's have a go at it! We could start with Sandy."

"Well how about Alex? That story he gave about Jeffrey in the bar was bizarre to say the least. I've seen Jeffrey in his cups from time to time, but the scene Alex described about him was disgraceful, way over the top."

Sydney sat down in his old familiar chair at the head of the conference table. "Let's back up a minute and think this thing through." Toby joined him at the table. "Jeffrey was behaving queer as a duck according to Alex. He must have been on his new medication like Harriet said. With all those martinis on board, Jeffrey was definitely on his way to the undertaker when he staggered into the locker room."

Toby remarked, "And I'll wager Harriet didn't tell him not to booze it up with his new prescription! Think about it, Sydney. I told you her other two husbands had a strange way of popping off. Stomach ailments—my foot!"

"Maybe you're right, Toby. But one thing we do have is a plausible explanation of why we thought Jeffrey was dead."

"Right now, I'm not absolutely sure if we're looking for someone who's alive or dead. If he really is dead, then someone else must have found him, moved the body, and disposed of poor old Jeffrey. It's not a very pleasant thought. I can't imagine anyone who'd want to do him in. But if there was, there's no reason to move the body unless that someone saw us laying him out on the seventeenth. If that is true, we could possibly end up being blackmailed for his demise."

"Good lord, Sydney! Who in the world would want to blackmail us?"

"Don't be too alarmed, Toby. It's highly unlikely. For persons of our standing in the community, we would hardly be suspected of anything, least of all a murder. Besides, what motive could we possibly have? None of course." Sydney folded his hands and stared at the ceiling. Toby hung on his every word. "Right now, I'm beginning to think there's a good possibility that Jeffrey is alive." Sydney stood up and began to pace around the conference table. "I'm almost certain of it and just as certain he must have been dead when we found him in the toilet stall!"

"You're having me on again!" exclaimed Toby, tilting back in his chair. "He's no Lazarus up from the dead." Toby was exasperated and tried to get a grip on what Sydney was saying. "Hold on, Sydney, we both thought he was dead when we found him." Sputtering he asked, "So, which is it, dead or alive?"

"I'll try to be more explicit. Try this on. Think about all the yanking and pulling we did to Jeffrey, pushing and shoving, scrubbing him up, jostling him about in a cart, and sliding him onto the ground. Well, I think we may have revived him and in the process saved his life!" Sydney paused to let his words sink in. "What other logical explanation can there be? He probably regained full consciousness out there on number 17." Sydney kept pacing and postulated that Jeffrey, in a state of total confusion, just wandered off someplace. "So, I think he's alive, and it would be in our interest to find him sooner rather than later."

"Well I'll be damned and go to hell! Thank heavens you've got the sagacity for this kind of thing. Solid straightforward logical thinking, Sydney. Ha—and last night you thought you were on the verge of senility."

"Just because I'm on the threshold of senility doesn't mean I've lost all my faculties. After all, I was a contract lawyer for a good number of years. So, let's work on the premise that Jeffrey is alive and start looking for clues. We've got to find him before this club is brought down around our ears."

"By all that's holy, maybe we really did end up doing the right thing for Jeffrey! Even if we find out he's the bastard I think he is."

*   *   *

Chief Bebee and Officer Sullivan were speeding their way back to the station. Warning lights flashed from the car's front bumper and the rear window. Bebee liked to put his new Chevy through the paces whether or not he was responding to an emergency. It seemed to provide him with relief from his usual mundane traffic control duties. Possibly he imagined himself chasing a van full of fleeing criminals. Folks in town thought he was releasing his suppressed teenage driving habits. Whenever he got caught out, he would explain his propensity to drive over the speed limit as a professional requirement to fine tune his driving skills. Nancy, however, being jostled around like a tossed green salad, hung grimly to her seat.

Halfway back to the station, he told Nancy to pick up the radiophone and call his deputy. "When you get him, Nancy, tell him to meet us at the station on the double. We've got work to do."

"Chief, I got him. He's at the station. "Wants to know if he should put a pot on."

"No, dammit. Hang up! I want you to make another call. Get the Brookside number from the operator." Turning at the next corner, his car lunged and swerved onto the shoulder to avoid an oncoming car. "Get that Sandy Cummings fellow. Tell him I've decided to move up the schedule. I want the club closed up by one o'clock today. No cars, trucks, people, nothing coming into the club. No golf. Got it?"

In spite of Bebee's erratic driving, Nancy tried her best to dial Cummings but was unsuccessful as Bebee continued to barrel toward the station. "I'm going to get to the bottom of this Jeffrey thing a lot quicker than anyone thinks. That includes draining the pond this afternoon. If it's a big pain in the ass for those fat cats over at Brookside—well, so be it. As far as I'm concerned, they can all use a little comeuppance!"

Bebee whipped into his parking space in front of the station and bumped into the sidewalk curb. He bolted through the front door, leaving it open for Nancy. Following in Bebee's back draft, she swung around behind her desk, plunked down in her oversized swivel chair, and tried calling Cummings again. The line was busy, and she turned her attention turned to typing up the notes she'd made earlier at Brookside.

The Livermore Falls Police Station was small by any measure. The front office was an obstacle course consisting of four desks and an ancient free standing safe for firearms, evidence, and office supplies. Hearing the arrival of Bebee and Nancy, Deputy Lester Sparks, better known as High Pockets, emerged from a bathroom carrying a handful of *True Detective* magazines.

"Lester," barked the chief. "I see you've been catching up on your reading for advancement."

"Right, Chief." Lester pointed at the bathroom. "I figure, though, when I'm in there I'm on my own time."

"Well, you're on my time now. I want you to get your tail over to Brookside Country Club on the double. Tell Cummings you're there to see that the pond gets drained—like now. I want you to take some of our barricades with you and throw them across the across the club driveway. Nobody's to come on the grounds. Got all that? And stay at the club and wait for my instructions."

Nancy looked up from her typewriter and challenged, "Chief, I thought you were going to start draining the pond tomorrow afternoon if we don't find Mr. B. today."

"So I changed my mind. That pond's a damn sight bigger than it looks. I've got to keep this investigation moving. No holdups." He swiveled around in his chair to yell after High Pockets. "Before you take off, Lester, were there any calls?"

"Not while I was here, Chief," he said opening the back door to leave. "No notes in the mail slot either."

"Nancy," Bebee said, his voice still shrill. "Try Cummings again and let him know Lester is on the way. Leave a message if you have to." Bebee always felt more in control of a situation when he could order someone to do something that he was perfectly capable of doing himself. Reminded of another piece of unfinished business, he said, "Nancy, when you're done typing, get hold of Judge Gillespie—I want a warrant delivered to Harriet Bartholomew just as soon as it's ready. Oh, and when you're not too busy, take the squad car down to Bob's Wrecking and get an estimate on my back bumper. I'll be using my pickup when you go."

"Bob's Wrecking?"

"I forgot you're new here. "It's Bob's Wrecking, Repair, & Rental Company on the flat road out of town. See if you can find that car we talked about getting for you, then call me."

He swung his feet up on his desk, lit a cigarette, and started making mental notes of what organizations he was going to call in to scour Brookside for clues to Jeffrey's disappearance. Being a Saturday, he thought, there should be a good turnout. Besides, the townsfolk that never ventured past the club entrance will be curious to see how these summer people while away their time.

*   *   *

Sandy Cummings sprinted into the conference room. "Good, I'm glad I found you, Mr. Worthington. I thought perhaps you'd left. There's a call for you in the club office. It's Mrs. Bartholomew." Sandy caught his breath. "I've been tied up all morning calling members when the operator interrupted and said this call was an emergency."

"Lead on, Sandy," said Toby.

Sydney rocked his chair forward to boost himself upright. "I'm right behind you, Toby! Oh Sandy, Sandy—Sandy, I want to have a word with you."

"Of course, Mr. Wadsworth." Sandy dropped back to walk by his side. Toby forged ahead to catch the extension phone in Sandy's office. "I'm very busy right now, but what can I do for you?"

"I'd be very appreciative if I could have a peek at the Bartholomew files. It could help us—shall we say—find Jeffrey."

"You don't have any idea how happy that would make me! It's against the rules of course, but help yourself. You know where they're kept." Sydney uttered a profuse thank you and entered the file room.

Toby lifted the open receiver on Sandy's desk, but before speaking he looked around to make sure no one could overhear his conversation. "Hello, Tobias Worthington here."

"Toby, this is Harriet. I thought you might still be there. I'm calling to apologize for my inexcusable behavior this morning. I made a complete fool of myself. I was terribly rude to you, and I want to make it up by inviting you to tea this afternoon."

Toby was completely taken off guard but managed to recover quickly. "Harriet, think nothing of it. I'm afraid it was I who reacted poorly. It was such a stressful meeting. You must be consumed with anxiety over Jeffrey's disappearance, yes?"

"Of course I am. It's so good of you to take notice, you dear man," she drawled. "At a time like this, I need to talk with someone of your sensibilities. Tea—say four o'clock?"

Vulnerable to flattery from a lady in distress was more than Toby could resist, even though he was contemptuous of Harriet and had suspicions about her past. "Off hand, I'd say there's nothing pressing on my agenda. I'll be there."

"Good," said Harriet, "I'm so looking forward to it. Ta-ta."

After saying his good-byes, he hung up the phone and joined Sydney in the file room. Sydney glanced up from Jeffrey Bartholomew's file. "Well, what was that call all about, Toby?"

"Don't be too shocked, Sydney. I'm off to Harriet's for tea this afternoon."

"Have you gone totally mad, Toby? That woman's a black widow spider. You know what a black widow does to its male counterpart. First she seduces him, and after he's shot his bolt"—Sydney snapped his fingers—"well bingo, she terminates him just like that!"

"Sydney, don't you worry yourself about me. I'm only going into that web of hers to do a little fact-finding about Jeffrey. I thought you might see this little tea party of hers as a golden opportunity."

"All right, Toby, but keep your guard up and use your wits. While you were dillydallying on the phone, I found a few things of interest in Jeffrey's personal file." Toby ignored Sydney's callous remark, and looked over his shoulder at the file. "It says here that Jeffrey's two sponsors were Mrs. Bartholomew and Malcolm Overton. You know, Overton's the president of the Cornerstone Bank."

"Isn't that the same bank that was robbed, in what, '39?"

"Yes, and Malcolm was president then too." He drew in a long breath. "It indicates here that Jeffrey filed his application for membership on 13 May 1940. So, eight years ago he showed up on our doorstep apparently out of the blue. Prior to his marriage to Harriet, he doesn't list any previous marriages or family members. No relatives mentioned. One of his two personal references lives in Argentina. A likely story. The other one's in Limestone Creek, Arizona—the address is probably some cemetery. Now this looks really bad, Toby. Note—not a single club member reference other than Harriet and Malcolm."

"How extraordinary." said Toby. "The membership committee accepted Jeffrey on some pretty slim pickings. Or maybe because he was married to Harriet, it was thumbs up all the way."

"Clumsy and inept on the committee's part, I'd say." Sydney shook his head. "Why would Overton sponsor him? Maybe you could find out this afternoon from Harriet."

Toby recalled that Overton was only one of three members at Brookside that claimed Livermore Falls as his residence. He knew that residents, in general, were not up for membership at Brookside, but out of necessity, the club's board sought a friendly relationship with a local bank. Rex Fulton was another local member, because Sydney thought the club should have an empathetic insurance broker on board. The third outsider, he remembered was Father Michael O'Connor an honorary member and listed as the club's chaplain. Being a chaplain for a number of country clubs in the region, Toby thought the good Father spent an inordinate amount of time playing golf among his flock.

Sydney moved on to rummage through Harriet's thick file. He noted that her second husband, Torrance P. Hadley, had joined Brookside in 1935. Sydney remarked, "Remember Terry Hadley? When the old buck died in '37, she retained the membership. The poor devil didn't get to play much golf, not at Brookside anyway. I think Terry was already ailing when he joined. On the downslope side of things so to speak. If my ciphering is right—according to her personal information sheet, Harriet would be just 48 today. Pretty young for someone you called an old trout this morning!"

Sydney looked up to see Toby's reaction, but Toby didn't rise to the bait. He looked down again to concentrate on the file. "Married to Jeffrey in '40. Not much else here, except for the number of times she lost her playing privileges. Looks like she had to be disciplined a half dozen times. Mostly for bad manners and cheating at bridge. Usually, you're sent packing after three times. "Let's move on, Toby. This foray isn't telling us very much." They replaced the files and slipped past Sandy at the front desk, where he had resumed phoning the membership. Out of Sandy's earshot he said, "Let's leave Alex for tomorrow. I'm bushed."

"Will you look at that?" said Toby, peering out into the portico. "There's Bebee's tall-drink-of-water deputy. He's dragging a barricade down the driveway entrance. Now, what in damnation is he doing that for?"

"I don't know, Toby, and right now I don't much care. It's out of our hands anyway. We'll talk to Alex on Saturday if he hasn't quit. Give things time. Bebee will get his comeuppance."

They had both lost their appetite for lunch and instead exited the front door and headed for the parking lot. Toby drove Sydney back to the 1876 House, where Sydney opted for an afternoon nap. No time to rest for Toby, however. He made a U-turn around the village green and headed back to his lodgings to freshen up and change for his rendezvous with Harriet.

*   *   *

At the same time Deputy Sparks was setting up barricades, Sandy Cummings was speaking with Officer Sullivan. Dutifully, she'd informed him of Bebee's orders to close the club by one o'clock and start draining the pond. Sandy was surprised but said he would comply. He immediately went about sending the kitchen help and other staff home for the day with instructions not to show up again until Monday, unless for some strange reason he called them back.

After the clubhouse staff was informed, he telephoned the golf shop to give the club pro, Johnny Palmerton, the latest edict. "Johnny, take all the caddies you've got left on the bench and send them out on the course with a message. Have the boys tell all the golfers to stop play, get back to the clubhouse, pack up, and leave the club on the double. It's the police chief's orders."

"Say, what's going on, Sandy? What's so damn important? Are the Russians coming?"

"No, but I haven't got time to explain something I don't fully understand myself. The caddies also need to let the members know that the police want Brookside closed for their investigation. That means you'll have to leave too. Your staff, the caddies, the whole lot. I'll lock things up for you. Oh, and I'll call you later on, when I can get a grip on things here."

Sandy rang Jacob Porter in the maintenance barn. "Jake, I want you to bring in all your people in from the course and let them go home early today. When you get through, come on down to the clubhouse. Deputy Sparks is here waiting for you."

"Right on it, Mr. Cummings. There's only four of my crew out on the course this afternoon raking traps. I'll take the pickup and have 'em back here and gone in a jiff."

When Jake picked up the grounds crew, they were elated with the news. Getting paid for time off didn't require any explanation, especially on a day that was hot and humid. Jake wished he had been let go too, but reasoned that, after all, he was the crew boss. He had been told to be at the club on Saturday to help drain the pond, but why was Sparks waiting for him this afternoon?

After the men left, Jake ambled his way down from the maintenance barn, which used to be home for a heard of Jerseys. That was before the farm was sold to become Brookside. He glanced back and mused about how it used to be filled with farm animals instead of tractors and mowers. Now, the barn was the only structure left standing from a collection of farm buildings that once occupied the site of the Brookside clubhouse. Jake smiled as he thought about the gas pump and tank standing where a proud old silo once did. He muttered aloud to himself, "No more smell of hay and manure, just gas and grease. No more horses—just horsepower."

Still a young man, he had been delighted to change from a life of farming to a much better paying job maintaining a golf course. He took pride in the fact that when the last course superintendent left for a better opportunity, he was chosen to fill his shoes. After all, he was a hard worker, a quick learner, and his skill with farm tractors was a real asset.

Spotting Lester Sparks wandering around the edge of the putting green, he shouted, "Hey, High Pockets. Remember me? Jacob Porter."

"Sure do, Jake. I had no idea you'd be working here. Haven't seen you in a dog's age. Maybe since high school, huh? I figured you might be working out on your pa's place."

Jake looked down at the ground. "It was time to move on. What's with you?"

"Me? I bummed around at odd jobs when I got out of the army. Here and there, you know. I was an MP in the service, goin' around bustin' heads in bars mostly, so when my folks wrote me about a deputy job opening up right here in town, I jumped at it."

Listening to Lester bluster, Jake concluded that High Pockets was content with his new station in life, and that when it came to punishment, he preferred to give rather than receive. "Jake, I hate to move on to business, but Cummings said you were going to give me a hand draining the pond."

"What—you mean today?"

"Yup, this afternoon, like right now. Chief's orders. How about it Jake?"

"OK, but that's going to be one mean job. The drain's on the bottom, and the gate valve that opens it is over there by the footbridge." Jake pointed it out. "It's been several years I'd guess since it's been used. I tried turning it myself an hour ago, just to see, but it's rusted up pretty good. Wouldn't budge. We can regulate the water level of the pond by lowering the spillway over the dam, but we can't drain the pond more than a couple of feet." Jake opened his snuff box and stuffed a plug in his cheek. "What are we doing this for anyway, some big shot lose his golf ball?"

"Truth be known, Jake, your club's lost one of its members."

"Might have guessed with all the uproar around here this morning. You don't expect to find somebody in the pond do you?"

"Well, the chief wants to eliminate it as a possibility. Said to empty it, quick's we can."

Jake spit and replied. "Empty yes, quick, maybe not. That pond's a lot deeper than it used to be when it was a watering hole for the old Benson farm. When they built the club, they dug it deep and used the excavation to make a cofferdam around a good part of the far end. My pa worked on it.

"That big drain I said was at the bottom—well, there's a pipe from it that goes under the spillway and back out into Snake Brook." Lester listened attentively. "There's a pathway on top of the dam with a footbridge over the spillway. Golfers use it to cross over. Come on let's go over there, and I'll lay things out for you."

Jake spoke first when they arrived at the footbridge. "Look at this spillway, Lester, I figure its some sixteen feet higher than Snake Brook." Lester nodded.

They walked out on the thirty-foot-long bridge and stopped in the center span of the wooden structure, which was anchored at each end by laid-up stone pillars. Lester said, "I'd wager that under a full load of golfers and caddies marching over it, these old timbers would really shake and groan. One of these fine days this bridge might just dump the lot of them in the pond." Facing the far end of the pond, the two men leaned on the handrail. Jake spat again, this time watching his tobacco ripple the mirrored surface of the water. "Yes, sir," Lester said, "The pond looks to be a good two hundred yards long. More like a lake than a pond. Maybe fifty yards wide."

"Good guess, Lester." Jake turned around to look out over the spillway. "You can see when the water leaves the pond, it drops down into Snake Brook on the flats. I can't figure out what possessed the club to stick nine holes down there where it's flatter'n a pool table. Look how the brook winds back and forth all over the map."

"Thanks for the geography lesson, Jake." Lester's voice registered his impatience. "I'm ready to get on with it if you are. Let's empty this big tub. It's Friday. I'll buy us a couple of beers tonight after we get this job behind us."

"OK, Lester. But the two of us ain't going to force that valve open. You wait for me here." Jake's aim to please others was a commendable attribute of his character, but it was also be one of his greatest weaknesses. His intentions were good, but in some cases he didn't think about something long enough to consider the consequences. "I'm going up to the barn and get me a tractor and a good long length of chain. If quick is what you want, Mr. Deputy, quick is what you'll get."

5

TEA for TWO

At precisely four o'clock, Toby pulled up in the driveway of Harriet's summer home. Her house was one of four that fronted on the nine holes down in the flats below the clubhouse and looked across at pastureland owned by the last remaining dairy farmer in Livermore Falls. After a quick appraisal of the house and gardens, Toby pressed the doorbell, which responded with a lengthy chorus of chimes to the strains of "O' Danny Boy."

Martha T., Harriet's housemaid and longtime village resident, answered the door. "Good afternoon. You are Mr. Worthington?"

"Yes, I'm expected," said Toby, shouldering his usual companion, a golf club.

"I'll announce you're here."

From another room a high-pitched voice echoed down the main hallway into the foyer, "No need, Martha. Come in, come in, Toby!" chirped Harriet prancing her way to the door. "So glad you could make it on such short notice." Harriet bubbled over. "Please, come on through to the conservatory. It has a lovely view of the course." Wearing a long-sleeved blouse, she paraded ahead of Toby, who was more interested in the cavernous house than her swaying posterior, sheathed in an overly tight-fitting brown leather skirt. "We'll have tea in the conservatory, Martha. Please bring it in there."

Toby stepped over the threshold of an open glass door to be greeted by a lush collection of indoor tropical plants. The white painted wicker furniture was upholstered with plush cushions and an excess of floral scatter pillows. The humid air was filled with a medley of subtle fragrances spread gently about by a slowly revolving ceiling fan.

"Absolutely charming place you have here," said Toby. "This room must be one of your favorite hideaways."

"You're so observant, Toby" Harriet replied softly. "Make yourself comfortable on the settee." Toby chose a far end. Harriet sat down close enough to Toby to make him a little uncomfortable since it had been a number of years since he had allowed himself to be in such close quarters with a woman, especially a woman who could be both disarming and domineering. Harriet's Chanel No. 5 dueled to a draw with Toby's Aqua Velva aftershave. Martha brought the tea service and placed it on the knee-high tabletop.

"Martha, it's almost the weekend," said Harriet. "I'm sure there are many things you'd like to attend to at home, so please feel free to leave. Oh, and take Mr. Worthington's golf club and put it in the umbrella stand on your way out."

Martha responded with a polite, "Yes, ma'am. Thank you, ma'am," and smiled as she closed the conservatory door gently behind her. An uneasy feeling came over Toby on finding himself alone and trapped with Harriet. To pour Toby's tea, Harriet inched ever closer. Toby had no room to retreat.

"Cream and sugar?" she purred.

Toby nodded. "Please, two lumps, and light on the cream."

"Of course, you must know Toby, I had another reason to ask you here today, besides apologizing for my inexcusable behavior this morning." When Harriet held out Toby's cup of tea, he noticed a slight tremor in her hands, which was accentuated by his spoon chattering on the saucer.

"I assume it has something to do with Jeffrey."

"Yes, and it's all so frightening. I don't know what to do or who to turn to. I don't know if he's just missing or maybe he's hurt out there somewhere. That gorilla Bebee's no help!" Harriet poured herself a cup of tea. "Jeffrey would never up and leave me. We've had a stormy eight years together, but we've always managed to see things through—even though he could be sweet as a canned peach one day and absolutely horrid the next. Until last night I didn't realize how much he really means to me." Harriet heaved a long wistful sigh. "Since then, I've reacted angrily to everything and everyone—including you, dear Toby. I'd be so relieved if you didn't think poorly of me."

"Of course not, Harriet. Don't be ridiculous, obviously you're deeply distressed. Perhaps it would help to talk about Jeffrey." Toby was pleased with himself that he found a wedge into the conversation that might provide some useful information. The question was, would she be forthcoming? "How did you two happen to get together?"

"It was the strangest thing. Now don't laugh!" Harriet giggled. "You know the annual street fair put on by all the churches in the village? Well, I stopped by, thinking I might pick up a cake or pie, certainly not a husband. It was a lovely Saturday afternoon, and I got caught up with the crowd. I found myself playing a ring toss game. Three rings for a quarter. Toss a ring over a duck paddling around in a makeshift pond, and you get a prize."

Harriet took Toby's empty cup and refilled it. "Hope I'm not boring you, Toby. Before my last toss, I looked up and saw this gorgeous creature of a man talking with Malcolm Overton. They started to make their way directly toward me. I just stood there, frozen, staring at him like some starstruck schoolgirl. After an eternity, we were face to face, and Malcolm introduced me to Jeffrey. He mesmerized me with his deep baritone voice and chiseled features like some Greek god. I hardly noticed when Malcolm left us alone.

"You probably don't recall, Toby, but it had been some two years since my previous husband, Terry, passed away. I was lonesome and admittedly in need of male companionship. Well, he took the ring from my hand and said, 'If I ring the duck, will you have dinner with me tonight?' I agreed. He ringed the duck, and that was the start of our romance! I remember it like it was yesterday. We were married right here in town a few weeks later at the Presbyterian Church! August 6, 1940.

"What a marvelous love story, Harriet. Did you know much about Jeffrey before you married?"

"No, Toby. I didn't feel I needed to. Malcolm did tell me that Jeffrey was financially comfortable. You know, all these wonderful memories are coming back to me now. Any more and I think I shall burst out in tears." Harriet reached across Toby's chest and removed his never-to-be-used handkerchief. She turned her head away from Toby to dab her eyes.

"There now, Harriet," said Toby softly, even though he suspected crocodile tears, "stiff lip. We'll find Jeffrey." He retrieved his handkerchief and carefully refolded it before returning it to its proper place, noticing more mascara than wetness of tears.

The front door chimed. Once, then twice more. "I'll have to get it, Toby. Now, don't you go running off. I'll be right back." Marching the length of the house, she opened the door and was not pleased to see Officer Sullivan standing there at attention.

Although Toby was some distance from the front door, he could easily overhear any conversation echoing down the long hallway. He disliked the idea of eavesdropping, unless of course it might prove useful to his mission.

"Let me see, you're Officer Nancy something."

"It's Sullivan, ma'am, and you are Harriet Bartholomew. I have a warrant here for you from Judge Gillespie. It bears the time and date you are to appear to answer charges filed by Officer Bebee."

"Is that so!" replied Harriet, cheeks flushed. Ripping open the envelope, she hastily read through the charges. "Nancy, you can take these silly pieces of paper back to Bebee, Gillespie, or whomever, and tell them these charges are baseless. I have no intention of accepting this warrant or appearing in court for that matter."

Harriet inhaled a deep-enough breath to exhale Nancy off the porch. "Let me be perfectly clear about this. First, I bumped into Bebee's damned car because he was parked too close to mine. The damages to my car are certainly more than his. Secondly, my town taxes should easily pay for a couple of scratches on his patrol car. In fact, the taxes I pay would buy your department a whole new fleet of cars! As for speeding, Nancy, I was on private property—my property in fact, since I'm a stockholder of Brookside."

Harriet drew in another deep breath for her closing statement. "I did not see or hear Bebee yelling, or waving behind me. Tell him I look where I'm going, not where I've been." She paused, looking straight into Nancy's eyes. "For the life of me, I don't understand why your boss has it in for me!"

Nancy replied quite calmly under the circumstances. "I guess it's because you rankled him. Like he said this morning, he doesn't like to be rankled."

"I have a guest, Nancy. You seem like a nice girl, and I can't stand here arguing with you all day. Now take this idiotic warrant back to Gillespie. Ask him to consider the consequences for issuing rubbish like this. Judges have to get elected—if you take my meaning."

"You'll have to keep the warrant, Mrs. Bartholomew, but I'll give the Judge your message." Nancy refused to be ruffled in kind. "By the way, would your guest be Mr. Worthington? That appears to be his car in the driveway."

"Is that any of your business?" Harriet slammed the door with a bang.

Having found Harriet's conversation with Nancy irrelevant and uninteresting, Toby seized the opportunity to examine the conservatory's visual gems. His gaze drifted among a variety of orchids, lush tropical plants, and flora uncommon in northern climates. Having followed an interest in botany at Cornell, Toby drank in their brilliant colors. A large brown spider darted from under the settee across the floor to find a sanctuary. Reminding himself of Sydney's admonishment about the similarity between dangerous spiders and certain women, Toby had the same impulse to flee. Besides, he had his own suspicions about Harriet. He could see that beneath her bravado was a tired face, weary with fear and concern that no amount of heavy makeup could hide.

The clicking of Harriet's heels down the long tiled hallway forewarned him of her return. "Toby, I'm so sorry to have left you here alone like this. I'm afraid there was a little unpleasantness at the door that needed taking care of. It was a bit unsettling. I wonder if you'd like to join me in having something a little stronger than tea? Of course, if you'd rather not—"

"Yes, Harriet, that would be nice. It's been quite a day up to now. Scotch and water, if you please."

The two drinks Harriet brought to the table had more scotch than water. "Now, before I tell you what's on my mind, I'd like to know more about you."

"Come to think of it, Harriet, not much to tell really." He stared at floor where the spider had fled and disappeared.

"Don't be silly, Toby. A good-looking man with your experience. I've only known you as a bachelor, but I imagine you've had your way with the ladies over the years—perhaps even now?"

Toby blushed and gulped his scotch. Harriet probed further, "Were you ever married?"

"Oh, yes but that was ages and ages ago. We were very young. Too young for marriage probably. At least I was. It only lasted a year." Toby started to reach for his pipe but thought better of it after his experience with her this morning. "Virginia up and walked out on me. The note she left said that she was bored and didn't give a hoot about me, my work, or golf, for that matter, even though I tried to get her to take lessons. She was full of fire, and I guess she expected me to put it out. Never heard from her again." Toby's voice quavered. "It really broke my heart, and I vowed I would never let it happen again."

"Well, it was her loss, the silly girl. Let me get you another scotch."

"Just a short one, please." Toby had surprised himself by revealing a part of his past that he hadn't shared before, even with his oldest and best friend, Sydney.

"You mentioned work. Surely a man of your means had a successful career."

"Not really Harriet—odds and ends. I had a short stint in the army when I felt a twinge of patriotism. When I graduated college, I was either overqualified for an entry-level job or not experienced enough to start half-way up the ladder. Double-edged sword so to speak."

"How terrible for you, Toby. Perhaps they thought you'd be taking a job away from someone who needed it more than you."

"Yes, but fortunately, an inheritance from my grandfather provided me with an opportunity to strike out on my own. Business wasn't the cut of my cloth, so I tried a self-funded political career, but for some reason the voters didn't really understand me. I've done public service work, of course, for various organizations, like the Red Cross. Little thanks, I tell you. They shuttled me to some other organization where they thought I would be more useful. Harriet, I finally came to the conclusion quite a number of years ago, that the best thing I could do with my life is to get out of the way of everyone else's—that and cash in my chips."

Harriet returned to the settee and eased her thigh next to Toby's. "Here we are, Toby. Cheers." She walked her fingers slowly, spiderlike, along the top of Toby's leg. Toby pretended not to notice. He was aroused, however, by an old familiar and provocative sensation he hadn't experienced for several years. Her hand then suddenly leapt from his pant leg to poke a finger gently on the end of his pudgy nose. "Now, Toby, I have a favor to ask of you."

"Certainly, Harriet, if I can oblige you in any way." said Toby, who by now was thoroughly confused. His thoughts raced back and forth between how much she professes to love Jeffrey and how much she's trying to flatter and seduce him. *Didn't she just say moments ago that her invitation to tea had to do with Jeffrey? But could she be trusted? Was it all really about me? Maybe I'm about to be used?*

"Toby, I need your help desperately, and it must be our little secret. Ours alone."

Toby was so relieved to know he might not be the object of her affection that he was prepared to do just about anything she asked. He drained the remaining scotch in his glass and reached unconsciously for hers and emptied it as well. "Sounds terribly foreboding, Harriet. You can count on my discretion."

"I just knew I could!" said Harriet. "Now then, I know that you and Sydney—and you must not tell Sydney—want to find Jeffrey as soon as possible. And so do I. I must. It's terribly important that when Jeffrey's found, I talk to him before anyone else does. I realize he may be hurt, delusional, or even suffering from amnesia. No matter. I think we both believe he's alive, and I wish, with all my heart, you could find Jeffrey for me. Toby, I don't know who else to turn to. If you can find him and bring him to me, or me to him, I'd be ever so grateful. Being grateful is something I'm good at, and I know how to show it."

"Harriet, Sydney and I are already on the hunt! In less than a day this whole tragic affair has devastated both of us and the club for that matter. Believe you me, we'll find him if anyone can. I dare say Sydney and I have come to know a lot more about Jeffrey than most. Except for you, of course. If there's anything you can add about his roots, his interests—outside the club I mean—it might be helpful."

Harriet paused to gather her thoughts. She rose from the settee and steered her way over to the conservatory bar carrying their empty glasses. "Like I said, I don't know much about his past. Malcolm didn't know much about Jeffrey either, except he said he was an independently wealthy bachelor. All I can really tell you is what I know about him since our marriage. He's still a bit of a diamond in the rough so's to speak. So I smoothed off some of the sharp edges. Besides golf, his other loves are fishing and playing poker. When we go to Florida for the winter, he's out tarpon fishing more often than golfing. He goes off on fishing trips from here too. Other times it's just an afternoon or evening, down on the Beaverkill."

Harriet weaved her way back to the settee, her arms outstretched like wings balancing two large tumblers of scotch. Toby sat mesmerized as she approached the far open end of the settee as if it was the deck of an aircraft carrier. She executed a rough bouncy landing coming to a full stop against Toby, without spilling a drop.

Picking up where she left off, Harriet continued. "Let's see, we were talking about fishing. Well, he goes away on long weekends, four or five days at a time, up north, fishing for trout. I don't pay much attention where he goes as long as he comes back. You know, Toby, I don't understand what men enjoy about fishing, do you?" Harriet paused then answered her own question. "If men love fish so much, why don't they just leave them alone?" Harriet was obviously pleased with her clever observation.

Not being a fisherman, Toby replied with a polite chuckle and an ambivalent nod of approval, then urged her to carry on.

"Well, I like to ride, as you might have guessed. Jeffrey thinks it's a bore. He plays poker with the boys, and I play bridge with the girls. So, you might say we have separate interests, except, of course, for our devotion to each other."

"Go on, Harriet. I just need to get up and stretch a bit. I'm listening." When he first got to his feet, he felt a bit wobbly, which he attributed to a sudden drop in blood pressure. He wandered through a loosely organized maze of foliage and ficus trees over to a window that looked out at the course. Harriet followed, carrying their unfinished drinks.

Before she could utter a word, Toby startled her. "Good god, Harriet. I don't believe what I'm seeing! The course is being totally flooded. The water's risen over the banks of Snake Brook. It's turning into a lake out there, the fairways are submerged. The sand traps, benches—everything's being washed down to the Beaverkill River!"

"Oh, Toby, you've got to do something," wailed Harriet. "The water's coming up to the patio!"

"I'm afraid there's no time to build an ark, Harriet." Toby rubbed his eyes to look again.

"It must be the work of that baboon, Bebee."

Draining the pond, my foot. He must have blown it up! I'll have to leave for the club now. Call to arms, don't you know." He spun around and started to breaststroke his way through the maze of foliage in the conservatory toward the front door.

"Would you be a good egg, Harriet, and call Sydney, at the '76 House? Tell him I'll pick him up on the way to the club. Ahhh . . . yes, let him know what's happening down here."

"Of course, I'll call, Sydney. I'm sure you can handle this quickly," she bawled, "we can't let this get in the way of finding Jeffrey now, can we?"

"Rotten shame this business. Sydney's worked so hard to keep the club afloat lately, and now it's under water." Weaving his way down the hallway to the front door, Toby fumbled through his jacket pockets until he found his car keys.

"Toby, do stop all this water! I know you will." Chasing after him, Harriet implored,

"Now, remember your promise!"

"Yes, yes," he stammered. "Thank you again for your kind invitation to tea. I'll see myself out." Toby closed the front door behind him only to spin around, reopen it, and reach into the umbrella stand to collect his golf club.

6

Water, Water Everywhere

During the few minutes it took Toby to arrive in front of the 1876 House, a drizzle began. Sydney was already waiting on the sidewalk. The wipers on Toby's Olds squeaked and struggled sporadically across his fogged-up windshield. Toby eased his car to a stop against the curb, as if he were docking the *Queen Mary*. Sydney collapsed his umbrella and, giving it a good shake, opened the door, and climbed in. Toby could see by the dour look on Sydney's face that Harriet had called him to say what was happening out on the course.

"Nasty change of weather eh, Sydney?" Toby forced a smile.

"Yes, but don't change the subject."

"What subject?"

"I'm coming to it, one of the many I'm about to bring up, which has nothing to do with the weather. Let's move along, Toby. By the way, when Harriet called she sounded hysterical, but then again that's not unusual for a woman of her temperament."

Here we go again, thought Toby, *another soliloquy on Brookside versus the world. Or will it be the lecture du jour? At least it's a short drive to the club.*

Sydney began his litany in somber tones like that of a preacher delivering a sermon on the pending doom of mankind. "I've got one of those nasty feelings that Brookside has a lot more problems than a flood. I heard an explosion about an hour or so ago. It was enough of a bang to wake me out of my nap. No one in the hotel could tell me what it was, but I have an uneasiness it has to do with the club."

"Good lord, Sydney, you haven't been thinking what I'm thinking—Bebee wouldn't dare blow up the dam."

"No, not today anyway." Sydney settled back in his seat. "I distinctly recall he was not going to drain the pond until tomorrow afternoon. And that was on the condition we didn't find Jeffrey somewhere on the premises."

"You're quite right, of course. Goes without saying. But the water flooding the front nine has to be coming out of our pond, either by an act of God, or Chief Bebee."

"God has better things to do I should think," snapped Sydney. "Why do you think Bebee took it on himself to drain the pond now, and with what—dynamite?"

"Damned if I know." Toby leaned forward to wipe off the fog on his windshield with his never-to-be-used handkerchief. "But I think we'll know soon enough. Something's stuck in Bebee's crop, I'd say." Toby was pleased with his explanation, and as if to punctuate it, released a loud scotch smelling belch.

Sydney turned to Toby and said in a voice filled with disdain, "I think something's stuck in your crop, and if I'm any judge, I'd say you're in your cups, and I don't mean they've been filled with tea." Sydney paused to let his observation sink in. "I've been very worried about you having tea with Harriet today, which so happens to be my next subject. Right now, I'm beginning to think she may be having her way with you."

"Nonsense, no need to worry about that. I had a couple of scotches just to play along, don't you know. Harriet consumed considerably more scotch than I did, and she divulged a great deal of useful information about Jeffrey, more perhaps than she intended. You know that old saying Sydney, 'Loose slips sink hips, loose hips sink ships.' Something like that. You figure it out, you're the navy man. Anyway, I found our brief tête-à-tête quite informative. For instance, I was able to draw out of her that Jeffrey likes to fish."

"Fish? How interesting," Sydney's patronizing response revealed his disappointment in Toby. "Try to keep focused on the road." he urged. "Now, besides apologizing to you for her rude behavior, what do you think was the real reason Harriet invited you to tea?"

"Whatever do you mean? Harriet just wants to find Jeffrey. Same as we do. Really, Sydney, I'm beginning to think we may have misjudged Harriet. She doesn't seem to be such a bad sort when you get to know her. Honestly, we've never made an effort to understand her in the past." As they approached the turnoff to the club, Toby continued, "She's a little volatile and over the top perhaps." He swerved the Olds to make the turn onto the road hole.

"Toby, Toby, Toby. You're so good hearted and vulnerable." Sydney stared past the windshield wipers with their monotonous metronome beat, weighing his words carefully, and said, "Has it occurred to you why she wants to find out where Jeffrey is?"

"No, I haven't exactly pushed myself over the edge of a cliff thinking about it. Why?"

"Well, if Jeffrey's gone missing, dead or alive, Harriet can't get any of his money for seven years."

"You don't say! But of course, you just did." Toby, chagrined by his naiveté, wheeled the Olds off onto the side of the road, set the hand brake, and left the engine idling. "This is an awful mess." Toby flung his arms over the steering wheel and buried his head. Turning his face toward Sydney, he said, "Do you realize if we had just reported Jeffrey dead to the police in the first place, none of this would be happening to us."

"Pull yourself together, Toby! Don't forget that what we did for Jeffrey saved his life—I think. I just hope he was worth saving. Now, we'd better get on down the road, or there may not be a club worth saving either."

"Sorry, old friend, I'll be all right. Just having a little mood swing." He sat straight up sucking in a deep breath. "In the end you know you can always depend on me!"

Toby slammed the Olds into first gear, glanced in the rear view mirror, and pulled back onto the road hole. The drizzle, now turning to rain, seemed to portend more terrible events to come for dear old Brookside. A bright fork of lightening lit their gloomy faces like an unwelcome flash bulb and was soon followed by a loud clap of thunder. For Sydney it was analogous to a warning shot fired across the bow of his old ship. Undaunted, they pressed on, arriving at a makeshift barrier in the clubhouse driveway. Standing behind an imposing row of barricades, Deputy Sparks, decked out in a yellow slicker, held up both hands and waved for them to stop.

Toby rolled down his window and barked, "Officer Sparks, isn't it? We're members here. Now if you would, please remove these barriers and let us pass."

"You're Worthington aren't you?" said Lester. "Is that Wadsworth with you?"

"Yes, you're right all around."

"Well, Chief Bebee is over by the pond, and he's been trying to get hold of both of you. Wants to see you right away." Lester dragged two of the barricades aside to open the road. "He's got a big problem, and he thinks you can help him out."

"Again, a big problem. Now why would that surprise me!" said Sydney, "Drive on, it's getting late in the day."

Toby stepped hard on the accelerator. As they approached the clubhouse, they noticed the flashing lights of a fire truck parked outside the portico. A limp fire hose was draped up the front steps and through the front doors of clubhouse. Volunteer firemen were standing under the portico drinking coffee. Toby braked to a stop in the traffic circle. Speechless, they emerged from the Olds and puddle-jumped their way past the fire truck to the entrance.

Looking as though he lost a fight with a waterfall, Sandy Cummings stumbled out of the club. Obviously elated to spot two familiar faces, Sandy picked up his pace and made his way toward them, waving with one hand and buttoning his blazer with the other. "Am I glad to see you, Mr. Worthington. You too, Mr. Wadsworth!"

"What the devil's going on here, Sandy?" exclaimed Sydney.

"We had an explosion in the kitchen," he stammered trying to picce things together.

"It was gas. It must have been left on while we were rushing around to shut down the club this noon. Could've been a spark from a motor or who knows what that ignited it."

"Anybody injured?" Toby asked.

"No. Thank God. The explosion blew out the whole outside back wall of the kitchen! It's just a mess of twisted stainless steel inside. Otherwise not a whole lot of fire damage, just all this fu—uh—foul bloody water everywhere!"

"Ha, Sandy," said Toby at his cynical best, "at least you won't have to worry about that sticky window in the scullery I told you about this morning."

Ignoring Toby's offhand boozy remark, Sydney observed that their new club manager was unnerved by the explosion, which could have taken his life. "Steady yourself, Sandy. You'll be all right. All is not lost, and you've still have your position. Remember that the directors voted to upgrade the kitchen this winter."

Sydney's mood piggybacked Toby's sarcasm, "Maybe the club'll manage some savings on demolition expenses."

"Excuse me, gentlemen, I don't know if I'm cut out for this job." Sandy rocked his head slowly from side to side. "I don't think I can handle this sh—stuff. It certainly wasn't in my job description. I've got a family you know."

"Sandy, the club really needs you now," said Sydney who was suddenly confronted with the reality of losing their manager. "Toby and I think you've got the mettle for it."

"Yes, I couldn't agree more," said Toby confirming Sydney's vote of confidence. "We're all going through a rough patch right now, but if you'll help the club see it through—well, young man you're on your way to very lucrative career! So, no more talk about throwing in the towel." He removed his never-to-be used handkerchief, wiped Sandy's water soaked brow, and stuffed the handkerchief in Sandy's breast pocket. "There you are, right as rain!"

"That's very kind of you, gentlemen. I appreciate your confidence in me." Sandy paused before responding further. He looked down at the handkerchief that had been pressed in his blazer pocket as if it were a medal awarded for courage above and beyond the call of duty. Unconsciously emulating Sydney's manner of speech, he said, "I'll give it my best, for now . . . wouldn't want to abandon a sinking ship, don't you know."

"We're both obliged to have you stay on board," replied Sydney.

"But I have to tell you," declared Sandy, "that we've got some other problems too. The members were really grumbling when they had to leave the course this afternoon. The Tinkers and the Stevensons told me they are tendering their stock and putting it up for sale. They said they are telling their friends they'd be wise to do the same."

"Good riddance, I say." Toby was indignant. "With this new crowd there's no tolerance for the slightest inconvenience."

Sydney's greatest fear was coming true—that the club was going to hell. The evening before he wasn't sure how or by what means it would come to pass. The sense of doom he held was certainly manifesting itself in today's events. He thought about Toby's no-tolerance remark. Perhaps Brookside has more than one road leading to hell. Maybe it was the coming of the nouveau riche, younger families expecting to be spoiled. Being more mobile since the war, people with a taste for what is new and different were easily seduced by a growing myriad of competitive choices, including other country clubs.

And then there was today's confrontation with Chief Bebee. He had left more than a superficial impression that the relationship between the community and the club was seriously conflicted and on a collision course. What could the club have done to prevent or deserve the town's tattered opinion of Brookside? No one could blame him or the club. It must be the changing times.

*   *   *

"Look Sandy, here comes Rex Fulton up the drive," said Sydney. "Lester must have let him through too."

"I know, I called him. Figured I'd better get our insurance broker up here right away."

"Good man. While you take care of Rex, Toby and I will see what Chief Bebee wants."

Sandy muttered under his breath, "If they only knew who else was there and why." Another boom of thunder rattled the clubhouse windows and rumbled down the valley. This time it was a signal the storm had moved on. The rain had let up, and a chilling breeze followed in the storm's path.

Each carrying an umbrella and his familiar club, Sydney and Toby walked abreast until they approached the shallow end of the pond where they stopped to survey the landscape. Up ahead a few men chatted alongside a number of vehicles that had been driven out onto the golf course. The cars were parked by the footbridge at the far end of the pond. Each vehicle left its own serpentine signature of muddy ruts.

"Just think, Sydney, we were here this morning looking forward to playing a decent round of golf. Now, here we are, it's almost six o'clock, and we're virtually up to our ankles in mud. It's deep enough to suck my shoes off!"

"I'd rather not think about golf if you don't mind. I'd rather concentrate on how to turn this fiasco around. Say, isn't that the town hearse up ahead?"

Toby squinted toward the footbridge. "You mean the ambulance? I found out from Alex it does double duty in Livermore Falls. In either case I don't think it bodes well for Brookside."

The ambulance, or hearse, was backed up a few yards from the edge of the pond not far from Chief Bebee's squad car. A chill came over Sydney. He shuddered and steadied himself using his golf club like a cane. His thoughts raced through the worst possible scenarios, all of which included the empty pond and the whereabouts of Jeffrey.

"Come on Toby, no sense dillydallying. Let's get up there and make our contribution." Silently, they picked their way, sidestepping puddles and ruts along the shoreline of the pond.

The pond was virtually empty. Snake Brook ran harmlessly along its bottom. The banks were covered with a thick layer of black ooze and green slime that reeked with the odor of decaying vegetation. A few gasping trout lay flopping near the outlet. Bewildered, a pair of mallards wandered along the edge. Perhaps they wondered how their home suddenly disappeared. Saturated sludge moved down the banks like lava revealing some of the objects the muck had devoured over the years—bottles, cans, a couple of worn-out tires, and a number of golf clubs thrown in anger.

As they worked their way along the edge of the pond, they marveled at the sight of hundreds of golf balls that had splashed harmlessly on the surface of the pond only to drift aimlessly down to a watery grave. The bottom bloomed like a field of white flowers in spring.

"You know, Sydney, I'd say most of those balls belong to you," mused Toby.

"Must you make light of everything?"

"No, but I didn't think a little levity would hurt under the circumstances. Come to think of it, it's been an age since you've cleared the pond with your tee shot."

"It so happens, Toby, that I cleared it with plenty to spare the last time I played. I didn't happen to be playing with you! If half those balls are mine, then the other half must be yours."

"Touché, Sydney. Have it your way."

*   *   *

Chief Bebee, appropriately attired in foul-weather gear, was pacing back and forth in front of his car, waiting impatiently for Sydney and Toby to arrive. Spotting them he bellowed, "Glad you boys could show up. Why is it I always have to end up dealing with you two?"

"Because we're always in the neighborhood?" answered Toby.

"Don't you people have a president, prime minister, or something?" Bebee asked.

Sydney, although irritated, replied politely, "Our president, Forest Eddy, is out of circulation for a few days. He happens to be back in Indiana for a family funeral. I don't think he's expected back until sometime Sunday. The board of directors is up in Stowe, Vermont, on a four-day planning retreat—left yesterday. So there you have it, Chief. You probably knew that anyway and just wanted to hear it from us. As you say, we'll just have to do in their place."

On the short walk to meet the other men, Sydney could not contain his anger. Devastated by surveying the empty pond, he knew he should hold his tongue but felt compelled to blurt out, "You realize, Chief, that today's destruction is all your doing! Not even a crack division of the Russian army could wreak this much havoc. It'll take years to stitch up the wounds you've opened. And for what?"

"Don't be so quick to pass judgment, Mr. Wadsworth. It was your man who managed to breach the dam." Bebee paused and looked Sydney in the eye. "It was your staff that led to the explosion in the clubhouse, and I don't mind telling you it was the town's fire department that saved the rest of the clubhouse. So let's give this whole subject a rest."

Reaching the others, Bebee began the introductions. "Now, if you'd gather 'round, I'd like these two gentlemen to get acquainted with you. Over here is Mayor Bill Yates, if you haven't met him already, and this is Chester Peabody. He's the town undertaker." Bebee swallowed hard, "This is Sydney Wadsworth and Toby Worthington, two of Brookside's oldest and most distinguished members."

Sydney and Toby exchanged greetings with the mayor whom they had previously met at a club reception. As they turned to shake hands with Peabody, they noticed what they surmised must be a corpse lying just a few feet away with a yellow canvass tarpaulin folded over it.

"How do," said Chester tipping his fedora before shaking hands. His face was etched in that perpetual look of sympathy characteristic of his trade. "Over there is my assistant, Walter Beckwith. He's a little shy around strangers, aren't you Walter? But, I couldn't manage without him. Come over here and shake hands with these two fine gentlemen." Walter approached and stared at the ground before extending his hand to Sydney, then Toby.

Growing impatient, Toby couldn't wait on Bebee to speak. "Chief, you don't mean to say that you've found Jeffrey?" He nodded in the direction of the tarp.

"We don't think so," said Bebee. "But we thought you fellows would know. That's why I had you two summoned. The deceased is a male probably in his fifties. If it isn't Jeffrey, you might be able to tell us if our John Doe is a member of Brookside." Bebee paused to be sure he had everyone's attention. "I sure as hell didn't want to get Harriet Bartholomew down here if it wasn't Jeffrey."

Toby's thoughts flashed back to the questions he'd raised with Sydney concerning the legality of moving of a dead body. "Somebody did call the county coroner, didn't they?"

"I know my duty," replied Bebee sharply. "Just so's you know, Jake and Deputy Sparks discovered the corpse. It was lying in the deepest part of the pond snagged up against the outflow drain right below the middle of the footbridge. Let's go check out the body and see what we've got."

Peabody and his assistant walked over to the tarp with all the pace and dignity required of their profession. Everyone followed reluctantly as if each was unsure this exercise was absolutely necessary. Each politely invited the others to proceed ahead of them, until finally Sydney and Toby found themselves at the head of line right behind Chester and Walter.

"Suicide?" Sydney inquired.

Bebee, bringing up the rear, suddenly looked amused by Sydney's question. "I don't think so, and I don't think you will either when you see this fellow."

Sydney still curious, "Was he dead when he was pulled out?"

Chester thought it was his place to answer and that he was the most qualified to do so. "Oh, yes, quite so. I'd say he's been dead for all of a week. Another thing, I think he was dead before he hit the water."

"So do I," said Bebee. "For the benefit of everyone here, I want you to know that Deputy Sparks was the one who called to tell me he'd found a body in the pond. I rushed over here and arrived right after Jake dragged the body out. Good thing Jake took the initiative to fish him out of there. Otherwise it could have been a helluva long time fetching a body out of this quagmire. The corpse was weighed down and was sinking in the mud."

Everyone listened intently, "To get our John Doe out of there, Jake waded down through all that muck to tie a length of rope around his waist. Lester and Jake couldn't drag him out, so Jake got the club tractor to pull him up on the bank." I had Jake hose him down so's we could get a decent look, maybe get a positive ID. You know the rest. I do know that if we didn't drain the pond, this poor devil might never have been found."

Bebee had seized the opportunity to exonerate himself for draining the pond and for the moment was quite pleased with himself. Everyone, including Sandy Cummings and Rex Fulton, who had walked up from the clubhouse a few minutes ago, jostled their way into a crude circle around the tarp.

Bebee began, "I want you people to know I got Chester Peabody over here before you arrived to lend us his expertise. It's good to get a jump on the state police before they show up. Sure as hell they'll be taking charge of this case, and I think we should show them we're on top of things in Livermore Falls, not a bunch of hicks botching things up." Bebee's eyes darted around the group searching for looks of approval, especially from the mayor, who found Bebee wanting of late. "I thought it would help an investigation to know if the victim was dead or alive before entering the pond. At my suggestion—and with Chester's approval—Walter obligingly stood on the back of the victim's chest. He rocked his weight back and forth while Chester here looked for signs of water coming out of his lungs and mouth. You didn't observe any, right, Mr. Peabody?"

"No, Chief. But I think we might have broken a couple of the victim's ribs with Walter prancing on his back."

"Murder then?" inquired a distraught mayor. Yates looked pale, unsteady, and ready to collapse. He managed to curb his long-held disdain for the chief and how he turned a simple missing person case into something that looked as if it could become a real debacle. His immediate problem, however, was holding back his deep-fried lunch that was rising in his throat like a gusher from an oil rig.

"No question about it," replied Bebee. "Chester, would you and Walter please remove the tarp?"

They slowly pulled the tarp back to reveal the entire torso, folding the tarp evenly and reverently as they went. Jaws dropped, eyes rolled back, heads turned away, breaths grew short, and the would-be exclamations of surprise and shock stuck in the throats of those who were viewing the victim for the first time. Bill Yates did a quick about face, took a few wobbly steps away from the group, and relieved his distress.

The victim was naked except for a pair of black slacks. The fly was open and the pockets were turned out. The bloated body lay prone, extended, bare-chested, ashen, no shoes or socks, no belt, watch, wallet, or even a tattoo to help identify him to the civilized world. Obviously, the murderer wanted to obscure the identity of the corpse as long as possible. What mystified everyone, more than anything else, was that the victim's pant legs were completely stuffed with a full set of golf clubs with the intent to weigh the body down.

Sydney was the first one able to speak. "Amazing—it's definitely not Jeffrey—thank God. I think I can speak for Toby that this man is not a member of Brookside. Plus, I doubt either of us has ever seen this person before, on or off these premises."

"Quite right, Sydney," said Toby, drawing closer to the body. "If I'm not mistaken, these clubs are made by Spaulding. Do you mind if I remove one and have a closer look?"

Bebee sighed, "Go ahead if you think it's important."

Toby slipped a loose midiron out of the victim's pants just as he would a club from his golf bag. He stepped to one side as the others fixed their gaze upon him. He waggled the club back and forth as if to take a shot; then he quickly whipped it over to inspect the club head up close.

"I was right, gentlemen, they're Spaulding Top Flites, this year's model. Quite expensive, so to speak. These clubs can only be purchased in a golf professional's shop. So I'd say if you want to identify this fellow, you might start by finding out from the pros in this area who sold any of these clubs recently." After a short pause before an attentive audience, "If you'll notice"—he pointed at the shaft near the club head, "there's a serial number on the hozzle. Spaulding should be able to tell you who they shipped these clubs to." Toby returned to the corpse. He carefully replaced the club by sliding its grip end back down inside the same pant leg he had taken it from. Chief Bebee was impressed. "I'll get Lester on it."

During Toby's animated observations, Sydney stared solemnly at the corpse. Unnoticed, he edged closer to the body, and with his reading glasses firmly affixed to his nose, he bent over a number of times for a closer inspection of the corpse. Right after Bebee finished his remark, Sydney stood erect and pocketed his glasses. "I think I know how he died."

The mayor, quite recovered from his temporary illness, had returned to the gathering and overheard Sydney's comment. "Oh, come on, Sydney, how'd you know that?"

"Simple, really. Look at the divot on the back of his head just above the right ear. Cut a swath of hair right off his scalp. The blow was obviously administered by an exceptionally strong, full swing with a golf club. May I illustrate?" Gripping his club and extending his arms he took a mighty swing like Casey at the bat. "To put a point on it, it was probably a 5-iron."

"Are you so sure about that?" said Toby turning his full attention to Sydney's observation. In order to get a better look, he knelt down on the edge of a tarp that was stretched out under the body. After a cursory examination and a long pause, he continued, "Based on the shape and depth of the wound, Sydney, I'd say it looks more like an 8- or 9-iron."

Bebee interrupted their conversation. "If you two gentlemen don't mind, I think I'll leave all these questions for the medical examiner's office. They're the experts. We're all through here. Oh, except I need to get Lester over here to take some pictures."

Bebee then set his sights on Peabody. "Chester, I'd like you to hang around here for a while. I'm going to send my deputy over here to take a few pictures of the body and crime scene. If the coroner doesn't show up by say seven o'clock, I'd appreciate it if you'd take our John Doe down to your mortuary and keep him there until the coroner finally does make an appearance."

"Glad to, Chief, I want to help any way I can. I'll be sending my bill to your office."

Sydney quietly snipped and lit a fresh cigar. Toby stood by while the others moved slowly away from the body and back to their cars. Bebee waved Sydney and Toby over to where he came to a halt, well out of the earshot of others.

"What seems to be the trouble, Chief?" asked Toby. "We're both pretty tired and hungry to boot."

"No trouble," replied Bebee with an unusual degree of civility. "I'd just like us to have a little chat over at the clubhouse where I can get in someplace dry. It won't take long—have you home by seven."

7

A Parley

Walking in single file, the three entered the open front door of the clubhouse with Sydney leading the way and the chief bringing up the rear. Absent electricity, the inside was dark except for the evening light filtering through the sagging wet sheer curtains. The air smelled of soot mixed with the pungent odor of water-soaked carpets and swelling wood floors. The volunteer firemen had left, but the evidence of their presence remained. The three could overhear Sandy and Rex who had gone to the main office to discuss damages, claims, and the process of clean up.

"Can we go some place private?" asked Bebee.

Looking around, Sydney was shocked at what he observed, and his voice tried to hide the dismay he felt in his heart. "Let's work our way over to the men's locker room. I don't expect there'll be very much damage there. But I do know it has a battery powered emergency lighting system. Latest thing I believe—state of the art."

"Well, Chief," said Toby, "you won't have much to search for in here tomorrow. Not if you're looking for clues to Jeffrey's disappearance anyway." Toby, who would know the way to the locker room blindfolded, took the initiative and forged ahead in the darkness.

As Sydney had suspected, the gas explosion in the kitchen had excused the men's locker room from the blast. Usually at this time of day, the locker room buzzed with conversation, frequently punctuated with the echoes of slamming locker doors. Bebee interrupted the eerie silence, "So this is what it looks like in here—nice, very nice." Bebee fashioned a clumsy pirouette; his eyes swept the room like the revolving light on top of his squad car.

"Listen, I'm going to talk to you off the record, you're both off the record too. Confidential, OK?" Sydney and Toby were so stunned that they both collapsed next to each other on the nearest bench.

"Certainly, Chief," replied Sydney. "And I think I can speak for Toby too. What's on your mind?"

"In your lingo, I'd be out-of-bounds if I didn't thank you for your help today. But I'm not so sure you boys are leveling with me. I think both of you know a lot more about what's going on here than you're telling me." Sydney and Toby ignored his accusation, and his words dropped on the floor like spent bullets falling short of their target.

"Since you're off duty, Chief," said Sydney, "why don't you join us for a nip? Take the edge off a bad day for all of us. The bar's locked up, but I keep a little scotch in my locker." Sydney rose to walk down the aisle to his locker. *Perhaps,* he thought to himself, *a dram or two of scotch might loosen Bebee's tongue.* "It's against club rules, but since my heart attack, I keep the necessary on board for emergencies and medicinal purposes."

Bebee thought to ingratiate himself by agreeing to Sydney's invitation. "Since I think we have a cordial understanding, don't mind if I do." Bebee took off his rain gear and tossed his hat up on a nearby coat hook. "By the way, Sydney, do you still have a driver's license?"

"Oh yes. But I prefer not to drive. I don't keep a car here just for the summer." Sydney returned with his hand around the neck of an open bottle of Johnny Walker. "Why'd you ask, Chief?"

"Now don't take offense, Toby, but I think you've boozed enough for one day. I think Sydney should drive you back to the village tonight."

Toby lied. "No offense taken—certainly not yet anyway. Sydney can handle the Olds almost as well as I can." Toby got up to move the benches closer to the lights over the exit doorway

"By the way, Toby, you don't mind if I ask you what you were doing up at Mrs. Bartholomew's this afternoon. Playing footsie? Makes me think that nasty exchange between you two this morning was just an act to throw me and the others off."

"Now see here, Two Bullets, let's not start getting off on the wrong foot again." Toby was miffed that anyone would accuse him of diddling around with a married woman. "How'd you know I was there anyway?"

"Maybe a little birdie told me." Bebee snickered returning to form. "I have ways of knowing what's going on in my town."

"Well, know this. Harriet—harumph—Mrs. Bartholomew and I are hardly an item! She's a married woman if that's managed to escape you.

I went to her house as any decent gentleman would do—to comfort her under extremely difficult circumstances."

"Of course you would, Toby, excuse my choice of words. No need to get rankled. For all I know you and Sydney may be an item."

Sydney was outraged and almost lost his grip on the bottle of scotch. "In the spirit of comity," he responded quietly and in a controlled voice, "you'd better change course Bebee, if you know how to set your sails. Remember, you're our guest on these premises unless you've come with a search warrant." He sat the bottle down on the end of the closest bench and asked Toby to get three paper cups from the water cooler. "You know, Chief, earlier today I was beginning to think those two pieces of lead you're carrying around in your ass might be lonesome for another one." Sydney let his words soak in before he cracked a thin smile. "At that time I would have been happy to oblige you with another bullet so it would make a threesome!"

"Is that so?" Bebee was startled that his offhand remark was met with such a firm rebuke. "I guess I deserve your getting sore. Sometimes my tongue jumps way ahead of what I'm thinking."

"I agree, it does, but since I understand we're here to get along," said Sydney, "hold out your cup and have a spot of this. Obviously, there's no ice, but if you really think you need water with a fine scotch, there's plenty of it over there in the cooler."

Not to have his manhood demeaned, Bebee extended his cup and exhorted Sydney to pour.

The three men raised their brimming paper cups toward each other in a silent toast to civility. They were weary of sparring with each other, and once again Johnny Walker, as referee, formed an unlikely brotherhood out of these sniping adversaries. Johnny bridged the gap between generations, social status, and old prejudices—at least for the time being.

"Now you two fellows," Bebee began, "probably know more about Jeffrey than anyone else around here. Can you tell me anything at all that might help me find him? It's been over 24 hours now since he's disappeared. Just before we walked down here, I put in a call to the state police to report a missing person." He took another long draft from his cup. "What a day. I no sooner finished calling them than I had to report a body found in the drink here! Can't wait to talk to those hot shot troopers and detectives when they show up." Bebee drained the remaining scotch in his cup. "I don't mind telling you that I'm up over my waders on this one."

"I agree with you, but frankly, Chief, we don't know that much about Jeffrey ourselves." Sydney got up and went over to replenish Bebee's cup. "Toby and I know what's mostly common knowledge. We've played golf with him, infrequently I might add, but we know his twenty-six handicap is legitimate. Outside the club, he's been married to Harriet about eight years. Every so often he gets sloshed, but who wouldn't under those circumstances, if you take my meaning."

Sydney returned to his bench, sat down, and folded his arms across his chest. "I saw no particular character flaws that were inconsistent with our club rules. His demeanor and dress were what we expect of all our members, but Toby has always had some reservations about Jeffrey." Sydney looked over at Toby. "Do you have anything to add?"

After a long pause and several glances back and forth with Sydney, Toby said, "Well, gents, I did learn today that Jeffrey likes to fish."

"Fish!" Once again, Bebee sensed he was being put off. The three observed a verbal cease-fire for the next few minutes. Each decided that maybe a good smoke was in order since talking wasn't going anywhere. The smoke from the heavy sweet pipe tobacco, the pungent exhaust from a glowing cigar, and a smell like burning newspapers from a cigarette commingled and rose to be trapped against the ceiling while the floor served as a convenient ashtray.

Toby got up and slouched against the doorway wall. With one hand grasping the back of his neck and the other wrapped around his pipe, he gave the appearance of one deep in thought. He abruptly broke the silence. "You know, Chief, as long as you're here, and we seem to be passing time chitchatting, why don't you have a look in Jeffrey's locker right now instead waiting until tomorrow?"

"Good thinking, Toby." Bebee, now energized, struggled to his feet. "No time like the present. I might even find a clue. Aren't the lockers locked up?"

"Hardly," said Sydney who once again had his usual sedate state of mind disturbed. "The members here are gentlemen, not thieves! Follow me, Chief, and I'll show you where Jeffrey hangs his hat. Oh, and pass me that flashlight in your belt. We might find it useful."

In the dim light, the three men felt their way down between a long row of lockers, sometimes stumbling over shoes left in the aisle, knocking a shin against a bench, or ricocheting off an open locker door. The beam from Bebee's flashlight was wasted much of the time flickering over the ceiling while the trio struggled for appropriate adjectives to curse the dark.

Arriving in the proximity of Jeffrey's locker, Sydney scanned the brass nameplates on the locker doors. "Here we are, men, this one's Jeffrey's. Thank heavens we found it before one of us got killed! You open it, Chief. Here, take back your flashlight. I want no part of invading Jeffrey's privacy."

Bebee swung the locker door open. Nothing seemed unusual as he reached inside to inspect the contents. There was a change of street clothes, club blazer and tie, rain slicker, rain pants, a pair of street shoes, golf shoes, and a pouch of golf balls with tees and markers. He turned his attention to the top shelf and beamed the light deep inside. A woolen golf cap was stuffed to one side in the back corner. Loose change and matchbooks surrounded a large bottle of aspirin.

"Whoaa—what have we here!" Bebee reached in to pull out a bottle of prescription medicine. "This must be the stuff Mrs. B. was squawking about this morning. I want to get a better look at this back in the light." This time, Bebee led the threesome stumbling and bumbling their way back. Sydney closed Jeffrey's locker door and brought up the rear.

Back at their three bench cluster, Sydney suggested they toast their discovery. Toby agreed, and Bebee thought another drink might help his vision in the poor light. The Chief gulped what little remained in his cup to make room for what he anticipated would be a generous refill from Sydney. He was not disappointed. Bebee set Jeffrey's prescription bottle down and proceeded to wipe the lenses of reading glasses with a tie that divulged the previous week's lunch specials at Sally's Diner. Toby sat down and held out his cup in Sydney's direction. On the way over to Toby, Sydney filled his cup at the water cooler. Returning, he winked at Toby and poured a mere smidgen of scotch into his cup. As he sat down next to Toby, he placed the almost empty bottle of scotch on the floor.

Chief Bebee was absorbed with the discovery of Jeffrey's prescription. He held it up to the light to get a reading, especially the fine print. "Well, the old witch was right this morning about his medication. It's definitely some sort of heart medicine. There's a warning down here at the bottom that goes on about not taking it with alcohol." Bebee dropped the bottle into his lap and stopped to ponder a moment about the meeting he held this morning in the club's conference room. In spite of his liberal consumption of scotch, he clearly recalled Mrs. Bartholomew's warning about the medication that she'd picked up for Jeffrey.

"The bottle's been opened too." Bebee observed the broken seal. Twisting the cap open, he stood up to peer inside. "Jeffrey must have taken one dose anyway. You don't suppose that's why he was acting crazy drunk yesterday in the bar with Alex?"

"Possibly," said Sydney. "Of course, but how bad off could he have been if he came in here, changed clothes, and went out to play a few holes of golf in the evening? As we all have reason to believe."

"Well, you can't expect me to understand what you people do. You club people are all a bit of a mystery to me." Bebee, wearing a smug smile, put away his glasses and sat down hard on the bench again. He clenched the prescription in both hands. "I really think this medicine rang Jeffrey's bell after he got out on the course. He went nuts and wandered off somewhere. Maybe he's dead. You two got any better ideas?"

Toby leaned forward to proffer a thought. "Chief, we don't really know what's in that bottle you're holding. It's been opened, as you say. Could it have been tampered with? Maybe there's no medicine in it at all. And you shouldn't rule out poison either."

"Jumping Jehoshaphat, you're right, Toby!" said Bebee. "I was just beginning to think along those same lines. First thing in the morning I'm going to send this bottle up to the crime lab in Albany."

Toby rose to his feet, went over to Bebee, and put his hand on his shoulder. "You might think about having it tested for oleander."

"Excuse my total stupidity, Mr. Worthington, but what in the hell is that?"

Sydney leaned forward to listen in. Toby took a deep breath before giving his professorial explanation. "Chief, oleander is a beautiful but lethal flowering plant that grows in southern climates. Nerium oleander, I believe, is the name it's recognized by in knowledgeable circles. Consuming just one of its leaves can be deadly. Basically, the leaves contain toxins that affect the heart."

Bebee looked mystified, "You sure know a lot more than you let on. Now how'd you come up with that fancy-dan idea, Toby?"

"Maybe a little birdie told me." Toby shot back. In his minor skirmishes of wit with Bebee, Toby felt he had at least drawn even. "Let's just say that it was a thought that dropped in on me."

Bebee looked up at Toby and slurred his reply, "Well, by God, I shtink it's a damn good thought."

Sydney looked at his pocket watch and proposed, "Men, it's after eight. I think it's about time to pack it in. Supper is getting high on my priority."

"Judas priest, you're right!" said Bebee looking at his watch. "Vera's gonna kill me."

"You know, Chief," Toby piped up, "ever since I was a kid, I wanted to drive a police car to see what it was like! How about you letting me have a run at it, and I'll drop you off at home. Sydney can follow us in my Olds and take me home from your place. Right, Sydney?"

"Great idea, and don't you worry none," replied Sydney. Toby presumptuously tossed his car keys in his Sydney's direction.

Still seated, Bebee said, "Well, I really don't see any harm in it. I live only a few blocks from here up on Cemetery Street. Here, Toby, take my keys. Bring the car 'round, and I'll meet you by the front door."

Toby found his way in the darkness back through the clubhouse. He strode out onto the course where Bebee had left his car. The fresh air gave him new life and energy. Caught up in the excitement and anxiety of driving a new vehicle, he wondered if he would be able to operate it with the same alacrity as his prewar coupe.

Sydney took charge of the chief's flashlight, and with Bebee's hand on his shoulder, he led their return to the entrance lobby. Sandy and Rex had left the club much earlier and, out of habit, locked up all the outside doors. Leaning his back against the panic hardware, Sydney opened the front door, and the two struggled out onto the portico to wait for Toby.

Watching Toby maneuver his new squad car with apparent abandon across a muddied fairway, Bebee's eyes rolled over like a bad trip on a roller coaster. Toby fishtailed and skidded dangerously near the edge of the empty pond. Sydney held his breath and wondered if Toby, floundering hell-bent-for-leather, was driving like this to annoy the chief or because of his recent consumption of scotch. Sydney closed his eyes and said to himself, *Where is St. Christopher when we need him?*

Whether Sydney's prayers had been answered or not, Toby locked up the brakes and brought the chief's car to a sliding stop past the portico. The Chevy spit mud on Sydney and Bebee, to the annoyance of both.

With the engine idling, Toby reached across the seat and flung the passenger door open.

"Nice rig you've got here, Chief. My old buggy is no match for this beauty. Hop in. These new plastic seat covers are a nice touch. Plaid, just like our lawn chairs at the Maple Leaf Inn."

Bebee, no longer in control of events, obediently slid in next to Toby.

"Wait for me to pull up behind you, Toby." Sydney started to walk away but turned to say, "When I drive up behind you, I'll blink my headlamps, and you can proceed—but don't drive too fast just because you're in a police car." Sydney laughed. Bebee sighed and slouched back in his seat.

Toby switched on the high beams and eased the Chevy into first gear. He adjusted the rear view mirror and noticed Sydney following. As the two cars inched their way down the club's entrance drive, Bebee waved at Toby who interpreted it to mean "pick up the pace." Obliging, Toby accelerated and inadvertently knocked over the wooden barricade that was lying in their path. As it tumbled over, it lodged itself on the chief's rear bumper. It went unnoticed by Toby and the chief, but Sydney saw it, and a lump rose in his throat that refused to go away.

As Toby and the chief reached the junction with the road hole, Toby sighted a car parked on the opposite side of the road. "Will you look at that, Chief? Someone's left a junker across the street."

Bebee opened his eyes for a moment but did not find it worthy of a serious comment. "Probably some kid in a jalopy ran out of gas and left it there." The two cars and one barricade turned out onto the road hole and headed for Cemetery Street.

Only Sydney noticed that their procession was joined by another car. He reasoned that the headlights he saw in his mirror had to be from the old wreck that was parked on the shoulder of the road outside the club entrance. The car behind mimed his every move of slowing down and speeding up. And when the car behind hung back and made no effort to pass, Sydney realized that he, or their convoy, was being followed. Another lump joined the one already lodged in Sydney's throat.

*　　*　　*

Up ahead, an oblivious Toby took delight in driving Bebee's new squad car. "Chief, if you don't mind I'd really like to turn on the flashing lights—the ones on top."

Bebee mumbled. "Go ahead, there are two switches on the dash above the radio telephone. Turn 'em both on for all I care. Let's just get moving."

"OK, Two Bullets, here we go." Toby punched the gas pedal to the floor, and the Chevy jumped forward, spinning its rear wheels and throwing a hail of gravel. With the sudden lurch of the squad car, the barricade dislodged from the rear bumper and tumbled down the road. Sydney, concentrating on the car following in the mirror, did not have time to swerve out of the way. Amidst flying gravel, it came to rest on the radiator grille of Toby's beloved Oldsmobile.

Startled by the rapid and unfamiliar acceleration from Bebee's souped up Chevy, Toby stomped on the brakes tossing them both forward. Toby's nose hit the horn. Bebee rammed his forehead into the knob on the glove box. The cars behind fishtailed to a stop.

"Jumping Jehoshaphat, Toby!" exclaimed Bebee. "Do you have any clue how to drive?"

"Of course I do, Chief. Remember I'm on my first date with this new set of wheels." Toby, not about to give up his station behind the wheel, quickly shifted down into first gear, and this time released the clutch as gently as he could. He added, "This little lady's quick on her feet. Packs quite a wallop, wouldn't you say?"

"Yeah, well let's get on up the road. I've got a big date myself—hic—tomorrow at your club with a search party of volunteers—maybe a hun'red to a hun'red and stiffy.

"Well, I don't think you're going to find Jeffrey in the clubhouse since a good chunk of it's blown up." Toby leaned forward on the wheel, squinting to focus on the road ahead. "Didn't find him in the pond either. Ha—at least we came close by finding a body. You might want to look for Jeffrey in our wood lot. There must be 20 acres we own on both sides of the road hole." Toby rambled on, "The front nine's turned into a swamp when the dam failed. Wouldn't even be able to walk it. So there's not many places left to find Jeffrey or even a clue for that matter." Toby didn't notice that Two Bullets had tuned him out a while back and was slipping in and out of sleep. "You know, Chief, our being on the same side of the law and all, I must tell you that you've managed to offend everyone associated with Jeffrey's disappearance. And that includes the golf god."

Bebee half opened one eye and mumbled. "Now just how do you figure that?"

"Obvious," replied Toby still staring straight ahead. "The golf god lives in the pond, and you're responsible for evicting him. As gods go, he's not the most pleasant one, and for the most part downright vengeful, especially if members unwittingly violate the rules of the game. He snatches a perfectly good golf shot out of the air, one that would obviously carry over the pond, then he drags the ball straight down into the mucky floor of his living room."

"You don't say." Bebee, indifferent to the golf god, dozed off.

"I do say. Certainly, you don't believe all the miserable things happening at the club are any fault of Sydney and me. It's the golf god. Yes, I'd watch my back if I were you."

The radiophone blinked followed by a woman's voice. "Chief Bebee, come in please. This is Officer Sullivan."

Bebee woke, fumbled with the phone and replied, "Yes, Nancy, what is it?"

"Are you aware sir that you're being followed by Toby Worthington?"

"Not very likely. Mr. Worthington is sitting right here beside me—hic—driving my car. Get your head on straight Nancy and meet me at the club in the morning, six-thirty sharp. Bebee out."

"See that house up there on the right Toby, the one with the porch light on—hic—that's my place. After I tell the old lady what I've been through today, she'll be glad to see me."

"I should think so," said Toby. He pulled up in front of house, shut off the motor, and turned out the headlights. Sydney drove up and parked a few feet behind. The car following Sydney had also come to a stop about fifty yards back on a deserted stretch of Cemetery Street.

"Say there, Toby, wasn't Sydney supposed to drive you home? You're in no shape to be driving, you know. I'd give you a ticket if I had my book."

"Don't worry, Chief, Sydney's going to drive me home as soon as I get out of the car. He's right behind us."

"Nancy just told me you were following right behind us. You aren't Sydney by any chance?"

"I don't think so," Toby replied.

Toby opened the door and slid out. As he did he noticed a woman, obviously Bebee's wife, parting the living room curtains to observe the shenanigans. Toby leaned back in around the open door and warned the chief to put ice on the lump rising on his forehead.

Leaving the Olds headlights on, Sydney stepped out of the car to remove the wooden barricade from Toby's radiator grille. Hunched over between the cars, he summoned up all his strength, took a deep breath, and ripped the damaged barricade from Toby's car. Fueled by angst, he swung it around and hooked one of the splintered legs between the bumper and trunk lid of Bebee's car.

Two Bullets was still firmly lodged in his seat when Sydney walked up beside Toby. He poked his head inside the open door and said, "Chief, I returned one of your barricades and hung it on your back bumper. By the way, the left side brake light's been smashed out. Must have been where Harriet ran into you this morning. And you should get some ice on your that forehead of yours."

Toby and Sydney waited patiently for some kind of response. The Chief appeared as if he either had a lot on his mind, or more likely, absolutely nothing.

"We'll say good night then, Chief," said Toby. "Glad we had a chance to have our little chat. Don't forget to file the evidence from Jeffrey's locker will you?"

Bebee turned slowly, leaning toward the pair. He opened his eyes and said. "I want you boys to stick around town until this case is wrapped up. Don't let me find out you've gone running off. Right?"

"Of course," said Sydney. "We'll be leaving now."

Toby didn't notice the bruised front end of his car as he walked back to get in on the passenger side. Sydney started up the Olds and wheeled it around the chief's car. "Maybe you didn't notice Toby, but we're being followed. There's a car parked back down the road from us. As soon as we stopped at the chief's house, it did too. I'm worried about that, and I don't like what it could mean."

"Good heavens," replied Toby, "why would anyone be following us? We never go anywhere. Not anywhere interesting anyway."

"Get serious, Toby! It could be anybody that thinks we have something to do with Jeffrey's disappearance. Or the murdered chap in the pond. Hasn't it occurred to anyone except me that Jeffrey and the murder victim might be connected? It's too much of a coincidence not to be. Any ignoramus can figure that out."

"Well it didn't occur to this ignoramus. I don't know Jeffrey all that well. So I don't know his friends, and I don't know any of his business acquaintances, except, of course, Malcolm Overton at the bank. I found out from Harriet at tea this afternoon that he was the chap who introduced her to Jeffrey. Harumph. Beyond that I can't think about much of anything right now."

They had only gone a couple of blocks when Toby piped up. "You do know, Sydney, don't you, at least every idiot knows Cemetery Street is a dead end. We'll have to turn around and go back past that parked car—the one that's been following us—so you say. Maybe we could do a slow drive by and get a make on whoever's sitting in it."

"You've been reading those hoary true detective magazines again. Haven't you? Keep up this kind of thinking, and the both of us'll end up in the club pond sharing a home with the golf god." Sydney swung the Olds around in a tight circle and sped back down Cemetery Street.

"Toby, you're coming to my place. I think both of us could use some food. Then we'll try to figure out our next move."

As they passed Chief Bebee's car, Sydney slowed down to look inside. Bebee was still slouched back in his seat. "Looks like old Two Bullets is either too scared to go in the house, or he can't." The welcome light was out on the porch. "Well, what do you make of that, Toby?"

"You said it this morning: 'Give it time, and Bebee will have his comeuppance.' But I can't say I'm very pleased about it."

Sydney sighed in agreement. "I must say not much good seems to come of a comeuppance. Can't say it gives me any satisfaction either." They continued their drive down Cemetery Street scanning both sides of the road looking for a parked car.

It had left.

8

On the Defensive

Sydney coasted the Olds up in front of the 1876 House and docked it, leaving the right front wheel up over the curb. As the pair steadied each other on the long trip to the front door, Gabriel, the hotel doorman known as the Ancient One, got in the coupe, and with due diligence, shut off the idling engine, turned out the headlights, removed the keys, and followed the two inside. Sydney and Toby were too busy ordering room service to notice Gabriel when he arrived at the front desk. Gabe shook his head and tossed the keys to the night clerk for safekeeping. Most of the hotel guests had retired early. Weaving their way around a few pieces of period furniture, Sydney and Toby managed their way to the stairs leading up to Sydney's second floor rooms.

Safely in the suite, Toby collapsed face down on the sofa. Sydney turned on a nearby floor lamp before settling into his overstuffed armchair.

"Well, Toby, we've had quite a day of it wouldn't you say?" There was no reply.

"The dawn is bound to bring a few more surprises, and we'll need to get our rest. That being the case, I'm afraid I'm going to insist that you spend the night here." Still no reply. "I'll take your silence for a yes."

On his second attempt, Sydney struggled to his feet and went into the bedroom to fetch a comforter from the linen closet. Dragging it on the floor, he returned and tucked in his old friend stretched out on the sofa. A half hour had passed before Oscar, the night clerk, knocked and announced, "Room service, Mr. Wadsworth."

As he entered, Sydney waved a hand and said, "Don't mind my friend Toby over there. He's a little unwell at the moment."

"I can see that, sir. I'll just leave the tray cart. The day clerk will pick it up in the morning. Anything else?"

"Very unlikely, I'd say," replied Sydney. As Oscar was leaving, Sydney said, "Ooooh, wake me at six o'clock and be sure I get the morning paper."

Sydney uncovered the linen-draped cart and removed the silver cover to reveal their late-night snack. The commotion in the room woke Toby, who was in a state of semiconsciousness. Silently, he rose to a sitting position.

On Sydney's tray was the judicious choice of a ham sandwich on crustless white bread. When they arrived at the hotel, Toby must have thought it was morning and unwisely ordered breakfast. Toby approached the service tray cautiously where his two poached eggs stared up at him like a reflection of his own bloodshot eyes.

Sydney, seeing Toby's anguished look, offered him half of his ham sandwich and said, "If you don't want your bacon, I'll take it." Toby turned pallid, leaned back on the sofa, and resumed his horizontal position. "At least have a cup of tea," Sydney pleaded. Toby's only reply was an unintentional belch. Sydney, sandwich in hand, got up and gently covered Toby again, turned out the lights, and toddled off to his bedroom.

* * *

Six o'clock Saturday morning arrived earlier than it should have. When the wake-up call failed to arouse either Sydney or Toby, the front desk clerk, Philip, came up to the suite, knocked several times and entered to make sure the pair had not died in the night. Hearing them both snore in concert, he left the morning *Weekender* on the coffee table and wheeled the messy service cart out of the suite.

It was 6:20 when Sydney sat up to look at the clock across the room. While both the wake-up call and clerk failed to arouse him, his bladder did not. Leaving the bathroom, Sydney walked back out into the parlor, rubbed his eyes and was alarmed to discover that Toby was not on the sofa. He panicked at the thought that Toby had gotten up and wandered off, or worse yet, picked up his keys at the front desk and drove off. "Toby, where on God's green earth did you bugger off to?"

A frail voice replied, "I'm down here on the floor, Sydney. I must have rolled off the sofa last night. I can't get up. Give me a hand will you?"

"You don't look well enough to stand up yet, Toby. I couldn't possibly lift you anyway. Try rolling over, then get on your hands and knees. While you're resting in that position, I'll order up some tea and toast, and you'll be right as rain in no time."

Sydney, still dressed in yesterday's attire, called room service and eased into his chair with the morning paper. He was not surprised to see that the events surrounding Brookside Country Club had pushed national news off the front page. There was a large photo of Jeffrey Bartholomew, and the article began with the headline, "MISSING."

MISSING
by Amy Trueblood
Intern/Assistant Reporter

Jeffrey Bartholomew, husband of Harriet Bartholomew, has been missing since late Thursday evening. He is a prominent citizen in Livermore Falls and is a longtime summer resident. Mr. Bartholomew is a member of the Brookside C.C., an exclusive golf club for the elite where it is believed he was last seen wearing golf attire. His car was found in the club parking lot. As of Friday 8:00 p.m., there were no clues concerning his disappearance.

Chief Bebee is organizing a search of the Brookside grounds and immediate area. Members of several town organizations were asked on Friday the 13th to volunteer and join in the search for Mr. Bartholomew or evidence leading to his whereabouts.

Members of the following groups will meet in the clubhouse parking lot to begin the search at 8:00 a.m. Saturday. If you have not yet been personally contacted by the organizations listed below, you are requested to show up at the registration table and participate.

Volunteer Fire Department   Masonic Lodge
Livermore Falls Rod and Gun Club   Knights of Columbus
Boy Scouts, Troop 29   American Red Cross
Veterans of Foreign Wars   International Order of
Odd Fellows   American Legion
Beaverkill Elks Club   Eagles Fraternal Order
Livermore Falls Minutemen

Ladies auxiliary organizations to the above groups are also invited to provide refreshments and emergency first-aid.

"What a circus," Sydney said to himself as he read on.

> Friday morning your reporter was present at Brookside C.C.
> when Chief Robert Bebee called a special meeting of key parties
> to ascertain details surrounding the mysterious disappearance of
> Jeffrey Bartholomew. Those present behind closed doors were
> Mrs. Bartholomew, Sandy Cummings, the club manager, and
> Alex Wiley, the locker room attendant. Also included were Sydney
> Wadsworth and Toby Worthington, two old and distinguished
> members of the club, who apparently figure prominently in the
> disappearance of Mr. Bartholomew. Chief Bebee and Officer
> Nancy Sullivan conducted the interrogation, which lasted
> approximately an hour.

Sydney was reluctant to read the balance of the article. "What could be more damning than a reporter implying that I and Toby might be complicit in Jeffrey's disappearance?"

> At press time for the Weekender Edition, the *Livermore
> Falls Journal* learned of a gas explosion in the Brookside C.C.
> kitchen. There were no injuries, but a side wall of the clubhouse
> was blown out, and a great deal of water damage was incurred,
> thanks to the Volunteer Fire Department who promptly put out
> the ensuing blaze. More disconcerting news from Brookside
> C.C. followed when this reporter learned from an anonymous
> source that an unidentified body was found at the bottom of
> a pond on the property. Details will become available in the
> Monday Evening Edition.
> Flooding of the Beaverkill River and the River Road businesses
> apparently was caused by the failure of a dam on the Brookside
> property. Litigation is all but a certainty. See page 2 for pictures
> and more.

Dropping the paper to the floor, Sydney turned his attention back to Toby, who managed to follow Sydney's instructions by rolling over onto all fours. "How are you coming along, Toby?"

"Quite well, thank you." Toby removed his unraveled bow tie. While Sydney read the paper, Toby stared at all the sundry items that had fallen out of his pockets when he rolled from the sofa onto the pine floor. He was devoting his full attention to returning each of these articles to his numerous pockets. They included his pipe, of course, glasses, an assortment of loose change, golf tees, a used pipe cleaner, and a book of matches that caught his eye more than the other items.

"Sydney, I think you'd better come over here and have a look. Put your glasses on while you're at it."

"If you want me to look at you, I'd rather not. Right now, you look worse than the front end of your car."

"Is that so? Well at least I can be consoled by the fact that I'm feeling a whole lot better than Two Bullets. And what's the matter with the front end of my car?"

"Later, Toby. What is it you want me to see?"

"This book of matches I found on the floor." His words struggled to get past his parched lips and a tongue that felt tacked to the roof of his mouth. "Look at the cover. 'Stoney Creek Rod & Gun Club, Exclusive, Members Only, Table Rock, New York.'" Toby, still on his hands and knees, struggled to a kneeling position and asked Sydney to give him a hand onto the sofa.

"Well, Toby, what seems to be so significant about this matchbook?"

"Don't you remember? When we found Jeffrey dead on the toilet, I asked you to hand me the matchbook that was lying on the floor next to his feet. I was fresh out of matches at the time and needed a light. These were his matches."

"I assume that you're going to make a point soon," Sydney said impatiently. "As a matter of fact I have a few points of my own we need to discuss."

"Dammit all, Sydney, the point is that Jeffrey likes to fish! I keep on telling you. He no doubt belongs to this trout club. For whatever reason, I think he could just as well be there as here."

"Cripes, Toby! I think you're on to something, you old bloodhound."

"Listen Sydney, I've got to take a whiz before I blow my tank. Why don't you find out where the devil Table Rock is?"

"Philip at the desk ought to know. I'll ask him to bring up a map with our breakfast."

Thanks to a rush of adrenalin and a book of matches, life and hope returned a flush to both men's cheeks. After calling room service, Sydney sat down to examine the matchbook with a magnifying glass. He noticed the high quality and feel of the glossy cover, not unlike what he had chosen for the Brookside match covers. Behind the matches, a string of eight numbers was written in pencil on the inside cover: 051041080. He thought Jeffrey must have scrawled some sort of cryptic message to remind himself of something pretty serious—something he didn't want anyone else to know.

Toby reentered the room, pulling up his britches. Yawning, he returned to the sofa and this time assumed an upright position. Sydney waited for him to get comfortable. "The matchbook has a chain of numbers written on the inside cover." He tossed it over to Toby, and asked, "What's your impression? Puzzles seem to be one of your fields of expertise."

After fumbling through several pockets for his glasses, Toby focused his eyes and attention on the matchbook cover, "Well, well, well. First of all, Sydney, if this is some sort of code, I would start by eliminating the cipher zero, because it probably means absolutely nothing, only occasionally something. That leaves 51418, which could mean anything like a combination to a lock or safe. It would take days to decipher it. Probably not a date, which would mean last May or next May. Unless of course . . . you reverse the numbers, which makes it the month of August the 14 and 15, which is this weekend. Too simple, child's play really."

"Perhaps, but just right for someone playing in Jeffrey's league, don't you know. Think on this for a moment. What if Jeffrey was planning to be at Stoney Creek on the fourteenth and fifteenth?"

"While you're thinking on that, Toby, I'm going to call Sandy Cummings. Here, read Amy's article on Jeffrey." While Sydney was dialing the club, Philip knocked and brought in a stack of toast, assorted jams, and a pot of tea. On the tray was a New York State foldout road map. "Hello, Sandy, this is Wadsworth. Glad I was able to catch you up. Not abandoning ship are we?"

"No, sir, it isn't quite seven o'clock yet, and it's getting awfully busy around here. It looks like the Normandy invasion. Almost everyone is in some kind of uniform." His voice began to crack. "There must be at least a hundred people here milling around in the parking lot, and they're making me a little nervous. You probably want to know Chief Bebee showed up an hour later than he said he would. Nancy Sullivan and Lester Sparks were here at six though, along with a state cop trying to direct traffic."

Sydney interrupted, "Where are you right now, Sandy?"

"I'm in the tower. I've got the club flag with me."

"Good, tell me what can you see from there?"

"I can see cars parked on both sides of the road hole." Still holding the phone, Sandy crossed the tower floor to look out the window facing the parking lot. "I can see Bebee down there now with his bull horn, but I can't hear what he's saying."

"Never mind him for now. Here's what I want you to do. Oh, hang on a minute." Sydney covered the phone with his hand and whispered to Toby, "Would you mind leaving me a least one piece of toast?" Embarrassed, Toby nodded.

"I'm back now. Be sure that you've locked up the silver and put the Wadsworth Cup in the safe."

"Right. I've already done that. What now?"

"Get Jake, if he's not there already. Have him take every truck, mower, and piece of machinery out of the maintenance building. Get him to form a tight circle around the clubhouse. Park the dump truck in front of the gap in the kitchen wall. That should discourage any notion that we're open for tours and souvenir hunters." Sydney took a long sip of his tea. "If you haven't already, be sure all the doors are locked and the windows secured."

"Are you expecting trouble, Mr. Wadsworth?"

"In these situations, my experience suggests we must expect the worst in human nature. With the Knights of Columbus and the Masons in close proximity, anything can happen."

"Certainly you don't mean there could be violence, do you?"

"Possibly. I anticipate there will be a great deal of competition to see which civic organization can help the most in searching for Mr. Bartholomew. So I'm hoping that any conflagration will be amongst themselves. On the other hand, Sandy, some of these groups might take it upon themselves to ignore Bebee's orders to stay clear of the clubhouse. Are you still on the line, Sandy?"

"I'm still here." His voice sounded a little shaky.

"Good." Sydney took a bite of cold, brittle toast. "Listen carefully. If any of the townsfolk try to enter the clubhouse, don't offer physical resistance. Politely ask them to leave. If they refuse, advise them you'll take their names and have them charged with trespassing. That should give them pause."

"You really think so, and where will you be?"

"Sorry, but Mr. Worthington and I can't be there with you, shoulder to shoulder and all that. We are going on a mission, incognito, to put an end to this public nightmare. If anyone asks for us, we're off to the symphony in New York. Got that?"

"Yes, but . . ."

"But, but, but no buts! You can handle it, Sandy. We're a team now, after all. I want you to know that after I hang up, Mr. Worthington and I are going to muster up help for Brookside. Bank on it."

"Shouldn't the mayor be included somewhere in the mix? He should carry some weight if Bebee can't handle the crowd."

"Good thinking, Sandy. Give him a call and explain the situation. I'll have to leave you now, so let's show our mettle and run up the club flag. Above all, be calm. Over and out."

A sad expression came over Sydney's face. He sighed deeply as his thoughts turned to the club flag. The pole in the center of the traffic circle was reserved, naturally, for Old Glory. She never had to share her rightful place with any other flag at Brookside, not even the state flag. However, the club flag that he and Toby designed one evening over several scotches, flew at another place of honor from a pole atop the highest point of the clubhouse the turret. The flag's design consisted of two crossed golf clubs on a field of dark green. The clubs formed a canopy over two overflowing beer flagons. These symbols of sport and camaraderie were enclosed by a circle of twenty-one golf balls under which the year "1921" was inscribed in Old English text.

How can it be, Sydney thought, that a town that welcomed his Brookside, now finds him and the members of the club some sort of rubbish that should be run out of town? How peaceful it was here in the 20s, a time when the club was flowering. Only now everything seems to be going to seed. His conversation with Toby on Thursday must have been an omen of things to come. Every summer day, the club flag was raised as a sign of welcome, but today, Saturday, it's raised as a sign of defiance.

Sydney turned his attention to Toby, who had finished reading the article on Jeffrey. "Well, Toby, what do you think? Shouldn't we head for Table Rock and get a move on?"

"You're so impulsive, Sydney, but you're probably right. It's a long shot, but it may be the only one we have."

"Why don't you go down to the desk, get your keys, go home and get cleaned up. I'll tidy up a few things here, and you can pick me up in say, half an hour."

"I just remembered," said Toby getting to his feet, "old Two Bullets told us last night not to leave town."

"He didn't say which town now, did he?"

"I don't think that'll stand up in court, but it's worth a try if it should come to that."

Soon after Toby left for the downstairs lobby, Sydney searched through his telephone book for the number of the governor's residence. He dialed the front desk and asked Phil to put him through to 469-9906.

*   *   *

"This is Governor Dewey's office, how may I direct your call."

"I wish to talk with the governor please on a matter of some urgency. Tell him this is Sydney Wadsworth."

"The governor is in an important strategy meeting right now." The woman's voice adopted an officious tone. "What is the nature of your business with the governor?"

"It's a rather sensitive nature, or I wouldn't be calling on a weekend. Just give Governor Dewey my name and say that it could involve calling out the Guard for a problem we're having in Livermore Falls."

"I'll relay that message to the governor's personal secretary. Mr. Skillings will discuss the matter with you." Her tone was now terse. "That's the best I can do, unless you wish to leave a number where you can be reached."

"No. I mentioned this is an urgent matter of some delicacy."

Madeline, the secretary put the phone down on the desk leaving the line open. Sydney could hear ongoing conversations in the background. Her disgruntled voice echoed down the mansion's long entrance hall to where Skillings was stationed outside the main conference room. "Mr. Skillings, could you take the phone? There's a real nutcase on the phone that wants the governor to call out the Guard." Sydney grit his teeth. "I don't know how he got the governor's private line."

Skillings replied, "I'd better ask the gov first if he even knows this guy. What's his name?"

"Wadsworth, I think—Sydney Wadsworth. He sounds ancient."

Sydney drummed his fingers impatiently.

*   *   *

Skillings knocked on the conference room door and slipped inside. The governor, fully engaged with his campaign manager and staff over the fall presidential election, looked up and said, "What now, Henry? This better be damned important."

Sheepishly, Skillings took a step back. "There's a man on the phone using your private telephone number. He says his name is Sydney Wadsworth, and that you may have to call out the Guard. I thought I'd better check with you before I speak with him."

"Good, except I don't recall any Sydney Wad—whatever. Where's he calling from?"

"Madeline said he was calling from Livermore Falls."

"Now where the hell is that?" said Dewey, raising his voice.

"New York," replied Emily, an eager young staffer. "It's downstate about an hour and a half drive from here on 87. Livermore Falls is a small town about a half hour west of Kingston."

Dewey was a little chagrined, and acknowledged Emily's comment with a nod of approval. His close friend and campaign finance director, Chip, leaned over to whisper in the governor's ear, "I seem to recall that Wadsworth is one of your biggest contributors. He put on a benefit dinner for you at the Highlands City Club—you and I were there. He is or was a close friend of Eric Robbins and Rodney Templeton."

Turning to Chip the governor whispered, "Yes, I didn't know it was *that* Sydney. I just have a lot on my mind right now." Dewey rose to his feet and gestured for the others to remain seated and keep working. Announcing that he had an important call to return, he departed to his private study and picked up the phone.

"Sydney, Sydney, Sydney! Sorry to keep you waiting. Glad you got through to me. Big election you know." He feigned a follow-up chuckle. "What's going on down in Livermore Falls?"

For the first time since talking to Madeline, Sydney's teeth ground to a halt. "To tell the truth, Governor, I'm not sure. But I know a lot of trouble is brewing at the Brookside Country Club. You no doubt know of our club."

"Yes, well, Sydney, can you give me some specifics?"

"As I speak, we have a missing member of our club. The golf course was flooded and a wall of the clubhouse was blown out. Oh yes, and some stranger was found in the bottom of our pond evidently murdered."

"My word. Aren't the local police following up?"

"That, Governor, is the problem!" said Sydney. "The chief of police Robert Bebee suspects foul play. He is determined to run roughshod over our property and relishes the idea of turning our club inside out searching for evidence, would you believe."

"Hold on, Sydney, isn't the state police involved in the investigation?"

"One would think so. There should be someone here besides Bebee looking into the disappearance of Jeffrey Bartholomew, and the last thing I know is that there's an unidentified corpse waiting for the county coroner over at the local funeral parlor. Bebee's enlisted virtually every civic organization in town except the Girl Scouts to volunteer in searching Brookside."

Greeted with the governor's silence, Sydney took a deep breath before going on. "There could be several hundred men, women, and children scouring our club today wreaking havoc, not to mention property damage. Before it's all over, there's bound to be a scuffle and possibly civil disobedience. I think I can speak for the club that we have no objections to their good intentions, but I feel that this little search party of Bebee's could be confrontational. Naturally, I wouldn't dream of disturbing you, Governor, if I didn't think the situation here could escalate into a matter for the Guard."

"I see what you mean, Sydney. Tell you what. I'm going to send my top aide down there immediately to size up the situation. You said the chief's name was Bebee?"

"Right, Governor, you can't miss him." Sydney chuckled to himself that a gunman in '39 couldn't. "Bebee's with his two deputies. And thanks for getting involved. I won't forget it."

"Don't mention it, Wadsworth. The man I'm sending down is Henry Skillings. He should be there in a couple of hours. I'll have him look you up at the club. You'll be there, yes?"

Slow to answer, Sydney contemplated a rapid change of plans. "You can count on it, Tom."

The governor shook his head and wondered if the conversation he just had was real or not. Sydney overheard him bellow, "Skillings, get in here, I've got a job for you."

*   *   *

Expressionless, Sydney walked over to the window that faced Main Street. From there he'd be able to see Toby drive up. A light canvas travel bag lay slumped next to his feet. He stared through the sun-filled sheer drapes contemplating a new strategy. The strategy was complicated now because he and Toby would be delayed leaving town. He remembered happier times as he gazed out on the kind of morning that reminded him of Brookside's opening day.

A dull pain traveled down his left arm, and his forehead began to sweat. He told himself to lie down and rest for a while, and perhaps the ache and discomfort would pass. It had before. He swallowed two aspirin and reminded himself to see his doctor when he returned to the city in the fall. On the couch he closed his eyes, and the pain subsided as he drifted in and out of sleep.

A half hour later Toby's familiar thump on the door woke him. "Come on, Sydney, old man, heave to!" He burst through the unlocked door. "It's eight-thirty already."

Sydney sat up on the sofa mopping his hair back with both hands. "We're not leaving for Table Rock just yet."

"And, why not? We're all gassed up and ready to go. You haven't overlooked something have you?"

"No, nothing like that. I'm ready except that we have to go to the club first. I've got to meet with the governor's personal aide before we can leave. Maybe he can put the brakes on Bebee better than we can."

Toby was taken back. "Very impressive, Sydney. I've got to hand it to you when it comes to playing your cards! Maybe Two Bullets won't be so uppity when he knows who he's up against." Toby suddenly forced a weak smile. "Listen, you look white as a ghost, so let's take it a little slow today. You have to admit you were in your cups last night."

"You're hardly one to judge. I don't know what's made you so chipper this morning."

On their way out the door, Toby turned to Sydney. "I've been thinking we may run into a spot of trouble up there in trout paradise. It may not be a bad idea to bring along your cane. Before coming over, I got out my old service revolver and stuck it in the glove box. Hasn't been fired in years, but it should still work."

9

The Pot Boils

The road hole was choked with cars and trucks trying to find a spot to park on the shoulder. Some folks were emboldened to drive through the roadside drainage swales and park on the edge of the course. Not all the people walking toward the clubhouse came there to participate in the search for Jeffrey. Small groups of chanting agitators were there to proselytize their social agenda. They carried signs full of foul language that railed against wealthy elitists. But coming from out of town, they were not welcome even by those who might be inclined to sympathize with their point of view.

Toby bobbed and weaved his Olds onto the road hole. His chin dropped and eyes popped in astonishment. He recovered to exclaim, "This is what Dunkirk must have looked like."

Sydney agreed. "I see the downstate commies have been reading our local paper. They're out in force this morning." His anger brought color back to his cheeks. "Double back, Toby, we're going into the club on the service road. You know, the one down on the flats. It may be washed out, but we stand a better chance of getting through."

The Olds responded to a sharp twist of the wheel as Toby U-turned back to Main Street. They whistled through the village and spun their way along the flat road. Less than five minutes later they swerved onto the club's one lane service road that wound its way up to the maintenance barn behind the clubhouse. The washboard road chattered their teeth and aggravated the headaches acquired the night before with Bebee.

As Toby wheeled the coupe inside the maintenance barn to keep it out of sight, Sydney smiled at the sight of the barn's empty interior because it meant all the vehicles and machinery were barricading the clubhouse. After a mighty struggle to close the big sliding door, they slipped outside and leaned back out of sight against the barn wall to catch their breath, thankful that with all the activity around the clubhouse, no one noticed their arrival.

Toby opened the conversation as usual, "What now, mastermind?"

"Toby, I'm going to sneak into the clubhouse through the service court. We need to find out exactly what's going on." Sydney reached for his cigar case in the belief that he could think more clearly when enveloped in a cloud of smoke. Reflecting on the gravity of the situation, he said, "We never should have considered leaving Sandy alone. It's not his job to face the likes of this."

"Speak for yourself, Sydney. I think we're blown way off course by coming back."

"Perhaps, but done's done. Be a good fellow, Toby. I want you to slip into the crowd, learn what you can, and meet me back inside the club, say, half an hour. Come in through the service court. I'll leave the scullery door open."

"Wouldn't it be easier if I just walk through the opening in the kitchen wall?"

"I believe that's the first thing Sandy would have blocked off." Sydney puffed nervously on his cigar. "Now then, if you see your caddy, Oliver, in the crowd, tell him we may have a lucrative job for him. Give him one of your generous tips, and ask him to hang out by the golf shop until one of us gets back to him. And Toby, whatever you do, steer clear of Bebee. Try to blend in. You know, be inconspicuous."

"I don't suppose you have any other little thing in mind, so to speak."

"Yes, I do as a matter of fact. It's the real reason we had to be here this morning." He flicked the white ash from his cigar and assumed another of his Churchillian poses. "If you see a state vehicle down there, and there's a chap in it who has government written all over his face, bring him with you. Name's Skillings. He should be here anytime now." Sydney squinted at his watch. "Check your timepiece, Toby, it's eight minutes past nine."

Toby clicked his heels together and saluted, "As you wish, Your Lordship. Half an hour it is, give or take." Toby tucked his club under his arm and started off toward the crowd. He stopped, turned to Sydney and said, "When I get back, I want an explanation about what happened to the front of my car."

*   *   *

Sandy had done a good job blocking off the service court by spreading kitchen garbage on the ground. Underneath the mounds of waste, he hid garden rakes with their tines up. If the rake were stepped on, the handle would come up to give an intruder a black eye and a new suit made of last week's cuisine. His second line of defense was a rudimentary fence made of waste barrels lashed together.

Sydney, club in hand, skipped over the open ground from the barn to the clubhouse. To gain access to the service court, he took what he thought to be the easiest access by sliding headfirst under one of the two big service carts blocking the entrance. He clenched his cigar tightly in his teeth and inched his way along on his back. Using his club head to hook on the undercarriage he pulled himself along. He wondered if it was the same cart that he and Toby used to haul Jeffrey onto the course on Thursday. Clear of the cart and out of breath, he rose to his feet, relit his cigar, and took inventory of his disheveled attire.

Being a founder, he was still in possession of a master key, which opened the scullery door of the clubhouse. Once inside, he took a deep breath and shouted, "If you're in here, Sandy, show yourself. It's Wadsworth."

Sandy's running footsteps and voice echoed down the main hall. "You don't know how glad I am you're here."

"On the contrary, I'm the one who's glad you're here. Are you alone?"

Finally, face to face, Sandy blurted out, "Yes. I let Jake and the grounds crew go after they finished blockading the clubhouse.

"Good man! Well then let's go up where we can survey the situation. I'm a bit off my game today, so let's take the elevator to the turret."

*   *   *

Traversing the gallery leading to the turret, Sydney and Sandy sidestepped soaked oriental carpets piled up in their path. The air was damp, heavy, and filled with a plethora of offensive odors—water-saturated wood, plaster, fabrics, ash and spoiled food. Sandy led the way into the atrium. Sadly, the grandeur of the space was suffering from the scars and indignities inflicted the day before by the Livermore Falls Fire Department. Glancing at the library, Sydney stopped for a moment to be sure that Sandy had indeed removed the trophies. *No newspapers today,* he thought, *no* Times *or* Tribune.

"Are you coming, Sydney?" said Sandy.

"Yes. Just having a look about. Will you listen to that mob out there?"

They took off crossing the atrium floor slick with water. Sydney held out his golf club like a hockey stick to steady himself. Skating to a stop in front of the elevator, he asked, "We aren't going to get electrocuted in this cage, are we?"

"We should be OK. I got it working this morning by tying it into the emergency generator. Would you rather use the stairs?"

"No thanks, Sandy. I think I'd rather take my chances and die right here than use the stairs."

The cage door closed, and as the elevator began grinding its way to the second floor, Sydney glanced up at the guest suites and was suddenly reminded that Baron Louis d'Chard was due to arrive here as a guest speaker Wednesday evening. "Hell's bells!" he said. "Too late to cancel."

"Cancel what?" replied Sandy.

"See, you've forgotten too? The baron—on Wednesday."

His old acquaintance d'Chard had recently established himself as a New York wine importer and was known for his impeccable taste and a nose for the grape. He was on the road now with his wine tasting, "smell and tell" show.

"Sandy, when you get a chance, put him up at the 1876 House and buy at least one case of everything he's got." He thought to himself how this would be one more embarrassment for the club. His only consolation at the moment was that it couldn't be worse than the wringer Bebee's going to be put through when Skillings shows up.

Arriving at the second floor balcony, the pair curled around the side of the elevator to the turret entrance, which was a gothic arched doorway replete with a display of medieval weaponry and a polished suit of armor symbolically guarding it. Sandy unlocked the heavy oak plank door with its oversized wrought iron hinges. They were greeted as usual by darkness and cool, dank air. Sandy lit a candelabra that was used in times of power outages. "Give me one end of your club, Sydney, and I'll lead you over to the staircase. Don't look around now, but I've got all the stuff in here you wanted brought up from the library. Try not to trip."

"Well done, Sandy. You'll be up for a good bonus this Christmas."

The turret was the centerpiece of Sydney's self-proclaimed design masterpiece even though it never received any architectural awards or accolades except from the local newspaper. Architecturally speaking, the tower was well-suited for a filming of Rapunzel. Stone walls made it safe from both fire and the fire department. A wrought iron staircase wound around the circumference to reach the topmost floor. There, another locked door waited, which led out onto an open walkway along the ridge of the clubhouse roof. Sandy led the way stopping several times to see how Sydney was progressing.

Looking back over his shoulder, Sandy inquired, "Are you sure you want to do this? If you must know, I'm not that certain I want to be up here."

"Go ahead, unlock the door, I'll be right along." said Sydney kneeling on a stair. Sandy shoved the door open leading out onto the walkway. Sunlight flooded the turret, and a refreshing breeze extinguished the candelabra. "Here, Sandy, take the end of my club and give me a pull up." Sandy obliged.

Commonly known in New England as a widow's walk, this walkway was never intended to be transgressed by a widow or any other female. It was an unwritten rule by the three founders that women were not allowed either up here or down in the men's locker room. It was never challenged, mostly because women had little interest in being in either place.

Now that Sydney was ensconced on the walkway, he felt that he was back in charge of events again. However, he became slightly delusional from exhaustion. In his mind's eye he envisioned that if he had to, he would make his final stand right here in the best tradition of Errol Flynn flailing away at his enemies. He leaned over the clubhouse ramparts and gazed down the steep slate roof to observe what appeared to him to be hostile villagers surrounding his fortifications. With his golf club at shoulder arms, he began parading back and forth pointing out obvious weaknesses in Brookside's fortifications to Sandy, who was the only soldier under his command.

Fortunately, Sandy was aware of this strange mood swing in him, "Sydney, I want you to sit down, put out your cigar, and take a few deep breaths. You've got to pull yourself together. I think you're beginning to hallucinate."

"Ridiculous, Sandy. This old girl of mine's been badly wounded, and I've got a duty to protect her. I'll be just fine. My vision gets blurred sometimes, so just let me rest here a minute or two while I gather my wits." After a few moments, Sydney collected himself. He straightened up and, with club in hand, headed for the terrace at the far end of the roof from the turret.

The walkway was wide enough for members to easily pass each other, and more importantly, wide enough to accommodate a beverage cart. At the far end, there was an open air terrace sufficient to comfortably seat a dozen gentlemen invited to observe tournament play or more often than not just to commiserate. There was storage for folding chairs, an old megaphone that singers used down below for club dances, a number of field glasses, and a loudspeaker system that Sydney didn't know how to use. Only members of the Founder's Club and special guests were invited to this place of privilege. And for the Wadsworth Cup, only the most reputable sports writers were invited to the terrace. Others were relegated to wandering the course for news.

When the finishing touches and amenities were being added to the construction of the terrace, it was Toby who came up with the idea of incorporating a small ceremonial cannon. Unquestionably, his inspiration came from his service as a gunnery officer in the Spanish-American War. He never saw combat or fired a round in anger. In terms of experience, the cannon and he were alike—all noise, no shot.

*   *   *

Down on the battlefield Bebee was still trying to organize the search for Jeffrey. By this time everyone in town knew that Bebee made a better buck private than a general. Bebee spotted Deputy Sullivan approaching him.

"Nancy, you're out of uniform." he exclaimed.

"I'm supposed to be, Chief. Remember? I'm tailing Worthington and Wadsworth. By the way, what happened to you? You look like you've been run over by a truck."

"Never you mind me, little lady," said a flustered Bebee. "I need you out here in your uniform. We've got to organize this search party before the natives get really restless. Half the town's milling around here. By the way, where are those two old coots?"

"The last time I saw them, they were dropping you off at your house." Bebee fell silent. Nancy thought hard about the chief calling her a "little lady." Maybe it's time for a career change, or at least a change of boss.

She was heading back to her car to get her uniform when the chief popped off, "Before you go get changed, have you seen High Pockets?"

"I'm pretty sure I just saw him go into some kind of new portable outhouse with a cup of coffee."

"Dammit, Nancy, with the kind of help I get in this town, I'm going to lose my goddamn job!" Bebee picked up his bullhorn and aimed it at the row of outhouses, "Deputy Sparks, since I don't have anything to do, can I bring you a magazine?"

Nancy carried her uniform up to the hospitality tent to change. The tent was set up in the back of the parking lot. Inside, it was brimming with tables laden with coffee and all kinds of confections. The Ladies Auxiliary of the American Legion arrived shortly after dawn to get themselves organized and spread out their homemades. The early arrivals got the best location to show off their wares and receive the icy stares of latecomers. Next to this tent was another smaller one occupied by the Red Cross and the Ladies Aid Society. Minor injuries, they thought, were bound to occur on a day like this one.

Not surprisingly, the scouts and various military organizations were in uniform gathered around their standard bearers anxiously waiting for Bebee's instructions. These groups occupied the center of the parking lot, with the Protestant sects on the right flank and the Catholic organizations on the left. Stretched out behind this loose collection of organizations were members of various business and civic clubs. Those who belonged to more than one organization wandered around looking for a home or a place to park with a face they recognized. Several women had long since left their posts to chase down their missing children.

The Veterans of Foreign Wars had already broken ranks to engage the out of town protesters as soon as they arrived at the club entrance. The vets quickly separated the outnumbered and disorganized protesters from their signs and battered them with their own placards. Signs that proffered Screw the Rich did not find favor. Even though such wicked thoughts had crossed the minds of many this Saturday, rich was what the majority wanted to be, and if they themselves became rich, they certainly didn't want to be screwed because of it. The victorious VFW swaggered back from the skirmish to a stirring round of applause and a musical salute from the high school fife and drum corps band.

Chief Bebee, armed once again with his bullhorn, walked over to a long folding table in front of the assemblage. In order to address his audience, he climbed a few rungs of a stepladder that High Pockets had placed there earlier that morning. The chief was about to speak when he felt a tug on his pant cuff. It was Mayor Yates. "Chief, is this your idea of an investigation?"

Looking back over his shoulder, Bebee said. "Well, it may not be your idea, Mr. Mayor, but it's the best idea I've got, and I'm going with it. So let me get on with my job." He raised his voice to the mayor, "People are waitin."

Yates wasn't through. "Stop being so stubborn, Chief. I just saw a trooper let a state vehicle drive in. You might want to know why before you turn this crowd loose." Bebee backed down the ladder to a chorus of boos. The mayor was startled to see Bebee's banged up forehead but thought better about calling attention to it. "Another thing, I want you to know that the town could be held responsible for any property damage done today."

"Hell, Mayor, look around this place, the pond's gone, one side of the clubhouse's blown out, and half the property's washed down into the Beaverkill River. What's left to damage?"

"Why is it that I feel you'll still be able to find something to wreck?"

"I'm going to find something all right. I'm going to find Jeffrey Bartholomew and whoever murdered that chap we found in the pond." Aggravated, Bebee started kicking the dirt around his feet like a frustrated baseball player at home plate. The mayor gave in to Bebee's resolve. Persuading Bebee to change his mind would be like convincing the captain of the Titanic to change course.

Unnoticed, Deputy Sparks sauntered up behind the chief. "Coffee, Chief? Gotcha a cup."

"No, and don't tell me where you've been because I already know."

"I've been doing some checking up on stuff. You know that old geyser Worthington? He might be onto something. You remember those clubs that were crammed in the stiff's pants? Well, I checked with the club manufacturer, Spaulding, like he said."

"Yeah, so get on with it Sparks. I'm trying to do things here."

"OK. Those clubs with serial numbers we found on the corpse. They were sent to a golf pro at a country club up in Buffalo. And guess what?" High Pockets took a drag of the coffee he had brought for Bebee. "The golf shop was robbed three weeks ago, and the only stuff taken were those clubs, a bag, and a dozen golf balls."

"So?"

"So, they think they've got the guy's prints. Chances are he's got a record. Sounds like a stupid thief to me."

"Thieves are stupid, Lester."

"Anyway, we might be getting a lead on our corpse. And before I forget it, Harriet Bartholomew wants to talk to you. Something about a warrant."

Bebee rolled his eyes and did not reply. Back on the ladder, he urged his army of volunteers to be patient just a few moments longer and said, "I want the leaders of each volunteer group to come down here to my table and get instructions. If you're not in a group, get in one, or you'll have to leave the grounds." Glancing back over his shoulder, he saw the top of a

black car surrounded by a number of curiosity seekers who had broken
ranks from Bebee's army.

*   *   *

The late-model Ford sedan inched its way through the crowd and
came to a stop about halfway to the portico. Toby worked his way over to
the driver's side of the car and tapped on the window. The driver rolled
the window half way down. Toby said, "You must be Mr. Skillings from the
governor's office."

"Yes, I am." He sounded moody, and his face had the anguished look
of one who was uncomfortable with his present surroundings. "And you
must be Sydney Wadsworth. I'm supposed to meet you here and report my
findings back to the governor."

"Sorry, Mr. Skillings, but I'm Toby Worthington."

"My apologies, Mr. Worthington." Skillings glanced away and looked
up at the roof of the clubhouse. His manner was overbearing and
judgmental. "Well, I certainly hope Wadsworth isn't that silly buffoon
marching back and forth up there on the roof. I guess he fashions himself
some sort of self-appointed general." Henry did not endear himself
to Toby when he continued, "Is he preparing to repel an imminent
attack?"

After the initial shock of his remarks passed, Toby's reply was civil but
stern. "I'm afraid it is Wadsworth—and in a way he is defending his castle."
Noticing Skillings's pinstriped business suit, Toby decided that this young
upstart probably finished first in law school but dead last in tact.

"Really, sorry to offend. I can see I'm getting off on the wrong foot here.
I do need to talk with him. Please, get in and show me how to get through
this mess." Toby battled his way around the back of the car and climbed in.
"Now, can you fill me in on Wadsworth and the situation here." Skillings
blew the horn, revved the engine, and started moving through the crowd
toward the clubhouse.

They had only gone a few yards when Toby raised his hand. "Please
stop here, Skillings. I see someone I need to talk to." He rolled down his
window and shouted, "Amy, over here."

"Yes, sir!" Amy exclaimed. "Coming Mr. Worthington. Is this a good
time for our interview? Remember, you promised."

"Not just now, Amy. Soon, really. But I really need a big favor. Is Oliver,
my caddy, around?"

"Sure is. He's right over there helping me with a story for the paper. Why?"

"I want you to give him these two quarters and ask him to standby at the pro shop until he hears from me. There may be an important job for him, that is, for me and Mr. Wadsworth.

"OK, but I want an exclusive. There's a lot of bigtime press floating around, you know."

Skillings, impatient, began tapping his fingers on the steering wheel. "Can we go now?"

"Not quite," said Toby. He rolled down the window again and called Amy back to the car and whispered so as not to be overheard. "I believe this is your lipstick. I found it in the seat of my car."

Her cheeks flushed, Amy snatched it from Toby's hand and rushed away.

Toby pointed to the entrance of the service road, which turned off the main drive to the clubhouse. It looped up to the service court and then on to the maintenance barn. "No doubt Chief Bebee's spotted us, but right now he's got his hands full keeping this crowd under control. Actually that's why Sydney called your boss this morning. He thinks we might need to call up the Guard if things start to boil over and get ugly."

Toby thought about the irony of the situation. "Funny isn't it—if it did get ugly—because undoubtedly a good number of the men here are in the Guard. This whole thing started out as a missing person investigation. But now it seems to be turning into some kind of a class war struggle. So, Skillings, there you have it."

"I'm sure you and Sydney must be imagining the seriousness of the situation."

"Could be. Keep on driving up to the barn. We'll park your car in there."

Skillings prodded Toby once again to fill him in on Wadsworth. "If I'm going to be any help diffusing this situation, I'd like to know a little more about him. Then I'll try to deal with Bebee."

"I know it may be difficult for you to understand a person you've described as a 'silly buffoon,' but I want you to appreciate what I'm going to tell you about Sydney. He began Brookside in 1921 and nurtured it every day since. Technically, he's a bachelor. But after he acquired this property to start a golf course, he might as well have married it.

"So, if Sydney seems a little quirky or overprotective when it comes to Brookside, I'd appreciate it if you'd temper your remarks and try to understand the man and the present circumstances."

"Of course, Toby. Here I am apologizing again. And I want you to know that I do respect the fact that he's a friend of the governor."

Toby and Skillings secured the car in the maintenance barn and headed for the clubhouse service court. With his field glasses in one hand, Sydney observed their arrival and waved them up with his free hand.

*   *   *

Sydney swung his attention back to the other side of the walkway to scan the club entrance. Still feeling faint, his knees wobbled at the sight of a huge white van and trailer as it struggled its way along the entrance road. "What in the hell is that!" he fumed and refocused his field glasses to read the identification on the side of the truck.

"Oh, oh. It's Baron d'Chard. He's not supposed to show up until Wednesday! He's certainly got a lot of moxie wading into this crowd with a truckload of wine, eh, Sandy? Well, that's the Frenchies for you."

"I'm afraid he's not our only uninvited visitor," said Sandy. "Look who's walking down the road hole. Isn't that Father Michael pulling his golf bag?"

For the first time today Sydney was visibly amused. "Father O'Connor picked a great day to show up for a free round of golf. But that's the Irish for you. On the other hand, his presence might be fortuitous. As our chaplain, we could use his blessing right about now." Sydney began slowly pacing again and resumed the look and bearing of a Churchill formulating a strategic plan of defense. "If we are clever, Mr. Cummings, perhaps these two allies could be used to our advantage."

*   *   *

Toby and Skillings entered the scullery door after working their way through an array of booby traps. Toby was almost as unsteady as Sydney when they reached the open door at the top of the turret. On seeing Sydney and Sandy conversing halfway down the walkway, they decided to join them. Skillings was the first to speak. "Mr. Worthington tells me you're Sydney Wadsworth. I've heard a great deal about you. I'm Henry Skillings, and I'm here representing the governor."

"Pleased to meet you, Mr. Skillings," Sydney replied, shaking Henry's hand. "We've been expecting you. I only hope you've arrived in time. Let me introduce you to Sandy Cummings, our club manager." After an exchange of greetings, Sydney explained the situation and asked if Henry had any authority to disperse the townspeople or at least keep them from invading the clubhouse."

"My authority here, I'm afraid, only extends as far as my power to persuade others to do the right or lawful thing. Of course, my instructions are to report to the governor if the state needs to intervene." Sydney and Toby blanched at his reply and the use of the word "if." Henry continued, "I assume Officer Bebee has declared Brookside a crime scene and has a search warrant for the clubhouse as well as the grounds."

Out of the blue Sandy said, "Henry, if I may interrupt, it appears that you may have stepped in something untoward when you came through the service court."

"That's an understatement, Sandy," replied Henry. "It's garbage served up on a rake handle."

"I'm afraid it's my fault. If you'll just send your cleaning bill to the club, I'll attend to it immediately."

"Thank you, Sandy, but right now my concern is resolving the situation at hand." He turned to address Sydney and Toby. "I understand that you two are in charge here until the president and the board of directors get back in town."

"Yes, quite so," said Sydney emphatically. "We rightfully assumed that role in the absence of anyone else taking the helm. Our president's train doesn't get into Albany until Sunday night. The board's golfing over in Vermont and won't be straggling back until next week."

"Well now, what seems to be the real trouble?" Skillings's eyes darted around his confreres. "The club apparently doesn't have anything unlawful to hide, right? Looking at this clubhouse closed up like a fortress, Chief Bebee might think so. Toby, what's your assessment?"

"Frankly, Skillings old dear, we don't want people running roughshod over our property like we're some sort of vermin to exterminate! At best those people down there are amateur detectives. Humph. Searching for evidence can turn into souvenir hunting, which is only a short putt from looting. How can Bebee get away with this unless he deputizes all these volunteers?"

"Actually, he can. But they need to be instructed against tampering with evidence. And they can be prosecuted for criminal activity, such as swiping your ashtrays."

"Come now, Skillings, we're talking about a lot more here than a couple of ashtrays!" Toby fiddled nervously straightening his tie. "Bebee's had it in for our club ever since one of our members climbed on his back yesterday. It didn't help either when she smacked into his new squad car. Apparently he thinks Brookside needs to be taken down a peg or two. He's as much as told Sydney and me that we're not being four square with him. Frankly, I think he's more interested in punishing the club than he is in finding Bartholomew or solving a murder."

"You think that's what it's all about?" said Henry. "What do you make of it, Mr. Wadsworth?"

"Well, Toby's right on the mark," replied Sydney speaking above the growing racket of the assemblage below. "We have some right to privacy." He leaned over the railing and pointed toward the crowd with his club. "Look at all those service organizations down there. In twenty-seven years there hasn't been one instance I know of where even one of our members invaded the privacy of their clubhouses."

Skillings looked over the edge, then back at Sydney and Toby. "I'd like to talk with Bebee now. It looks like he's pulling out all the stops on this search party of his."

Sydney raised his field glasses. "You're right. The Boy Scouts are already marching toward our stand of maples to the east. There's a long line of people in front of Bebee's command post for who knows what. Instructions?"

"I'd better get Bebee's attention and stop him right now before this goes any further." Skillings was emphatic. "This whole thing of Bebee's could end up being counterproductive to an investigation and do a lot more harm than good."

Sandy, who had been standing motionless and away from the conversation shouted, "There's a new loud speaker system installed over here, but I don't think anyone knows how to use it yet. Not me anyway."

"Perhaps I can. Let me have a look." Skillings forced a smile. "Politics and loud speakers go together."

Sandy opened an undercounter cabinet revealing a microphone and a forest of dials and toggle switches ultimately connected to four outdoor speakers mounted on the far edges of the roof. Sydney and Toby remained perched on the walkway while Skillings kneeled on the terrace deck, stuck his head in the cabinet, and began familiarizing himself with the system. "This should only take a minute."

It seemed an age for the watchful trio before Henry exclaimed. "I think I've got it! See if you can get the crowd's attention."

"I know how to get their undivided attention!" said Toby. Sydney knew exactly what he meant. They sprinted down the walkway to the terrace like a walrus and a sea otter heading for open water. Unnoticed they slipped past Skillings to the cannon mount. Toby swung it around in the direction of the crowd. "Pass me a charge, Sydney."

"Double shot it is. Just one left." Sydney plugged his ears, crouched behind the rail and, in the manner of Admiral Dewey's famous command, exclaimed, "You may fire when ready, Toby."

The blast echoed down the valley like rolling thunder; blue smoke billowed from the barrel. Terrified women shrieked. Children stopped in their tracks; boys playing cowboys and Indians dropped their cap pistols. Men looked up staring in silence. Bebee, his jaw slack, dropped his bullhorn. High Pockets had taken cover and peered out from under Bebee's sign up table. Nancy, accustomed to loud explosions in her childhood neighborhood, stared in disbelief at the source. The acrid smell of cannon powder filled the air.

Pleased with himself, Toby surveyed the scene below and said, "All right, Skillings, you can start your speech now. All eyes and ears are up here."

"I'm afraid he can't," said Sandy. "When the cannon went off, he banged his head on the cabinet and knocked himself out, either that or he fainted. I wouldn't blame him if he did faint. But he didn't. Look here, he's got a nasty gash on the back of his head."

"He'll be all right, Sandy," said Sydney taking command. "Here's what we're going to do. Toby, help Sandy drag Skillings out onto the walkway. Sandy, take off your blazer and put Skillings suit coat on. Jump to it, man. Skip the tie and vest. I'm going to hunch down behind the railing, and you're going to take Skillings' place and give the speech of your life."

"I am?"

"You are! Now, put on his sunglasses, take his cap, and pull it down tight over your forehead. Hurry up. Grab this microphone and then say exactly what I tell you to say, right?"

Although Sandy was following Sydney's instructions, his voice quavered with apprehension. "Isn't this being deceitful?"

"Of course it is," said Toby. "Let's get on with it. Hell, Sandy, nobody will know, not even your wife would recognize your voice on a loudspeaker."

Toby took back the never-to-be-used-handkerchief he'd given Sandy earlier, then knelt beside Skillings to clean his wound, avoiding Harriet's obvious spots of mascara.

*   *   *

In less time than it takes for a one-minute egg, Sandy was positioned next to Sydney with microphone in hand.

"OK, Sandy, here we go. Repeat after me. I'll have to make this up as I go," said Sydney. "Chief Bebee and citizens of Livermore Falls."

Sandy repeated, "Chief Bebee and citizens of Livermore Falls."

"Now say, 'I'm Henry Skillings, Governor Dewey's personal aide and representative.'" Sandy delivered it on message.

"Now you've got to get this right, Sandy. 'I've come down today from the capitol to assist this community and law enforcement authorities with an investigation into the murder of a person unknown and the disappearance of Jeffrey Bartholomew, a resident of Livermore Falls.'"

Sandy delivered it perfectly, and he seemed to be enjoying his theatrical impersonation. An approving murmur passed through the attentive crowd, the kind that sounded like one of acceptance and approval. Bebee had fallen silent. His deputy, Lester, slowly crawled out from under the table to hear the proclamations coming from the roof of the clubhouse.

Taken with his new position of authority, Sandy said, "Sorry about the cannon, folks, just wanted to get your attention."

"Dammit, Sandy, don't ad-lib!" said Sydney. "And don't get chummy. Now start again after me. 'I have just concluded the following arrangements with Sandy Cummings of Brookside C.C., who will be assisting your chief and the investigation.'" Sandy looked down again at Sydney and blurted out over the megaphone, "But, I'm the . . ."

"Stop!" said Sydney, tugging on Sandy's pant leg. "Of course you are. But right now you're Skillings. For God's sake remember that! Now let's get back on message.

"Next, repeat this, 'You are all invited to witness a nine hole exhibition golf match between Sydney Wadsworth and his partner Toby Worthington against Baron Louis d'Chard and Father Michael O'Connor.'"

Sandy prefaced his delivery by inadvertently saying "What!" into the microphone, but recovered quickly and delivered the invitation.

"We're almost through, Sandy, now repeat this. 'Play will begin at ten o'clock sharp, so please everyone clear the tenth tee.'" Sandy recited his lines confident in the knowledge that the end was near.

"Here's the big one, Sandy. 'Also, at ten o'clock, Sandy Cummings, the manager of Brookside will give tours of the clubhouse in groups of twenty. One of Chief Bebee's deputies will assist him as an escort.'"

Sandy began and finished his lines all right until he comprehended what he just announced. Bending over to Sydney, he said, "I'm giving tours?"

"Of course you can," said Sydney. "Don't you see? You'll be in control of folks from the front door until you whisk them out the back, and Bebee's going to help you. Think of it as giving a tour to prospective members. Now straighten up and deliver this next one with some gusto. 'In appreciation for this community's effort to help the investigation, Brookside will host,' now pause here for emphasis, 'a free wine-tasting event in the hospitality tent beginning at noon.'"

When Sandy finished his invitation, the crowd began to buzz. At first there was a smattering of light applause, which grew until people actually broke out cheering. Bebee was upstaged, outspent, and once again, no longer in charge.

Sandy was pleased by the crowd's response, and continued on to say, "The governor and I, along with Mr. Wadsworth and Toby Worthington, thank you all for your kind cooperation."

"You went a little over the top with that ad lib, Sandy, but well done nonetheless." Sydney, seated with his back to the railing, rolled over on his side and then up onto his knees. He rested there a moment in anticipation of getting to his feet, but not until after he felt his body was ready to respond.

A groan from Skillings meant that he was regaining consciousness. "Toby, get him some water, and Sandy you need to get out of his suit coat. When he comes to, we've got to get him out of here and on his way back to Albany."

Skillings, still lying on the deck, opened his eyes and slowly reached behind his head. When he drew his bloodied hand back to look at it, he gasped, "I've been shot!"

"Negative," said Toby sympathetically. "You're all right, Henry, you just got a bad knock on the head from the speaker cabinet when the cannon went off."

"Cannon? What cannon? What are you doing with my coat, Sandy?"

Sydney, standing now, answered for Sandy. "He just wanted to clean it up for you, blood and all, don't you know. We don't want to send you back to the governor looking like damaged goods now, do we? Come along, we'll help you put your jacket back on. When you've got your sea legs, you and Sandy can go down to the Red Cross tent and get that gash on your head stitched up."

Toby played along filling in the blanks, "Thanks to you, Skillings, things are shaping up, and all for the better I might add. That was quite a speech you gave."

"I don't remember giving any speech."

"Of course you don't. Temporary memory loss, no doubt. You're just a little shell-shocked so to speak. You were talking to the crowd out of pure guts and instinct. Thank heavens. You've resolved our little dilemma here single-handedly." Toby reached for his pipe.

"Look. Down there, people are lining up in the portico for the clubhouse tour. Some are even leaving. Ha! I wouldn't be surprised if they're back at noon for a little sip of the grape." Toby lit his pipe and secured the cannon tying down its canvas cover.

"Toby's quite right, Skillings. You've managed to come down here and diffuse our problem."

"I did, did I? Well thanks, Sydney, glad I could help."

Sydney, standing behind Skillings, winked at Sandy, hoping he could lip-read "Not a word, Sandy." Sandy nodded as though he understood.

"By the way, Skillings," said Toby, "you might also let Governor Dewey know that your collaboration with us will most likely deliver Livermore Falls into his camp come the election."

Sydney followed up, "Yes, and after this whole mess settles down, I'm going to put in a good word for you with your boss. Now off you go."

*　　*　　*

Toby helped Sydney to his feet. "Sydney, are you sure that d'Chard and Father O'Connor will play along with this ruse?"

"I'd be very surprised if they don't. Louis will make a fortune at my expense, and our association's good club chaplain . . . well, he wouldn't show up here and leave without grounding a club on our course."

"No doubt you're right. I'll get word to my caddy, Oliver, to meet us on the tenth tee with our clubs. I put him on standby this morning, like you said. Oliver'll have to carry double for us. I'll have him try to round up couple of caddies for d'Chard and Father O'Connor. Sydney, I can't quite put my finger on your change of strategy with the locals. It was brilliant! Was this one of your backup plans?"

"In a manner of speaking, yes. It occurred to me that I might have misjudged the motives of the townspeople. Except for a few employees at the club, most of them have never set foot on the premises. Bebee unwittingly provided the town with an opportunity. Think about it, Toby. How many people do you really believe want to come out here to look for Bartholomew?"

"I haven't devoted a whole lot of time to think about it. Curses, Sydney, thinking's your department." Toby headed back for the turret. "I don't expect a whole lot of folks would come here actually hoping to find Jeffrey. Maybe he's a big shot around town, but I always thought of him as sort of a blight on the club."

"Good, we're agreed then on our strategy. Look, why would these community clubs bring a hospitality tent? It occurred to me that this whole mishmash is a social event like some village treasure hunt. I could be dead wrong, but I think they're mainly curious about Brookside." Sydney tailed along behind Toby.

"Very perceptive on your part, you old fox," remarked Toby.

"Thank you, my friend. I don't like to choose between a fight to the death or unconditional surrender. We'd end up loosing either way. This approach at least gives us a chance to salvage the day."

During the elevator's slow descent, Toby inquired, "Do you think Skillings is going to come to and figure out what really happened?"

"It doesn't matter, Toby. If he does sort it out, he's not going to tell the governor. After all, he's a success, a hero, about to receive the club's undying gratitude."

"Well, Sydney, all we have to do is play out our part this morning and get out of town." On the way to the locker room, Toby waited for Sydney to catch up. "You feeling up to this match? I'm whipped myself."

"Me too, Toby. Thank God we're only playing nine holes. I don't think I've ever been this beat in my life, and it's still morning. At least we'll be finished by noon, and we can hit the road." Sydney smiled. "You drive, I'll sleep."

Toby stopped to survey the grounds. "Sydney, you're right on about d'Chard. Look who's heading for the locker room with Father O'Connor hot on his heels." Toby chuckled. "You can't miss the Baron in that gadfly outfit he's wearing."

"Just as I thought, let's beat them over to the locker room."

10

The Game

Baron Louis d'Chard was a tall slender man. He had an elongated nose under which he frequently parked an ivory cigarette holder. In his early forties, his dark complexion and leathery folded skin earned him the nickname of Mummy, which only his closest friends were privileged to use in his presence. Since his father was French and his mother English, he was fluent in both languages. A thick French accent appeared only when it was to his romantic or monetary advantage. Inheriting his father's prewar wine brokerage business, Louis decided to resurrect it and invade the United States. Livermore Falls was not to be spared as he marketed his wares to the finest establishments across New York and New England.

Moments after Sydney and Toby arrived in the locker room, d'Chard burst through the door flaunting his pleated robin's egg blue suit, white vest, cobalt blue ascot, and white wingtip shoes, all topped off with a broad brimmed panama hat. The only thing missing was a white carnation, which was probably a simple oversight on his part. Toby always viewed him as someone quite enamored with himself. Sydney's opinion was even less charitable.

"Good to see you again, Baron d'Chard," said Sydney. "You couldn't have shown up at a more propitious time."

"I might take issue with that. What the devil's going on here anyway? The club's a shambles."

"Later, Louis. I'll fill you in after we get off the tee."

Father O'Connor, now sixtyish, trailed in behind Louis. Carrying his golf shoes, he backed his way through the swinging locker room door, smoking one of d'Chard's cigarettes. He was garbed in his simple, worn-out at the elbows and knees rumpled black wool travel suit, which doubled as his golf attire. After dropping his shoes on the floor, he pulled out a golf cap tucked in his back pocket and sailed his straw boater hat toward a row of coat hooks.

"Good shot, Father." said Sydney. "You haven't lost your touch. I'm delighted you could make up our fourth this morning. Obviously, you've met the Baron, and I believe you know Toby Worthington from past encounters."

"Greetings to ya, Mr. Wadsworth. It's nice of you to accommodate me on such a fine morning." His cigarette wobbled on his lower lip as he spoke. "I had a bit of trouble, though, making me way through that congregation of yours outside. With the tents and all the commotion I thought you might be holding a revival meeting." He smiled good naturedly. "Not that the holy church is afraid of a little competition."

"No need to concern yourself, Father Michael. A good measure of that congregation may be in our gallery today."

"Is that so? I'd best be on me game," he said picking up a handful of tees, pencils, and ball markers from a basket. "By the way, I won't be needing a caddie. I'll pack me own as always. A servant of the Lord has no servants." On further reflection he added, "I think it goes something like that."

Toby managed to get Louis' attention. "So good of you, d'Chard to play along with us."

"Of course, *mon ami*. As you Yanks are fond of saying, my time is your time—until noon that is! Anyway, Toby, it is Toby? Because of you and Sydney, I'm really looking forward to introducing some of my new table wines to the area. I must apologize for showing up a couple of days early, but I had a cancellation downstate."

Toby inquired, "Will you be needing a change of attire?" hoping that he would. "Also, I possibly have a caddy arranged for you, and we can get you a set of clubs if you don't have any with you."

"Kind of you to ask, but that won't be necessary," Louis assured him. "My driver will be caddying for me, and all I need are my shoes and a cardigan sweater from my bag."

"My word," said Sydney, "you've certainly hit the high road in the last couple of years. You have a driver that doubles as your caddie?"

"Yes, and she's my masseuse as well. I tire so easily now on these long road trips. Her name is Simone."

Toby gasped, "Simone?"

"Yes, I rescued the poor thing working at a sidewalk bistro in Paris. She performs quite well for me in sales too. You don't mind if I have her drop my things off in here do you?"

Sydney coughed several times, stalling to consider his reply. "Why, Louis, you old rake! Please ask her to leave your belongings outside the door. Club rules, if you don't mind."

HOLE NO. 10—PAR 4 380 YDS. THE ROAD HOLE

On the way out of the locker room, the foursome settled on a best ball match pitting, Sydney and Toby against Louis and Father Michael. It was Father Michael who suggested a five-dollar wager. Toby needled good-naturedly, "Tell me Father, you smoke, drink, and gamble—is there anything else you do that you're not telling us about?" Father Michael's blank stare conveyed a distinct lack of amusement.

As they sauntered out of the clubhouse approaching the tenth tee, Sydney and Toby were relieved to see a number of townspeople lining both sides of the fairway. Between the street and the road hole fairway, several people were watching from their cars. Some honked their horns to welcome the arrival of Sydney's foursome. A number of youths climbed on top of trucks and car bumpers to get a better view.

At first sight of the large gallery, Father O'Connor became visibly uncomfortable and turned around to his playing partners mumbling, "Gentlemen, don't you think we should have a wee drop of the Irish before we start—just to mark such an auspicious occasion?"

"Father, don't be nervous," said Toby. "I want you to think of those people out there watching you as your devoted parishioners and that you're here to conduct them in holy communion with nature."

"Yes, yes. But what if I hit one of them?"

"Well then, if need be, who better to give the last rights? Let's play on. I'll hit first if it makes you more comfortable."

Toby strode across the tee to where Oliver was standing and held out his hand for the driver. No words were exchanged. Oliver knew Mr. Worthington insisted that he not encounter the slightest distraction prior to or during his shot-making. After going through his exacting preshot routine, Toby addressed the ball and took a sweeping roundhouse swing. The shot arced high out over the gallery hooking to the left toward the road hole. All eyes followed it as came crashing down on the windshield of a Studebaker sedan parked on the edge of the course.

"Well, gents, I dare say that'll be an unplayable lie. If you don't mind, I think I'll take a mulligan." This time he plucked a few blades of grass and dropped them to check the wind direction. When he teed up another ball, the gallery moved back for fear of getting beaned. This time the gallery was safe as his tee shot cheated the wind by dribbling harmlessly 50 yards up the middle of the fairway.

The onlookers suddenly lost all interest in Toby's golfing exploits when Simone emerged from the clubhouse carrying Louis' golf bag. Tall, tan, and athletic, her long legs and Amazonian proportions were handsomely accentuated by her one-size-too-small white shorts and sleeveless top. As she strode across the tee to deliver a club to the waiting Baron, the men in the gallery moved in as one for a closer look.

Before he teed off, d'Chard took notice of the gallery's interest in Simone and felt assured of a good turnout for the noon wine tasting event. The men, he told himself, would be there and their female counterparts would be there too, making sure the men behaved. Louis was a remarkable golfer in the sense that he could make a relatively normal golf swing with his cigarette holder firmly clenched in his teeth. He made a respectable drive down the right side of the fairway, but since the appearance of Simone on the course, it predictably went unnoticed.

Sydney was sure that the gallery would tease the Baron about his dandy attire, but their attention was too focused on Simone's lack of attire to bother assessing Louis' outfit. Sydney, who also went unnoticed, felt a twinge of jealousy. But as he took his place on the tee, the sight of Bebee lining up behind the first group to tour the clubhouse gave him a sense of relief. Taking his driver from Oliver, he stood behind the ball and went through his twelve-point mental checklist. Unfortunately, his drive took on the low trajectory of what is known in golfing parlance as a worm raper.

Father Michael, having witnessed the tee shots of his companions, was seriously considering giving this exhibition match a pass. *I can't do any worse,* he said to himself. *Besides, a walk-off now may mean no more walk-ons.* Although aging and slight of build, he was a strong man and prided himself on his physical fitness. Wielding a golf club, he was able to coil up like a snake and strike like a rattler. He approached the tee with trepidation, glanced heavenward, closed his eyes, and prayed for his imaginary patron saint of golf to give his ball the wings of a guardian angel. To his delight and the chagrin of his opponents, his ball floated into the center of the fairway considerably beyond those of his companions.

Toby muttered to himself that only Catholics with direct connections to the Almighty could be that lucky. He conceded politely, "Good shot, Father Michael. Keep it up."

Four abreast, the men left the tee and paraded down the fairway. Simone marched out in front of them like a majorette. Oliver, head down and carrying two bags, brought up the rear. He didn't notice that his girlfriend, Amy, was following the match still looking for a front-page story.

When Toby approached the location of his first ball, a very irate Studebaker owner accosted him. "Well, Mr. Bigshot, what are you going to do about the ball you hit through my windshield? It's sitting right over there on my front seat!"

Toby accepted the verbal assault like a gentleman, and said. "Actually, sir, I'm not obliged to do anything for you. You see, you placed your car in bounds on the field of play, which by the way, you did at your own risk. I could have taken a free drop from your car no nearer the hole, but I elected to take a mulligan. My ball striking your car, a movable object, is of no consequence, it's just what we call the rub of the green."

"Well, maybe I should rub your nose in some of the green."

"See here. There's no need to be hostile. I'm just acquainting you with the rules of the game." A small group of people gathered around the altercation. Oliver stood frozen but glanced around for an escape route in case the situation became physical. "My ball obviously ended up in an unplayable lie, and as a gesture of good will, you may have it as a keepsake."

"That ain't going to be good enough!"

"I think you should let me finish," said Toby. "I would never tarnish my reputation or that of the club if I didn't hold myself responsible for any damage I cause."

"That's more like it. Why didn't you say so to begin with?"

"Because I want you to understand the game and the reason things like this are bound to happen. There are rules, protocols, and manners to iron them out. Here is my card. Call me when you get your windshield fixed."

Sydney shouted across the fairway, "Come along, Toby, no time for idle chitchat."

HOLE NO. 15—PAR 3 146 YDS. DEAD MAN'S CAT

Arriving at number 15, the foursome was delayed by a number of kids from the gallery who were emptying the sand traps onto the putting green. It was a short hole across a natural ravine inhabited by a thicket of blackberry bushes. Oliver, with bags in tow, trotted over the wooden bridge to the far side and began chasing the youngsters out of harm's way and back into the gallery.

While Simone was reraking the traps, Louis took the opportunity to query Sydney. "What's going on with Brookside? The police and townspeople are all over the place. I found out there's a missing club member and a murder victim in the pond. Are you sure it's safe for me to be here?"

"Of course it is, Louis. Don't be ridiculous. I've got things here pretty much back under my control."

"Is that so? Well then, I'm glad to hear it, because I would suggest the way you are playing, your mind is someplace else. My real concern, of course, is for Simone. I wouldn't want her to suffer any indignities while she's here—I'm sure you understand."

"Of course, Louis. A beautiful young woman with so many talents must be of considerable concern. I must say I envy you. I gave much thought to having my own manservant a few years ago, but that was becoming the way of the past." Sydney lit one of his cigars and offered one to the others milling around on the tee, knowing full well they would refuse the offer.

"I'd enjoy one since you're offerin'," came a voice from the gallery behind the tee box. Sydney was trapped and held out his cigar case to the man with a Studebaker. Toby smiled; Sydney grimaced.

As the green was cleared and they were about ready to tee off, Sydney probed Louis further about Simone. "She's a remarkable, shall we say, multitalented woman. Is there anything she wouldn't do for you?"

"Sydney, how could you ask such a thing? That is a question gentlemen neither ask nor are they obliged to answer."

"Naturally, let me rephrase my question. Toby and I have to leave town as soon as this little exhibition match of ours is over, and it may require a diversion for us to slip away unnoticed. Who better than your Simone?"

"So you really are in trouble. Leave it to me," said Louis.

HOLE NO. 18—PAR 4 416 YDS. THE BERM

As the teams approached their final shots to the eighteenth green, a number of people who had already been through the clubhouse tour came over to join the gallery that formed a horseshoe of spectators to witness the finish.

Father Michael played first with his ball coming to rest on the green a good thirty-five feet away from the hole. His partner Louis overshot the hole, but his ball was still on the green. Toby, Sydney's partner, dribbled his third shot barely onto the front edge of the green.

Meanwhile, Sydney was still vacillating over which club to take. In a quandary, he sought Oliver's advice. With his partner Toby in difficulty, Sydney had to shoot for the pin. For the first time in the match, he was actually focused. After several disagreements with Oliver as to which club he should choose, Sydney selected an 8-iron over his caddy's objections. The shot fell short and rolled into a deep greenside bunker. Sydney groaned, "Oliver, I should have listened to you!"

Sydney, farthest away, was the first to play. He tiptoed into the sand trap delicately, careful not to ground his club and incur a penalty. Oliver removed the rake from the trap. From where his ball came to rest, Sydney could barely see over the front edge of the trap to the green beyond. He addressed the ball and took a healthy swing, hitting the sand about four inches behind the ball. Sand flew onto the green but the ball didn't. It caught the front edge of the trap and rolled back down into the divot he'd just taken. Exasperated, he took another full swing. This time his club cleanly propelled the ball out over the gallery hitting the roof of the clubhouse.

Sydney stepped out of the trap and declared. "Well at least I'm out. I'll take a drop over by the clubhouse and play up."

"I'm afraid not," said Father Michael. "Your shot's gone out of bounds. It'll cost you two strokes."

"You're right of course," replied Sydney climbing back into the sand trap. Oliver tossed him another ball and reminded Sydney, "Mr. Wadsworth, sir, remember the rules require you to drop it in the same divot hole you've been digging." Sydney frowned and grit his teeth. The last two things he needed were lectures on the rules of golf from a priest and a caddy.

The hole got deeper after two more failures to extricate himself from the trap. The ball would roll down back down the steep sand bank and funnel into the same divot that no longer had sand in it. In total frustration, he took a wild swing, which flew gravel and loose dirt up on the green.

"Did I get out?" Sydney implored.

"Yes, you're ball's on the green, partner," said Toby. "Good work. Don't worry, Sydney, I'll keep our opponents at bay."

Sydney walked up on the green to mark his ball and clear away the sand and gravel that lay between his ball and the hole. As he was brushing away the sand he came upon an object that consumed his interest.

"What is it, Sydney?" said Toby.

"It's a finger."

"Sydney, don't you dare be having me on!"

"Hardly at a time like this. You can see it's obviously from a hand. I'd say it's a thumb severed just below the first knuckle."

"Oh, good god! There's got to be a body buried in the sand trap!"

"What's going on?" said Louis. "Did I hear Toby say there's a body in the trap? I don't wish to be flippant, but has your town cemetery run out of room?"

Father Michael walked over to join the discussion. "I don't think we should alarm these good people out here watching us. When the moment's right, we can let the police in on it."

"So when do you think that might be?" said Toby. "Sometime later today?"

"After we finish the match obviously," said Father Michael lowering his voice. "The gallery will leave when we do." He paused to reinforce his suggestion. "Besides, there's a fiver riding on the match."

Sydney interrupted, "So good of you to remind us of the wager, Father. But how am I supposed to putt when somebody's thumb is lying directly in line between my ball and the hole?"

"Sydney, just treat it as you would someone else's ball." Toby declared. "Use your ball marker, remove the thumb and replace it after you putt."

"Thank you, Toby, of course. It's all so damn disconcerting—I should have known." Sydney marked the thumb and rolled it out of the way with his putter. "I hope to God we're not disturbing some crime scene. Up to now, the only crime here seems to be my poor play."

"Speaking of the authorities," exclaimed Louis, "here comes a gendarme headed for us, and he's got company not far behind. Two plainclothesmen—I think you call them dicks."

"Good grief," squawked Sydney. "It's Bebee and a couple of plainclothesmen! Louis, it's time for Toby and me to haul anchor, so if you have a diversion in mind for our departure, now's the time for it."

Simone, on Louis signal, strode slowly toward center of the green. With a hand on her brow, she sighed and staged a fainting spell worthy of a Hollywood actress. She alit on the ground as softly as a butterfly and arranged herself in a seductive pose before coming to rest. The crowd rushed forward surrounding Simone and completely engulfed Bebee and the detectives. Sydney and Toby worked their way off the green where they encountered Oliver. They chucked their clubs to him for safekeeping.

Toby gave him ten dollars and another ten for him to split between Father Michael and Louis d'Chard for forfeiting the match because he and Toby left the field of play before its conclusion.

Toby caught his breath after forging his way through a few onlookers. "Sydney, don't you think we should take a quick check of the trap before we bail out of here?"

"There's hardly time for it, but you're right. Let's have a look-see."

In the trap, Sydney took one of the rakes and began pulling the sand away from the spot where he took his last swing that lofted a thumb onto the green. "Lend me a hand in here, Toby. Two rakes are better than one." At first a hand was revealed, then an arm, and finally the torso of a middle-aged man that had been buried rather clumsily. The grave was shallow, just inches below the sand and obviously dug in haste without any regard for the dignity of the corpse. Raking the head into view, Sydney remarked, "It's not our Jeffrey Bartholomew."

"Well, Sydney," drawled Toby, "this poor chap's not a member of the club either. Just look at his togs. If he met his demise on the course, he wasn't playing golf. He's wearing loafers. God knows how long he's been in here, the bugs are working on him already. Damnation! There are people who must think our club can be used as some sort of pauper's graveyard."

Amy, breaking out of the crowd, spied Sydney and Toby. She shouted, "Mr. Worthington, is this a good time for that interview?"

"Not just now, Amy. I know I've promised a couple of times, but I think you'll have more than enough to write about without my interview."

"Like what?"

"Like a dead man's thumb on the green and a body we found in this sand trap. That should suffice for now."

"Jeeeez. I guess!

"You'd better skeedadle out of here right now, young lady," said Sydney. That's what we're going to do. Now I suggest you get on back to your folks if they're here. On the double."

                              *   *   *

"What in tarnation's going on here!" exclaimed Bebee as he elbowed his way through the crowd surrounding the eighteenth green.

"My Simone's fainted." said Baron d'Chard. "Please, everyone, stand back. Will someone get her some water?"

"I want everyone out of here, now," bellowed Bebee. "The only ones I want to see around here are Wadsworth and Worthington. The gallery began to move slowly up in the direction of the hospitality tent.

D'Chard rose to his feet and said, "You must be Chief Bebee. I'm Baron Louis d'Chard. Even though I'm new to this village, I've already heard a great deal about you."

"I bet you have." Bebee made no effort to be polite. "Now what seems to be the matter with this Simone?"

"She's exhausted, and I think she was overcome by all the excitement. That and a little something she may have picked up on our tour of Indonesia. We've been assured it's nothing contagious." Louis knelt again beside Simone. "I think my poor little kitten is starting to come out of it. If you don't mind, Chief, I'll tend to her now."

"Good idea," said Bebee backing away. "I'd get her up to the Red Cross tent and have her checked out if I were you."

Bebee spun around and turned his attention to Father Michael, who didn't leave with the others but remained standing on the edge of the green lighting a cigarette. The two detectives had also arrived on the scene and suddenly became preoccupied with helping Simone to her feet.

"What are you hanging around for, Father? Your exhibition match is over isn't it?"

"That it is, that it is, and a very satisfactory conclusion I might add." He fingered a five dollar bill folding it neatly into his wallet."

"Father O'Connor, isn't it? I'm looking for Wadsworth and Worthington."

"Ya just missed 'em. Bailed out of here like their pants were on fire."

"You won't mind telling me what started the blaze in their britches? I'd really like to get my hands on that pair for a little chat."

"Do you now?" replied Father Michael. "They'd be best at telling what happened. But I thought someone the likes of you would be coming along, so I waited up to let ya' know what all the real commotion is about."

"Well, here I am, out with it."

"Somewhere over there on the green is a dead man's finger—a thumb actually. I don't suppose it's still around where I saw it last. Lot's of scuffling went on after the young lady fainted. That thumb's probably been stepped on and kicked dozens of times. No telling where it is now." Bebee went speechless and stared up at the sky. Father Michael imagined that the chief was asking the Lord's assistance but dismissed the thought as being out of character. Waiting for Bebee to come back to the conversation, he pinched out his cigarette, field stripped it, and put the balled-up white paper wrapper in his pocket. Father Michael got Bebee's attention again when he remarked, "But we do know who the thumb belongs to."

"Yes, yes, well!" Bebee pulled out a handkerchief, took off his hat, and wiped the sweat off the liner.

"It belongs to a body that's been buried not fifty feet away from here in a greenside bunker. Look over your shoulder, to the left. The trap is deep and you can just see a young girl gawking into it." He pointed to where Amy was standing. "Worthington told her to get on out of here. She did but then she doubled back." Amy was shaken, pale, and obviously too frightened to move. "I was about to go over there to lead her away when I saw you coming."

"I'll tend to her in a minute. I know her. Amy's a reporter for the local paper. Always looking for a big scoop when she should be covering Girl Scout campouts. Right now you need to tell me what you know."

"Well, Chief, it was Wadsworth who discovered the body. Shall we say he found it the hard way. His ball was in the trap, and he was chopping at it like he was trying to send it to China instead of up on the green. But if it weren't for Sydney's predicament and lack of skill, the body might not have been discovered for some time. I think Sydney should get a reward of some kind, but he's a shy, modest man—probably why he shot out of here in such a hurry."

"Enough." Bebee couldn't be more stunned if the Brookside cannon were fired again.

Father Michael lowered his head and said, "I'll bid you a good day, Chief. I have my duties to attend to. By the way, you'd do well to escort that girl off the course." Having seen enough death for a lifetime, he walked away from Bebee, Amy, and the sand trap, picked up his golf bag and left for the village.

Bebee trotted over to Amy where she stood with her gaze still fixed on the body. "Amy, you shouldn't be here. You run off now, get on home, or find your folks if you know where they are. Reporter or not, this is no place for you, not yet anyway. I'll take care of things here."

Ignoring Bebee's plea, Amy stood silent, glassy eyed and continued to stare at the half-buried body lying face up. Sydney and Toby had neatly raked the sand into an even halolike pile around the man's exposed edges. Suddenly, Amy found her tongue, "I've seen this man before, in the village."

"Go on."

"I don't know who he is. I'd never seen him before until I saw him a couple of weeks ago in front of the post office. I noticed him because he was arguing with another man I've never seen either. They were really mad at each other. I wondered what they could be doing in Livermore Falls. They weren't dressed like us or the summer people. Look at his clothes, kind of weird don't you think?"

"Yes, I do think, Amy. You're being very helpful. Anything else you can remember about him? What happened after they argued?"

"Not much," said Amy. Her voice trailed off. "I remember seeing them walk off together. Then I watched them get into a car up the street. They looked kind of creepy, and I just hoped they'd leave town."

"Good work, Amy. Could you tell me what kind of car they got into?"

"I don't know too much about cars, just Mr. Worthington's. It was a black four-door sedan, and it was old, I know that. And it didn't have New York license plates." She turned her eyes away from the trap and pointed to the man. Words stuck in her throat, "This man got in on the passenger side." Amy began to shiver. She'd never seen a dead person before. When Bebee heard her voice tremble, he put his arm around Amy to steady her.

"That's enough for now, Amy." Together they began to walk slowly toward the clubhouse. "Detectives Soldano, Rivera! Get back here. You're needed!

11

On The Road

With the clutch in neutral, Sydney and Toby coaxed the Olds out of the barn and jumped in as it silently rolled down the gentle slope of the maintenance road. Out of sight from the clubhouse, Toby slipped the engine into low gear. The engine turned over and responded with a comforting purr. "I'm glad we're pulling out of here, Sydney. I don't think there's much more we can contribute by staying on. Probably just get in the way. It's up to Sandy and d'Chard to hold the fort now."

"Quite right, Toby. Being out of town on Sunday when our president shows up is a pleasure I can easily forego. It would almost be worth it, though, to see him wet his pants."

Toby laughed at the thought. "Forest never was much good in a pinch. He never got in over his head as long as we were around to pull his ass out of the fire."

"Strong language but well put, Toby. I have a hunch that what's waiting for him at Brookside will help Forest grow into his position." Sydney smiled.

Toby said, "Off the subject, what did you tell Sandy about our plans?"

"As little as possible of course. I didn't have time to elaborate anyway. What we're doing doesn't need to get blabbed to Bebee, not that Sandy would. As I told him before, we're on a mission and we'll be back in a couple of days." To get their bearings and chart a course, Sydney retrieved the road map from the glove box. "Keep your eyes on the road, Toby. You're starting to drift off. We'd better make an early night of it. I need the rest even if you don't."

Toby grunted his approval as they approached the turn onto the Flat Road heading toward the village. "We're going to have to do a stopover. It's much too late to make Table Rock tonight." When they drove past Harriet Bartholomew's place, Toby remembered his promise to her, and he began to question his judgment. Why had he promised to deliver Jeffrey to her or take her to him before telling anyone else, even Sydney? he asked himself. At first he thought he could excuse himself by saying he promised her in a moment of weakness, but on reflection he knew it wasn't out of fondness for her. *Why did Harriet insist on such secrecy? Perhaps she's responsible for Jeffrey's disappearance and wants to frame the story before the truth comes out. Maybe she knows he's dead and wants me to think she believes he's alive to throw me off—not likely, much too confusing.* He shook his head, hoping that all the loose pieces floating around in his mind would fall into place. *I can't dismiss the fact that she may have poisoned or at least tried to poison Jeffrey, which after all was my own theory. If I could only know what the test results were on Jeffrey's heart medication. Well, I may have a higher calling, because I do have an obligation to society: to see that justice is done. Certainly that should trump my promise to Harriet. I think I'll hold on to that thought.*

While the debate raged in Toby's mind, Sydney fumbled with the road map trying to refold it into its original configuration. "Confound it, Toby, only some sadistic bastard could design something as simple as a road map into a conundrum."

"Get a grip, Sydney. You're sounding constipated again. I'm amazed that you seem more troubled by folding that map than finding a body in a sand trap. We've got to focus on the big picture here, don't you know."

"Toby, we need to concentrate on the immediacy of what we're doing right this minute. I refuse to be annoyed by your shallow remark only because I know it's well intentioned. Of course I'm deeply concerned by some strange person buried on our course." Sydney shoved the crumpled road map back into the glove box. "While you were driving through town, I did manage to select a couple of possible stopovers for us tonight, assuming we can drive on for another three or four hours." Sydney yawned.

Toby managed to dodge several potholes in the two-lane road leading out of town, but like any good mine field it was impossible to escape them all. The occasional jostling of the coupe only served to scramble their thoughts and feed their anxiety about what may lie ahead. As the Olds danced and swayed down the road over multiple old frost swells, they focused increasingly on the relief that Highway 87 promised.

*   *   *

Both were gratified to head north. Sydney broke a long period of silence, "If you don't mind Toby, I'd appreciate it if you'd continue to take the first watch at the wheel. We can switch off when we need to stop for the necessary."

"Fine by me. But when I'm smoking my pipe, it would be nice if you didn't smoke your cigar at the same time. It's hard enough to see in here with just one of us lit up." Toby, after some difficulty and fiddling, finished stoking his tobacco furnace and struck a match to it. "You know Sydney, your cigars bugger the aroma of my tobacco. And there's no opening the windows. It blows hot ash all over everything and burns holes in your clothes where you least want them."

"Oh, for heaven's sake, Toby, if there's absolutely nothing else troubling you about my cigars, I'm going to get a little shut-eye." Sydney slouched down in his seat, rolled up an old sweater from the rear window shelf, and tucked it behind his head. He wondered if Bebee was looking for them. *Perhaps the chief has enough on his plate without worrying about us. At least the coroner and medical examiner should be at Brookside by now.* Exhausted, Sydney began to drift off to sleep, but visions of more corpses being discovered on the course startled him back to consciousness again. What if a rash of members put their stock up for sale or if Bebee dug up all the sand traps looking for more bodies? He imagined what might happen if d'Chard put out too many bottles of wine, and the town went wild on the golf course. *No,* he thought, *that wouldn't happen. The Baron isn't that generous, not even with my money.*

While Sydney intermittently dozed and snorted as if he were having a bad dream, Toby sped on through the afternoon with a careful eye on the gas gauge. The monotony of smooth straight stretches of road and the persistent droning of an engine running at a constant speed had a hypnotic effect on Toby that he fought by turning on the radio. After some difficulty, he located a station that could be heard above the static interference. The tobacco in his pipe had burned its way to the bottom, and the smoke that found its way through the dregs to Toby's tongue was bitter. As he tapped his pipe on the small ashtray, a considerable amount of the hot ash fell unnoticed onto Sydney's white knickers.

Toby struggled to keep awake as he fought the fatigue of the day's events. An hour of driving mesmerized took its toll on him. But he pressed on knowing that Sydney needed all the rest he could get. Harriet and Jeffrey had long since exited Toby's thought processes. He read the Burma Shave homilies along the regularly spaced roadside signs. "HIGHWAYS . . .

ARE . . . NO PLACE . . . TO SLEEP, STOP YOUR CAR . . . TO COUNT . . . YOUR SHEEP. Trying to keep some measure of concentration on the road and constantly rubbing his eyes to keep them open, Toby didn't realize he was losing a battle that couldn't be won. He weaved across the centerline and was rudely awakened by a horn from an oncoming truck. Struggling with the wheel, he overcompensated and swerved out of control. The Olds left the road and careened its way over and down the loose gravel shoulder. Slamming on the brakes, Sydney was tossed into the dashboard while Toby introduced himself to the steering wheel.

"Sorry, Sydney, I thought I'd pull over to catch a little nap. My turn, so to speak."

"I think you started your little nap before we arrived here, if you don't mind my saying."

"Yes, well, I'm afraid we're stuck." Toby turned off the ignition.

No longer parallel with the road, the car angled nose down and was pitched over to the passenger side. Reeds and tall cat-o'-ninc-tails stared at them through the windshield. "We're high centered, Sydney, so we're not going to back out of here even if I could get traction on all this loose gravel. You'd think the state cold do a better job maintaining the shoulders." Toby leaned over to retrieve his pipe from the floorboards.

Sydney alternately rubbed the back of his neck and the bump on his forehead. Glowering like a wounded buffalo, he asked, "How long should we wait here before we go up on the road and ask for help? Can anyone even see us down here?"

Toby looked in the rear view mirror. "Not much traffic up there. But I don't think wc should be in a rush to ask. I hate to be beholden."

"Am I hearing this right? You are being facetious, aren't you? This isn't my first choice of a place to starve to death."

"All right then, I'll go. After all we are on a schedule. If worse comes to worse, I can flag someone down with my pistol." Toby was still in the process of regaining his senses.

"Really, Toby, you must have scrambled your brains on the steering wheel."

Before Toby could formulate a rational response, he glanced again in the mirror and saw a state patrol car parked above with its lights flashing. "We don't need to go looking for help Sydney. It's here. There's a patrolman scrambling down the bank toward us. I say we just act natural and be calm as if nothing happened. I'll do the talking." Sydney shook his head.

Toby rolled down the window and spoke first. "What seems to be the trouble, officer? We just pulled over to get a little rest."

"I can see that," replied the trooper. "I hate to disturb your nap, but I'd like both of you to step out of the car and show me your identification and car registration. I'm James Barnes, and you, behind the wheel, I'll need your driver's license." Barnes pulled Toby's door open to let him out. Because Sydney's door wouldn't open, he was excused from leaving the car. "I've been following you two from a couple of miles back. When I saw your car wandering back and forth over the center line, I was going to pull you over, but you beat me to it." Toby handed the trooper a fistful of identification cards. Sydney reluctantly passed his identification over to Toby along with the registration from the glove box.

"Very interesting. Everything seems to be in order, Mr. Worthington. Hmmmm. I see you're an honorary member of the South Bend Police Department, and you're entitled to every courtesy by other law enforcement agencies. 1923. Did you know you've got an old driver's license purchased in a drug store? I've heard about things like this, but I've never actually seen one before."

"Well, it was perfectly legal when I bought it, believe you me. I renew it every year, and I would appreciate you keeping your tone a little more civil."

"Certainly, sir, I'll give it my best try. And the other gentleman is Sydney Wadsworth?" Sydney nodded. "You fellows might not know it, but there's a lot of law enforcement folks just like me looking for you two."

Toby steadied himself against the car, assuming a nonchalant pose. "Whatever on earth for, officer?"

"Why don't you tell me?"

"Of course, now let me see, I think I know what it's all about. Chief Bebee in Livermore Falls, yes. He must have wanted to get in touch with me about my sister-in-law. The old girl is on her last legs, but fortunately her brother already got in touch with me." Toby took a deep breath. "Bebee couldn't have known that, but his concern is much appreciated—thoughtful man that he is. Right now we're on our way up to Maxine's nursing home in Saratoga Springs, aren't we Sydney?"

"Oh yes." Sydney drawled.

Trooper Barnes interrupted their conversation. "You two must be pretty important fellows getting that kind of attention. You're lucky too. Another fifty feet through this thicket and you'd be floating in Purdy Lake." His remark startled both Sydney and Toby and commanded their full attention.

"Now you two don't go running off. I have to get up to my car and do some checking." Trooper Barnes turned away and scrambled up the bank.

"A bit patronizing, wouldn't you say?" said Toby. "Do you think he's running a check on us?"

"Of course he is. But that story of yours was quick thinking on your part. After all these years, I'm still impressed. But there's not a chance in hell he believes it anymore than I do."

Toby wagged a finger at Sydney. "You know the part about my sister-in-law, Maxine? Well, it's true. She's been dying for years. Sometimes, I wish she would pop off. I thought we might stop by on the way back to see how she is. My brother Alfred, rest his soul, went to an early grave because of her." Toby wiped his brow and swatted his cap at a collection of mosquitoes swarming around him for an afternoon snack. "So you see, Sydney, my explanation to Trooper Barnes is not a fabrication but has a foundation built on the truth. I just omitted some of the salient details of our trip when he interrupted me and went packing off."

*   *   *

Up on the highway, another car pulled up behind the trooper's car, stopped, and cut the engine. It was an old prewar Plymouth with a personality, like its faded gray color. Nancy Sullivan, still in uniform, stepped out to greet the state trooper snaking his way up the shoulder of the highway. "I'm Officer Sullivan from Livermore Falls," she said. Are the two men in the Oldsmobile, OK?"

"Yeah, there's nothing wrong with those old boys that a shrink and a good night's sleep wouldn't cure. What's your interest?"

"My chief wants me to tail them in connection with a murder and a missing person down in Livermore Falls. I saw them sneakin' out of the Brookside Country Club. That's when I took off after them. I'm supposed to be undercover, but I didn't have time to change out of uniform."

"You're not kidding, are you? No wonder your chief's got half the state looking for them. What are they, material witnesses or something? They look pretty harmless." He brushed the dust and brambles from his pants. "By the way, I'm James Barnes. Friends call me, Jim. And don't apologize for being in uniform, it suits you fine."

"Hi, Jim. Please call me Nancy. With your permission I'd like to use your radio and check in with my chief. Mine's on the fritz, and he doesn't know where I am."

"Sure, I'll give you a hand. Get in on my side." Jim opened the door for Nancy to slide in. "You wouldn't believe the story Worthington handed me."

"No, I probably wouldn't. Frankly, I think they're up to some mischief, and the chief thinks they're giving him a snow job. They have this inflated sense of their own worth, and it drives my boss crazy. Tell me, Jim, is their car drivable?"

"I think so as long as they've got gas. I'll pull them out of there or get a tow truck if I can't."

Nancy couldn't get through to Bebee but left a message with Lester that she was following Sydney and Toby, as ordered, and advised that she could be more effectual if he called off the search for them.

"You know Jim, all kidding aside, I'm actually worried about these guys. They could be way in over their heads depending on what they're up to."

"Nancy, wouldn't it be better if I just brought them in?"

"Could be. But let me work this out on my own. Forty-eight hours, OK? Just tell me how I can get in touch with you if I need help."

Jim, a young bachelor, responded eagerly, "Sure, you can get in touch with me anytime by phone. Here's my number at the station. They know how to reach me. But how can I get in touch with you?"

"I guess you can't, but I have a feeling we'll be meeting up again." Her reply was shaped by her instincts, experience, and intuition. "I can't believe I'm worried about these two guys. They must represent some father figure of mine." She laughed and bounced out of the car.

Jim laughed too. "Say you probably could use a cup of coffee. Why don't you take my thermos with you? It'll give us a reason to meet up again."

"Good idea, Jim. Thanks. I'll back down the road out of sight and wait 'til they're out on the road again."

Smiling, Jim headed down the bank to where Sydney and Toby were marooned.

*   *   *

By now Toby had rejoined Sydney in the car. The windows were rolled up and each was smoking furiously to discourage bloodthirsty mosquitoes. "Behind you, Toby. Here comes our trooper. I can barely make him out in the mirror. I'll wager he talked to Bebee, and we're going out of here in handcuffs. The thought of finishing out my days disgraced and rotting in some hoosegow is totally repulsive to me."

"Sydney, there's no reason to talk rubbish like that."

Barnes approached the driver's side of the car and tipped his hat back. He tapped on the window, and Toby rolled it down a few inches. "I should be giving you boys a healthy ticket, but you're going to get off with a warning this time. Everything checks out on you two."

"It"—cough, cough—"does?" said Toby.

"Don't act so surprised," whispered Sydney.

"I brought down a length of rope to get you out of here. Just stay in the car. I'm going to wrap it around your back bumper and drag you out of here ass end first. Got it? So you, Worthington, start 'er up when I give you the signal. When I get up on top, shift into reverse and when you feel the rope pull tight, let out the clutch and gun it, OK? Oh, and clear the smoke out of your cab so you can see where you're going or more like where you've been. Now when you're back on the road, I want you fellows to stop where you can get some rest, all right?"

"You got it," said Toby.

12

Back on the Road

Back on the highway a half hour later, Sydney and Toby watched the trooper speed out of sight. Sydney was behind the wheel as they cautiously resumed their journey north. The Olds responded relatively well after surviving such a traumatic experience. However, it did suffer a debilitating side effect from the accident. The front-end wheels were thrown out of alignment so badly that the car couldn't go over 40 mph without a severe shimmy.

"At least we can't get a speeding ticket," said Sydney gripping the wheel with both hands. "I don't suppose you have any grub on board. I'm starved. You know we haven't had anything to eat since breakfast."

"Tea and burnt toast wasn't my idea of a breakfast," said Toby. "I think I've got a bag of pretzels in the trunk if you're desperate."

"No thanks. The first decent town we come to, we're getting supper and a good night's sleep. That is if we can find a place with indoor plumbing and screens on the windows."

"I'll go along with that." Toby was attending to several mosquito bites on his ankles and the back of his hands by rubbing them with freshly burnt out matches. "For some reason they're allergic to your tired blood. With all those bloodthirsty buggers on me, I'll be lucky not to come down with malaria."

"That may be the least of our worries, Toby. There was another trooper hiding behind that billboard we just passed. Maybe it was our trooper friend, Barnes, maybe not. I've got another one of those nagging feelings that Bebee and the cops are onto us, and we're being followed."

"Aren't you being a little paranoid, Sydney? You think Barnes didn't buy our story back there in the bulrushes—just a ploy to set us up so we could be followed?"

"Most emphatically, yes."

"Well, I never! Here we are, two law-abiding citizens on what may be a wild goose chase, and we're suspected of involvement in criminal activity."

"Toby, I agree with your indignation. Right now, I hope you'll agree with me that we need to give the authorities the slip. We can't outrun them. But if we duck off 87 and head northeast around Albany and Schenectady, we just might lose them long enough to get to our destination."

"Good thinking. Take the road less traveled by and all that. You pick the turnoff, and I'll do the navigating. I'm quite awake for the moment." Toby groped in the glove box, first for his glasses and then the crumpled road map. "Now then, where the hell are we?"

"I don't know, Toby. But I wonder what we're doing out here dodging the law and trying to pick our way out of one mess after another. All I can say is that this is a defining moment for both of us. Our reputation is on the decline. Brookside may be irrevocably ruined. And to top it all off, your ashes are all over my new knickers."

"Easy, Sydney. If all else fails, we've got each other to fall back on."

"Sometimes that bothers me." Sydney paused to check the mirror. "But not in the way you might think. I've said many times over what a solid friend you are, and I'm sorry for getting you involved in this caper."

"No regrets or apologies necessary, Sydney. You couldn't have gotten us in this much trouble without my help. We'll see it through this rough patch. The key to everything is Jeffrey."

After going through a sharp S-curve, Sydney didn't spy any cars in his mirror. He took the opportunity to swerve left off 87 onto a country road with a sign inviting them to the village of Peach Hill, a mere nine miles ahead. The landscape was changing, becoming ever more rural. It was hilly farm country, and the road followed a gentle stream most likely headed for the Hudson River. After five miles, the road unexpectedly changed from asphalt to gravel. "I hope to hell this road doesn't end in Peach Hill. What's the map say, Toby?"

"I can't read the map unless you stop, Sydney. I need to get out and take a whiz anyway."

"All right, I'll pull over up ahead by the stone wall. You go, I'll read the map, and when you get back, I'll go." Sydney was relieved to discover that the road connected to a number of small communities heading northwesterly before heading north again to their target, Table Rock.

Back on the road again, Sydney noticed that the Olds was not behaving like it's usual self. "Toby, your car's overheating. Look at the temperature gauge, it's up in the red zone."

"Well you can't always go by that. We'll give 'er a good drink of water when we get in town, and she'll be right as rain."

"I don't think so, Toby. She's beginning to sputter. I'm going to stop before we seize up the engine and do some real damage."

"You're right. The old girl's been through a lot in the last couple of days. No telling what's the trouble."

On the side of the road with the engine turned off, steam hissed out of the radiator grille and the side vents like a wounded dragon. They raised the hood and circled around the engine compartment several times. Sydney peered under the car to look at the belly of the beast as if he actually knew what he was looking for. Toby, disgusted, flung open the door and sat on the running board. "What is it about us, Sydney? Just when we think things couldn't get worse, they do."

"Yes, and right now I think I understand how Job felt." Totally out of character, Sydney walked out into the center of the road and looked both ways before raising his hands heavenward. "I lift up mine eyes unto the hills from whence cometh my help. Haven't I always been, at least tried to be your faithful servant?" Seldom if ever animated, he visibly showed signs of stress when he pointed both index fingers at the ground, like a Pentecostal preacher. "Lord, we could use a little help down here." Sydney went back to the car and slumped down next to Toby. "Under these circumstances, I should have asked for a lot of help, specific help."

Ten minutes elapsed, and no vehicle passed them in either direction. Thirsty and bone weary, they decided to work their way down to the stream below on the opposite side of the road to get a drink and freshen up. They resigned themselves to the fact that they might have to walk to Peach Hill. Out of sight from the road, they heard a car roar by. Sydney shook his fist, "Wouldn't you just know it? God sends us a car, and we're not around to get in it."

Back up on the side of the road, Toby scraped the caked mud off his shoes, while Sydney pulled brambles off his high top cotton socks.

"Look, Sydney, I think help's on the way! There's a tractor heading in our direction. Sounds like an old three-cycle engine. "Maybe that prayer of yours is being answered, providing this chap'll give us a hand. It was your supplication to the Lord, Sydney, so I think it behooves you to wave the driver down. And try not to muff it."

"All right, but someday you'll have to tell me how you know so much about tractors and don't know a damned thing about your own car." He stepped out into the road and flagged the approaching tractor.

Silence prevailed between the two until the antiquated tractor pulled up alongside the Olds. The two large wheels that flanked the driver told of the day's work in a nearby field. Their tracks left a muddy residue on the road behind. The driver and the tractor appeared to be the same age. Both suffered from that ancient struggle between a man who wants to cultivate and an earth that doesn't want to be cultivated.

"Broke down, eh? Where ya headed?" His words were clipped.

"The same direction you are," said Sydney. "We could use a lift into town."

"I can do better than that. I can give you a tow into town, long's you got the time."

Toby perked up. "We certainly do have time, and we'd be delighted to show our gratitude and compensate you for kindness."

"I'm not sure 'xactly what you meant, but why don't you both get in your car, put it in neutral, and I'll drop you off in town at Jenkins Emporium. Should take us about half an hour. Amos has a fix-it garage behind the store." He jockeyed his tractor up in front of the Olds. "No sense you waitin' for Amos to come way out here with his tow truck. So's you know, my name is Clyde Bebee. Who'd you fellows be, not from around here?"

"Yes—I mean—no," said Toby whose words choked in his throat on hearing the name Bebee. "We're just passing through." He struggled to formulate a reply wondering if Clyde could be an upstate relative of Two Bullets or if his name just happened to be a remarkable coincidence. Not taking a chance on the latter, he replied, looking over at Sydney with an obvious wink for him to play along with whatever came out of his mouth. "I'm Pinky and this is my friend Rodney." Clyde and Toby smiled at each other.

Sydney got behind the wheel again and followed Clyde's instructions. Toby climbed in the other side while Clyde stepped down from the tractor and threw a rope around their front bumper.

Toby said, "You know, Sydney, I think God sent the first car for us, and when we didn't show up to meet it, he let the devil send Clyde up the road for us. Is that too cynical an observation on my part?" Searching for a pat on the back, he continued. "Seriously, I believe it was pretty quick thinking on my part to change our names, just in case Clyde really is a relative of the chief."

"Who's paranoid now, Toby?"

"No need to be snippy, Rodney old dear."

"Well, P-i-n-k-y, now we've got something else to remember like our new names. Thank God it's only 'til we get out of town."

The rope tied to the Olds gently tightened as Clyde urged his tortoise to pull their crippled old hare up the road to Peach Hill. "Listen, Toby, perhaps we've taken this whole business too far. It's probably not too late to turn back."

"Just me talking, but I think we've passed the point of no return." Toby reached for his beloved pipe. Like Sydney, his best thinking usually took place when he was engaged in smoking. "What would we face if we turn around now? I think what's waiting for us back in Livermore Falls could be a lot worse than what's facing us up ahead. To go back and confront Two Bullets empty-handed with a handful of excuses for bailing out of town—well it's more than my pride could bear. You know that Jeffrey's got to be seriously mixed up in everything that's happened since Thursday night. After we laid him out on the course, it's been all downhill for us." Puff . . . puff . . . cough. "We still have an outside shot to pull the reputation of Brookside out of the fire if we can find him. Dead or alive. So, my vote is to soldier on."

"Well put, Toby. You've got my vote. We can't go back anymore than we can go back to being 40 again. We'll just have to think smarter and work twice as hard." The pair, deep in thought, barely noticed a car honk and flash by them going north.

"You have to admit though, Sydney, the odds of our finding Jeffrey are slimmer than Two Bullets finding his ass with both hands."

"Yes, and you know we're rolling the dice on a string of numbers you deciphered on Jeffrey's matchbook."

"Sydney, why don't you just have a smoke? Go ahead, have one of your ropes." As the outskirts of town came into sight, their spirits began to improve. A small weather-beaten sign greeted their arrival: "Welcome to Peach Hill, Population 163."

As the tallest building in Peach Hill, the roof of the Emporium came into view above the summit of a gentle foothill. Once over the crest, they could see the two-story building on the west side of the main drag. In front of its broad front stoop stood a lone abandoned gas pump, a relic of the '30s. Adjoining the south end of the dominant two-story structure leaned an unmanned post office. The north end of the Emporium stood at the corner intersection of a dirt road leading west out of town. As they crept to a stop in front of the Emporium, Toby said, "Sydney, look to your left on the other side of the dirt road, the Mountainview Inn. Vacancy. Our luck must be taking a turn for the better."

Before he could respond, Sydney's attention turned to Clyde, who jumped off the tractor, unhitched the towrope, and coiled it up on his arm. Coming over to Sydney, he said, "OK, Rodney, this is where I leave you two. Amos'll take it from here."

Toby leaned over and said, "There must be some way we can thank you for giving us a hand."

"Nope, it was on my way, Pinky. I 'spect you might be thinking of staying overnight. You might want to stay at The Mountainview Inn. My daughter works there, and she says the food's good. I see they've got a vacancy."

"That sounds like an excellent suggestion. Thank you, Clyde." As he walked back to the tractor, Sydney turned to Toby who had slouched down in his seat and said in a low voice, "She's a Bebee. Do you get the feeling we're being surrounded by them?"

"Yes, and they seem to be closing in," said Toby. "Oh well, we just have to tough it out. I'll go talk to Jenkins about the car if you'll make arrangements for tonight's lodging."

Sydney climbed out and decided to stretch his legs before going to the inn. "You know, Toby, this town could fit on the head of a pin." He could see on the dirt road behind the Emporium there were two attached buildings obviously built years ago to house two related businesses, one for a repair garage, the other for storing animal feed. Sydney looked further up the dirt road and saw what he guessed was a nondenominational Protestant church with its white steeple and black shuttered windows. A grassy hillside beyond the church was home to rows of tilted marble and granite headstones staring down at the village.

On the east side of the road opposite the Emporium, a vacant attorney's office caught his eye along with a butcher shop, a bookstore, and a small, obviously struggling, bakery. A collection of large homes flanked both sides of the road leading north out of town. Their carpenter Gothic architectural style reflected a more prosperous period for the town before the turn of the century. Most of the homes had been converted into rooming houses or ground floor cottage industry businesses and offices as indicated by street signs and signs hung from porches. The remaining few homes still had barns and out buildings, home to horses, hens, and domestic farm animals.

Toby extricated himself from the passenger side and wobbled across the street like a cruise ship passenger trying to gather his sea legs. He weaved his way up the front steps of the store among a group of men who found some amusement in observing life's passing parade on Main Street. Inside he found Amos behind the counter slicing into a wheel of cheese for a lady customer. "Be with you in a minute," he said looking up at Toby.

The general store was fairly typical of the time, especially for one that didn't have competition and specialized in everything, from men's underwear to fishing tackle. Out-of-favor items found their way to display shelves on the balcony. Toby could see that the Emporium also had a thriving business as a feed store. A sign over the cash register put the record straight: "If We Don't Have It, You Don't Need It."

"Now, sir, what can I do for you? I suppose it has to do with your car across the street."

"Yes, but how do you know?" said Toby rather mystified.

"News travels fast." Amos finished ringing up the customer. "If you want, I'll get my rig and tow you into my garage behind the store. No sense starting her up again until we know what ails her."

"Yes, by all means, Amos. Good thinking. Clyde said you might be able to fix up the old girl. We'd be most grateful if you can get us back on the road again."

"Sound's urgent."

"Not terribly urgent. Rodney and I, well, we're anxious to get up north to do some trout fishing. No time to waste, don't you know." Toby reminded himself that he'd better be careful not to expose his true identity and where he and Sydney were headed. Toby repacked his pipe and stepped out onto the stoop along with the men who sat stoically on the front steps to watch Amos tow the Olds. Meanwhile, Sydney, rumpled knickers and all, had meandered across the street into the Mountainview Inn.

After opening a stubborn sliding barn door, Amos skillfully backed Toby's Oldsmobile into his garage. The inside looked more suited to repairing buggies and farm wagons than autos. Hand forged tools hung on the wall that told of a blacksmith age. Only one whitewashed window graced the back wall. Amos flicked on a light hanging from an overhead chord. Toby's confidence in Amos was on the wane. At the same time, he felt he didn't have a choice and was at his mercy.

Hands behind his back, Toby fidgeted and his nose twitched involuntarily. Amos must have read the look of doubt on Toby's face when he said, "You know, those folks down the street with the new filling station on the way out of town, they don't know much about fixin' a car, just pumping gas. By the way, if I'm going to work on your Olds, I'll need your name and where you're from."

"Pinky . . . Pinky Robbins . . . New York City."

"New York City's a big place. Got any street address to go with it?"

While Toby was conjuring up an address, Amos said, "You don't happen to have another name you go by?" He smiled and said, "Pinky, hell, what kind of a name is that? I wouldn't know if I'm talking to your johnson or your little finger."

Toby flushed. "Well, my given name is Eric. That should suit your purposes. By the way, those two cars in the drive, are they yours?" Toby thought he might be able to rent one of them in a jam.

"Nope, they're crippled up, waitin' for service ahead of you. They can wait though. No big rush on 'em."

Amos raised the hood and hung a light over the engine. After a lengthy discussion with Toby and some diagnostic head scratching, Amos surgically removed a number of parts and carried them over to his workbench for a closer inspection. Several minutes passed before he looked at Toby, who was pacing back and forth in front of the garage door. With his usual economy of words, Amos shouted, "Water pump, Eric."

"Is that bad?" replied Toby.

"Yes and no. No, because it can be replaced, and yes, because I don't have one." Toby's face fell along with his hopes for an early departure from Peach Hill. Anxiously, Toby spoke first. "How far out is it before we can get one?"

"Let's see, today's Saturday. Too late to call my supplier. Have to wait till Monday morning. We'd be real lucky to get it delivered same day on the bus. Only one a day goes through here. So it looks like sometime Tuesday you fellas could be on your way. On the other hand maybe not that soon. In any case wherever you're going, the trout will still be there."

His words plunged into Toby's heart like a Turkish dagger. He steadied himself by grasping the workbench with both hands. Breathing deeply, he tried to collect his thoughts. With a dry throat and raspy voice he said, "Doesn't that beat all? Well, you might as well go ahead and order the water pump anyway."

"I thought so," said Amos, then changing the subject in midstream. "Staying across the street, I see."

"Yes, but I was hoping just for the night. Perhaps you might know of some way we can get up to the old fishing hole and pick up our car on the way back. Maybe rent a car."

"Not likely. You won't have any luck in that department. Most people here are fortunate to have just one. I can't tow you up to Albany. My wife's lame, and I can't leave her alone in the store that long. As for the bus, I can write tickets for you fellas but you won't get into Albany 'til late Sunday night." Amos shook his head and spit out the garage door. "We were hoping to get a taxi 'round here, but the town's too damn small. Peach Hill has another problem. We don't have an ambulance yet either, so if you get sick or hurt in this town, you're on your own hunt. Folks say, 'Most of what happens here stays here—up in the Meadow Rest Cemetery.'"

Toby's head was reeling. Every option he could think of for getting to Table Rock was shot down like geese, one by one, until the sky was empty. Completely buffaloed, he began to wander aimlessly through the shop while a puzzled Amos watched him march around the tools and clutter of generations.

"I think we're finished here, aren't we?" declared Amos. "I need to close the store and wash up before supper. Going on five-thirty."

After a lengthy silence, Toby replied. "Yes, yes, of course. If you don't mind, I'm curious about what's under the tarp over here in the corner."

"Oh, that. That happens to be one of my pet projects. Only God knows how long I've been working on it. Don't know that I'll ever finish it. Pull the cover off it, if you've got a mind to.

Toby took up his offer. The tarp, heavy with grease and soot, was obstinate and reluctant to reveal the jewel it concealed. A motorcycle with a sidecar. Toby's eyes bulged. "Good lord, man! I haven't driven one of these for over twenty years."

Amos joined Toby and declared, "I was riding these in World War I! When I enlisted they shipped my ass off to Texas to train on bikes."

"I don't believe it. In my younger days, I used to be something of a wild hare with motorcycles. When I tried to enlist, I visualized being a dispatch rider, racing behind German lines, dodging enemy fire, saving the day for my buddies in the trenches." His immediate and obvious glee fell just as sharply as it rose when he recounted, "But I was turned down for WW I—too old. How about you, Amos?"

"Me? Well I was tinkering with motorcycles a long time before I enlisted, so I had what you call aptitude. But the bastards had me spend most of the war on a bike like this with a sidecar—chauffeuring big shots and officers around. Never did see England or France."

"You're probably lucky, Amos. Lot of our boys didn't make it back from that one." I got in the Spanish-American War as a young buck but too late to fire a shot."

Both men stood back to quietly admire the meticulously restored thirty-year-old motorcycle, an unlikely catalyst for an equally unlikely camaraderie between two old veterans who, outside of war, had very little in common.

"How did you come by this old sweetheart, Amos?"

"You mean Ugly Annie? I ran across her in an army surplus outlet up in Schenectady of all places. The engine was seized up, had to rebore it, thought I'd never get a set of tires I could run on." Amos circled the bike admiring its lean lines. "Much as I hate side cars, I thought my wife Helen would take to it, and we'd go on trips together. That's why I rebuilt it—to use it. I even spent two years building a little custom overnight trailer." He smiled as he recalled it was harder to get a license for his rig than to build it. "You know, Eric, after all the effort, she wouldn't even get in it."

"Damn shame," said Toby sympathetically. "Quite an unusual name for your bike too, wouldn't you say?"

Amos scowled, turned to look out the garage door, and replied, "Just to encourage Helen to at least take a test run, I let her name it and promised on my mother's grave I wouldn't change it. Damn if she didn't decide to name it after what I used to call my first wife! I probably deserved it."

Toby laughed and thought a change of subject was in order. "One thing's for sure. This is a real work of art, hand-rubbed paint and all. Have you put her to the test?"

"Ohhh . . . ya. If the tires'll stand up it, she'll do fifty all day." Amos appreciated the flattery and walked back over to Toby. "It wasn't designed to be like the big crotch rockets they're coming out with these days."

Wistfully Toby said, "I'd like to take it for a spin sometime, but I know it's late, I'm beat, and you've got supper waiting." Dejected, he turned to walk away and say goodnight when he suddenly turned to Amos and said, "You know, I keep a flask in the trunk for emergencies. Maybe you'd like to join me in a toast to your Annie?"

"Now, that's the best idea of the day," replied Amos.

Toby raised the trunk of the Olds to look for his flask that was buried somewhere in a sack of roadside repair tools. Amos peered in the trunk too, more out of curiosity than to be helpful. "Hmmmm," he said, "I don't see any fishing tackle, Eric."

"Oh, that's a little oversight on our part. We were in such a rush to leave we plumb forgot the necessary. I mentioned it to Rodney, and he suggested we pick something up on the way rather than go back for it. You must have some gear you could sell us." Toby was pleased with his quick thinking. He was becoming as deft at lying as a low-level criminal on the lam.

Amos was quick on the uptake. "Gear I got, but it's mostly for worming, live bait, and hardware."

"Well, I think we're after trout. We're headed for a camp upstate near Table Rock." Finding his flask, Toby said, "What's hardware?"

"You know, like spoons, fenders, wire leaders."

"Yes, of course, well here's to your Ugly Annie, Amos. Have a swig of scotch, you first."

Amos obliged and took two long drags before handing the flask back and said with a gravelly voice, "That was very good of you, Eric. Tell you what I'm going to do. You're in a pickle here, and I just got an idea that can work to both our advantage."

"Yes, and what would that be, Amos?" Toby shut the trunk lid, turned around, and took a generous swig from his flask, followed by a long wheeze and several follow-up deep breaths.

"I need some cash to finish out my Annie. I'd like to take it to collector shows, and I need the kind of dough that my old lady doesn't need to know about. For a hundred bucks you can have my Annie for a week. Your car's my collateral, and I'll have it fixed for ya when you get back. Whatcha say?"

"I'd say you've got a deal!" Elated, Toby quickly peeled off five twenties before Amos could have a change of heart.

"Good," said Amos. "Let's drink on it. Now why don't you and Rodney come over after supper, and I'll open up the store? I'm pretty sure I can find you a couple of fly rods, reels, and stuff to get you started. You'll need vests and clothes too. All cash naturally. After that we can come in here and pack up only what you really need to take in the trailer. Watch out it doesn't fish tail on you. Pack up tonight—that way you'll be ready fire out of here first thing in morning." Amos couldn't be happier than a trapper finding a mink in his skunk trap.

"Amos, I'm truly relieved we've come to this arrangement. Rodney will be delighted, especially since he counts on me for almost everything. Come to think of it, Amos we're not exactly dressed for riding a motorcycle or fishing."

"Right," said Amos. "You can borrow my goggles and gloves. Rodney can wear the goggles I got for Helen. They're pink, but I'm sure he won't mind."

Toby could hardly wait to tell Sydney of their good fortune.

13

A Night at the Inn

While Toby spent an inordinate time at the Emporium garage, Sydney sauntered into the Mountainview Inn. At a makeshift reception desk he rang the service bell. Under the glass countertop he read about the features of the inn and the local points of interest while he waited. Home cooking was the number 1 attribute touted by the inn, closely followed by "comfortable, spacious rooms with country charm." A two-mile nature walk headed up the list of the best things to do while visiting Peach Hill. For history buffs, a visit to the local cemetery would reveal the gravesite of the town's only citizen who participated in the Revolutionary War. He fought on the side of the Crown. Interrupting Sydney's preoccupation, the owner appeared through a door leading from the kitchen and offered the usual "how do" of an innkeeper.

Requesting lodging for the evening, Sydney indicated that he required two rooms, one for himself and one for his friend. "I understand from a certain Clyde Bebee that you serve meals here. Is it on the European plan or the American plan?"

"Yes we do, but let's put it this way: it's five dollars per room per night, two-fifty for supper and a dollar twenty-five for breakfast. All family style, and what we serve is whatever we have in the larder."

"Excellent," said Sydney placing a $20 on the counter, "Hopefully, we'll be moving on tomorrow morning." Sydney swung the register around and fortunately remembered to sign it in his newly adopted name, that of his old friend, Rodney Templeton. "Thank you, Mr. Templeton. I'm the proprietor here. My name is Frank, Frank Hapgood. If you need anything, ring the bell on the desk. My wife Eunice does the cooking, and Lilly takes care of the rest."

Through the open door to the kitchen, Sydney saw Eunice preparing the evening meal. A plain middle-aged woman, she was unkempt and bent, obviously from years hovering over her wood-fired stove. Steam rose from a boiling pot that waited anxiously for the garden vegetables she chopped with a measured cadence. Her pace and movements seemed habitual and almost mindless. Old for her age, he thought. A wave of sympathy came over Sydney for a woman whose life apparently was void of joy and laughter. He sighed and glanced into the dining room where a young buxom girl in her twenties, obviously Lilly, was setting the table.

Frank handed Sydney his change and said. "You'll be in rooms 5 and 6 upstairs to the left. No need for keys. The bathroom's at the end of the hall if you want to freshen up for supper. Better tell your friend that supper's on the table at six fifteen sharp."

Sydney was just starting up the stairs when Toby burst through the door. "I've got a lot of news, Sydney. You'll find it most interesting!"

Frank, overhearing Toby, stepped back to the front desk and remarked, "Sydney is it? Not that I really care, but I thought you were Rodney."

"Yes"—cough, cough—"but, my good friend Eric, for some strange reason, persists in using my middle name, and I'm too damn old to give a whit what he calls me." Sydney glared sternly at Toby and suggested he sign the register and come upstairs with him. Both men puffed their way up and stopped briefly on the generous landing to check their timepieces against the grandfather clock parked in the hallway at the top of the stairs.

Sydney spoke first, "I'll take number 5, you've got 6. Now come to my room and tell me how in hell, if and when in hell, we're ever going to get out of here." Toby headed straight for the foot of Sydney's bed and flung himself face down crosswise on the white chenille bedspread. "Nice landing, Toby. You could have left a little room for me."

Undeterred, Sydney dropped lengthwise on the bed, gathered a pillow under his head and slowly swung his feet up over Toby until they unceremoniously came to rest on Toby's buttocks. Sydney stared blankly at the ceiling where a number of mosquitoes and black flies were trapped in the overhead light canopy. Feeling sequestered in the Mountainview Inn, he wondered if he were any different than they, and if he and Toby would endure a comparable fate, either baked to a crisp or snared up as an easy dinner for a spider. "Did you bring up the scotch, Toby?"

"I'm afraid, old dear, that flask is now running on empty," replied Toby, his voice muffled by the bedspread.

"I might have guessed." Sydney grew more sullen. "No doubt it disappeared for a worthy cause I trust."

"Oh, indeed, indeed it did." Raising his head toward Sydney, Toby delighted in regaling Sydney with the contents of his conversation with Amos over at the Emporium and the deal he made to move them on down the road.

Sydney immediately perked up, then suddenly winced at the idea of mounting a motorcycle. And the last thing he wanted to do after supper was to go over to the Emporium to pick out fishing tackle. "You get something for me, Toby. Nice but not extravagant." He put a point on it, saying, "I doubt we'll ever find a use for any of it. Probably end up in some benefit auction at the club."

*   *   *

Later, having refreshed themselves with tepid tap water and starched hand towels, they were prepared to engage the outside world once more. Both were too tired to sleep, too hungry not to eat, and too unsteady to descend the staircase without latching on to each other's arm.

Entering the dining room through the curtained glass doors, they spied another guest already seated, fumbling to reach his napkin that had dropped to the floor. Lilly was quick to retrieve it, yet spent an overindulgent amount of time smoothing it out on the young man's lap. This did not go unnoticed by Toby.

Frank was already seated near the kitchen door at the far end of a table that accommodated a dozen places. He acknowledged their presence with a forced smile and nod. Without a word he pointed with his fork at two open seats next to him on his left. Too tired to consider other seating arrangements or risk offending their innkeeper host, they settled in the designated chairs.

They politely introduced themselves to the stranger sitting across from them. Jack was a strapping young man who, Sydney discovered by way of polite conversation, was a frequent guest at the Mountainview Inn. He was a neatly dressed gregarious chap, which suited his aspirations of being the world's foremost farm implement salesman in upstate New York. Lilly obviously shared his dream. Selections of sausages, mashed potatoes, and a medley of boiled vegetables from the kitchen were delivered to him first, a fact that went unnoticed by Frank, who customarily batted cleanup after everyone else had been served. Toby and Sydney found light entertainment in the not-so-subtle flirtations between Lilly and Jack. Toby whispered to Sydney, "Have you taken notice of our waitress, Lilly? Quite a nice chassis, wouldn't you say?"

"Very observant, Toby. Rather nice headlights," said Sydney cracking his first smile in an age. He turned to Toby and cupped his hand over his mouth and whispered, "But I'm not sure if she's built for comfort or for speed."

Toby chuckled. "No matter. The only comfort I'm interested in tonight is a comfortable bed. As for speed, I only care about how fast I can get to sleep." He produced a gaping yawn as he passed a tray of relishes from Sydney to Frank. "We've got to be on our toes tomorrow, Frank. Leaving early, don't you know? Could someone give us a knock in time for breakfast?"

Frank looked surprised. "I thought you fellows might be laid up here awhile with your car in the shop."

"Well, we've been able to make other arrangements," Toby quickly replied.

"Fine, I'll see to it then."

Lilly circled the table with a pot of coffee before bringing everyone a dish of tapioca smothered in whipped cream. Jack's dish had an extra dollop. For serving Sydney and Toby, her walk was strident and martial, whereas for Jack, her approach and departure had the gait of a fashion model on a New York runway.

Sydney and Toby nodded to each other that it was time to retire and rose from the table. Sydney spoke first, "You'll excuse us, won't you, if we retire early, it's been a most tiring day? Please extend our thanks to Mrs. Hapgood for her excellent fare."

Frank could only manage a hand gesture to acknowledge their departure, while Jack responded with a crafty smile. His overly polite good night signified that he was not disappointed at their early departure.

Toby responded with a knowing wink to Jack. He suspected a romance was kindling, and Jack was about to strike a match to it as soon as Frank left the table. But Jack's patience was tested when Frank looked up from his desert, raised his cup, and motioned to Lilly to bring another round of coffee.

While Frank and Jack lingered over coffee, Sydney went upstairs, and Toby scooted out the front door and over to the Emporium as planned.

Amos had already switched on the store lights in anticipation of his arrival. "Where's your buddy, Rodney?" he said, obviously disappointed.

"Don't you worry about him. He's on board," said Toby. "His boat just slipped over the falls, and he needs his rest for tomorrow."

"By the way, where did you say you were headed on this trip?

"It's a little place up by Table Rock. Forgot the name of it."

"No matter. I hope you don't mind, Eric, I've already put two outfits together for you. I loaded the reels with fifty yards of backing and float lines including two good bamboo rods made over in Vermont. I know they're good. I've used them myself. The vests are full of fly boxes, flies, leaders, everything you need including dope to keep the skeeters off. I even got you two aluminum traveling cases for the rods."

"Amos, I really appreciate all you've done for us. Tell you what. How about fitting me up with the works, you know, a hat, shirt, trousers, braces, and a pair of field boots? Sydney, I mean Rodney, can fend for himself in the morning before we leave."

With a considerably lighter wallet, Toby settled up with Amos. Before returning to the inn, he went into the garage to stuff as much as he could in the trailer. Suddenly, he stopped in his tracks and debated whether he should put his pistol in the trailer or keep it on himself. Deciding on the latter, he turned his attention to finding a place for Sydney's cane. Eventually he strapped it to the sidecar with a length of rawhide. Flush with success, anticipating a good night's rest, and tomorrow's ride out, he ambled back to the inn.

Sydney had already retired for the night. After a prerequisite visit to the communal bathroom, Toby shuffled down the hall to his room. Passing Sydney's room, he heard snoring and thought better about disturbing him. Once in his Spartan room, Toby turned down the bed covers and laid out the contents of his pockets on a highboy bureau. His sensitive nose twitched at the repugnant smell of camphor rising from the empty drawers below. He put his wallet and pistol under his pillow and changed into his pinstripe flannel nightshirt. Taking note of the wood plank floor, he decided to leave his socks on to avoid drawing a splinter. After a couple of feeble efforts to crack the window behind a roll down shade, he realized it was painted shut, and he would have to endure a humid night's sleep.

Toby yawned and tossed fitfully trying to find a comfortable spot on a mattress with the shape of a country road. Visualizing himself mounted on Ugly Annie blazing out of town, spitting gravel in every direction, dodging Bebee and the enemy behind the lines, saving the day for Brookside and the boys, he drifted off into a deep sleep. He never heard the clatter of the kitchen cleanup activity directly beneath his room or the occasional truck or car passing by or the old gray Plymouth coming to a stop across the street from the inn.

By dusk the town and the inn had fallen silent. Although the Mountainview Inn had a few empty rooms, a No Vacancy placard was hooked over the sign standing on the inn's front lawn. At dinner, Frank had stated he never wanted to answer the door after ten o'clock. Sydney surmised that was Frank's self-appointed time to be in pajamas. More aptly the yard sign should have read Do Not Disturb.

*   *   *

It was ten-thirty when Nancy Sullivan pulled her Plymouth off the road across the street from the Mountainview Inn. Looking for a place to phone from, she saw a booth in front of the Emporium under Peach Hill's only streetlight. Everything in town was buttoned up like an undertaker's vest. She ached from several hours of driving trying to catch up with Sydney and Toby. Slowly she climbed out of her car to cross the deserted street.

Dialing the operator, she said, "Long distance please, collect." Her first instinct was to call the Livermore Falls Police Station and report in. There was no answer. She was not surprised but not all that displeased since she would have to report that she lost track of two old curmudgeons. Her next call was to Trooper Barnes at the number he had given her. It connected with his station. "Could you please put me through to Trooper Jim Barnes? I realize he's probably off duty, but this is Officer Nancy Sullivan from Livermore Falls, and it's case related. He knows me."

"Hold on," an officer replied. "He's off duty, but he's hanging out here someplace. Three dimes later, Nancy was relieved and delighted to hear a phone being picked up followed by Jim's greeting. "Hi, Nancy, what's up, and where the devil are you calling from?"

"Jim, you can't believe how glad I am to hear your voice. I'm in Peach Hill calling from a pay phone. Maybe you know where that is? I've been on the road all day racing up and down the state trying to find Wadsworth and Worthington."

"You're not kidding are you? No one here's reported a sighting. Not on 87 anyway."

"I think they must have given me the slip right after we split up. But I kept going north on 87 hoping to catch up to them at a filling station or a roadside stand. No luck, so I decided to double back south. They must have turned off 87 heading west. Nothing. So here I am." Nancy sighed, then continued, "I was hoping you might have some news or an idea I could follow up on."

There was a short silence before Barnes replied. "Maybe we should have brought them in when we had the chance, but it was your call—it still is. You must be hungry, and how are you going to get some sleep?"

"I guess I haven't given it much thought, nothing's open around here for miles."

"Well, I got off duty at nine. I live less than half an hour from Peach Hill. Why don't I pick you up at your car? Back at my place, I'll make you some eggs, and you can catch up on your shut-eye. Don't worry, I'll take the couch. I'll get you back early in the morning so you can get a fresh start."

Nancy, hungry and tired, weighed her situation against her attraction for Jim. "I think I'd like that, Jim, but no candlelight, OK? Anyway, I want to return your thermos."

"Oh, that's right," Jim said, "I'd almost forgotten, Nancy. See you soon."

Relieved, Nancy returned to her car. Inside she adjusted the rearview mirror and did battle with her unkempt hair. She decided a fresh coat of lipstick might help compensate for her otherwise ragged appearance. Leaning her head back against the seat, she closed her eyes and tried to imagine what Jim's place would look like. Was he going to dash home first to tidy up, take down his Gibson Girl calendar, and put up photographs of his parents? She wondered what he read—probably detective magazines, she thought. Nancy, confident of her martial arts ability, decided not to worry if Jim started to take advantage of the situation. On the other hand, she questioned her resolve to put up a credible defense.

Wadsworth and Worthington suddenly jumped into her thoughts and put a chill on her anticipated meeting with Jim. She twisted uncomfortably in her seat and said to herself, "I don't care if those two characters are across the street staring me in the face. I'm off duty!" Nancy quickly returned to her previous euphoric state of mind and dozed off waiting for Trooper Barnes.

The familiar quiet of summer evenings in Peach Hill was reserved for a concert of singing crickets and trumpeting frogs. An audience of stars blinked their approval, while fireflies on the dew-damp lawn winked back through space. A time for sleep, a time for dreams, and a time for romance.

*   *   *

Sydney and Toby hadn't noticed the fireflies and stars. Nor had they heard the crickets orchestrating in the surrounding fields. Neither did the crickets hear the off-key rhythmic sawlike snoring and snorting of Sydney and Toby inside the inn.

Toby, sleeping with his back to the door, did not hear the knob slowly turn or the door shut softly behind an intruder. He did not stir at the sound of slippers shuffling across the floor. Nor did he stir with the weight of someone entering his bed and crawling deftly under his covers. A soft caressing hand slipped under Toby's nightshirt and danced its way across his leg toward his groin.

Perhaps it was the familiar waft of Chanel No. 5 that stirred Toby's senses or the last time a woman touched him in the region of his privates that his eyes blinked open and exclaimed, "Harriet!"

"Oh, God! You're not Jack!" she screamed.

"No, and you're not Harriet. Whoever you are, get the hell out of my bed!" Flailing in the dark, he exclaimed, "Lilly is that you?" Toby jumped up on the bed and stood against the wall, his feet sunk in his pillow. "For God's sake woman, stop your screaming!"

Panicking in the dark, Lilly began flopping around the room like a decapitated chicken, all the while screeching at the top of her lungs. Disoriented, she tried to find the door out. Toppling over a floor lamp, she slipped on a scatter rug and ended up in a heap of blankets at the foot of the bed. The sound of running footsteps in the hallway mingled with her whining sobs. "Please, please, please—don't give me away," she begged.

Toby, still reeling and not fully conscious replied, "Give away what?"

Frank could be heard charging down the hallway. Eunice, carrying her slippers, was right behind him when he burst through the door and flipped the light switch. "Well, what have we here? Mr. Eric whoever-you-are, by the looks of things, I'd say you're in one heap of trouble." Frank clenched his fists and walked deliberately toward a speechless, Toby. "Think you're a real ladies' man, do you?"

Out of breath, Eunice gasped when she entered the room. She stopped and then went directly to Lilly. "You poor dear child. Whatever did he do to you?" Lilly did not, could not respond. Her face was wet from streaming tears and rivers of makeup. Sensing her life and dreams had been shattered forever, she fell silent. Her eyes stared off into the distance as if there was no one in the room.

Eunice took off her bathrobe and wrapped it around Lilly. "Did this man give you this skimpy black thing you've got on? He probably knows all about the kind of women that wear undies like these." Lilly began sobbing again. "You know, Lilly, you can't trust men, not like this one anyway. No matter how old they get, they still let that—that thing in their pants do their thinking."

Frank was about to haul Toby off the bed, when Jack came through the doorway, still fumbling with the cord on his pajama bottoms. "What's going on here!" he exclaimed as his eyes darted around the room for answers. When he saw Lilly, he rushed to comfort her and snatched her out of the arms of Eunice.

Lilly whispered, "I didn't do anything, Jack, really." In an heroic display of masculinity Jack said, "If he so much as laid a hand on you, I'll thrash him senseless!"

"Help yourself, Jack," said Frank. "Saves me the trouble. I bet Clyde Bebee would like a shot at him too. An old bastard like him still thinks he's a big stud, when he belongs out to pasture."

Trapped, and still standing on the bed, Toby hadn't moved a muscle since Frank came through the door. He wondered where Sydney was. Could he sleep through all this ruckus? Desperate to avoid bodily harm, he considered reaching beneath his pillow, brandishing his pistol and effecting some sort of escape. Out of the question he decided. He'd have to try another avenue. "Now see here, Mr. Hapgood, while you're thinking about different ways to have me drawn and quartered, I have something to say."

Just as he was about to speak, Sydney walked into the room fully dressed except for shoes. He announced his arrival with a voice of authority, "Now, what seems to be the trouble in here? Toby, jump down from the bed, you look ridiculous up there."

Toby scrambled down to floor to meet his adversaries face to face. "I'll handle this, Sydney—I mean—Rodney. As I was about to say, all this fuss is over absolutely nothing." Toby began speaking quietly and deliberately, "Before I retired for the evening, I asked Lilly to bring up a glass of water for my medications. Isn't that right, Lilly?"

Not having a clue where Toby was going with his explanation, she gulped and agreed, "Yes." She seemed to know it was the only answer she could give that might rescue her from a dire predicament.

Toby pointed to the water glass on the floor. "On the way to her room, Lilly, from the hallway, heard me sleeping and entered my room hoping not to disturb me. Placing the glass on the night table woke me, and I was so startled I literally erupted out of bed. Poor Lilly thought she had entered the wrong room, and in the dark she behaved almost as berserk as I did." Toby began pacing and delivered his explanation like a lawyer, making his summation in front of a hostile jury. "Under the same circumstances, you, yes you, may have reacted the same way. Lilly does not deserve the slightest admonishment from anyone here."

Frank was quick to speak. "Maybe she doesn't, but I'm not so sure about you with the silver tongue." Frank paused, "I don't think we're quite done here yet. I think we'll let the law sort things out. I'm calling the state police." Staring at Toby, he continued, "I'm sure our two new guests here have no objections. Right?"

"Certainly not from Rodney and me." Toby raised his nightshirt to wipe the sweat from his brow. Inadvertently, for one brief moment his plumbing was on display.

Eunice, eyes bulging, shrieked, "You beast!" She took off her slippers and threw them at Toby, hitting Sydney instead. Lilly sighed and went limp in Jack's arms.

"You just can't stop, can you?" Frank growled through a wicked snicker.

"Stop what, Frank, trying to be reasonable?" Unaware that he had just displayed his genitalia, he implored, "All I'm asking is that you don't put Lilly and Jack through the wringer of a police investigation over a bit of nonsense. Wouldn't you agree, Lilly?"

Looking up Lilly replied, "Oh, yes. It all seems so silly now. Don't you agree, Jack?" Lilly moved closer to Jack and dried her eyes on Jack's pajama tops.

Jack's outrage disappeared once he developed the whole picture and understood that his Lilly had innocently gone into the wrong room. He would just as soon this whole debacle go away and told Frank as much, but Frank would have none of it.

Sydney, silent until now, said, "Frank, you might want to reconsider calling the police. A scene like this on the police blotter won't help the reputation of you or your establishment. Think on it."

Frank scowled and replied sharply, "I don't need the likes of you to help me do my thinking. I suggest everyone get back to their rooms and stay there. I'll call you when a trooper shows up. It could take a couple of hours or more, so don't get any ideas."

Eunice left her bathrobe with Lilly, retrieved her slippers, straightened her hair net, and followed Frank out of the room. Without a word to anyone, Jack put his arm around Lilly and escorted her down the hall.

*   *   *

Alone together, Sydney said, "Well, so much for a good night's rest." It's already after eleven by my ticker, and I don't see us getting any more sleep tonight." Out of his inbred natural curiosity, he walked over to the window and rolled the shade part way up for a look-see. "Would you believe this, Toby? A trooper just pulled up behind a car parked across the street. No one, not even Frank, could have gotten one here this fast. God knows we're in for it now."

Toby tripped his way across the room to peer out. "Good lord, Sydney, look again!" That trooper walked up behind the parked car and tapped on the driver's side of the window." A woman in uniform got out. Because the vehicles were parked near the streetlight, it was easy for the boys to recognize Trooper Barnes and Nancy Sullivan. They watched intently as Nancy got into Jim's car.

Seeing them drive off together, Sydney whispered, "I told you they might be on to us. You know old friend, we're surrounded by the law and a gaggle of Bebees."

"Yes, and I think you'd agree we've worn out our welcome here."

Sydncy rolled the shade back down and said, "Toby, get dressed. Meet me in the hall. We're leaving Peach Hill in thirty minutes."

14

In Full Flight

Arms full of their overnight belongings, they crept down the squeaky wood stairs. Only a desk lamp at the reception counter lit their way. Sydney tucked a 10-dollar bill under it. "This should be sufficient to cover our bar bill," he whispered.

"What bar bill?"

"This one," said Sydney. Reaching down behind the counter he pulled out a partially consumed bottle of Old Rocking Chair he'd seen Frank stash there earlier in the evening.

As they crossed the street, Toby remarked, "I hate leaving things here all topsy-turvy. You don't think Frank will really call the police?"

"I'd like to give him the benefit of the doubt, but he's so goddamn ornery! And narrow-minded. He could see through a keyhole with both eyes open."

"What you said goes double for me. Since our good deed Thursday evening, we're now considered—I think they call it—persons of interest in two homicides and a missing person report. Now I, Tobias Worthington, may be labeled as some sort of pervert who sexually assaulted a woman not old enough to drink. Well, really!" Exasperated by the thought of going to trial, he visualized the trauma of having to explain that his tallywhacker had long since gone into retirement.

"Stop worrying, Toby. Lilly wouldn't dream of bringing a charge. After all, you covered for her. Lilly's chance for a decent future with Jack depended on your quick thinking. Buck up, old man. Right now she's thanking her lucky stars it was you and not someone like Frank. If anything, I think you did Jack and Lilly a favor getting their romance out in the open."

They slid the garage door open and fumbled around in the dim moonlight that filtered inside. Tripping over loose tools on the floor, they cursed the darkness until they finally stumbled on Ugly Annie. "Are you sure you know how to launch this thing?" Sydney whispered.

"Of course I do. It's been over twenty-five years, but there are some things you never forget."

Toby put on the gauntlets Amos left for him on the seat. He handed the pink goggles to Sydney and exhorted, "Here, you're going to need these. When we leave, this baby's going to make a big racket. As you say, the best thing we can do is put a lot of distance between us and this town, so as soon as the engine turns over I'm going to give it the gas—all she's got, so to speak."

"You're right of course. But I wonder if I've got enough gas left in my tank." Sweating, Sydney felt the ache of a recurring dull pain starting in his left shoulder. It had been occurring more frequently now, twice since Friday. The pain traveled down his arm. "I might have been hasty in my suggestion that we jump ship. Perhaps you should leave me here. I could do a more than a credible rear guard action while you go on, unfettered so to speak."

"Tired blood again, Sydney?" Toby chided. "Certainly not cold feet. When and if we meet up with Jeffrey, we're going to need each other." He lit a match to make sure he had clear a path to the open garage door. "I think you're just reluctant to get in the sidecar."

"Don't be silly," Sydney was not about to reveal an aching chest. Toby would insist on scuttling the whole mission. Accustomed now to carrying aspirin, he opened the small tin, placed two tablets in his mouth and washed them down with a swig of Frank's bourbon.

After a few indecisive attempts to step into the sidecar Sydney discovered the grab handles and entered it as if he were squatting into a tub of scalding hot water. He did not relish the thought of skipping through back roads in the middle of the night the next few hours with his britches only a few inches above a roadbed. "Have we got everything, Toby?"

"If not, it's too late anyway. Don't worry, Sydney, when we get out on the road, you can take a good nap in that cocoon of yours. After we slip past Albany, we should be in Table Rock before dawn."

"With you driving, you want me to sleep in this contraption?"

Toby let the remark slide. With his foot on the kick-starter, he brought his weight to bear. After two more failed attempts to start the engine, Ugly Annie began to cough and bark at her frustrated passengers. The fourth attempt produced the desired roar and bleating of the engine as well as the disagreeable exhaust that filled the garage and billowed out onto the street.

Gasping for air, Toby gunned the engine and slipped the bike into gear. Sydney's head snapped back in response. As they burst through a cloud of blue smoke in the doorway, Toby was so surprised by the sudden acceleration, he could not make the first turn and instead shot across the street onto the Mountainview Inn lawn. Squirreling the bike through the soft grass, Toby executed a number of turns leaving a trail of deep ruts before he gained control and returned to the main road heading out of town.

"That was a nice farewell touch of yours, Toby," shouted Sydney. "I think I'm feeling better now." He scrunched down and pulled his blazer up around his neck like a blanket for protection against the night air.

At the inn, lights blinked on through the second floor windows. In Toby's mirror the Plymouth parked under the streetlight patiently waiting for its driver to return faded from view. Speeding away, Toby was euphoric and overcome with a sense of youth and power long since expunged from his memory. A fresh supply of adrenalin leapt into every fiber of his body. The vibration of the engine coursed through his limbs as the engine purred seductively. "Faster, faster," she seemed to say. "Later, later, old girl," he repeated over and over to himself. "The night is long." The lonesome small beacon of a headlight sped on feeling its way through the darkness like a shooting star searching for a home.

*   *   *

While Ugly Annie and her two passengers sped north, Nancy and Jim turned into the driveway to his apartment. It was in a new complex off Highway 87 some eight miles north and east of Peach Hill. Turning into the parking lot, she said politely, "Nice place you have here, Jim."

"Thanks," he replied parking his squad car. "It's late, so we should keep the noise down. We're upstairs on the left, 208."

"Sure thing." The thought of how often he brought girlfriends home late at night bothered her, but she decided to dismiss it, partly in the hope that it was out of character for him. In any case, she was determined not to be one of his conquests, and after all, she had nothing to fear from an officer of the law. Suddenly she cringed when she reminded herself—Chief Bebee is one too.

Jim unlocked the door and switched on the hallway light. Nancy brushed past him closer than need be and tossed her overnight bag on an armchair. "Very comfortable, Jim. You have a decorator?" she asked, exploring whether another woman had an influence.

"Oh no. Maybe the last tenant did. I just moved in a few weeks ago. I bet you'd have some good ideas though." He removed his tie and hung it on the bedroom doorknob. Returning, he stepped into the open kitchen. "It's late. How about I fix you some scrambled eggs and toast? My mom's recipe."

"Please don't fuss, Jim, but that sounds perfect. I'd like to wash up and change if you don't mind."

"Help yourself, Nancy. There are fresh towels under the bathroom sink."

She mused, *he can cook and loves his mom. Good.* Nancy's mind raced through a scenario that went from a first date to the altar. *OK, girl, calm down, so what if he is handsome and has thick black wavy hair you'd love to run your fingers through, nice high cheekbones and eyes black as sin? Why fret about anything? A guy this good must have some conniving bitch with her hooks in him by now. On the other hand, if that were true, he wouldn't be bringing me home, now would he? En garde, Nancy.* When she emerged from the bathroom, Jim already had her late dinner waiting on the table. "Nothing for you, Jim?" she asked.

"No, I ate earlier. I'll just have a coke. Can I get anything else for you? If you're OK, I'll get a blanket and pillow for the couch." As he left the room, Jim thought he must be careful not to appear forward. *Independent women are fine, but I've got to avoid being overly protective if I'm going to build a real relationship—God knows I've been disappointed by enough shallow ones. Nancy could be right for me, but how am I going to make it work out?*

Jim returned from the bedroom, tossed the bedding on the couch, and sat down at the dining table across from Nancy. He couldn't stop thinking about her or staring at her while she consumed every morsel. "Nancy, I know you're new on the job, but I wonder if you'd given some thought to taking the state police exam?"

"Not until you just mentioned it."

"I don't sense that you're really satisfied in your job right now. The department's looking for qualified women on the force. To me, you're smart as a whip, and I think you'd pass our muster in a snap." Jim watched her eyes for an answer.

"I just might do that, if you could help me through the process."

"Of course I would." Jim tried not to show his elation as his mind fleeted to the vision of their working together and being geographically closer. Spontaneously, he reached across the table and clutched her hand. She suppressed her surprise and did not withdraw her hand. His was warm; hers trembled.

"Damn, who'd be calling me at this hour?" Jim picked up the receiver and asked, "This is Jim, who's calling?" Jim's face fell. "Nancy, it's for you. Chief Bebee, and he's on fire. Better take it."

Nancy rose slowly from the table, fearing the worst. Answering, "Hello, Chief, I'm glad you were able to get in touch with me." Trying to be on the offensive she said, "You got the message I left this afternoon? I'm surprised you were you able to find me."

"I just did a little checking around with the state police. I found out you called me on Trooper Barnes phone, then I found out at his station you called in to him later." His voice raised an octave. "The station gave me his home number, and now I can only conclude you're shacked up with him for the night!"

"It's not like that, Chief," Nancy fumed but resisted hanging up on him.

"Well, what the hell is it like, and it better be good?"

Nancy collected her thoughts. "First of all, you're not my mother. You wanted me to tail Wadsworth and Worthington. I did, right out of the club parking lot. That was just after noon. They were heading north on 87, but somehow they gave me the slip, and there's no way they could have known I was tailing them."

"Well, where are they now?"

"I really have no idea. I've been all up and down the state. You know I have no authority to do anything, even if I find them."

"So, you've lost them. Two wandering old farts. Great! Since you do know you're way out of our jurisdiction, you'd better get your tail wagging back here first thing. I'd fire you on the spot if you weren't needed. Where the hell are you?"

"I'm a few miles north and east of Peach Hill. My car's parked on the street over there."

Bebee was startled. "Well, don't that beat all. My brother has a farm there, and my niece, Lilly, works for some jackass owner of the Mountainview Inn. Back to business, what in the devil is your car doing in Peach Hill? Getting its rest while you play patty-cake with Barnes?"

"I'm tired of your carping, Chief. If you know Peach Hill like you say, you'd know there's no place open late for gas, and your precious

Mountainview Inn across the street was closed up for the night. I'd be stuck in the car all night if it wasn't for Jim."

"OK, but I'm calling my brother Clyde first thing in the morning to make sure you get gassed up and on your way back to town."

"Really, Chief. I don't need a baby-sitter."

"Maybe not, but I've got a pot full of things to do here Sunday morning."

"So, go ahead clue me in."

Nancy could hear Bebee take in a deep breath to unload his woes. "First off, my jail's full, and there's a waiting list to get in. Those two Frenchies, d'Chard and Simone somebody, passed out all the wine they had in their trailer. Emptied it by five o'clock. Half the men in town were jammed into the hospitality tent swilling wine or drooling over Simone. Even the mayor got himself sloshed. Inside the Masons and the Knights of Columbus got into a shoving match and took their scrap outside. Lester broke it up if you can believe that. High Pockets marched them down to the station and cuffed four of them to a lamp post."

Before Nancy could get a word in, Bebee got his second wind. "But there is some good news. We got an ID on the body in the lake. The autopsy report confirmed that the guys you're supposed to be tailing were right. He was killed with a golf club. They were right too, about tracing the registration numbers on the clubs. You know, the ones stuffed in the pants of the corpse. Lester followed up and found out the dead man had to be the one who stole clubs from a golf shop in Buffalo. It's hard to tell, but the prints in the golf shop seem to match up with the victim's. Turns out he's a two-bit in and out of jail hoodlum from Gary, Indiana. Name's Norman 'Knuckles' Nelson. He worked as a nightclub bouncer. Never held a job more than a month." Bebee chuckled, "I thought the name 'Knuckles' might be short for 'Knucklehead,' but no. Amused he chuckled again, "Autopsy showed this creep had ten fingers and twelve knuckles. How positive an ID do you need?"

"That's all very interesting, Chief." Nancy was posturing to hang up. "But I need some sleep tonight, so I want to know what you actually need me for tomorrow."

"Yes, I almost forgot about that. Well, just keep your drawers on until I finish." Nancy flushed and turned away from Jim who had busied himself in the kitchen. "You'd already taken off after our two Brookside boys, so you don't know that we found another body on the golf course. Guess what? It was Wadsworth who discovered the body just before they skipped. Get this, on the last hole of this big exhibition match, Wadsworth was in

a sand trap when he whacked the thumb off the corpse with his club."
Bebee waited for Nancy's reaction, but only her silence was forthcoming.
"Are you still with me?"

"Yes, Chief, go on." Startled, Nancy thought this is incredible but
amusing if it weren't so ghastly.

"You might remember Amy, the cub reporter? Well, a couple of weeks
ago she saw two men in town squabbling with each other in front of the
post office and recognized the dead guy in the sand trap as one of them.
Knuckles might have been the other one. Nobody's been able to ID the
body in the sand trap or determine the cause of death. Not yet anyway.
For all I know, there may be more bodies out on the course—some big city
mob dumping their garbage in my town."

"Easy, Chief." Nancy raised her hand to let Jim know she'd only be a
couple of more minutes. "I know you think Wadsworth and Worthington are
deeply involved in this whole mess, but Jim—I mean trooper Barnes—and
I think they're pretty innocent and may be exposing themselves to real
danger."

"Think what you want. I'm tired of pussyfooting around with those two.
I still don't like the idea of them knowing something I don't. I want you to
know I rescinded my previous order for the state police not to pick them
up. I want Wadsworth and Worthington in custody, and you're not needed
for that." Nancy could hear Two Bullets fuming and sputtering. "For their
own good, they should be put behind bars where they'll be safe."

"Understood. But one more time, what do you have in mind for me to
do tomorrow?" "Plenty," Bebee said emphatically. "You're going to help
Mayor Yates with the renovation of Brookside. He got himself all cranked
up at the wine tasting party and decided to make a reelection speech.
In the middle of the hospitality tent he climbed up on a table. Then he
asked everyone in town to volunteer for a Sunday after-church work party."
Bebee continued by mimicking Yates, "In two weeks, Brookside hosts the
Wadsworth Cup. Players and spectators for many years have come to our
town from all over creation. They fill up all the restaurants and guest rooms
for miles."

Bebee added, "Yates did a 360 degree spin on the table, raised his arms
to the top of the tent and said, 'It would be an economic disaster and a
black eye for our community if the event didn't come to pass. Brookside,
my friends, lies crippled. So, men and women of Livermore Falls, let's put
our shoulders to the wheel and resurrect this club to its former glory in a
common cause—the Wadsworth Cup.'"

"Nancy, truth is, he sounds better inebriated than when he's sober. The idea, he told me, is to clean up all the damage caused by the flood on the golf course. Sandy, the club manager, and staff will do most of the supervision. But I need you here to keep law and order. When the club president shows up tomorrow, I'm letting him know, he'd better get his members off their duffs and pulling their weight. You're there to see there's no trouble."

"All right. I'll be there in the morning. Can I say good night now?"

"Yeah, good night, Nancy. I hope I can get some sleep. That witch Harriet really rankles me. Calls me every hour, day and night. It's a mystery to me why she worries a helluva lot more about Toby Worthington than her husband Jeffrey." Click.

Nancy put down the phone and walked slowly across the room to Jim. Her eyes welled up with tears of frustration and disappointment. Everything was going so well between her and Jim, when one phone call seemed to bring her whole life crashing down around her. She felt a gap growing between her newfound dreams for the future and the grim reality of her present situation.

"What is it, Nancy?" Jim asked. Seeing her obvious distress, he dropped his apron on the kitchen counter and instinctively raised his arms to embrace and comfort her.

"Oh, nothing." she quavered. At Jim's open-arm invitation she buried her face against his shoulder to hide her tears. "If you're really willing to help me, I think I better get ready to take that test you told me about."

Jim said softly, "Let's go study for it right now."

Miles north of Nancy and Jim, a motorcycle steadily bore its way through the black of night.

15

Sunday Drivers

A little past midnight, Toby cleverly skirted the old bike along the back streets of Albany. Table Rock, their destination, still lay another 120 miles north near the Canadian boarder. Toby pulled over to see what time it was and check his fuel supply. "Getting late and getting low," he muttered to himself. "Maybe got another hour of gas. Better keep my eyes open for a station." He glanced over at Sydney and noticed he was present in body only. An occasional grunt interrupted his snoring. Toby reached over and gently tucked Sydney's blazer back up around his neck. "I should know by now he can sleep through anything," Toby chuckled. "Ugly Annie has no trouble keeping me awake."

Coasting into a little town twenty miles north of Albany, Toby spotted a small establishment called the Blue Bird Cafe, its lighted sign urging the reader to Eat Here. Get Gas. Another sign advertised Blue Bird Cabins. Modern Plumbing. In front of the roadside café, a glowing gas pump emblazoned with Mobil Oil's flying red horse greeted late night travelers. Although the cafe was obviously closed, he was relieved to see the neon Open sign flickering in a window. Stopping in front of the lone pump, he ordered his stiff arms and legs to dismount. Reluctantly they obeyed.

A young unshaven man approached, wiping his hands with a greasy rag. "Fill it?" he asked with a yawn. His name was sewn into his bib overalls.

"Top it off, Harold," said Toby. "And if you don't mind, we'd like to use your facilities."

"If you mean the toilet, sure. Here's the key. It's in the back to your left. And my name's not Harold, it's Mike. These overalls belong to the owner."

Toby returned, paid the attendant, and went over to wake up Sydney. Toby reasoned there might not be too many opportunities to empty one's own tank further up the road. He shook Sydney hard. "Wake up, Sydney, last chance to take a whiz."

"Really," he muttered. "Well, help me out of this sardine can." Once out, Sydney couldn't straighten up, but with Toby's help tottered through the darkness to the restroom. Leaving Sydney there, Toby reemerged out front to engage in small talk with Mike, who was leaning on the pump scratching his stubbled face.

It occurred to Toby that they could get a few hours shuteye and still make Table Rock by early morning, though it would take a couple of hours hard ride. "Say, Mike, who runs the cabins?"

"Right now, I do. I've got one I can let you have. Six bucks, but you can have it for five–being it's this late. It's not made up, but I can get you sheets and towels if you want to do it yourselves."

Toby peeled off a fiver and handed it to Mike. "It'll have to do. We'll be on the road early. We're not here for comfort or pleasure."

"I can see that. I'll get you a key. No need to sign the book this time of night." Returning from a check-in office attached to the cafe, Mike said, "Drive in behind cabin number 7. Here's your key, clean sheets and towels." Mike then queried, "Who's that character you're with in the pink goggles and white knickers? Some old movie star?"

"Not even close." Toby grimaced. "He happens to be a very good personal friend, and that's all there is to it." Taking out his pipe, he considered a long-overdue smoke, but being near the pump he thought better of it.

"You know," Mike drawled, "a lot of our late night customers are cops. They drop in here from time to time and ask if I've noticed anything or anybody unusual passing through. Being a good citizen I try to help them out when I can."

"Very noble of you Mike. What's your point?"

"Well, I was wondering what I should say about you two fellows. You're not exactly our run-of-the-mill customers."

"Are you insinuating we're some sort of criminals on the lam? Sized us up have you? It sounds to me like you require a little hush money. Come to think of it, you may be the kind of person who'd take it and squeal your head off anyway—assuming there's anything for you to spill to the cops—which there isn't. So say what you will if the law shows up here tonight."

"Hey, suit yourself. It's your hide. I just do my civic duty." Mike began to walk away, then stopped to remark, "Say, when is your friend coming out of the can?"

Before replying, Toby thought that Mike could turn out to be a real problem. He could put the state police right in their pockets, especially if Frank alerted them about what happened earlier at the Mountainview Inn. "All right, Mike, let's go get him out of there. We can't be dawdling around here all night." Together they approached the bathroom door.

"Sydney, it's time to shake a leg." Toby said in a loud voice. His mind flashed back to Thursday evening when they found Jeffrey slumped over on a toilet in the clubhouse. Relieved to hear the rhythmic sound of snoring, he knew his old friend was all right and must have fallen asleep while seated on the throne.

"I'll open the door and wake him. Mike, you give me a hand, and we'll yank him out of there."

"Get him yourself."

When the door swung open, Sydney woke with a start. "Where am I?"

Toby replied, "Never mind, give me your hand. And while you're at it, hoist your sails before you trip on them." Shaking his head, Mike stepped back and had a good laugh.

Holding on to Sydney who was trying to regain his sea legs, Toby asked Mike to step inside the restroom to see if Sydney left anything behind.

Mike hesitated. His grinning face turned into a sour look of disgust, "Well if it'll get you guys out of my hair. Jeeezus lord of mercy." Reluctantly he stepped inside. Suddenly, the door slammed shut behind him. "Hey, what's going on!" yelled Mike.

"I'm afraid you're locked in—accidentally—as it were. It seems that I have the key. Silly of me isn't it, and here I was going to give it back to you."

Mike pounded on the door furiously. "You bastards better let me out of here, or I'll have the law on you. By god, I'll see you two up to your ass in alligators! Now let me out of here!"

Toby, pleased with himself, took the key and tossed it through the open transom above the door. "There you go, Mike. Let yourself out."

"You crazy old fart, it doesn't unlock from inside."

"Damn, I should have known that. Shame isn't it? I'll leave a note on the cafe door to have someone let you out in the morning." Sydney, still in low gear, was unaware of what was happening. He didn't particularly care since it seemed Toby had control of the situation.

Mike's tone suddenly became conciliatory. "Hey, you seem like nice-enough guys, really—don't leave me locked up in here all night. The place stinks!"

Toby, walking away with Sydney, hollered back, "I know. Someone should take better care of it."

*   *   *

Toby opened the back door to cabin number seven. Switching on the light, he was more than dismayed by what greeted his eyes, and his nose began to twitch at the reeking smell. He left the door open and sprinted across the bedroom to open the front door that went out onto a porch. He took a deep breath and went back inside hoping that the two open doors would eventually flush out the stench left by previous occupants.

"Phewww," sniveled Sydney as he entered. "What kind of a stable is this?"

"So it isn't the Waldorf. Obviously, the Blue Bird is a truck stop. Just look what's parked outside. If you're not doing anything right now, Sydney, you could help me get rid of the old sheets. Put them out on the porch swing. Pillow cases too."

It didn't help matters when Toby walked into the flypaper roll hanging from the ceiling light fixture. Peeling it from his forehead, he noticed that it was fully occupied. He said, "Look, Sydney, these poor devils couldn't get out of here and decided to commit suicide."

Sydney worked up a weak laugh and, when he stared at the soiled horsehair mattress, remarked, "If you expect me to sleep on this, I think I'll go back to the motorcycle."

"If you're going to start whining, Sydney, I wish you would."

"All right, I give up, Toby. I'd better bring our things inside before the rats walk off with them."

A light came on in number 8. Another in number 6. A loud voice reverberated through their thin-shelled cabin from number eight. "If you guys don't shut up, I'm coming over there and put you to sleep for a week!"

Sydney whispered to Toby, "I wish I could sleep for a week." He tiptoed over to the front door and latched it. Toby did the same to the back door and doused the light. After some arguing about which side of the bed each would sleep on, they removed their shoes and climbed in.

"Toby," Sydney grumbled, "what in hell was going on between you and the gas attendant?"

"For our own good, Sydney, and his too, I had to lock him up for the night or he'd have spilled the beans about us to the state police. Fortunately, no one can hear him yelling his head off behind the café."

"Good god, man, don't you know that's illegal."

"Well, in this particular case it shouldn't be. The nerve of him, Sydney—he tried to shake me down."

"Nice work, Toby. Don't know what I'd do without you."

"By the way, I left a note at the café letting the owner know this young man was both ill-mannered and had a definite penchant for extortion. I told the owner his continued employment at this establishment should be reviewed. Oh, I also mentioned Michael was so inept that he got himself locked in the toilet room, and he has the key."

*　　*　　*

Both had forgotten to set the alarm clock on the dresser, but it wasn't necessary to wake Sydney and Toby in the morning. The truck parked in back of cabin number 8 roared to life at five-thirty and was left running while its driver packed up. The rhythmic cadence of the diesel engine was loud enough to vibrate the loose window panes in their cabin.

Thinking he was on the opposite side of the bed, Toby rolled over and greeted the floor below with a thud. He lay there for several moments while he checked to see if his body was in working order. "Now that I'm up, Sydney, we might as well get a move on."

"Where the hell are you?" asked Sydney raising himself to a sitting position.

"Down here on the floor looking for my shoes. At least we don't have to waste time getting dressed. You can have the bathroom first. Be sure to shake out your shoes. I think there's a roach-like thing coming out of one of mine, but then again I'm not an entomologist."

"I think I must be having a nightmare," replied Sydney. "Let's high-step it out of here before I go mad."

Toby got to his feet with some difficulty and moved to the porch door and rolled up the window shade to greet the dawn. The lawn stretching out in front of the cabins was graced by a flock of plastic pink flamingos. Cracking the door open, he was pleasantly greeted with the pungent smell of thick farm country air. He yawned and gazed at the tiny collection of buildings up and down the town's empty main street.

Sydney lugged his shaving kit into the cramped bathroom. He clutched his sore back with his other hand. "Toby, there's no toilet paper in here!"

"Well, don't talk to me. Find something. You're not about to have my handkerchief—use your own." Toby continued to look out the window trying to ignore Sydney's nagging.

Suddenly Toby sputtered, "Good god almighty! The café's opened up already. Mike must be out of the toilet room by now—or will be pretty damn soon. Come on Sydney, we've got to get out of here, and there's not a moment to lose!"

A mad scramble to reload the motorcycle ensued. In a flurry of activity, fear drove them to the brink of panic as armloads of baggage and paraphernalia were carried, dropped, picked up again and stuffed into the luggage carrier. Toby shouted back into the cabin, "Don't forget your cane."

"Got it. Did you get the goggles? By the way, it's your turn to wear those god-awful pink ones you gave me, thank you. And damned if I'm going to leave a tip for the maid."

The driver in number 8 came over to watch their frantic departure. He laughed and yelled to them from the driveway, "Don't you guys ever shut up?"

"Not really," said Toby mounting the bike, "but we're sorry we disturbed you last night. There are some real nasty characters after the likes of us. If they show up before you leave . . . well . . . we'd be grateful if you told them we're headed north."

Toby revved Annie's engine. This time Sydney crawled in the sidecar as if it were his second home. "You know, Toby, my back doesn't seem to hurt anymore. Let's get the hell out of this dump."

Trying not to attract too much attention, Toby crept their motorcycle out of the Blue Bird lot and eased back onto the road out of town. After a few hundred yards, Toby opened the throttle and Annie responded beautifully. "Tell me, Toby," Sydney shouted over the racket of the bike, "why did you tell that driver we were heading north, when we're heading north?"

"Simple logic, Sydney." Toby glanced at the rear view mirror. "Mike and whoever will think we lied to the driver and that we would be too stupid to keep going in the same direction we were headed in last night."

"Well, I'm beginning to think we are stupid." He chuckled. "Look how far our superior intellect has gotten us so far. No offense, Toby."

Deflated, Toby failed to see the humor of Sydney's remark and showed his disgust by giving the gas to Annie.

*   *   *

When the phone rang in Jim Barnes' kitchen, Nancy woke with a start. For a brief moment she didn't know where she was, let alone whose bed she was in. She was under a blanket but on top of a bedspread when her memory of last night clicked in. She was relieved to discover that she had her street clothes on. Jim must have removed her shoes. Awkwardly, she squirmed and reached her hand across the bed to know if Jim was there. A wave of disappointment swept over her to find out that he wasn't. The phone continued to ring.

It was dark in the bedroom except for a thin streak of brilliant light bursting through a slot between the roll-down shade and the window frame. Nancy sat up and put her feet to the floor. She asked herself if she should answer the phone. Suddenly, her heart leapt. Where in God's name was he? *The phone's still ringing—oh damn. And double damn, he couldn't have left me here alone, or could he? I'm not going to panic, and I'm not going to call Bebee or my mother!*

She heard Jim say from the next room, "Barnes, here." At the sound of his voice, Nancy heaved a sigh of relief and fell back on the bed. Jim must have been sleeping on the couch in the living room. She sat up again and stretched. I must have fallen asleep on the bed while we were chitchatting. He must think I'm an awful bore. She yawned and walked over to the window, wondering what time it was. From behind the shade she could see Jim's patrol car was still covered with morning dew. Jim's conversation filtered through the bedroom door. His somber tone must mean that it was work related, especially since he was doing more listening than talking. She whispered to herself, "Come on, Nancy, pull yourself together. That call's nothing to do with you. You're headed back to Livermore Falls."

She heard Jim hang up and cross the living room floor. He rushed through the bedroom door grabbing his tie off the knob. "Oh, you're up already," he said. "Good. It looks like we're going to be working together sooner that we thought." Jim ran his eyes over Nancy. "Perhaps it would be a good idea to stay in uniform. Official business. Chief Bebee will just have to be disappointed today."

"But I'll lose my job, Jim! I can't afford to botch my first assignment."

"Don't worry, you'll still be on your first assignment. Aren't you supposed to be after those two geezers from Livermore Falls?" He smiled broadly as he buttoned his collar and seemed especially energized to meet the day head on.

"Yes, but . . ." Nancy moved in close to work on his tie.

"No buts. You have to go with me or stay here. I can't take you back to Peach Hill now." He took her by the shoulders and gently pulled her towards him. Giving her a quick kiss on the cheek, he ran a hand down her back, gave her fanny a playful swat, turned, and dashed out.

"OK, I won't be minute." She surprised herself by how quickly her anxiety and apprehension had acceded to his will. Nancy flushed as she reached up to touch the place where his lips had touched her face. Why would he kiss her as if they were teenagers on a first date and then swat her butt like sending a football player into the big game?

She took her duffel bag into the bathroom to change. From inside, she asked, "Jim, are you going to tell me what's going on?"

"Later, when we're in the car. Now hop to it, Officer Sullivan!" He returned to the living room and folded the quilt on the divan where he had slept. On the way out of the apartment, he glanced around the kitchen for something to eat on the road but came up empty.

Nancy was glad to shed the clothes she'd slept in and would have given a month's salary for a hot shower. No time for that. Only time for a quick sponge off and a change of underwear. Naked, she caught sight of herself in the full-length mirror on bathroom door. The view did not please and made her wonder how any man could find her attractive, let alone Jim. Stocky and muscular, she mused about auditioning for Jane in a Tarzan movie. She laughed at the thought, congratulated herself on her wit, and firmly resolved that if she was going to capture Jim or any man with her sexuality, she'd definitely need a new bra and a pair of high heels.

Slipping into her uniform, she could not drive Jim out of her thoughts. Wistfully, she wanted to know him better but was afraid to because it might spoil her image of him. She was afraid to care too much too soon. He seemed to care for her, she thought, but did he really and in what way? That pat on her rump seemed to have more friendship in it than passion or desire.

While Nancy puckered up to apply lipstick, her thoughts suddenly turned to her Irish mother's no-nonsense advice, "Remember this. Men cruise, women choose. Nancy, darlin', men are full of hormones, sweet talk, and promises. They're always on the prowl trying to lift our skirt. But when it comes to marriage, a man may propose, but it's the woman that got him to." *Simple,* Nancy thought, *but Mom's got a point.*

"Nancy, come on. I'll be down in the car. Just slam the door shut behind you."

By the time Nancy reached the car, Jim already had it running. Nancy tossed her duffel bag into the rear seat and jumped in next to Jim. "Ready," she said.

"Ha, but are you ready for this?" He gunned the patrol car out of the parking lot onto the dirt road headed toward Highway 87. "The two old men you were following—the guys I pulled out of the ditch Saturday—well, it seems they've started their own crime wave." Nancy's jaw dropped. "Come on, Jim, this has got to be some kind of sick joke."

"Nope, that call I got this morning was all about them. Worthington and Wadsworth, isn't it? You know, I'm supposed to be off duty today, but the station called and told me to find these two and bring them in."

"Yes, that's them, but what in God's name are they wanted for now?"

"Enough." Jim pulled out onto 87 heading north with lights flashing. "Would you believe we're shorthanded today because of them?"

"No. Not really. They may be in trouble, but how much trouble could they possibly cause on their own?" She could not hide the consternation in her voice. "I know, they're implicated some way in a club member's disappearance and material to possibly two murders, but is there something else?"

"Yep, now here's the kicker. You'll love the irony of this." Jim seemed to enjoy teasing Nancy with his drawn out answers as much as he appeared to relish the nature of this assignment. "We'll be stopping up ahead for coffee."

"Damn the coffee, Jim. Love the irony of what?"

"It seems that when you were parked last night outside the Mountainview Inn in Peach Hill, your quarry had registered there a few hours earlier." Jim's grin, one of those that asks, "Why aren't you smiling too?" didn't help.

"Oh god, are you trying to make me sick?" Nancy's empty stomach echoed the question with an angry growl. "Jim, this puts me in a jam. I think I'm going to need your to help to get me out of it. You will, won't you?"

` "Don't fret, Nancy, sure I will—and we'll find them too." Jim's demeanor and confident voice reassured her. "Now don't laugh. Apparently one of them attempted to rape a waitress who was in his room. There's also a charge of indecent exposure. On top of that, they blew out of town on a motorcycle, destroyed the inn's front yard, and here's the closer—they stole the owner's whiskey!"

"Wait a minute. You made this up, didn't you? Actually it's so stupid it's kind of funny." Nancy cracked a wicked smile. Already giggling, she raised a hand to cup her mouth before bursting out laughing.

Jim noticed and began to laugh with her until, for safety's sake, he pulled over on the side of the road where they could laugh at length. Every time they told each other they had to stop laughing, they would start in all over again. "Nancy, can you imagine their faces on wanted posters in the post office?"

"Yes, and the crimes they're wanted for gets even better."

"Country club duo wanted by police in connection with murder, rape, theft, and indecent exposure. Last seen together on a motorcycle. Dangerous. Do not approach. Contact your local police."

Nancy spun around in her seat laughing uncontrollably. It took a couple of minutes before they calmed down enough to stop laughing and return to the reality of their situation. Her face wet with tears, Nancy wiped her cheeks with the bottom of her tie, rearranged her skirt, and settled back in her seat.

Jim throttled his patrol car back on the road north again, until it was flying along quietly at sixty miles an hour. "One of our troopers went down to Peach Hill last night to investigate, and he's still there. The allegedly raped girl evidently took off with her salesman boyfriend. Remember Worthington's Oldsmobile coupe? It was left in a garage across the street for repairs. The garage owner said they were going fishing and thought it was some place around Table Rock."

"I gotcha." Nancy had refocused and returned to the hunt. "So we're headed for Table Rock?"

"Right. I don't know much about the area. But there can't be too many fish camps or places the locals don't know about." Jim tucked in his chin. "I've got another stop on the way up there, and unfortunately it has to do with the same two fellows we're chasing."

"Don't tell me. Does this have to do with the crime wave you're talking about?"

"Nancy, it's more like a tidal wave. That call I got this morning—well, my dispatcher asked me to investigate some criminal activity reported by the local constable in Hammerville. Their chief must be out of town. The perpetrators are described as two well-dressed elderly gentlemen in an old green motorcycle with a sidecar. Recognize our nefarious poster boys?"

"Yes, and I know what nefarious means too." Nancy emitted a deep, soft sigh. "I guess you'd better bring me up to speed."

"Evidently they robbed a gas station attendant and locked him in a restroom. No mention of them being armed. The owner of the Blue Bird Cafe said they were believed to be heading south."

"So they may be coming our way?"

"I certainly don't expect to run into them, not if they're still heading for Table Rock."

"You've got that right. They seem to be on a mission, and they're deadly serious about it. And from what I know about these guys, going fishing is pure fiction."

"I'm sure you're right, Nancy." He glanced over and flashed a smile. "I've got a sneaky feeling if they're going fishing, it's in water over their head. Think about this. We're after two old, crotchety country club characters on the run. Don't you think it's rather strange they'd leave that posh lifestyle of theirs for whatever in hell they're up to now? It must be pretty damned important."

"Yes. But I want to know if you care about them. You do, don't you?" Nancy turned to look for any kind of an empathetic response.

"I suppose so—as long as you do." He bit his lip. "Nancy, you know that it could be dangerous to let your feelings get in the way of doing your job." She looked sheepish and fell silent. Jim went on speaking, "One thing's certain. We're going to limit our time in Hammerville and move on. You can be a big help with the interviews while I talk with the constable. Try to keep them short and to the point."

"I guess that makes me your unofficial deputy. I like that. How far is Hammerville anyway? I could use that cup of coffee you promised."

"We should be there inside of thirty minutes if I step on it."

16

Gone Fishing

Toby coasted Annie up in front of a sign reading, "Table Rock Country Store: Established 1887." It was one of those typical picturesque buildings whose entrepreneur owners lived on the second floor. Against a dark blue sky, a column of spiraling white smoke spewed from its chimney. "Wake up and look at this, Sydney. We're in the middle of town and you can see both ends of it at the same time."

Sydney only yawned and rubbed his eyes. He looked across the street where a black rock the size of a bus was imbedded in the middle of an unkempt small park. Its top was flat and noticeably rectangular in shape. "Well, they didn't have to spend a lot of time naming the town. Do you think we can find something to eat inside?"

"Maybe," snapped Toby. "It doesn't look like they're open yet. The Sunday papers are still stacked outside the front door."

"So grab one off the top, maybe we made the front page."

"You really do need some breakfast. Perhaps some pepperoni and pickled eggs would sweeten your disposition."

The screen door in front of the general store slowly creaked open. From the porch Thaddeus Warner gazed down the flight of wood steps to greet his arrivals. "Mornin'. Heard you two coming from ten miles out. It's Sunday morning here you know." He stooped to drag the papers inside. "Since you fellas stopped, you must want something, so come on inside. I'm not going to stand here all day and hold the door open for ya."

"Of course," said Toby. "Much obliged and all that. Come along, Sydney."

Thaddeus, a heavyset man, wormed a way through his cluttered merchandise to stand behind the counter. His receding hairline reached the summit between his brow and the nape of his neck. A yellow Ticonderoga pencil was imbedded in his thick white locks. With his forearm, he swept aside an assortment of knickknack items to clear a place to conduct business. After wiping his nose on his soiled bib apron, he said, "Now, what can I do for you, gents?"

"We're hungry, to put a point on it." A growl from Sydney's stomach echoed his sentiment.

"No problem." Thaddeus cracked his first smile since they met. "I've got a wheel of good sharp cheddar cheese. Soda crackers on the shelf. Homemade strawberry jam sittin' in front of ya. What else d' ya want? I've got some dried kippers in the back."

"Any chance of coffee?" said Toby.

"My wife's got a pot going upstairs. If you ask real nice she might let you have a cup."

"Sydney and I wouldn't think of imposing, but we would be appreciative. Perhaps we could replace it with a pound of your best."

"That'll work," said Thaddeus, grabbing a can of Maxwell House off the shelf. Give me a minute, and I'll be right back with your coffee. Help yourself, and if you need the restroom, it's in the back."

"Very kind of you," said Sydney. "Both of us could use a tidy-up and shave."

*   *   *

Sydney and Toby consumed their cheese, jam, and cracker breakfast on the front stoop and surprisingly found it quite agreeable.

Washing down his last bite of cheese with coffee, Toby observed, "You realize, Sydney, that we haven't the faintest notion where the Stoney Creek Rod & Gun Club is."

"Thaddeus must know, I'll ask him. He's probably a town father." Inside, Sydney hailed Thaddeus, who had obviously retreated back up stairs again. "Could we trouble you for some directions?"

"I thought you might be askin'," he bellowed. "Everybody comin' to town can't wait to find a way out." Thaddeus trundled down stairs and resumed his place of authority behind the counter. "Now, where is it you'd be wanting to go?"

"We're up here to do a little fishing and thought perhaps you could direct us to the Stoney Creek Rod & Gun Club. First timers, don't you know. We're expected, but it seems we've left our directions behind."

"Very interesting you should ask. Strange doings up there. Some fishermen and hunters like yourselves who stop here on the way to Stoney Creek, I never see them come back through. And I don't miss much. The road to it's a dead end, and this is the only road through town. Then again, I see some folks come zipping out of there I didn't see going in. No explanation. It's either my bad eyes, or I'm drinking cheap whiskey."

Baffled, Sydney inquired how the fishing was before asking for directions.

"Dunno. Not for a lot of years. The people out there keep to themselves. And they keep everyone else out unless you're a big shot member. The owners come into town from time to time to get groceries. Sometimes they phone in here asking for an electrician to come out or something complicated they can't take care of themselves."

"Now, I'm really curious. Sounds like it might have an interesting past."

"Yep. In the early 1900s, what's now called Quarry Lake was not much more than an oversized beaver pond—about five acres. Upland from the pond, a decent grade of white marble was discovered, and a quarry operation was started. Teams of draft horses used to drag the marble out on sleds down to the road out of town. After about ten years they'd quarried deep enough to hit spring water. Flooding put an end to the quarry business."

"So then what happened?" Sydney asked.

"I'm comin' to it. The owners back then decided to log off the property. To dwarf a long tale, they built an earth dam at the outlet of the old beaver pond. It was fed by Stoney Creek. The pond became a lake, and because of the rise in elevation, it backed into the old quarry. It must cover one hundred acres. Logs were fed into the lake and floated to a sawmill at the foot of the dam. They split 'em up there before takin' 'em into Table Rock. It was successful for a lot of years until the timber ran out. When it did, the owners sold it out to the bunch that's up there now running it as a lodge for people like you. Can ya believe it, the state even lets them write their own hunting and fishing licenses?"

"I assure you, Thaddeus, if my partner and I catch any fish at the club, we'll be sure to stop by and let you know."

"I'm not going to hold my breath." He walked out onto the porch and pointed. "Since you're determined to go, just keep goin' east 'til you come to a fork in the road. Take the dirt road to the right, it's about a mile in."

When Sydney got back to Toby, he decided not to sound the alarm or elaborate on his conversation with Thaddeus. "Let's haul anchor, Toby."

As Thaddeus turned to enter his store, he called. "Watch out for Waldo. He's a little off."

*   *   *

Following instructions, Toby guided Annie gently along the unmarked dirt road. Lacking traffic, native grass and weeds grew in its undisturbed crown. At the end of the road, there was a turnaround in front of a swinging gate wide enough to let a large truck through and tall enough to discourage someone from trying to scale it. Toby slowed the motorcycle to a stop and aimed at the imposing entrance. On each side of the gate ran a long straight stone wall. Sydney noted several strands of barbed wire augmented the top. "Evidently, Toby, it must have served at one time to contain livestock."

Toby squinted and pointed at a small rusty white sign framed with blackberry bushes. "If I'm reading it right, Sydney, I think it says, Warning! Electrified!"

Sydney shook his head. Thaddeus hadn't mentioned farming or dairying. "I don't think it's electrified any more. Look at the meadows on both sides of the fence, they're fallow. Still, I suppose the sign serves the purpose of warding off would-be intruders."

The early morning sun cast long finger shadows across the road. Dew sparkled like strings of diamonds along the strands of barbed wire. Two deer were feasting on a distant apple tree completing the pastoral scene. For an August morning the air was crisp, invigorating, and heavy with the scent of tall grasses. The sound and sight of a struggling Ugly Annie had already scattered partridges and pheasants from their habitat. Brazenly, a flock of crows objected to Annie's arrival at the gate.

Finally, they were within reach of their destination. Neither spoke a word while taking in the surrounds, nor could they look at each other and ask the inevitable question of the other—"Well, what do we do now?" Having endured challenging events requiring endurance of heroic proportions for men of their age and drift, each wondered if they had come the end of the road, mentally and physically. But out of pride and respect for the other, neither was about to admit the slightest intent to withdraw from their objective to find Jeffrey.

Toby, as usual, broke the silence. "It's a good thing we've got fishing equipment with us. Need to pass as fishermen, so to speak, otherwise we might not be able—to coin a phrase—worm our way in. In an effort to be uplifting, he smiled conceitedly at his own wit.

"Please, Toby, that pun was unworthy of you. If that's the best you can do, well I'm very disappointed. Besides we're supposed to be fly fishermen not bait fishermen. For heaven's sake, let's get on the same page."

His feelings wounded, Toby replied, "Now you're sounding more like yourself, crabby."

After a silent spell, Sydney, who was brought up short by the truth, said, "You're right. Actually, your characterization of me is flattering, considering my attitude of late." He took out a long overdue cigar, one of his last. "Driving this motorcycle all night deserves my thanks, not my sniping."

"Forget it, Sydney. Actually I rather enjoyed the ride up here." Toby plucked out his pipe from his side pocket and gently prepared the bowl and stem with an assortment of cleaning tools. He packed in a mixture of his favorite Three Nuns tobacco and said, "You see, I look at it this way. I had a date with Ugly Annie, and I just thought of you as an indifferent chaperon."

Sydney ignored Toby's remark. He had been focusing his attention on the portal sign above the entrance gate. "Stoney Creek Rod & Gun Club. Trespassers Will Be Shot."

"What is this," he said, "a fish camp or a prison camp?"

"I think we'll find out soon enough. Here comes a truck. I hope it's a member and not someone from the village. Let's be sharp." A black postwar Ford pickup chugged into view.

Stopping just short of the gate, the driver rolled down his window and shouted, "Hi, gents. I'm Karl Zecher." A slightly built man who looked to be in his early 50s was garbed in the usual telltale khaki accouterments of a well-dressed fly fisherman. He slid out the door and said, "From the looks of things, you must be guests trying to get in."

"Right. This is Sydney Wadsworth, and I'm Toby Worthington. Pleased to meet you, not to mention how glad we are to see you come along."

"Obviously, you didn't blow your horn yet."

"No, should we have?"

"Your host must have forgotten to tell you. If you had, he or someone on staff would have come to fetch you. With all that gear you're toting, I guess you're ready to do a little fishing. Who invited you up?"

Sydney replied, "Jeffrey Bartholomew asked us to join him."

"Can't say that I know him. But then again, I don't know every member." Karl tipped his wide brimmed hat back and walked to the gate.

While Sydney struggled out of the side car, Toby dismounted and followed Karl to the gate. "That sign of yours, I can't say that I enjoy the thought of being mistaken for a trespasser."

"Oh, that. Club policy. Don't worry, it has to do with Waldo. He's our gamekeeper."

"Should we be worried about Waldo?"

"He's all right." Karl chuckled. "Just a little touched in the head. Whatever he does to keep poachers out seems to work. Sunday's his day off, so he'll be practice shooting around here today." Karl activated the gate by pressing several buttons on a pipe stanchion. Waiting for the gate to swing open, Karl spoke more seriously. "Waldo prides himself as a crack shot, so he likes to keep sharp. One of his little quirks is to set up scarecrow targets around the property to shoot at."

"Isn't he taking his job a little too seriously?" Sydney asked.

"Oh, not really. He's not trying to hit one of these targets. Waldo tries to hit something real close to it. The idea is not to kill a trespasser, he just wants to scare the crap out of them. I'm sure there must be times when he accidentally hits the scarecrow, but that's why he needs to practice."

Toby sensed that Karl was firing a warning shot of his own at them. Smiling weakly, fear flooded into his voice. "I'd say your Waldo has already scared the crap out of us."

Karl laughed, that ominous kind of laugh that meant he was glad his message sunk in. "You chaps being guests, Waldo probably wouldn't recognize you, so I wouldn't go wandering off too far from the lake for a while. Bertha will tell you the same thing at the lodge." He climbed back into his pickup and waved for Sydney and Toby to follow him. "Come on through. I'll show you where to park that three-wheeler."

After they passed through the gate, Karl reached through his open window and pressed a single button on another pipe stanchion, which activated the gate motor again. "Getting out's easy. Just tap this button once, and you're on your way. Oh, yes, it gives you twenty seconds to get out, so don't dillydally." Sydney and Toby glanced at each other for a moment. Neither had any intention of staying here one moment longer than necessary.

Sydney held tightly to the grab bars of the side car and grumbled, "Honestly, Toby, I don't know how many more times I can crawl in and out of this sardine can without causing permanent damage to my back. If we get out of this with our skins, my golf game is really going to end up in the toilet."

"If you think you're setting me up to get strokes from me, forget it. You only give me six shots as it is. Three months from now my legs will still be vibrating. When this little mission of ours sorts itself out, you may end up having to give me at least eight strokes instead of six." Toby kick-started Ugly Annie's engine, and only her sputtering engine spoke for the rest of the trip to the lodge.

About three hundred yards up the gravel drive, the lodge came into view. It was a typical two-story Adirondack-style building of rough-hewn siding, log posts, and beams. Apple green shutters stood out in contrast to the otherwise bland building that sported a dark brown oil finish.

Toby followed Karl around a gravel traffic circle that led to a narrow opening through a row of pine trees into a grassy parking area. Pine logs resting on large native rocks defined its perimeter. Back on solid ground again, Karl led them up a long marble-slab entrance walkway that was flanked on both sides with tall white birches. He waited for them at the top of a dozen stairs to hold the front door open leading into a main hall.

It was a large woodsy two-story space, beyond which a pair of doors opened into a dining room. A candlelit wagon wheel chandelier crudely suspended by chains embellished the center of the room attracting their attention. Sydney's expression indicated that it was trite and miserably failed his taste quotient.

"Well, boys," said Karl, flipping his hat onto a coat hook, "This is where I leave you. Bertha's my wife and our club secretary. She'll be happy to get you started. I don't see her now, but she should be close by." Karl skipped up the stairs to the second floor where there were probably lodgings for a dozen or so guests.

"Thanks for all your good help, Karl," said Toby with a salute. He dropped two rod cases on the floor along with a few essentials he'd brought along from the motorcycle. "OK, Sydney, I drove all night. Can you take it from here?"

"All right. I know how to handle this. You just flop yourself down over there and pull yourself together." Approaching what apparently was Bertha's reception desk, Sydney decided to examine what was to him a very foreign environment.

This club was definitely a contrast to his Brookside Country Club. The walls were lined with stuffed fish and wild game common to the region. Above a cavernous wood fireplace, a mounted moose head gazed dispassionately. In front of the hearth a bearskin rug was stretched out with its yellow teeth and glass eyes staring up ominously at the fireplace, no doubt angry at the flying embers that had burned their way through his shiny black coat. On the wall opposite the entry hung another large bearskin flanked by pelts of beaver, fox, and raccoon. The library table sported a leaping moth-eaten wildcat surrounded by dozens of old wildlife magazines. Sydney imagined this room must be a taxidermist's dream of heaven, overstuffed.

Side tables were home to a variety of lamps concocted out of wood sculptures featuring leaping trout, swimming loons, and various game birds taking flight. In an alcove by the staircase, there was a small fly-tying desk for those whose hobby was tying their own lures. Above the tying vise were carefully labeled drawers of hooks and spools of thread. Higher up, open boxes contained feathers and skins of peacock, partridge, pheasant, and jungle cock. Sydney suddenly felt smothered and claustrophobic.

Finding it difficult to breathe the stale gamy air, Sydney bolted for the pair of doors opening out onto a broad screened-in veranda. Outside, he said to himself, "God, surrounded by all those dead critters, the silence in there is stifling." Sydney took several deep breaths. "Toby must love it in there, if he were wearing a lampshade on his head, he'd even look like he belonged. Oh, for the sound of some living thing, a bird, a squirrel, or anything that wasn't about to have its life abruptly terminated by a club member." He wondered what was making his skin crawl and why he felt suspicious of everything. Maybe it had to do with the possibility that Jeffrey may not even be a member.

On the veranda, Sydney looked out across Quarry Lake. The morning sun shimmered across the placid water. Several empty wicker rocking chairs lined the back wall. How lonesome they looked. Pillowed with pine needle cushions, the rocker closest to him moved slightly for no apparent reason other than a gust from a passing breeze. He smiled and reflected on the notion that perhaps a ghost occupied it. Sydney resolved that he had no intention of becoming a ghost at Stoney Creek. He concluded that the rocker was lonesome, and its motion was merely an invitation to come and sit a spell. Rocking and breathing comfortably now, he took solace in the sound of water rushing over the lake's nearby spillway, listening to its steady rhythmic song as it went about its preordained business. Across from the spillway dam stood the sawmill building Thaddeus told him about. Its waterwheel turned hypnotically. Overhead wires to the club explained its latest task of generating electricity. Visually, the scene was as serene and enchanting as a tourist bureau postcard. *Beauty is a temptress,* Sydney reminded himself, *and often a veiled disguise for what is sinister.* Victims of the Venus flytrap discover this fact too late. With Toby dozing in the lobby, Sydney closed his eyes and drifted off into a contemplative mood.

"Can I help you?" said Bertha announcing her presence.

Sydney flinched at the sound of her deep icy voice. Startled, he looked up and flinched again.

"Yes, yes, of course." He shot out of the rocking chair, "You must be Bertha. Mr. Worthington and I are guests."

"I see. And you are?"

"I'm Wadsworth, Sydney Wadsworth. My friend and I just drove up from Livermore Falls."

She motioned Sydney to follow her back to her desk. Passing by Toby, she muttered, "Perhaps we shouldn't disturb your friend."

Her broad shoulders, thick neck, and strident gate led him to believe she might have been a weight lifter in the Berlin Olympics. Her hair, tightly pulled back in a bun, did nothing to compliment her puffy powdered face or alter his first-impression of her as a formidable force. Bertha squeezed in behind her stand-up reception desk, took out her guest book, and appraised Sydney that, "Strange, but we weren't expecting you. Actually, no one is due in for several days." Which of our members invited you?"

"Oh, that would be Jeffrey Bartholomew. We're members of the same golf club."

Bertha clenched a pencil between her teeth while she shuffled through the membership roster. Her heavy eyebrows suddenly dove toward the center of her pudgy nose, and a grimace crossed her chalky face that would intimidate the bravest of souls. She spun the club roster around and very emphatically said, "See, no Bartholomew. The only Jeffrey we have here is Jeffrey Barstow."

Tongue-tied, Sydney turned as white as his knickers and was as speechless as the stuffed trout glaring at him from the opposite wall. He felt Bertha's eyes staring right through his eyes into a recently vacated mind. Meanwhile, every sinew of his being drained down into his toes that begged him to make a run for it.

"Barstow, that's him!" bellowed Toby from across the room. Feigning to be asleep, he was listening in on their conversation.

"Of course, it is!" said Sydney. "How utterly stupid of me. Bartholomew is an old college chum of mine. I don't know how I suddenly conjured up his name. I hope you'll excuse me, Bertha. It's been a difficult trip for us."

"I should imagine—considering that contraption you're driving."

The chicanery employed by Sydney and Toby seemed to work. But Sydney sensed that Bertha was not totally convinced, and obviously she wouldn't stand for any claptrap. His color and courage returned enough to say, "May I assume Jeffrey is hereabouts?"

"Mr. Barstow's down at the boat launch. He's working in his cabin right now. Before I check you in, I'm going to buzz him on the intercom to come up here and straighten out any confusion." Forcibly polite, she said, "Make yourselves comfortable on the veranda while you're waiting."

Feet dragging, they traipsed out onto the veranda where they slumped into adjacent rockers. Both were relieved to be out of Bertha's presence. Sydney tapped Toby on the forearm and said, "Quick thinking, Toby, but what's our take on this Barstow chap? And what makes you think Barstow is Bartholomew?"

"Well, it flashed across my mind that it's unlikely that a club this small would have two Jeffreys, now would it? If I wanted two identities, I would keep my first name. That way it would be perfectly natural for me to respond to it when I'm being addressed, right? Very simple deduction, really. Surprises me that you didn't think of it. You're the brains of this outfit."

"By George, I think you're right on target. Barstow could be our Bartholomew."

"Indeed. As you know I've had my suspicions about Jeffrey not being who or what he claims to be. At the club I've always found him ill-mannered and rough on the edges. After eight years there you'd think he'd do a better job observing the dress code, let alone the rules of the game. I'm beginning to wonder if he had any respect at all for Brookside. My biggest regret right now is that we went to a lot trouble lugging him out onto the golf course."

"No doubt you're right, but what if this Barstow isn't our Jeffrey?"

"Then we'd better get our sorry asses out of here and fast. Speaking of fast, I didn't like the way Annie's engine was spitting at us coming up the drive. We must have picked up some bad gas back in Hammerville. Could be water, maybe sediment in the tank. Off that subject, have you noticed something strange about this place? Plenty, and it's not just the owner's wife, Bertha. I saw a tall nasty looking chap sneaking around the back of the lodge. I've a hunch it's Waldo."

"Very observant, Toby. Yes, there most certainly is something fishy, and I don't mean the trout. Maybe fishing isn't the primary pursuit of this club."

"You certainly don't mean this is some sort of hanky-panky club, do you?"

Sydney muffled a laugh. "No, but I'd be careful that Bertha doesn't take a shine to you. You do seem to attract women."

"There you go again, having me as sport." He flushed but finally managed a laugh. "Now seriously, did you notice that none of the mounted trophy fish was identified? I can't think of one fisherman who wouldn't have his name engraved all over a trophy fish. Seems everything in the lodge was shot or caught by those who wish anonymity. Totally out of character I'd say."

"Not many golf trophies at Brookside go nameless—ha." To confirm his observation, Sydney rocked his chair back to peek into the lobby. "Uh-oh, look out, Toby, here comes the Bismarck."

Bertha's heavy steps across the club's creaking pine floor heralded her arrival. Barely civil she said, "Mr. Barstow's busy packing down in his cabin—number 4. He wants both of you to meet him down there." Then pointing to the far end of the veranda, she said, "Follow the trail down to the lake."

"Thank you, Bertha. We'll be off then," replied Sydney. "I suppose our luggage is all right where we left it?" She only nodded and marched off.

As soon as Bertha disappeared out of earshot, Toby said, "The last thing I need is a nature walk. My legs haven't stopped shaking since I got off Annie."

"Well, like I said, Annie didn't do much for my back either." He groaned as he got to his feet and took a few baby steps. "I can't say that I like this change of venue. But I believe, as the saying goes, it's time to fish or cut bait. Before I go down there, I'm fetching my cane from the bike. How about you, Toby, have you got everything you need?"

"If you mean my service revolver, yes. Remember when we left your hotel, I said there might be a spot of trouble in Jeffrey's piscatorial paradise. Well, I'm ready."

"Please, Toby, try not to be quite so clever. We've come a long way since Saturday morning. For the club's sake we can't afford to louse things up. This may be the match of our lives, and we're in the finals. Wait here for me."

A few minutes later, Sydney, with cane in hand, arrived to rejoin Toby at the foot of the veranda steps. Waldo, rifle on shoulder, left the lodge unobserved through the kitchen service door.

17

The Face Off

The carefully maintained trail down to the lake, wide enough for the pair to march alongside each other, was freshly covered with crushed gravel. Quarry Lake was calm and quiet this morning except for the cackling of a mother duck warning her brood of approaching strangers. The bank leading from the lodge down to the water's edge was steep and arduous until it reached the shallows of a wetland area choked with cattails and tall sepia colored reeds. In the soft marshy areas between the trail and the lake, deer tracks mapped where they had come to drink in the early morning hours. Alongside the trail, small frogs sprang from decaying rain puddles to escape from the intruders into the deep grass. Moving beyond the spongy undergrowth, the trail narrowed and stretched out to follow the winding shoreline towards deeper water. Oblivious to the presence of Sydney and Toby, water spiders skated along the mirrorlike edge of the shoreline. The trail skirted around an elderly uprooted pine tree that had fallen into the lake from an eroded undercut bank. No longer a home for birds of prey, it provided a refuge for trout from the likes of their arch enemy, the kingfisher.

Ahead, six wood-framed boathouses sat on pilings extended out over the water. Each sheltered a dock long enough to accommodate four wooden rowboats. Sydney observed how clever it was that during off-season the boats could be hoisted up from the lake and stored in the rafters for the winter. As the pair strode past the first two, Toby said, "How odd—the boats are already hanging under the eaves. I thought this was the height of the fishing season."

"Do you see anyone out on the lake, Toby?"

"No, and haven't seen a soul since we left the lodge. Rather nice, isn't it, considering the company we've been in lately? I've seen a couple of trout rise though."

It suddenly occurred to Toby that there were only a few vehicles in the parking lot, and that might be the reason for the absence of fishermen. "You know Sydney, besides us, there was only Karl's pickup, a jeep, and a couple of other cars. Staff probably. I noticed one of them had out-of-state plates."

"Yes, it's all rather strange." Sydney stopped to rest and look back toward the lodge. Only the top floor was visible through a corridor of trees and dense foliage. Turning his attention back to the nest of boathouses, he remarked, "Toby, look at this will you? Each boathouse has a cabin for storage opposite the path. Must be a lockup where they store their oars, anchors, and whatnot." They were small twelve-by-twelve shingled cabins spaced about twenty yards apart with a small clearing in front of each. On opposite sides of the cabin there was a small window with whitewashed panes to let in light. The trail, now a worn-down dirt footpath between the docks and the cabins, wound its way into the heavily forested shoreline. Sydney was very impressed with the degree of sophistication and preparedness required to fish for something as ordinary as a trout. "Toby, this is quite a classy setup."

Toby shrugged. "Well it certainly isn't a very good investment, when you're expected to throw back your catch. Says so on a sign in the lodge."

"I think it's time we quit stalling around," said Sydney. "We're coming up on number four. Before we try to find out whether it's Jeffrey in there or someone else, I think I'll take a precautionary leak to avoid any potential embarrassment."

"Good idea, Sydney. We don't need any accidental discharge. I'll take a whiz too."

While Sydney urinated, he took yet another opportunity to reflect on the status of their situation. "If our Jeffrey is in there, he could be a real rotter. All the same we have to keep him from disgracing Brookside. Yes? Well, I hope this doesn't wind up being the end of the road for us, Toby. Out here in the wild. But we've certainly had a good run, haven't we?"

"There you go again," said Toby, zipping up. "Of course we've had a good life. But I have no intention of shedding my mortal coil out here for the likes of Jeffrey. Now pick up your cane, muster up your courage, go over there, climb the stairs, and knock on the door. I'll be right here to back you up."

Before Sydney could rap on the door, it swung open, and there stood Jeffrey Bartholomew. "Well, if it isn't my old pal Sydney—and Toby too. Now how in the devil did you find me?"

Toby was nonplused even though he expected to find Bartholomew. He recovered quickly, walked up next to Sydney, and tossed him the book of matches they found next to him Thursday evening in the locker room. "Jeffrey, I believe these are yours."

Jeffrey chuckled as he plucked the matches from midair. "Now, I know you're not here to return my matches. Bertha tells me you two are my guests. I didn't think either of you had an interest in fishing. I certainly don't recall our ever discussing it." Jeffrey continued to stand in the doorway.

"You know there's always a first time." said Toby. "Sorry to barge in like this on impulse, but we hoped you might be pleased to see us."

"I should be, but you've come at an awkward time. Maybe one of you can tell me why you're really here." He moved out of the doorway and down onto the front step.

"Actually, Jeffrey," said Sydney, "we're not here to impose on your hospitality. We're here to collect you."

Jeffrey smiled and broke into a laugh, "Collect me for what? Maybe you'd better come inside and tell me about it." He stepped back through the door and held it open for them. Hesitant at first, they each nodded and accepted the invitation.

"We've gone to a lot of trouble finding you," said Toby. "Actually, after you disappeared on Thursday, we managed to get ourselves into a lot of trouble chasing you down."

Jeffrey's face flushed as if he'd just swallowed a mouthful of jalapeño peppers. "I didn't disappear, I just took off for a few days' fishing." He walked to the back of the cabin and sat down on a steamer trunk against the wall. "How much do you know about Thursday anyway?"

"Enough," said Toby.

"OK then, why don't you fill me in. Grab a chair."

On Jeffrey's right against the wall there was a small worktable where a pair of kerosene lanterns kept each other company. On the opposite wall stood a small one-lid potbellied wood stove covered by a teakettle. Toby slid a crude armless wooden chair from the table and moved it next to the open door. Sydney did the same and crumpled into it on the opposite side of the door from Toby.

Sydney opened the conversation. "To begin with, Jeffrey, Toby and I found you dead on a toilet seat in the locker room. At my insistence, I convinced Toby that this was no place for a member of Brookside to have drawn his last breath, don't you know."

"My god, you're serious aren't you?" Completely taken by surprise he shook his head in disbelief. "What are you saying? All I remember is going into the clubhouse and waking up out on the course."

Sydney took out the last cigar in his case and fondled it affectionately. "It's true, we tidied you up and laid you out to the seventeenth hole. Even said words over you. I remember you saying that when you were called to the Lord, you hoped it would be out there on your favorite hole."

"I can't . . . I just can't believe that's what happened, and you really did this for me?"

"Don't be so surprised," remarked Toby. "And there's no need to thank us. We'd feel obliged to do that out of respect for any member of the club. We called the police to gather you up, but you were nowhere to be found. Sydney figured that with all the jostling getting you from the locker room out onto the course, we somehow managed to get your ticker started again, revive you back from the dead so to speak."

"I'll be goddamn. I guess I do owe you my life." Jeffrey's eyes rolled up to the ceiling. Speechless, he appeared bewildered at first and fidgeted for a pack of cigarettes in his shirt pocket. The look of disbelief on his face turned somber. "Maybe for both your sakes, you should have let me die. I wasn't having a very good day Thursday."

"I should think not. You were saturated with booze and whatever. Made quite a display of yourself in front of Alex in the lounge. And I must say right now, I'm not at all that sure you're grateful we saved your life."

"Oh, but I am, really I am! Try to understand. It's pretty difficult for me to put all the pieces together." He paused to light a cigarette. "When I regained consciousness on the course, I was sick. I'm still sick. My head was splitting. I seem to remember rolling over and over down into a thicket. That's where I puked my brains out. I couldn't think coherently at all, but I had a strange feeling that someone was trying to kill me."

"What in the deuce made you think someone wanted to do you in?" Sydney slouched back in his chair while he snipped off the fresh end of his cigar.

"Well, first of all there's Harriet. Did you know her first two husbands ended up dead under some rather mysterious circumstances?"

"Yes, we did." said Toby. "Stomach ailment, I believe, was the cause of death—both cases."

"Well there you have it," said Jeffrey. "Recently, I've suspected that she's been lacing my heart medication with some foul-tasting crap. I've got a bad ticker, you know. I always felt rotten right after taking it."

"I had the impression from Harriet your marriage was rock solid," said Toby. Suspecting the likelihood that she might have been poisoning Jeffrey, he decided to follow it up. "When you went missing, I found her to be quite distraught. So, why on earth do you think she wants to do you in?"

"I don't know. We've always gotten along rather well, whether it's been in or out of the sack. I know I'd be tits up if I got caught cheating on her. Maybe it was for the money, huh? We kept separate accounts, so this would be one way to get her hands on what little money I brought to the marriage. I know my life insurance doesn't amount to much." He got up and went over to the table to get an ashtray. "Don't you think, since her modus operandi worked so well before, why not try it again? Maybe it's something ingrained in her nature." Jeffrey crushed his cigarette out and stared toward the open door. "I guess I panicked and drove up here to get my mind sorted out. Can you appreciate that?"

"Of course," said Sydney. "What you've just said sort of makes me glad I never tied the knot. But I'm afraid your explanation doesn't quite wash. There are a lot of people looking for you, including the state police."

"What? Just because I decided to skip out of town for a couple of days?" He sputtered, "I've been coming up here for years. It's been my little secret, until you two showed up."

"I'm afraid it's the way you skipped out of town," said Toby. "Why did you leave your car in the parking lot? Was it to throw Bebee and everyone else off your track? And while we're at it, what's all this Barstow business?"

"Take it easy, Toby. You're getting yourself all worked up." Jeffrey began to pace around the small cabin like a caged cat. "All right, I came up here in a friend's car. I thought if I left my car in the parking lot, anyone looking for me would guess I was still in the neighborhood, and under the circumstances, I didn't want Harriet to think any differently. Hell, I was only planning on going for a couple of nights." Jeffrey took out his last cigarette, crumpled the empty package, and threw it angrily at the wastebasket across the room.

"Those cigarettes will kill you, Jeffrey," said Sydney.

"And, what if they do?"

"Well before they do, we'd still like to know what all this Barstow business is about?"

"I suppose I do owe you that much." His words were accompanied with a stream of exhaled smoke. "I've assumed a few names in the past, but Barstow's my real name. You probably guessed I had a checkered past when I slipped into Brookside on the back of Harriet's membership." Jeffrey stared at the floor like a repentant sinner.

Sydney suspected this admission was just the tip of an iceberg and the beginning of a shallow attempt to gain their sympathy and shove them out the door back to Brookside. He decided to wait out Jeffrey and hear where he was going with his explanation. Having just confessed to his real name, returning to Harriet and Brookside was no longer an option, unless Harriet knew he was Barstow and Sydney and Toby kept his secret to protect the club from embarrassment.

Just above a whisper, Jeffrey continued, "When I showed up in Livermore Falls, I hoped I could start a new life—a respectable one for a change. I think I was forty-eight back then. It occurred to me that I might not get another chance, and I didn't need my past catching up with me. A good part of my past involved separating wealthy people from money they had trouble holding on to anyway. In the end, very few ever complained or called in the law. It would be too embarrassing for them to reveal their own stupidity. Sooner or later, I usually had to move on down the road. Some people just wrote me off as a bad investment, like one of their stocks that tanked." He smiled wryly. "For women, I was nothing more than the price of a good time. I'm not particularly proud of my past, but it gave me a fairly decent income."

Toby shook his head. "That's really shameful of you, Jeffrey. Very disappointing. In my book, you've sunk even further beneath the low esteem I already had for you. Harriet, Brookside, us—just another easy mark for you?"

"Well, Toby, I suppose you've never jilted a dame or welshed on a deal?" He tossed his head back and laughed momentarily. "Of course you haven't!" He leaned back against the wall, and his mood turned serious again. "Listen, to make short of all this, when I landed in Livermore Falls, I simply changed my identity and became Jeffrey Bartholomew. Is that really so terrible?" Jeffrey glanced up to make eye contact. "To put it in terms you guys might understand, doesn't everyone deserve a mulligan?"

Sydney was resolved not to be bamboozled or thrown off course by Jeffrey's simplistic plea for sympathy and forgiveness. Taking a moment to ponder a reply, Sydney said, "Jeffrey, a mulligan, as you should know by now, is a second chance to hit your first tee shot over again. You don't get to take a mulligan anywhere you please during the round, or to put a point on it, in life for that matter."

Toby took to the floor to chime in. "Sydney's right, you know. Certainly in terms we all understand, you know that when you hit a ball off the course and out of bounds, you're penalized two shots—rule 27.1, I believe. In life, Jeffrey, you knock your ball out of bounds, and you get to stand in front of a judge. As to your past, we have good reason to believe it may have already caught up with you."

Jeffrey's eyes blinked, and his voice registered his irritation. "I'm getting a little tired of being lectured to about rules for this and rules for that. So what does your little playbook say if you didn't intend to hit your ball out of bounds?"

Sydney leaned back and made himself comfortable. "Nothing obviously. Like the law, it's silent about one's good intentions."

"Really. Well, I'd like to wrap up this chitchat of ours." Jeffrey's eyes burned with anger enough to make his inquisitors shiver, all the while pounding his fist into the palm of his hand.

So far the discourse between the adversaries had all the properties of a sparring match that degenerates into a no-holds-barred fight. Sydney and Toby had the offensive and the numerical advantage, while Jeffrey's strategy was to counterpunch until his opponents' fatigue became an ally. Even though Jeffrey was back on his heels, this bout could go several rounds before the outcome was decided. The mat was in Jeffrey's ring, and the referee was in his corner.

Toby turned up the heat, "After your disappearance, Chief Bebee closed the course and then set about wreaking all kinds of havoc on the club looking for you. Bringing you up to date, Friday afternoon, a murdered man was found in our pond." Toby paused to weigh Jeffrey's reaction, only to be rewarded with a blank stare. "We even had to get the governor involved. You can't begin to imagine the chaos Bebee caused."

"I don't believe it," responded Jeffrey. "All this is obviously a coincidence. You don't think I'm connected in any way?"

Sydney kept up the pressure. "Toby and I are of the mind that it's a possibility." He leaned forward and with the help of his cane, rose to his feet. "That's why we originally came here, Jeffrey—to get to the bottom of this miserable damned mess. And with your help, we might be able to right the ship."

"Why do I get the impression that you two are more concerned about Brookside than me?"

"Your impression, for the moment, is correct and for a number of reasons. If you stayed dead, as we thought you were, no one would be looking for you, and Two Bullets Bebee wouldn't have drained the pond where we found the murder victim. Everything's been unraveling from that point on." Sydney got up and walked over to the table where he flicked his cigar ashes into an empty pop bottle.

"When we left Brookside Saturday noon, the club was under duress, and with all the problems we've had trying to locate you, we've ended up dodging the law ourselves." Between puffs on his cigar, Sydney resumed, "I didn't want to bring it up, Jeffrey, but through a series of unfortunate events getting here, our reputations have been besmirched as well as the club's. That aside, as a founder of Brookside, whatever happens to me either elevates or taints every member of the club, including you."

Jeffrey's mouth fell open then gaped like a goldfish. "Excuse me for returning from the dead. One moment I'm supposed to be grateful to you for saving my life, and then, in the very same breath, you're teed off at mc because I survived? I think I know what all this is about. It's all about your damn rules and manners with you fancy-dan twits, and I don't fill the bill. Saving face for yourselves and your precious Brookside is all you really care about." He snapped, "Well, you can take all that rubbish and stuff it you know where!"

Toby said, "No call for you to be uncivil, Jeffrey, you made your point. So did Sydney. The problem, you see, was exacerbated when on Saturday we found another body. This poor devil was buried in a greenside sand trap on the ninth hole. Sydney discovered the body when he lopped the victim's thumb off with his wedge trying to get his ball out of the trap. The thumb came to rest on the green about twenty feet from the hole. Now, I'd like to know, what do you have to say about that?"

"What should I say? Nice shot! I don't know how any of this concerns me in the slightest."

Sydney raised an eyebrow and returned to his chair. "For members like us, finding a body in a sand trap is a sign that it's time for the members to circle the wagons. You always were a little slow in this department, but as a new member, I gave you some latitude." His hands cupped over his cane, he leaned forward and continued. "The chap in the pond was killed with one swing of a golf club, probably a 5-iron. Based on the depth of the wound, Toby believed it was an 8- or 9-iron. Which one of us is right remains to be seen. The autopsy no doubt will establish that."

"So, would either of you please tell me what in hell my connection is to all this crap?"

Sydney responded, "Jeffrey, calm down, let me explain. The corpse in the pond was naked except for a pair of pants, which were stuffed with a new set of golf clubs to weigh the body down. Obviously this was a crime of passion. First, Toby and I knew a murderer in his right mind wouldn't throw away a brand new set of clubs. Secondly, the perpetrator of this crime probably didn't know that the serial numbers on the clubs are traceable. You, of course, would know, yes? More than likely the clubs belonged to the victim, and the police should learn his identity soon. Since you turned up missing, Bebee and the police have several theories about what happened to you. They include the possibility that you're a hostage, another victim, or even a murderer." Sydney tossed out these scenarios to catch Jeffrey's reaction. Flirting with the truth, he continued, "Of course Toby and I would have nothing to do with such speculative nonsense. We reckoned that you might have amnesia or something and couldn't find your way home. We have since come to the conclusion, however, that you and the two bodies may be related." He coughed while he relit his cigar. "That's one of the reasons we're here—to bring you back and help us clear everything up."

Jeffrey slammed his fist against the wall. "Should I really care? Look, I'm innocent. You can see for yourselves. I'm not a victim or a hostage, and murder is not in my repertoire." He took a deep breath then spoke deliberately, "I'd like to help you fellows out, but I've got some serious personal business I need to iron out here."

"We understand," said Toby, "but time is of the essence. Even as we speak, your clubs are probably being tested for traces of the victim's blood and hair, obviously to implicate you. And I must tell you, Jeffrey, that the medication you left in your locker is on its way to Albany for analysis to see if there's been tampering. From all appearances, there aren't a whole lot of things stacking up in your favor. To put it politely to a fellow member, we really must insist that you return with us as soon as you can gather your things."

"Insist do you? You're joking." There was a hollow ring to Jeffrey's laughter. "Insist all you want, I have no intention of going back with you. I'm sorry to say this, gentlemen, but later on today I will be in Canada, and you're hardly in a position to stop me."

Jeffrey's announcement came like a body blow knocking the wind out of Sydney and Toby, only to be followed up and punctuated by the unmistakable report of a high-powered rifle.

Kapow!

"Waldo is it?" said Sydney trying to compose his thoughts, which were rolling around in his head like an open sack of marbles.

"So, you know about him," replied Jeffrey.

"Yes, just enough to make us rather uncomfortable," said Toby.

While the shot that rang out unnerved the pair, it seemed to settle Jeffrey, who got up and sauntered his way to the open door, "I need some fresh air. Let's step outside."

Sydney agreed, "No argument from me. Let's go, Toby." Stepping out the door, he noticed a small puff of bluish smoke rising from the trees across the lake and surmised it must have come from Waldo's rifle. He winced at the thought. Leaning against a birch tree, he hung his cane on one of its low overhanging branches. He stroked his chest briskly with both hands and drew in several deep breaths of woodland air.

Inside, the cabin had the aura of a boxing ring with the combatants exchanging verbal blows, but outside, the adversarial mood of the trio diminished considerably. Was it the healing effect of nature? It seemed as if they had left the fight and gone to their respective corners to recuperate between rounds. Jeffrey noticed a morning hatch of mosquitoes and reached into a shirt pocket for a small plastic bottle of insect repellent. "Here, you guys better smear some of this on, or you'll get eaten alive."

"That's considerate of you, Jeffrey," said Toby, who was shadow boxing with a number of mosquitoes he managed to attract. He noticed a tin cup hanging from a water spigot on the side of the cabin. "I think I'll do with a drink of water first, if you don't mind." After quenching his thirst, he splashed his face with water and took out his never-to-be-used handkerchief to dry off the excess. Covered with Harriet's makeup and Ugly Annie's grease, he was barely able to discern his richly embroidered initials. Rather than use it, he decided to rinse it out and draped it over the handle of Sydney's cane to dry.

*   *   *

Deciding to split up, Jeffrey ambled out onto the boat dock to stretch his legs. He wondered how his two visitors would react to his leaving for Canada and needed time to contemplate their reaction. Before rejoining the battle, he sought a friendly face and bent over the end of the dock to stare at his reflection in the water. He was disappointed, however. The image staring back at him was that of a tired man at the end of his tether, an unwelcome portrait. He sighed at the thought of having to reinvent himself again, this time in Canada. Once a relatively easy task, it was complicated now by two stubborn old goats trying to skewer him. He sensed that hightailing it to Canada would only fuel their suspicions about him, and they'd definitely blab his whereabouts to the cops—if they haven't already.

He decided to find out if they divulged where they were to anyone before he contemplated his next move. One thing was certain—he could not allow them to foil his escape to Montreal. Frustrated, he wished that for their own good, they would decide to shut up, mind their own business, and go home. But knowing them, that was too much to hope for, just as returning to Livermore Falls and the good life was not an option. That train left the station several days ago.

Jeffrey felt on the defensive and outnumbered. But he did have a trump card he was hoping he wouldn't have to play. Sydney and Toby were far from the safety of the walls of the Brookside Country Club. He smiled at the vision of these two quixotic knights riding out of their castle to save the day. But they were at Jeffrey's club now, and like the victims of the trapdoor spider, they had no idea of the perilous trap they wandered into.

Perhaps it was time to put the Stoney Creek Rod & Gun Club to the test. Ten years of dues had to be worth more than a few baskets of trout. Up to now, his membership entitled him to services he never dreamed he would ever use. It gave him comfort to know that he could trust his club to do much more than get him to Canada safely.

He took a last look at his reflection in the lake and spit in it. He said to himself, "I'm not much to look at, but it's all I've got left. Not much time in life left for me, and damn if I'm not going to make the best of it." Turning back toward the cabin, he saw Sydney and Toby pacing back and forth along the shore.

* * *

Watching Jeffrey approach, Toby said, "Well, Sydney, what do you make of all this Canada business?"

"I know we're not following him there, and he's not about to take us with him. So that leaves us with one of two options." Looking grim as a seasick deckhand, Sydney continued, "He knows by fleeing the country that we'll peg him for a murderer. So, old friend, we can try to take him with us forcibly or turn tail and make a run for it back home. That assumes, of course, he lets us go, and I don't think he has any intention of turning us loose. That possibility ended when he said was leaving the country. He knows we could spoil his "Canadian Sunset" if he turns us loose."

"I don't suppose there's another option?" Toby sensed an unpleasant showdown coming. "Let's suppose we get the drop on Jeffrey, how can we sneak him out of this place? Harrumph, we certainly can't trust anyone around here to help us. Quite the opposite I think."

"You're right, of course, on that count." Doffing his cap, Sydney swatted helplessly at the hoard of mosquitoes taunting him. "Remember, Jeffrey said he came up here in a car. If we get Jeffrey past the clubhouse, I can drive the car out of here with him in it, and you can follow behind in Ugly Annie until we get to Table Rock and call the police."

"Good thinking, Sydney. Sounds like the only plan we've got. I don't know which way this is all going to play out, but I feel we're about to give it our best shot." Toby affectionately knocked his friend on the shoulder and patted the revolver in his pocket. "Heads up, here comes Jeffrey."

Kapow!

Just as Jeffrey stepped ashore, another rifle shot echoed across the lake, this time from a different location. Jeffrey pointed to the cabin door, "Let's get back inside and wrap up this conversation. All this talk is all very interesting, but it's not leading anywhere."

Sydney didn't require urging, "Between mosquitoes and stray bullets, inside seems like a damn good suggestion." He collected his cane, handed Toby his handkerchief, and quick-stepped into the cabin behind them.

Before Jeffrey had a chance to sit down, Toby challenged him. "So the idea that you were just popping up here for a few days was just a ruse to send us packing. Having us on, so to speak."

"Yes, I was. But believe what you want, it was damned good advice at the time. You could even call it a missed opportunity on your part." Jeffrey crossed the room to an upright steel locker and opened the combination lock. "Go ahead and sit down. We're going to be a while."

"Perhaps you'd care to explain that remark, Jeffrey," said Sydney. He felt his heart race ahead of his words. "Apparently, you're resolved not to return with us, yes?"

"Right, and to screw up my plans further, I suppose you've told everyone in earshot that you've followed me here."

"Of course not!" said Toby. Reluctantly he sat down and shot back, "After all these years you still don't get it do you, Jeffrey? This is an internal affair to be worked out among club members. Club business is private business! We came up here in good faith to appeal to your better nature."

Sydney wondered what Toby was thinking, if at all, when he tipped off Jeffrey that nobody knew of their whereabouts. He thought it better not to refute Toby by conjuring up a lie, because Toby would likely take issue with it and become argumentative. At the moment nothing was more important than their solidarity.

"Yes, Toby's right," said Sydney. "No one knows we're here. And if you don't mind my saying so, I think this rather bizarre trout club of yours has muddled your senses."

"Obviously, I disagree," replied Jeffrey, "but before we get down to brass tacks, I want you both to know that Brookside was the best eight years of my life. I actually care for Harriet even though she is an argument waiting to happen." He pulled out another pack of cigarettes from the top shelf of the locker. "You know, I avoided playing golf with either of you two because I always ended up being lectured on some damn protocol or flaw in my golf swing." Smiling, he sat down again on his steamer trunk and struck a match on the floor next to an open suitcase. Lighting his cigarette, he inhaled deeply. His voice was conciliatory when he said, "Except for my infrequent golf matches with you two, I had one hell of a good time at the club. I think I actually developed a conscience along the way—you should be proud of me—but in the last couple of weeks everything's turned to crap."

Sydney and Toby didn't know quite how to respond, but it was obvious from their deadpan glance at each other that they were incensed to learn that someone or anyone could possibly be offended by their play or helpful lessons along the way. Since their initial meeting outside the cabin, Jeffrey's mind had wandered, and his mood vacillated unpredictably from being contrite and grateful to being angry and vengeful—from one with a pathological disorder to suddenly a person of conscience.

Jeffrey stood to face the open locker. Inside, fishing rods wrapped in cloth sacks hung from coat hooks along with the usual required garments for fishing—vest, pants, and a straw hat. He slowly knelt down to reach into a leather duffel bag on the lowest shelf just above his boots, and after some fumbling, his search abruptly ended. Rising up and turning around, he brandished a small pistol in his right hand, waving it back and forth around the room aiming it at various objects until he brought it to bear a foot away from the tip of Sydney's nose. It was the kind of gesture that suggested it was a practice run of what Jeffrey might actually do, with all its deadly consequences.

"Good thing you're just having sport," said Sydney. "That's a fine piece you've got there—.38 special? Your hand's a little shaky, Jeffrey. Wouldn't want an accident, don't you know."

"I'm not having sport, and if I shoot anybody, it won't be an accident."

"Listen," said Sydney, "you seem unsettled by our visit. Perhaps it will help things if you tell us what kind of crap you've stepped in? It might do you good to scrape some of it off your shoes, in a manner of speaking."

"Well, it won't help, and since it won't make any difference if I do or don't, maybe you should know the whole story. You boys don't know as much as you think you do. And you, Toby, you can pick your eyeballs back up off the floor." Jeffrey returned to his locker to retrieve a small open box of cartridges. He scooped some out and began loading the empty cylinder.

Toby watched intently. "I'm beginning to lose interest in your story, Jeffrey, if the conclusion involves a bullet." He slowly reached into his jacket pocket seeking the comfort of his old service revolver. His mind raced back to the time when he decided to bring his pistol on the trip. He said to himself, *Good god! I did load it, didn't I? I must have. After all, why wouldn't I? I can't remember. Just relax—hell, if I have to pull it out, Jeffrey will have to believe it's loaded.*

"You'll like this story, Toby. I wasn't always a lightweight conman. When you guys first knew me, I really wanted to turn my life around. A few years ago I used to look like a Charles Atlas ad. But I was running out of looks and assets. I thought if I could make just one big score, I could retire, and everything would be easy street after that. Right?"

Jeffrey began pacing again. His eyes twitched nervously as they glanced back and forth between Sydney and Toby. "I was in a bar in Buffalo when I ran into a couple of real hoods back in '39. They seemed comic to me at first, like low-life gangsters in an Abbott and Costello film. Come to find out these guys were true to their looks. Specialized in armed robbery. I found out that knocking off a small town bank or a liquor store on the weekend ranked high on their list of things to do. They often laughed about their experiences in the big house, but once outside they kept practicing their trade hoping somehow to perfect it. It was obvious in talking to them that they had grown up with a mob mentality.

We kept crossing paths after that, until we decided to team up on a job that would either set us up for life or jail us for life. I'd never used a gun before—ha—or even fired one, but they gave me this one from their collection. I didn't realize how much I was going to need it. Hey, what did I have to lose? Back then, I was headed down a dead-end street."

Once again Waldo's shooting startled the trio.

Kapow! Kapow! Kapow!

It seemed closer now and portended some danger. Paper-thin walls were their only protection.

Toby piped up, "Who were these Damon Runyon characters, not that it matters?" He thought if Jeffrey could purge himself of the recent past, there might be some hope of diffusing a situation that was headed downhill.

"Not the types you'd find in our locker room. They weren't club members, unless you think of organized crime as a club." Jeffrey laughed at the thought of them at a dinner dance. "One was Knuckles Nelson. He was something of an ape—had six knuckles on each hand. His pal, Timmy Moynahan, was known in his circle of friends as Rat Face, for obvious reasons."

"Jeffrey," said Sydney, "just now you used the past tense when you said Knuckles was something of an ape. May I assume he still is?"

"Don't play word games with me, Sydney. You know damn well he's dead! So's Rat Face. Don't you know it's rude to interrupt someone when they're speaking? Keep it up and you'll miss the best part." He whirled around and placed the pistol on the top shelf of the locker. Grabbing clothing indiscriminately from the shelves and hooks, he tossed them one after another into the open suitcase on the floor. Picking up the pistol again, he swiveled around and held it out in front of Toby. "Now, just how do you think Two Bullets Bebee got his name?"

"You mean he got it from that gun?" Toby gasped.

"Yeah, this is the one. Those two bullets he's carrying around are .38's from the bank holdup of '39, right in good old Livermore Falls." He leaned back against the far wall laughing again. "Surprised? I never meant to shoot anyone, but in the heat of the moment I started blasting away at anything that moved."

"I never took you for a violent man, Jeffrey. Whatever possessed you to cross the line?"

"I didn't think I could, but since I did, I have to deal with it now. Anyway, now that I have your complete attention, I can tell you that holdup was my entrée into your precious Brookside. I finally had enough money of my own to call the shots my way. Can you think of a better place to hide my share of the robbery than in the bank I stole it from? Every so often I'd deposit a small amount out of my safe deposit box and reinvest it in bank notes and securities. You guys know Overton. Well, he worshipped me ever since the day I walked into his bank, except this time I was an out-of-town entrepreneur. He introduced me to Harriet, and the rest I think you know."

Sydney could hardly muster a retort. "So this Knuckles and Rat Face were your confederates? You might as well tell us how they ended up dead on the course."

"I suppose." He began casually while tossing the gun back and forth between his hands, saying that he never dreamed of making such a big haul, how he and Knuckles could hardly carry it all. Rat Face was the driver and lookout. All agreed to a three-way split and never to see each other again and if caught not to squeal. That was 1939. Until a month ago things worked out well. Jeffrey claimed he had no way of knowing they were blowing their share on dames and horses.

Jeffrey laughed that short pathetic kind that turns into a snicker. "Ironically, by investing over the years, I've made half again as much as I stole. In fact I've got a big share of it right here in the liner of my steamer trunk."

Sydney squirmed in his chair. His mouth was parched and ached for a prenoon scotch. He felt his nerves beating on each other. "So something must have gone terribly wrong for you."

"As wrong as it can get." He closed his suitcase and set it by the door. "Knuckles spotted me upstate on a business trip and followed me back home. He looked up Rat Face, and right after that the two of them show up in Livermore Falls. They were both broke and slept nights in their car on back roads. Based on my lifestyle, they evidently thought it would be simple for me to bail them out of their present dilemma."

Toby said, "You must have looked like an easy mark compared to robbing a bank. What a nasty kettle of fish for you."

"Don't try to be funny, Toby. Can you imagine? Knuckles actually wanted to move in with Harriet and me! He even had the audacity to suggest that I should get him into Brookside because he always had a hankering to take up golf seriously."

Sydney sighed, "Thank heaven that didn't come to pass!"

"Of course I couldn't let that happen. Funny isn't it? I actually did Brookside a good turn when I introduced Knuckles' head to a 5-iron."

"See, Toby, I told you it was a 5-iron."

"I'll take Jeffrey's word for it," Toby conceded. "But where was Rat Face while all this was going on?"

"Knuckles told me he was already dead. They had a meeting down by the road hole and quarreled over who should get what and how much from me. Rat Face lost. Knuckles said he shot him because he was too greedy. Of all the idiotic places, he buried Rat Face right on the course because no one would ever think to look for a body there, *ha*! Knuckles still had the gun on him when I gave him a haircut with my club. Best shot I hit all week." He grinned. "After I stripped the bastard, I tossed the gun into the far end of the pond. I thought it was pretty clever of me to put his pants back on and load them up with his new clubs. Weighed him down perfectly. When I dumped him in the pond he dove to the bottom like a submarine. What a relief. I didn't think there was a chance in hell of anyone finding—"

Several loud knocks on the door interrupted Jeffrey's soliloquy. Engrossed, both Sydney and Toby flinched.

Jeffrey jumped up and said, "Is that you, Karl? Open the door."

Karl poked his head inside. "Are you going to be ready to go? We leave in just about an hour. I've got your other luggage loaded up." He glanced around the room. "Everything OK in here?"

"Yes, thanks Karl, I'll only be a few more minutes. Oh, you might tell Bertha that my two guests will be staying over. They're exhausted from their trip, and I'm sure they'd like to get some rest now. Perhaps they'd like a scotch first just to relax."

"I get the picture. Bertha will have everything waiting for them when you come up to the lodge."

When Karl slammed the door shut, Sydney and Toby turned to stare apprehensively at each other. Neither wanted to find out what Bertha might have in store for them, and their faces sagged.

*   *   *

Karl came in the back door of the lodge and called out, "Bertha, we've got another assignment for you."

"What is it?" she yelled back. "Is it about those two old goats with Jeffrey?"

"Well, who else?" He crossed the main room and slammed his hat down on her desk. "Dammit all to hell, I thought by now we'd be out of this side of the business. Of course," he said, "you seem to actually enjoy doing this, and after all I want you to be happy. You couldn't put down that fleabag dog of yours, but you don't mind bumping off a few guys from time to time."

"Why don't you shut up, love? You seem to like the money, so just lock your shaky little knees together and do your job." Karl trailed behind Bertha as she strode over to a small storage room off the kitchen. Unlocking it, she let a smile slowly cross her face like a crack on a frozen lake.

He kept carping, "That stupid ass Waldo is always gone when we need him."

"I know that," she huffed. "If we have to, do you think you can stop shaking long enough to hold a gun on those two useless old farts? You know I have to give them their sleepy-time medicine." She moved deliberately about her tiny laboratory stocked with potions, vials, and hypodermic needles. "As far as I'm concerned, they're no different from the rest of the creeps we put on the bottom of the lake."

"Bertha, why do I think of you sometimes as a nurse gone bad in a previous life?"

"Listen and listen good, my little prince—don't get funny with me." Preparing two deadly hypos, she paused to rebuke her usually obedient husband. "We've been at this game a lot of years. One more time won't kill the goose."

"All right, all right, Bertha. We've filled up the lake with all kinds of crooks and bad apples, but these two guys are a little diffcrent."

"Is that sooooo? And I say, so what! We're under contract. Remember? Every dues-paying member is entitled to three things, and it's the third thing that carries a nice fat service charge. Number one is fishing. Number two is getting them back and forth across the boarder with new identities, etc., and the third thing is?"

"Eliminating their problem associates and disposing of them. Well, I say we've pushed our luck far enough. It's time to retire. Cancel the goddamn contracts. We've got enough to walk away from this place and the one in Canada too. Our people at Four Meadows are getting long in the tooth at this business. They've started making mistakcs, and you know it. It's not too late to make a new life."

She turncd and gave him a look that said he was wasting his breath. "And where do you think we'd go? Or can't you think that far ahead? We've got 250 members of the world's worst crooks and gangsters who might think we know just a little too much." Defeated for an answer, Karl could only walk away.

Finished, she set her tray of instruments down, locked the laboratory door, and handed Karl four tablets. "Offer them a scotch and slip 'em a mickey like we've done with the others. You know the routine." Karl nodded. "By the way, don't you think it's much more humane if our guests have gone beddy-bye before they get their lethal injection?" She smiled knowing that would make Karl squirm. "Anyway, I think so."

18

Showdown at Quarry Lake

Jeffrey stood up and said, "You heard Karl. I'm ready to go, and we're due up at the lodge. I'm afraid you're going to be permanent guests of the Stoney Creek Rod & Gun Club. Sorry men, you know it's not my choice, not now anyway."

"It's not our choice either, Jeffrey." Toby felt a certain sadness attached to Jeffrey's voice, thinking that perhaps he regretted the event that he was about to initiate. "It's hard for me to believe that you would deliberately set out to harm us. I can understand your overreacting to Knuckles, but I must say that I'm very disappointed in you. Sydney and I are hardly in the same camp with the likes of him."

Contemplating the prospects of their demise, Toby felt a rush of adrenalin that put every fiber of his body on red alert. Self-preservation was foremost in his mind. Not able to outrun a bullet, he decided that it would be significantly better for them to put up a fight than make a dash for it. Still seated, he placed a firm grip on the revolver in his jacket pocket.

Sydney reached for his cane as if he needed it to help him stand. He winked across the room at Toby. "We won't be bargaining for our lives, Jeffrey. It's too out of character for Toby and me anyway. And you may have underestimated us, Jeffrey."

"Underestimate you two—I don't think that's possible." He laughed cockily while trying to shrug off the smidgen of doubt that just crept into his mind. Was he being too anxious and impatient to escape to Canada? Maybe there were unturned stones and information they knew that he didn't. For a brief moment he thought about letting Bertha have her persuasive ways with them, knowing that she'd like that. The idea was suddenly repulsive. "All right, boys, the stalling's over—out the door."

"Not just yet!" said Toby, his voice trembling with anger. During a brief instant when Jeffrey turned his attention to Sydney, Toby pulled out his revolver and pointed it directly at Jeffrey only a few feet away. In an effort to keep it steady he held it with both hands.

"Hey, Toby, don't try to scare me off with that antique. It'll probably blow up in your face if you try to fire it." Shocked, Jeffrey tried to make light of Toby's threat.

"Well, I'm sure you don't want to find out. In the Spanish-American War, it was a damned good firearm. Plenty good enough against that pea shooter of yours, I'll tell you."

Their gun barrels were aimed so close at each other that should one go off, the other one probably would too, and both men would suffer the same dire consequence. Jeffrey flashed a cocky smile, which belied the knot in his stomach. "I can't believe you'd shoot me." He joked, "Hell, I'm still a member of the club. You wouldn't want it on your dossier that you shot a member. Harriet might not think well of it either. Besides, knowing you two as I do, I might change my mind and decide to blast Sydney first. Toby, you wouldn't like to live with Sydney's death on your conscience even if you did manage to drop me. So why don't you just put your pistol down?"

Sydney had been busily removing a cap from the bottom of his cane. "Jeffrey, before you do something rash, there's something I should explain to you."

"And what would that be?" Jeffrey turned and pointed his .38 at Sydney. "Hey, what do you think you're doing with your cane?"

"That's what I want to explain to you. I'm loading it." Suddenly, Jeffrey was transfixed. Sydney had slipped a single shotgun shell into the breach near the grip of the cane. "You see, Jeffrey, this cane can be a handy weapon in an emergency." He raised the barrel of the cane with one hand to point it at Jeffrey. "Notice my forefinger on the shaft below the grip? My friend, Buster, has a hair trigger, so you really don't want to make me any more upset with you than I already am."

"OK so we've got a Mexican standoff." His feigned smile wilted.

Toby, emboldened and still firmly gripping his pistol said, "Sydney, I believe his appraisal refers to a no-win confrontation? However, this happens to be the two of us against you, Jeffrey. Under these circumstances and considering the locale, I'd call this a Canadian standoff."

"He's right, Jeffrey, two against one. You might as well surrender your weapon." Anticipating the possibility of having to fire a shot, Sydney braced the cane firmly against his side. An old familiar dull ache rippled across his left shoulder, and his pulse raced ahead of his words. He did not want his voice to quaver or register any sense of fear. "At this range, Jeffrey, my cane will blow a hole through you the size of a saucer. Shred your innards like a cabbage salad. I know—this wouldn't be the first time I've fired Buster."

Leaving his suitcase by the doorway, Jeffrey retreated awkwardly as he backed off toward his steamer trunk. Bewildered and embarrassed at letting these two old schlemiels get the drop on him, he sat down and laid his gun on the floor. "This isn't going to get you anywhere you know. If you think you're getting out of here with me, you might as well know you'll never make it past the lodge. Karl's going to be coming down here soon if we don't show up. If you've got something on your mind, you'd better spill it out fast."

"Gladly," Sydney replied. "In the meantime, just take your foot and gently slide your gun over to Toby for safekeeping." He scooted his chair around to train Buster on Jeffrey and keep an eye on the door as well.

Toby picked up Jeffrey's gun and pocketed it. "Sydney, you won't mind if I step outside for a pee, will you?" Nature was calling Toby, but his real mission was to see if he had indeed loaded his pistol.

"No, but stay out of sight and don't dillydally!" Sydney's eyes remained fixed on Jeffrey, "Now then, Mr. Bartholomew, you've been going about this all the wrong way."

"And that is?"

"First of all, we now know that you killed a man. When you're apprehended, and you will be, it's very conceivable that you will face the death penalty and the electric chair. Having witnessed an execution, I can tell you, being strapped in that chair is not an enviable way to end one's life. When they throw the switch, you'll light up like a Christmas tree."

"So, if we all make it out of here alive and back to civilization, I might get life instead of the chair. I think I'll take my chances."

"Harriet says you have a weak heart. How much time do you have left? Days, weeks, perhaps months? It's a bloody miracle that you survived the first time you died."

Jeffrey interrupted, "I can ask you guys the same question. How much time have you got left. For Christ's sake you're both short-timers!"

Toby opened the door and latched it behind him. "Short, short, who's short?"

"Jeffrey thinks we are—short of time to live that is, and he's on point with that." His eyes remained locked on Jeffrey's. "If I may indulge you with a metaphor, Toby and I understand that our life's already been one long plane ride. We are on the glide path now, approaching the terminal, don't you know. Nothing would suit us better than a soft landing instead of the one you've concocted for us." As a show of their determination, Sydney continued, "Nevertheless, and maybe because we are short-timers, we don't mind dying in a hail of lead for a good cause, right, Toby?" Before Toby could agree, Sydney motioned to Jeffrey with his cane, "Now move away from your locker." From the look on Jeffrey's face, Sydney's bravado had stung him like a swarm of bees. Steadying his grip on Buster, he asked Toby to rummage through Jeffrey's locker for either aspirin or scotch.

Toby reopened the locker and with one hand dug through what Jeffrey hadn't packed. "Bourbon, OK? Half empty bottle, no aspirin."

"Thanks, Toby, that'll have to do. Just give me two fingers. That stuff's probably not good for much except stripping paint."

While Toby poured a quantity into a used glass and passed it over to Sydney, he managed to keep his pistol aimed at Jeffrey's vitals.

Sydney chucked down the warm bourbon, which resulted in a long wheezing sound, a signal of resentment from deep within his fragile innards. He resumed, "As I started to say Jeffrey, you're going about this the wrong way. Let's look at the options. One, you have us killed, you escape to Canada, in which case you either die at the hands of the law or the grim reaper, who, according to you, may have first crack. Two, some of us or all of us die, including Karl, Big Bang Bertha, and that nutso Waldo. Three, Toby and I manage to escape with you and bring you to justice."

"Option three's a laugh," said Jeffrey. "You've got quite an imagination!"

Sydney's face puckered. "Is that so? Well it's served me pretty well up to now. We simply slip past the lodge together. You and I leave in the car you drove up here in, and Toby follows us on the motorcycle. After you've been taken into custody, Toby and I will put in a good word for you only because, as you just reminded us, you're still a member of Brookside."

Jeffrey shook his head in disbelief and looked dejectedly at his two captors. He didn't like any of the scenarios Sydney had suggested so far, but he couldn't devise one of his own that didn't include the help of Karl, Bertha, and Waldo. "I don't suppose you have any other options with a different outcome?" Stalling for time, he played to Sydney's weakness for storytelling and listening to his own voice.

Sydney took a moment to test his memory. "As a matter of fact, there is another option. It may not be applicable in this situation, but perhaps it's worth the effort to explore. There is one particular instance that comes to mind of a gentleman who slipped off the straight and narrow. It sort of relates to your situation, but you may not agree. Toby knows of whom I speak."

"Are you thinking of Deacon Witherspoon?" said Toby.

"Precisely. That was a lot of years ago, but I think it's a fit. For your information Jeffrey, Deacon Sebastian Witherspoon was a man of impeccable character and high standing in our community. During all his fifty or so earthly years, he was true to his marriage, family, and position at the bank. As a deacon of the church he was not a man of the cloth, but no mortal man held more steadfastly to his Christian faith than he did. In every sense of the word he was a real gentleman."

Toby fidgeted impatiently. "You'd better get on with it, Sydney."

"Yes, yes! I was just setting the table, don't you know. So here's the meat of the coconut. Witherspoon was the treasurer of the Gentlemen's Commercial Club, and it was discovered that he was filching funds from the club to pay blackmail, to a woman of disrepute I believe, not that he couldn't afford it out of his own comfortable means. What he couldn't afford was to have funds of that ilk on his books and risk a chance of exposure. That would destroy him, ruin everything, and leave his family shattered and destitute. Sebastian was perched on a high wire of respectability, and he only had to fall off it once. Very sad state of affairs. Well, the board of directors and I met with Witherspoon in the club library and confronted him with the issue at hand." Sydney paused a minute to let his long-winded narrative sink in for Jeffrey's benefit. Reluctantly, Jeffrey listened to Sydney pontificate on this anecdotal parable, perhaps thinking that time was on his side and that Karl would become concerned. He was, by his silence, evidently mystified by Sydney's lengthy discourse and couldn't understand where it was leading. It could be his curiosity was aroused.

To quench a growing thirst, Toby took advantage of the momentary intermission to sidestep his way over to the bourbon on the table. Jeffrey probably humored himself with the thought of them getting plastered and falling asleep.

Before resuming his spiel, Sydney cleared his throat and swallowed hard. "Witherspoon had been flushed out and knew that his misdeed could not go unpunished, even if he could make amends with the club. He was crushed and emotionally distraught. We left it to him as a gentleman of conscience to pronounce his own sentence. The board and I retired to the bar and left him alone in the library to give him time to do some soul searching.

"Moments later when we heard a gunshot, we knew the path he had chosen. We found him lying on the terrace with the club's service revolver in hand. On the library table was a neatly penned note and a check to cover the club's losses and his current month's dues."

Jeffrey blinked. "Hey, wait just a minute you two. That little fairy tale wasn't for my benefit was it? You're not suggesting I blow my brains out?"

"Most certainly not," replied Toby. "You were the one suggesting another option, and Sydney just gave you an illustration."

"What if I don't like the picture? Good Christ, don't you think it never crossed my mind?" His voice rose to a fever pitch. "Well, screw you both! I do happen to have some conscience. I haven't been able to face up to a lot of things I've done in my life. That and I'm too much of a coward to kill myself. After what I did to Knuckles, my solution, of course, was to go on a drunk. He was a rotten little bastard, but I'm sick about what I did to him. I couldn't kill myself, especially over that miserable dickhead, but the way I was drinking I was doing a pretty good job of trying, right?" Jeffrey's shoulders slumped forward, and his eyes fell to the floor. "Speaking of drinking, Toby, how about letting me have a shot of my own bourbon?"

"I see no harm in it." Toby set the bottle down on the floor in front of Jeffrey, who took a healthy swig and grimaced as it burned its way down his throat. Deciding to take a mulligan, he guzzled down another shot before returning the bottle to the floor, then he folded his hands and dropped them between his outstretched legs.

"After I clobbered Knuckles," Jeffrey began, "I had no choice but to make a run for it. Sooner or later even that dolt Bebee would catch on to me. I only had a few days to collect as much cash as I could and haul ass. Stoney Creek's been part of my exit strategy for a lot of years—my insurance policy in case I ever had to move on or get out of the country. I hoped I wouldn't have to, but gentlemen, here we are."

Jeffrey took a deep breath and let out a long sigh of relief usually reserved for the confessional booth. "When I woke up on the seventeenth hole and cleared my head, I decided there couldn't be a better opportunity to hit the road. If you haven't guessed by now, running's instinctive with me. I drove off in Knuckles car. I already had it packed. I found it where he'd left it parked a couple of hundred yards from the Brookside entrance. It's sitting up at the lodge now. You see, with my car left in the Brookside lot, no one would suspect I had left the area, and that would buy me time. You had that part right." Jeffrey hoisted the bottle of bourbon and availed himself of two more quick belts. "Another thing, I just couldn't come to grips with the idea that Harriet could be poisoning me. But the thought of it put a little more fire to my feet. I never figured you two birds in the equation. I can see now how you might figure out where I was going, but how did you know when I'd be here? You tell me."

"Quite simple really," said Toby puffing up. "I was able to translate the coded numbers you'd penciled on your matchbook cover. These had to be the dates you'd arranged to be here. I surmised it was a careful reminder to yourself."

Jeffrey laughed at the irony. "I hate to deflate you, but that was the number of my bank account you were looking at. I think your calculations just turned out to be lucky, don't you?"

Toby flushed, "Perhaps you're really the lucky fellow."

"Maybe you'd like to spell that out for me, Toby."

"Jeffrey, I'd like to remind you that you've already died once, and now you've been given a second chance to make amends. Not too many chaps have had such an opportunity I dare say. Sydney and I gave you that chance." He paused, "I have to concede, though, it was quite unintentional. So, now that life's dealt you a new hand, how do you want to play your cards?"

"Right now, I don't see any options, and you boys are holding the winning hand—for now. I think I'll fold and see what kind of hand Stoney Creek's holding."

Sydney's arms ached from holding a bead on Jeffrey. "Toby, I think the time's approaching to take the initiative. Jeffrey's right. It may not be much longer before Karl and Bertha show us their cards."

*   *   *

Bertha beelined from her lab to her desk off the main hall and opened Jeffrey's file folder. She scanned through a package of new identification documents Jeffrey needed to cross the Canadian border and establish himself in Montreal as Jeffrey Barstow. His pretext for crossing the border was simply to go fishing with Karl for a few days at Four Meadows, their sister fishing club a few miles into Canada.

Karl crossed the main hall and detoured into an overstuffed chair. Sulking, he pulled his guide hat down over his eyes and mumbled several of his favorite curses. It was eleven ten when Bertha glanced up to check the time and saw that Jeffrey should have been up at the lodge and on his way by now.

"Karl," she snarled, "have you got Jeffrey's stuff loaded yet?"

"All except some odds and ends—fishing stuff, suitcase, and a trunk."

"Don't forget to go through it. All of it. No slipups in case you get searched. Unlikely, but god, you can be careless. I don't have to do everything, now do I?"

"No. You didn't have to arrange for Jeffrey's car to be disposed of, did you?" Karl was more annoyed with Bertha than usual. It was his job to drive cars like Jeffrey's to a junkyard in the hinterland that would pay cash and ask no questions. "Waldo's taking my truck and following me over to Walt's Body Shop on Tuesday. We'll be getting back a little later than usual." He rose from his chair and walked over to Bertha, who was still engrossed in the contents of Jeffrey's file. "In case you're listening, we've got to be more careful how we dispose of our member's cars. Except for the car Jeffrey showed up in, the guests aren't coming in junkers anymore." Karl pocketed his hands and smiled wryly. "Maybe we're getting a better class of crooks passing through here, either that or the economy's looking better."

His comment went unheeded. The forged documents she had carefully crafted engaged all her attention. She held Jeffrey's army discharge papers up to the light with the calm satisfaction of a boa that had just swallowed a rabbit. "I added to his resume that he served with distinction." She laughed, "I decided to give him a battlefield promotion too. He deserves one just for paying his dues on time."

"Well, he certainly got his money's worth," he shrugged. "He's one of the few members who ever came here to actually fish. I think he'll even miss this place. I've noticed him sitting out there in the lake 'til dusk."

The same simple pleasures of fishing at twilight appealed to Karl, and he envied Jeffrey. Karl's times away from the club were limited to business trips in order to keep a low profile and their real activities from being disclosed. There was no way for him to indulge in his favorite sport away from Stoney Creek. An avid fisherman from the time he was a boy, he could not bring himself to cast a line on Quarry Lake, even with its abundance of native rainbows. Once he rowed out on the water, he was reminded what lay beneath the surface. Faces of the men he'd buried in the watery depths rose to the surface like leaping trout to haunt him with visions that drove him back to shore.

"Know what I think, Karl? Jeffrey must have had a lot on his mind," she replied. "An unhappy man, I think. Anyway he knows how to get in touch with us if he wants to get stateside again." She raked her straight hair back with both hands and refocused her attention on the tray of hypodermic needles. "Karl, dear," she said ever so sweetly, "don't you think it's time to fetch Jeffrey and our guests? Now!" Suddenly her face flushed and puckered up like an overripe plum. "And if you see Waldo, kick his goddamn ass up here!"

"Your little prince is on his way." Karl sighed. "Give Jeffrey a buzz and tell him I'm coming." As the back porch screen door closed behind him, another shot rang out from Waldo's Sunday practice session.

*   *   *

The intercom rang three times before Toby waved his pistol at Jeffrey and said, "Get it."

Jeffrey rose slowly and picked up the receiver. "Yes, Bertha what is it?" He held the receiver away from his ear to listen while Bertha barked at him. From across the room Sydney and Toby could only catch snatches of what Bertha said and were resigned to imagine what Jeffrey heard. They were both shocked when he said, "Karl might as well take his time, I'm going to take a last turn around the lake before leaving. I probably won't be coming this way again for a long time. Give me an hour, and I'll be up with our guests." He hung up, evidently before Bertha could get a word in.

Toby exclaimed, "A turn around the lake? Well, I never!"

"Never?" said Jeffrey. "You laid me out on the seventeenth because I said a long time ago that if I had to choose a place to die, that's where I would like to cash in my chips. Well, that isn't quite true. I lied. It's my second choice. My first choice is out there on Quarry Lake. I love fishing, but I love being out there on the water even more. This club actually grew on me because I'm at peace with myself when I'm out on the lake." Jeffrey's tone became uncharacteristically meditative. "I don't understand a lot of things about you two antiques, but I've got a feeling you both know what I'm talking about. If either of you had to leave Brookside, wouldn't you be up for one last round of golf? How about it guys?"

Like well-placed arrows, Jeffrey's words pierced their thin sentimental armor. Sydney's attitude toward Jeffrey suddenly softened. "What's come over, Jeffrey?" he thought. Perhaps Jeffrey really did have a soul after all. "What do you think, Toby? My vote is to give him a turn out on the lake. There's no place else he can go except back here. I see no harm in it."

"Right," said Jeffrey.

"I am reminded," said Toby, "that we are unwelcome guests here, not unlike some other places we've been recently. I wouldn't be surprised if Bertha plans to feed us to the trout instead of the other way around. No thanks to you Jeffrey, by the way. But I'll go along with Sydney as long as we have your word that you will return, yes?"

"You know my word hasn't been very good up to now, but this one will be easy to keep. You've got my money in the trunk for collateral, and Karl's got my passage to Canada."

"Well get going then," said Sydney. "We want you back here when Karl shows up."

Jeffrey got up and walked to the door, "Thanks, this means a lot to me. I'll be back in half an hour, OK?"

Sydney and Toby both nodded and followed Jeffrey out of the cabin. They watched him amble down the dock to a rowboat tethered at the far end. Jeffrey methodically lifted an anchor from the dock and put it in the bow. He untied the boat's lashing and gently pushed away from the dock with an oar.

Exhausted from lack of sleep and the standoff with Jeffrey, the pair collapsed in two nearby camp chairs. Toby closed his eyes and wiped his brow. His shoulders sagged and his left arm hung limp. Sydney rubbed his two sore arms vigorously, hoping to return their circulation.

Alone for the first time in over an hour of confrontation that could have escalated into a shootout, Sydney cleared his throat to get Toby's attention. "You know, Toby, Jeffrey may have something untoward up his sleeve. Maybe that's why he's changed tactics—appealing to our better nature. Any thoughts?"

Toby managed to open his eyes enough to let in a sliver of light. "For heaven's sake, Sydney, do we have to be suspicious of every act of civility and decency? Anyway, it's a little late to have second thoughts." Seeking comfort, Toby scrunched further down in the canvas folding chair that was totally inadequate for his corpulent frame.

"All right, but listen up, Toby. When Karl comes down here looking for us, we'll have to get the drop on him." Sydney sighed and rested Buster across the arms of his chair. He rubbed his eyes vigorously before they shut involuntarily.

*   *   *

Karl arrived much sooner than either Sydney or Toby expected. Deliberately sneaking up behind them to catch them unawares, he exclaimed, "Hey, what's going on here?"

Startled, Toby leaned forward and tried to stand up, but the camp chair stuck to his buttocks and rose with him. Unable to stand erect, he pushed down on the arms to no avail. Forced to crouch over, he discovered his sleeve was fully engaged in the folding device. Exasperated by an effort to release himself, he began spinning around like a dog chasing his tail until he rotated into a tree. The impact released the chair from his rump, and although he could stand upright again, the chair remained attached to his sleeve like a crab with a death grip. Dangling the chair from his extended arm, he dashed it against the tree several times until its severed parts lay at his feet. "Thank God I'm free of that beast!"

Sydney smiled and said, "Good work, Toby. I never did like these contraptions."

Karl was not amused by Toby's antics. He threw his hands in the air and yelled, "What in hell is Jeffrey doing out on the lake?"

Groping for an answer, Sydney cranked his head around and said, "You don't know? Humph—you must not travel in the right circles. We heard Jeffrey tell Bertha he was going to take a spin around the lake before leaving today. So calm down, go in the cabin, and call that charming wife of yours, if you don't believe me."

"That's just what I'm going to do," said Karl. Flustered, he spun around and headed toward the cabin. "And I don't need any sarcasm or advice from either of you."

Sydney followed him. Karl was reaching for the intercom when Sydney stuck his cane sharply into Karl's ribs. "I'm not used to a display of force when I make a request, but in this case I find it necessary because I don't think you will cooperate otherwise."

"All right, just what in hell do you want?" He muttered over his shoulder to Sydney, "You're friends of Jeffrey? Fine guests you turned out to be."

Toby came through the door in time to overhear Karl's remark. "I wouldn't be too quick to judge us Karl or whatever your real name is. We're on to your little game. Rod and gun club—ha!"

Sydney thought Toby's adrenaline would have run out after the fight he just had with the camp chair, but instead he was pleased that Toby found a new well to tap. "When I step back, check his pockets and see if he has a weapon." Sydney's heart was racing again, and he breathed deeply to calm his nerves.

Toby had Karl empty his personal effects on the floor. "Besides his wallet, there's nothing on him of interest except a pocket knife and a key ring. Poor devil, probably all that Bertha'll let him have."

Sydney sat down in a chair by the door, "All right, Karl, you can turn around."

"You stuck that stupid cane in my back?"

"Careful how you talk about Buster. He's a shotgun with a nasty temperament." He aimed at Karl and said, "Now go ahead and ring up Bertha, and after you have your small talk, I want you to tell her that you're watching Jeffrey taking a sentimental journey around the lake, and you'll return to the lodge with everyone when Jeffrey gets back. No tricks."

"OK!" Karl rang the lodge and said softly, "Bertha, it's me. Jeffrey's gone out for a row. As soon as he returns, we'll be right up." There was a long silent period, and while Karl was listening, he put his hand over the receiver to turn and ask Sydney, "She wants to know if you two are giving me any trouble."

"You're asking me? You idiot, you're supposed to say, no!"

"No," Karl told Bertha, "nothing I can't handle. Bye for now."

"Thanks for tipping her off," said Sydney, "I think she already knows you can't handle much of anything."

"Maybe yes, maybe no." Karl, who'd been embarrassed at finding himself a captive, turned downright gleeful. "Up 'til now I had a soft spot for you two. Pretty stupid of me. But you might as well know you'll never make it out of here alive. You don't know my Bertha."

"Under the circumstances, I'd prefer not to know her if you don't mind," replied Sydney. "Let's all be calm and go outside to wait for Jeffrey."

Back at the dock, Toby cracked the wall of silence. "What's Jeffrey's thinking about out there? He just shipped his oars."

"God only knows," Sydney replied. "I make it he's been gone about twenty minutes. Now he's just sitting there like he's waiting for something to happen." A gentle southerly wind stirred his boat, and along with the current it began to drift toward the sawmill. "Maybe he wants to get to a certain spot before turning back."

Karl offered, "Not that it makes any difference, but he's over the deepest part of the lake now where the old quarry was. Look at the trout rising all around him. I bet he wished he had a rod."

"Now why on earth's he standing up in the boat?" said Toby. Jeffrey stood motionless for several minutes, facing a bluff of white marble rising out of the lake. "Now he's waving his hat over his head. Something very strange is going on here, Sydney." There was not long to wait for the unmistakable sound of a high-powered rife sending a bullet with deadly accuracy to its target.

Kapow!

The birds heard the shot that Jeffrey couldn't as it ripped its way through the back of his chest. He could not see his hat float from his outstretched hand. Nor could he feel his falling body crumple against the gunwale of the boat and tumble over into the lake. Earthbound and helpless, the three men stared in silence as Jeffrey slowly slipped beneath the surface. Frozen in place like statues, their ashen, expressionless faces watched the horrific scene unfold like witnesses at a prisoner's execution. Jeffrey's boat twisted and hovered over his watery grave like a macabre floating tombstone, until at length it resumed its course to the outlet, while Jeffrey continued his voyage to the bottom of Quarry Lake.

19

Final Confrontation

It seemed like an eternity passed before anyone could speak or move. Toby was the first to find his voice. "Nothing can be said I suppose, except that he got his wish to die out there. Ironic, isn't it, he got to die in his two favorite places?"

"Twice dead," said Sydney. "Quite a feat—and can you believe it, not a week apart?"

Even though he had taken part in the death of dozens over the years, Karl was shaking. "I don't believe any of this is happening. It can't. Waldo must have shot him. If he were going to shoot anybody, it would have been you two. God, I wonder if Bertha saw what happened."

"Toby, keep your pistol on Karl. We've got to focus on getting out of here alive, and he might have some value as a hostage." Sydney's attention turned from the lake to the surrounding woods searching for a clue as to Waldo's whereabouts. "Where do you think Waldo would go, Karl?"

"If not here, probably to his mother's house in the village. Lives with her in the winter. He's dumb as a rock and unpredictable. And that's all you're gonna get out of me!"

Toby observed, "It looked to me like Jeffrey was shot in the back because he fell forward away from us. That tells me Waldo shot Jeffrey from this side of the lake. So, Sydney, this is what I think—it doesn't matter whether he's headed home or back to the lodge, he'd still have to come through right where we're standing. Simple logic."

"Good thinking, Toby. I've got an idea how we can get the drop on Waldo, and I don't have time to explain. Toby, I need you to fetch the fishing reel I saw on the table in Jeffrey's cabin." Sydney kept his cane pointed at Karl while Toby, clutching his pistol, took off on his errand.

Trotting back from the cabin, he held out the reel and said, "Well, what now, Mr. Brains?"

"Toby, we're going to wrap Karl up like an Egyptian mummy."

Karl began shaking his head violently. "Hey, what are you guys trying to do? Bertha's going to roast you on a skewer if any harm comes to me. You'll see."

"Shut up, Karl," said Sydney. "I think you'll survive. Quickly, Toby, tie the line around Karl's shoulders—make it tight—and Karl, you'll save yourself some pain by putting your feet together and your hands down at your side. And if you don't stop that motor mouth of yours, I'm going to let Buster turn your chest into a train tunnel." Sydney took pleasure in his use of Hollywood tough guy lingo.

"That should do it, Sydney. I'm finished."

"All right, Karl, start turning around. We're not here to lollygag. I'll feed out the line, Toby, and you wind him like a spool of thread all the way down to his ankles." Karl was spinning like a wobbling top. "What in the devil gave you the idea to do this?" Toby asked.

"Never mind, Toby, not now. If he's not dizzy enough by now to fall over, tip him over and turn him face up. Then, Toby, would you please stuff your handkerchief in that overworked mouth of his. It needs a rest."

Sydney approached with a tie-down stake he found lying near the dock. He worked it through the tightly wound fishing lines and slipped it between Karl's legs near his crotch. "It's not a good idea to move about, Karl." Finding a rock nearby, he pounded the stake down between his legs into the path. "This way, Toby, Karl can't roll over." The task was demanding, and his breath came heavy and fast. Yet he remained focused on the work with determination, knowing that his and Toby's life might depend on how successfully he completed his task. Satisfied that Karl was immobile, Sydney beckoned Toby to follow him into hiding behind Jeffrey's cabin. "Come to it, Toby. We're setting a trap for Waldo. I can't believe you haven't guessed what kind of a trap it is by now."

"With so much going on, I can't say that I've given it a great deal of thought."

"Honestly, Toby, you've seen it a hundred times in big game films. It's a tiger trap—or is it a lion trap? Either way, the natives stake out a live goat as bait, and when the quarry shows up for a tasty meal—bam! End of story."

"Allegorically speaking then, Karl is our goat. Ha—I like it!"

"Now keep your voice down." Putting a finger to his lips, Sydney shushed him. Taking advantage of the silence, birds, in their ignorance, began to chirp again.

*　　*　　*

"Listen, there's someone coming from up lake," whispered Toby. "It must be Waldo."

"Yes, and with all the racket he's making, it sounds like he's running."

Waldo came crashing out of the thicket into the clearing where Karl was squirming like a worm on a fishhook. Running full tilt, he stumbled over Karl and sprawled out on the ground next to him. He left his rifle on the ground and went over to kneel beside Karl.

"What happened to you, Mr. Zecher?" Waldo took off his wool hunting cap to wipe his sweat-drenched forehead. "Bertha must be really mad at you. I don't know if I should untie you or not." His long blond hair flopped down over his weathered cheeks. "Maybe I better go up to the lodge and ask her first." Karl moaned through Toby's handkerchief shaking his head violently back and forth. His eyes were big as chicken eggs. "I guess it wouldn't hurt to take that hanky out of your mouth." Karl moaned again, nodding his head up and down. "Before I do, though, I want you to know that I'm the one who shot Mr. Barstow—just like he asked me to. Can ya believe it? He gave me fifty dollars. Heck, I'd have done it for nothin'. I always liked him, and he was really good t' me."

"Do you believe your ears?" Sydney whispered to Toby, "Let me handle this. I'm going over there."

"Do I have a choice? And what in the name of Hades am I supposed to do in the meantime?"

"You'll know, just follow my drift." Sydney, accompanied by Buster, slipped out from behind the cabin and walked casually up behind Waldo, who was still carrying on a one-way conversation with Karl.

"Waldo, isn't it? Allow me to introduce myself. I'm Sydney Wadsworth." He held out his hand as a gesture of friendship to the thoroughly confused gamekeeper. "It's a good thing my friend, Toby Worthington, and I came along. We're the ones who tied Karl up. If it wasn't for the two of us, he would have stopped you from shooting our friend, Jeffrey."

Waldo blinked, stood up, and brushed his scraggly hair back over his shoulders. "Now, why would Mr. Zecher want t' do something mean like that?"

"You'll have to ask him, but it looks to me like Karl's just fainted. In any case, I want you to meet my friend, Toby. He's a crackerjack marksman like you, and I know he's wanted to meet you ever since we arrived. Excuse him if he seems a little shy. Come on over Toby, and be kind enough to pick up Waldo's rifle and bring it with you."

Waldo was a tall, imposing figure outfitted in tattered hunting clothes. Sinewy and strong, it was immediately obvious from his weathered hands and face that he was suited to an outdoor life in the woods. Sydney judged from Waldo's level of cultivation that the less contact he had with the outside world, the happier he would be.

Toby emerged and picked up Waldo's .30-06 bolt-action rifle. He stopped to open the chamber to make sure it wasn't loaded. "Don't want to be pointing a loaded rifle," he said, walking over to Waldo and handing it to him. "Well hello, I'm Toby. It's good to meet you, Waldo. I've heard a lot about you. Perhaps we could have a little competition one day?"

"Nope, haven't the time. I've got t' git on home to Ma now so I can mail Jeffrey's letter Monday mornin'. He said it was real important, and I'm goin' t' do it. It's already got a stamp on it. By the Cheesuz, after what you told me, I ain't goin' t' let Mr. Zecher take it t' the post office."

"I couldn't agree with you more, Waldo," said Sydney. "You know, Mr. Zecher is married to Bertha Zecher. You've worked for them long enough to know that they must think alike. If he tried to stop you from shooting Jeffrey, it wouldn't surprise me if she'd try to stop you from mailing Jeffrey's letter."

"Judas priest. I didn't think of that. You're right." Waldo scratched behind his ear. "She's damn good with a gun too. That woman's shot most everything on the wall or floor of the lodge. Took her a few years to do it, though. She skinned 'em too. Her daddy taught her how. He was one of those people that got paid to stuff animals." Grimly, he looked out over the lake. "Said she'd skin me too if I didn't keep my mouth shut about the club, and I'd better do whatever damn well she said."

Toby said, "Waldo, after what you did for our friend Jeffrey, we'd like to help you deliver that letter. When did he give it to you?"

"Oh, he'd give me one every time he came up here. I guess it's all right to talk to you. If Jeffrey asks me to shoot him, and I do, then I'm supposed t' mail it. If he doesn't ask me t' shoot him, I give him the letter back when he leaves."

"Those were your instructions?"

"Yup. I'm not too smart, but I've got a good memory. I'll tell ya what the two of us worked out. He told me he could never shoot himself if he had t'. Then he asked me if I would—that is, should the time ever come. Said he'd like to die at the hands of a friend. I couldn't say no. Did I tell ya he gave me fifty dollars to cover expenses?"

Sydney and Toby listened spellbound. Sydney said, "Please go on."

"Well"—Waldo paused at length to watch Jeffrey's boat drift closer to the sawmill—"he told me if he couldn't see a clear way out of his problems, he wanted me t' keep an eye out fer him whenever he was out on the lake. If he stood up and waved his hat several times, that meant I was t' shoot him. Hardest thing I ever had t' do in my whole life was t' pull the trigger."

Toby put his arm around Waldo to comfort him. "Waldo, we know how difficult this must have been for you. You did something we couldn't imagine doing ourselves. What a good friend you've been to Jeffrey!" He could see by looking into Waldo's eyes they had earned his trust. Toby began again slowly, "As Jeffrey's friends, I hope you won't mind telling us who the letter is being sent to."

Waldo took the folded up enveloped from a pocket inside his vest. "I never wasted my time learning t' read, I was too busy working for Pa. If you can read, have at it, but don't open it because I want it back."

"Certainly," said Toby taking the letter. His hands shaking, he groped for his reading glasses. His eyes opened so wide at what he saw, his glasses slid down to the end of his nose. *Good heavens,* he thought, *why in God's name would he send a letter addressed to "Father O'Connor, Chaplain of Brookside Country Club" etc., etc.?* "I don't believe it!" exclaimed Toby.

"Believe what, Toby?"

"Jeffrey's written a letter to Father O'Connor. I had no idea Jeffrey might be Catholic."

*   *   *

At the lodge Bertha was in a stew and asked herself, "Where in hell is Jeffrey?" From her desk drawer she retrieved a pair of binoculars to get a closer look at the lake. To her way of thinking, Jeffrey's short loop around the lake was taking much too long.

Bertha was sure that if Jeffrey were back on shore, Karl would call to let her know, but then again her opinion of Karl had dropped several notches below that of a klutz ever since he lost his stomach for their operation. Through her binoculars, the upper part of the lake was partially obscured from the veranda by tall pines, but when Jeffrey's empty rowboat drifted into view, it jolted her otherwise steely nerves. For her, the sight alone was cause enough for her jaw to drop and the binoculars to follow suit. Only the lanyards kept the glasses from crashing to the floor.

She speculated that Jeffrey probably was dead, that he either drowned, or worse, been shot by their village idiot gamekeeper, Waldo. Waldo wouldn't shoot Jeffrey. They always seemed so buddy-buddy. The only people he might take a shot at were Sydney and Toby because she told Waldo not to let them leave camp, which, to her way of thinking, was the same as issuing a death sentence.

Ordinarily Waldo would be back at the lodge since it was approaching noon, and he always showed up early for his grub on Sunday. Not hearing a shot for a while might be a sign that he's on his way back. Resigned to wait things out, Bertha needed Waldo almost as much as she needed Karl but couldn't decide which of the two she could trust more. Never one to admit a mistake, Bertha allowed herself a brief moment of self-recrimination when she cursed herself for not kicking those two old farts out of her club the minute they walked through the front door.

She retreated to her office and took out her favorite Winchester pump-action shotgun from the gun case. If she had to fight this one out alone, she wanted to fight it out with something she could depend on—her dad's gun. Reminding herself that Freda, the camp cook from hell, always made a lunch for Waldo on Saturday night before she left, Bertha decided to go to the fridge and eat Waldo's grub. Served him right. Besides, she never went into any scrap on an empty stomach. Opening Waldo's sandwich, she discovered a huge slab of roast beef and a love note inside. "Freda's fired when she gets back," Bertha mumbled to herself. "She drinks too much, writes too much, and screws too much. Obviously she's hung up on Waldo, who can't read a stop sign."

Bertha decided there might not be that much to worry about. If Jeffrey's dead, she felt she could deal with that better than any undertaker in Clinton County. Although extremely rare, it wouldn't be the first time the club sent a member to the bottom of the lake, and there was time enough when the dust settled to have a long talk with Karl. As for those two phony fishermen, she hoped they had their last will and testaments in order. Fortified with lunch, she licked her greasy fingers and picked up the intercom to ring Jeffrey's cabin.

After a number of rings, a scratchy voice responded, "Hello, this is cabin number 4."

"I know that!" Bertha was curt and impatient. "I'm looking for Karl. Put him on."

"Is that you, Bertha? This is Sydney Worthington. To answer your question, I'd like to, but he's tied up right now."

"What do you mean 'tied up'?"

"As in tied up."

"Is that so?" Surprised, Bertha's voice quavered slightly, and her tone changed to one a lot less demanding, "Well please untie him and tell me what's happened to Jeffrey."

"I'm afraid I can't oblige you, Bertha. You see Karl offended Waldo in the worst manner possible, and he wants to make sure that Karl remains in his present state of immobility."

"Well, just put Waldo on the line, and I'll straighten this whole thing out."

There was an extended pause before Sydney answered. "He refuses to, and truthfully we are in no position to argue with him."

"I see. You still haven't told me what's happened to Jeffrey. His boat's adrift, and he isn't in it."

After another, but significantly longer, pause, Sydney said, "We know. It's all very sad."

Bertha's worst suspicions were realized, and trying to find out what happened was like pulling teeth out of a hungry bear. "Jeffrey's dead, isn't he?"

"I'm afraid so, Bertha. It's come as quite a shock to Toby and me, especially under the circumstances."

"I understand. You know he was a good friend of mine too. Losing a dear man like Jeffrey must be much too difficult for you to talk about."

Bertha thought if she could get them in her sights for only a moment, it would be goodbye for her two uninvited guests. She smiled when the thought crossed her mind that it would be the first time in sixteen years anyone got a free funeral at Stoney Creek. Conjuring up a special eulogy for them had to wait while her thoughts shifted to baiting a trap for Sydney and Toby.

"Why don't you two dears come up to the lodge? You probably want to get on home. And all your luggage is still waiting here for you. We could have cocktails together, and I'll fix both of you a nice box lunch to go."

"How considerate, Bertha? Thank you. But what about Karl and Waldo?"

"I'd let them sort things out between themselves. It sounds like they both need to do a little cooling off. I'm disgusted with both of them. Karl can be so confrontational when he doesn't get his way."

"In that case we'll come along shortly. Regarding Jeffrey, I assume you'll take care of any inquiry by the authorities?"

"Of course," she said, as sweetly as her "I do" at the wedding where a few guests thought they heard her say, "You'll do." With a new semblance of politeness and civility, she said, "I'll be expecting you then. Bye-bye."

After hanging up, she returned to the gun locker to grab an extra box of shells and her hunting vest from the office cloakroom. She couldn't believe what she just said, but it pleased her to know that she could when she had to. Men—what fools, so easily manipulated they deserve whatever they get. Except for her dad. In her eyes, he was the gold standard, and she missed him terribly.

From the screened-in veranda, Bertha propped a side table against the door leading down to the lake. She knew instinctively that her best shot was from where Sydney and Toby couldn't see her until it was too late. "Ha," she muttered, "I can look right down the throat of the path they'll be on. I can see those two poor bastards now, slowly moving up the final grade as unsuspecting as deer coming to a salt lick. Take a bead at thirty yards—bam, bam—both'll go down like two sacks of grain falling off the back of a pickup." The thought amused her as she took the last bite of Waldo's sandwich.

*   *   *

Sydney hung up the receiver and returned to Toby and Waldo standing next to Karl. "I just got off the telly with Bertha."

"What's the good word, Sydney?" Toby fidgeted with his moustache.

"Not very much on the good side. Bertha's invited us up for a drink and a box lunch to see us on our way out of the club. Generous, but she seems awfully anxious to get rid of us, don't you think?"

Toby said, "Getting rid of us has a whole different meaning according to Karl, doesn't it?" Although Toby felt more secure now with their numerical advantage by virtue of Karl's capture and Waldo's allegiance, it was clear to him that Bertha had a tactical advantage. "If she wants us to leave hastily, she probably means she wants us to stay—permanently."

"You got that right," said Waldo shaking his head. "A lot of people that come here do just that and end up on the bottom of the lake—six or seven a year I calculate." On further reflection he said, "September seems t' be our busiest month."

In utter disbelief, "Really" was the only reply Toby could muster.

Sydney turned bleach white. Steadying himself against a tree, he said, "By the way, Waldo, I've some news for you too. Bertha doesn't seem to care if you leave Karl tied up for a while."

"Suits me fine," said Waldo cracking a smile.

Sydney, relieved, nodded to Waldo and quickly turned to Toby. "I don't think we should accept Bertha's invitation."

"No argument from me. I'd rather charge up San Juan Hill with a bull's-eye tattooed on my forehead than go up against Bertha." Toby reckoned that his remark would place some urgency on Sydney to come up with a plan other than leisurely walking into the wrong end of a shooting gallery.

Sydney pondered how he could use Waldo and Karl as assets instead of liabilities on his balance sheet. *I must be careful not to let Waldo talk to Karl,* he thought. *His allegiance is to the last person he talks to or at best from whomever he gets instruction, so I must keep his mind focused on a one-way track, which is to get Jeffrey's letter mailed. Now Karl's a different kettle of fish. There's certainly no love lost between the mister and missus. He can't help us much being tied up here. With us bottled up, I don't think she's dumb enough to waltz down here to rescue him even though there's no reason for her to think we're armed. Still she may think Waldo's turned into a wild card and can be a danger. Maybe if I went to take a leak, I could come up with a decent scheme.* He glanced at Toby, who must be contemplating something—like coming up with a plan to get them out of there—but more than likely he's daydreaming about an aperitif and lunch at Brookside.

Toby suddenly came to and waved both hands and arms in front of Sydney like a loon taking off, which interrupted Sydney's deep concentration illustrated by his blank hypnotic stare into space. "Sydney, you know a frontal assault is doomed if she's sitting up there with an arsenal of firearms. Do you think one of us could do an end run and go for help?"

"Good thinking, Toby," said Sydney loud enough that Waldo could easily overhear. "If one of us can escape from here with Waldo . . . Jeffrey's letter would get to the post office. Brilliant."

"It is? Yes it is, isn't it?" Toby hadn't the foggiest idea how to follow up his remark with a coherent plan.

"Listen carefully, Toby—Waldo too. It's much too far for us to skirt around the lake, and we don't have that kind of time. Besides, I doubt if either Toby or I have enough left in our tank to walk more than two holes let alone two miles." Sydney's plan evolved as he spoke. He was not in the position of ship's captain as he had been in the navy, so whatever he proffered required Toby's approval and Waldo's cooperation. "Waldo, you could row Toby and yourself across the lake. From here it's out of sight from the lodge. Then you could sneak along the shoreline to the old sawmill."

"That don't sound so good t' me!" said Waldo. "She could pick us off easy with a rifle. Maybe one of you two guys should take the letter to the post office."

"Waldo, we're all in this together—for our friend Jeffrey. A bit of advice though. When this is over, you might want to consider employment someplace else." Waldo banged his forehead with the heel of his hand. It may have been a gesture that indicated he was trying to think of where that elsewhere might be.

"Now then," said Sydney, "back to the plan. True, like Waldo says, it is a risk. But I'll be here to divert Bertha's attention away from the lake. I thought about each of us rowing down the lake, but realistically it will take Toby and me a week to get to the sawmill. Besides, a flotilla like that has a better chance crossing the Dardanelles. Look, Toby"—he pointed to a boat tied up at the dock—"obviously these boats are designed to be operated by one man fishing, max two. They have wide beams, but I dare say aren't more than twelve feet long. There's no freeboard. As an old navy man, I'd say two would be a crowd, and three'd turn it into the *Titanic*, with or without Bertha's help. I think you'll agree our chances are better if we split up." Waldo looked confused and was lost in the conversation long before Sydney got to the Dardanelles.

Greeted with silence, Sydney took it to mean they agreed. Either that or they couldn't come up with a better idea. He looked at Waldo. "Good, it's settled then. The mail will go through." Turning to Toby, he became full of himself again. "Bertha probably thinks we're easy prey, but that's nonsense. I can't think of a single reason why we should consider ourselves underdogs."

"Indeed," Toby agreed. "But, but, I don't like leaving you here, Sydney. I can hold the fort here every bit as well as you."

"I know, Toby, but you go. You're a couple of years younger than I am, and you've got your whole life ahead of you." Sydney thought he was being witty and laughed. "Besides," he continued, "I don't think you have it in you to shoot a woman even if it means saving your own life—no disrespect."

"You're probably right, I don't. I always thought it bad form, but in Bertha's case I might make an exception."

"We're wasting time, no more debating. After you arrive at the sawmill you should be able to get up to the parking lot without Bertha knowing."

Waldo spoke deliberately, "Why don't we open the main gate while we're at it. From the sawmill it's on the way up to lodge. If we're driving out of here, I don't want to be stoppin' for nothin'."

"Thanks, Waldo, now you're on board. You'll be riding out on our motorcycle—Toby drives, you're in the sidecar. Now then how long do think it'll take to row across the lake and down the far side to the sawmill?"

Waldo wiped his nose on his shirtsleeve and gazed up and down the lake. "Maybe ten minutes t' cross and fifteen goin' down lake. I'm not good figurin' time, so put on another five minutes for luggin' your friend here. You can forget the whole time thing if she starts shooting at us because that's when I'll be rowin' up the bank and through the trees."

"Understood, Waldo," said Sydney checking his watch. "Oh, Toby, give Waldo his rifle back, and while you're at it, check your timepiece. I'll give you fifteen minutes before I attract Bertha's attention. Off you go now. I've got a couple of things I need to do first."

With his turned up eyebrows and drooping mustache, Toby resembled a wounded basset hound. "Be careful, Sydney. Even if she is a woman, she can be treacherous, so to speak. And don't you worry one whit about us, we'll get through."

Armed with his cane, Buster, and Jeffrey's pistol, Sydney's fear was overcome by a growing confidence that he could prove himself a worthy adversary. As he watched the rowboat slip away from the dock, he felt a pang of loneliness. For over thirty years, Toby had been constantly at his elbow, dependable in a pinch, and he could always count on him for something as simple as a game of golf.

He said to himself, *I wonder if I'll ever see the old fellow again. Just as well we didn't say good-bye. Nevertheless he could have at least waved back to me. Damn, I don't know if that man can survive without me. I have to hold his hand from one crisis to another. Well, he's on his own now, and so am I. Aha, it looks like Karl's coming around, he's beginning to twitch.*

*   *   *

Bertha was anxiously waiting to see a pair of heads pop up the path into her gun sight. She noticed that it had been a good fifteen minutes since she'd talked to Sydney. "I know it can't take more than five minutes to walk up from the lake," she muttered. "What in hell is taking so long? I asked them real nice." If she called down there again, they'd become suspicious. Bertha suddenly felt, although only for only an instant, that she was getting too old for this kind of work. As a perfectionist, it was becoming harder all the time to live up to her own high standards.

"Dammit," she groaned, "my leg's cramping." Reaching up she grabbed a chair cushion off the nearest rocker and tucked it under her knees. She rose up again to glance over the veranda rail and scan the lake. Nothing unusual, just Jeffrey's boat caught against the outfall at the sawmill. Worried about Karl and Waldo, she figured that it was Waldo who must be screwing everything up, and she didn't know why he was all of a sudden mad at her. Disgruntled, she uttered, "I'm going to find out just how big a vacuum head Waldo is soon enough. There's been too much friggin' in the riggin' going on around here."

This wait with a shotgun in front of an open door gave her more time than she wanted to let her thoughts drift over her twenty years in a hard-up marriage, one that her dad had warned her against. Resigned to the fact that she had been young and a little pig headed, she nonetheless was sorry that she had let Karl con her into marrying him. Now, out of the blue, Karl wanted to pack everything in and start a new life. "Oh, joy, just a couple of decades late for that."

Anxiously, Bertha looked at her watch. Several more minutes had ticked off. By this time Karl should have crossed into Canada on his way to Four Meadows with Jeffrey. She was inflamed at just the thought of it. Like a lightning bolt ready to strike, all her pent-up fury focused on the cause of her problems: Sydney and Toby.

The familiar call of a loon was all that disturbed the silence dominating Quarry Lake. Yet the sense of tranquility was not unlike that of being in the eye of a hurricane. Bertha's ears twitched like that of a frightened hare when she heard the faint voices of men approaching from the boathouses. "Ahhhhh. I may not have much longer to wait," she whispered. "I think my guests are finally about to arrive. They're a little late, but after all, I'm the forgiving type."

The usually unflappable Bertha was paralyzed when Karl popped into view with Sydney following tight behind him. "Karl," she shouted, "I almost shot you, you goddamn idiot! Get out of the way."

"He's got a cane in my back. For God's sake don't try a shot, Bertha, it's too risky."

"A cane? You're kidding? I ought to drop you too. Now move!"

"Bertha, it's a gun! A shotgun."

"Well, let's find out. I don't do Mexican standoffs." His wife shouldered her shotgun. Karl panicked and dove for the shrubbery on the side of the trail, toppling Sydney backwards.

Sydney inadvertently tripped the hair trigger on Buster.

Kaboomm!

The recoil sent Sydney spiraling further back down the trail.

At the same instant, Bertha fired twice.

Kablamm! Kablamm!

One of Bertha's shots winged Karl in full flight, shattering his right arm. The other shot flew well over Sydney and crashed into an overhead pine tree that dropped small twigs and showered him with needles. His wild shot peppered the lodge siding only a few feet away from Bertha. Karl, moaning in pain, grasped his bleeding arm and stopped to glance back over his shoulder at Sydney, looking as if he didn't know who posed more danger—his wife or Sydney? Karl decided to crawl toward the lodge.

Sydney hollered up to the veranda, "Now you've gone and done it. My blazer's ruined. I'm afraid I'll have to decline your invitation for cocktails."

Bertha could not see Sydney from her position. Ignoring Karl, she bellowed, "I invited you and your friend. What happened to him?"

"He asked me to send you his regrets along with a message." Sydney, hurt and lying on his back where he'd come to rest, got off two quick shots with Jeffrey's revolver.

Bang! Bang!

Off line they ripped their way harmlessly high up into the pine branches near the roof of the lodge.

Karl inched his way up the stairs to the veranda where Bertha, with her free hand, jerked him inside. He glared at her. "You crazy bitch, you shot me! Didn't I tell you not to underestimate them? Didn't I?"

"Listen to me, Karl. Get in the kitchen—now—and clean up that wound. It doesn't look that bad. I'll dress it later. I've got other things to do besides fight with you." Wobbly, Karl stumbled off clutching his arm. Bertha, keeping her eye on the trail, called back to Karl, "Sorry you got hit, you know I didn't mean to. Now hurry up and get in there. You're dripping blood all over the floor. I might need your help after I pop these two weasels you let in the gate." Bertha smiled at the thought even though she had suffered a setback in the initial confrontation. Karl was already out of earshot when she asked him what happened to Waldo.

Sydney, still on his back with his feet facing up toward the lodge, decided to keep Bertha's attention focused on him. Buster, lying several feet away, was visibly crippled and out of service. With the revolver held in both hands, he aimed up the slope at the lodge and squeezed the trigger.

Bang!

The shot flew high and to the right of Bertha into the attic space above the main hall. She noticed that the shots fired by Sydney sounded like a small-caliber pistol or a police revolver, and they seemed to come from the same location. Maybe there was a good chance that she winged Sydney too. A protracted standoff with Sydney wasn't a workable solution with his sidekick on the loose somewhere. She observed that his last shot hit the attic and decided to move up there. From the vent hatch she would have a clear shot at him on the trail. Ha, just like finishing off a skunk in a trap. Before she could move, a sharp unfamiliar voice came from the main hall behind her.

"State police. Put the gun down slowly." Shocked, she lowered the shotgun to the floor. "Now, put your hands up behind your head."

"Police? Oh, thank God you're here. You're just in time to help. I caught two trespassers trying to rob us. One of the thieving bastards shot my husband! He'll tell you. I've got one of them nailed down now on the trail." Hesitantly, she turned toward the officer, "Well, are you just going to stand here and let him get away?"

"It won't work, Mrs. Zecher." Jim Barnes steadied his revolver on Bertha. "In the last few minutes we've learned a great deal about your operation here."

"Now that you think you know so goddamn much, you stupid ape, show me your warrant!"

"Sorry, old girl, under the circumstances I don't need one."

Jim yelled from the veranda, "Wadsworth, state police, you can put down your weapon now. It's all over. Are you hurt?"

Painfully raising himself to sitting position, Sydney shouted back, "Not exactly, but I'm glad you came along, officer. Toby and I are very much beholden to you."

"You may not think so when I get my hands on you two. I've got a few questions I'd like answered." Jim turned his attention back to Bertha, "As for you, Mrs. Zecher, get up and back away from the door nice and slow."

Nancy bounded onto the veranda and moved in next to Jim. "I've already had the pleasure of meeting your husband, Bertha, and I'm happy to report that Mr. Zecher is handcuffed to the kitchen range."

Without looking away from Bertha, Jim told her that Officer Sullivan was going to pat her down for weapons.

"My pleasure, Officer Barnes," said Nancy, "and Mrs. Zecher, when I tell you I'm finished, I want you to drop your hands behind your back. Then I will be placing you in handcuffs."

Like an electric blender set on high, Bertha's mind tried to whip up any way possible to break out of her present dilemma. *God almighty, Daddy! I could use a little of your help right now.* She squirmed and shuddered as Nancy removed a hunting knife strapped to the outside of one of her boots. She reacted to the handcuffs like an animal in a hunter's trap and struggled against them though she knew it would only create further discomfort.

Her mind raced on ahead. She surmised that no hack attorney was going to get her out of this jam. Karl no doubt would spill his guts to save his own skin. She guessed she couldn't blame him after she shot him. Ha, she realized that she'd have been better off if she killed him. After all these years, how did this business blow up in her face? It's that damn Sydney and Toby. She vowed those two country club dandies would pay dearly even if she had to come back from the dead. Bertha gritted her teeth and resolved that for her dad's sake she wouldn't let her life come down to the finish line like this.

She groused to Nancy, "I don't deserve this kind of treatment. No judge will send me to prison for bumping off crooks. Ha, when I tell a jury how I've been doing the law's dirty work for them all these years, their attitude's going change a whole bunch. I might even get a medal."

*   *   *

During the fracas, Sydney had wrenched his back and pinched a nerve for good measure. Painfully, he worked his way up the path to the bottom step of the veranda, where he decided to go no further. Hearing voices on the veranda, he called out, "Officer, whatever your name is, tell me please what's happened to my friend, Toby."

"My name's Barnes, Jim Barnes." He walked through the open veranda door and went down the steps to join Sydney. "We met Thursday, remember? I'm too busy to talk right now, so I'll have to get back to you." Looking at Sydney's tattered clothes and scraped up hands and face, he said, "Give me your hand, and I'll drop you off in the main hall with your friend."

"For that, I'd be most appreciative. Is Toby all right?"

"Mr. Worthington's all right, just bunged up and wiped out. He's resting, so don't be alarmed." Jim steadied Sydney's slow and painful climb up the stairs and steered him on a course to the main hall where Toby was sprawled out on a divan.

Sydney noticed that Toby had closed his eyes, and his open mouth fluttered as he breathed in huge chunks of air. Toby appeared oblivious to the racket Bertha was making while Nancy literally dragged her off to Jim's patrol car. For once, Bertha had met her match physically, and she showed her displeasure by screaming a stream of blue epithets.

Sydney was shocked to see how pale and worn-out Toby looked. For a man who took so much pride in his appearance regardless of the place or occasion, it was not often that Toby appeared disheveled. Toby didn't stir when Sydney slumped down into the same sofa. He thought it best not to disturb a resting volcano and decided he could use a breather too.

Half awake, Sydney noticed Nancy coming back in the front door. As she whisked by Sydney he called out, "Hello, are you lost, girl?" She stopped short when he asked, "What in blazes are you doing in this human cesspool? I can understand your wanting to get away from Chief Bebee, but this is no place for a nice, attractive young woman like yourself—contending with the likes of these villainous crooks."

"I guess that's a compliment, Mr. Wadsworth, but what I'm doing right now has a lot to do with you. We can discuss that later. We've got two in custody now, and one of them needs medical attention."

"Good, well you keep an eye on Bertha. She's a real dreadnought if there ever was one. Oh, and on your way, would you please tell Officer Barnes I'd like a word."

"Luckily, he just walked up behind you. I have to go."

Sydney got the trooper's attention with a hand wave, "Officer Barnes, have you come across a chap by the name of Waldo?"

"Oh, yes. Nancy, ah . . . I mean Officer Sullivan. She and I were down at the main gate trying to figure out how to get through when he ran up out of nowhere and opened it. Lucky for you, right?"

"Indeed, and you arrived not a moment too soon. But if Waldo's outside, go easy with him. He's not a bad sort. Just fell off the balance beam if you take my meaning. And I want to be sure the letter he's been given to mail gets to the post office."

"Post office?" Jim registered a quizzical look. "We'll worry about the post office later after I get some backup here and find a doctor for Zecher.

I've got a whole lot of stuff here that needs to get nailed down." Shaking his head, Jim smiled as he turned away and joked, "Don't leave town."

After Jim left to make his calls, Sydney rose from the sofa with a painful groan. He stumbled over to Bertha's reception desk where he removed the club membership ledger and opened it. Sure enough, he said to himself, this is all the evidence the state needed to electrocute Karl and Bertha several times over. Hmmmm, it wouldn't surprise me if these are the names of some of America's most wanted gangsters. Huh, no wonder the law couldn't find these goons. They're members of Karl and Bertha's perfectly innocent little rod and gun club. Sydney felt dizzy and weak. *My, my, looky here. She's marked off those who went fishing in Canada and came back to try their luck again in the States.* He turned the page to discover a few members left for Canada and didn't bother to come back, or the Mounties got them and they couldn't renew their membership. *Hmmmm—not many.* Ahhh-ha, and the big black *X* marked the names of guests and the dates they were sent to the bottom of Quarry Lake. Sydney dry swallowed when he saw that the last two entries at the bottom of that list were his and Toby's as "Guests of Jeffrey Barstow."

Sydney returned to the sofa with the ledger and collapsed. He clutched it tightly to his chest with both hands and closed his eyes, content with the knowledge that their mission was rapidly approaching a satisfactory conclusion.

20

Return to Brookside

Ten days had passed since Sydney and Toby returned to Brookside. Their newfound aches and pains had subsided to the point where they could appreciate their old persistent ones. With the book closed on Jeffrey, Chief Bebee went back to writing traffic tickets and was well advised to leave Brookside in peace.

On the club veranda overlooking the course, Sydney and Toby were seated in their usual after-lunch rocking chairs. Anticipating a warm day, Toby was decked out in his ancient seersucker club blazer punctuated with a fresh red carnation and a new never-to-be used handkerchief. Sydney's attire was much less flamboyant. His starched white togs made a perfect canvas for a splash of color in the form of a paisley ascot and cordovan wingtips, and to complete his outfit he topped it all off with a straw boater and black-rimmed sunglasses. Toby was busy packing his pipe when Sydney asked, "How did you like the obit I wrote up for Jeffrey? I cleared it with Harriet. She seemed disinterested and told me to go do whatever."

Toby leaned back in the rocker to reflect on the question. "I thought it said all that really needed to be said. Nice personal touches as I recall." To refresh his memory, he picked the local newspaper off the deck where he'd left it and turned to the obituary section.

Jeffrey Masters Bartholomew 18__-8/15/1948

Eight years a resident of Livermore Falls, New York, Jeffrey M. Bartholomew died suddenly in a fishing accident in Table Rock, New York. The body was not recovered. A lifelong sporting enthusiast, he was a proud member of the Brookside Country Club for eight years, and he will be missed by many of the club members who knew him. He maintained a 26 golf handicap. He is survived by his wife and sole beneficiary, Harriet Bartholomew, also a member of Brookside Country Club and longtime resident of Livermore Falls.

A memorial service will be held in the chapel of the First Congregational Church on Main Street followed by a tea in the church parlor. August 27, 1948, 3:00 p.m. Please: No flowers.

"I thought it hit the mark. No need to put all the laundry out on the line to dry." Sydney was quite pleased with himself and decided that a fresh cigar would be a proper reward for his adept writing skill. "Sad though, isn't it? Jeffrey was such a tragic figure."

"So was Waldo. Never did get his last name. When the time comes we'll have to put a good word in for him. The poor devil deserves some consideration. Besides saving our lives, I thought he had a lot of admirable qualities."

"You're quite right, Toby. Some ambitious prosecutor might like to feather his nest by portraying Waldo as some sort of hit man. But I think our testimony can knock that issue off the table." He took several puffs on his cigar while Toby worked on relighting his pipe. "Since you brought up the subject of Waldo, I think I've just spawned an idea that might appeal to the governor. I'll broach it with him when we get together Saturday."

"Well, what is it, or am I going to be left guessing all day?"

"Don't you think the Stony Creek Rod & Gun Club would make a good psychiatric care facility for the state? It's all there—the rooms, kitchen, recreation, fences, the whole nine yards."

"You always amaze me, Sydney. I think the gov just might go for it. Ha—wouldn't it drive Bertha and Karl crazy if they wound up incarcerated there?"

"Wouldn't it just." Sydney smiled. "It's getting a bit hot out here. Let's move to the tea room where we can chat about the governor's visit."

Inside, workmen were scrubbing away ash and soot from windowsills. The collapsed outside wall of the kitchen was still lying on the ground, which demonstrated how badly wounded the clubhouse was from the explosion on Friday the thirteenth. Large floor fans pushed damp moldy air out through doors and windows that were jammed open. The tea room was relatively unscathed, and the club manager saw to it that it was stocked with complimentary beverages and light fare from the town's hospitality tent, mostly for the likes of Sydney and Toby, who relished privacy and personal attention. Toby lifted the damp napkin on a tray of finger sandwiches to view the selection while Sydney banged on the wing chair seat cushions checking for dust.

"Coffee or tea, Toby?" With most of the employees on temporary leave or cleaning up the premises, members served themselves.

"Tea. Too early for a scotch I suppose. I'm not sure how all this business of a visit from the governor came about. And why? According to Sandy, he more or less invited himself and his entourage to the club before you even had a chance to get your sea legs back. That took a lot of brass."

"Yes, well it seems that I'm always on some politician's hit list when they want a favor or contribution, especially during an election year." Sydney sat down, put his teacup on a side table and dropped his cigar butt into a pedestal ashtray. "I think it was last Wednesday when the club got a follow-up call from his man Skillings. First off, Sandy told me that the governor wants to help shoot off our cannon to start the tournament on September 3."

"Oh well, there can't be much harm in it. The board's sure to go along," said Toby before tossing down a ham and cheese sandwich. "He knows there'll be a crowd, and it'll be an opportunity for him to do some backslapping politicking."

"It may have slipped my mind at the time, Toby, but Skillings also told Sandy that the governor was having a special medal struck for us. It's to honor our service as some sort of civilian crime fighters. The governor describes us as heroes and wants to present them to us in a public ceremony here."

"How awkward," fumed Toby. "This is after all still a private club, and frankly I have all the medals I require. I don't need another campaign button stamped out of recycled bottle caps." He sighed. "Something else we'll have to soldier through."

"Relax, Toby. Have another sandwich." Sydney saw through Toby's objections as part of his reluctance to be in the limelight for anything. "Apparently, we were instrumental in breaking up one of the largest crime operations in the country. Dewey's built quite a reputation as a crime fighter, don't you know. Obviously, he wants to acknowledge how modest citizens like us can be a great asset to law enforcement. If he wants to show us off as role models, let's suffer through it and give the subject a rest for now."

Before entering the tea room, Sandy Cummings stopped to adjust his club tie and announce his presence by clearing his throat. "I'm glad I found both of you here. You're celebrities all over the country. It's in all the papers. But of course you know that." Sandy mistakenly thought they would be pleased to learn about their fame. Observing their dour looks, Sandy's smile wilted. He decided to quickly change the subject. "Anyway, Mr. Worthington, you'll be pleased to know that I've been able to lay in a new supply of charges for the cannon."

"Good work, Sandy, said Toby. I want you to know how pleased I am with everything you've done to bring the club back to form. Sydney is too. I see you got the front nine back in play for the Wadsworth Cup. And to your credit you've got the whole damn town behind the effort." Toby broke out laughing. "Sandy, have a sandwich."

He declined politely and turned to leave when he remembered that "Father O'Connor is looking for both of you. He's been out playing the back nine by himself. He should be finishing his round soon."

Sydney nodded. "Thanks, Sandy. We'll go out now to wait for him." Whatever it was, he suspected that it must have to do with the letter Waldo mailed from Jeffrey. Both men, with their hands clasped behind their backs, began a leisurely stroll around the grounds. There was a great deal for them to reflect upon in the past week, and their homecoming was awash with interviews and intensive interrogations by both Bebee and the state police.

"Getting back to Harriet," said Toby, "I find the results of the test on Jeffrey's medication rather baffling, don't you? The report gave no conclusive evidence of tampering according to Bebee."

"Baffling, yes. But that doesn't mean she didn't try or even succeed for that matter. For someone with a bad heart, the mere suggestion that one's medication was tampered with could in itself cause severe stress and a coronary. Hence, old fellow, speech becomes a perfect murder weapon. But now that Harriet's in the clear, and with Jeffrey out of the way, you may have risen to the top of her list of potential consorts."

"Really, Sydney, you go too far!"

"Sorry, just musing. We're lucky to be in the clear ourselves. If it wasn't for Nancy and Jim, we might be swimming with Jeffrey."

"Good lord, yes." Toby, breaking into a sweat, borrowed Sydney's handkerchief to wipe his dripping brow. "And if it weren't for her testimony, both of us could have wound up in the hoosegow."

"Especially you, Toby." Sydney smiled as he thought back to Toby's several recent misadventures. "Your antics in the Mountainview Inn come to mind."

Suddenly Sydney stopped in his tracks. His tone was vexed and serious. "Did you know that clutz Bebee was torn between giving Nancy a promotion and firing her? When I found that out, the chief and I came to a little understanding—if he wanted my $500 contribution to the policeman's ball."

"I heard about her promotion, but I didn't know you were influential." Toby laughed so hard and at such length he began to cough and snort. "Lester got a promotion too."

"Not a word about my involvement, Toby. Frankly, if I know anything about human nature, that state policeman, Jim what's-his-name, is going to pluck Nancy right out of Livermore Falls anyway. I've never personally known love, but I think I know what it is when I see it."

*　　*　　*

Instead of chipping up to the eighteenth green, Father O'Connor picked up his ball and headed straight to where Sydney and Toby stood waiting. After a few cordial exchanges, Father O'Connor returned to his golf bag and withdrew an envelope. As he brought it back he asked, "Why do you suppose I got a letter from Jeffrey Barstow?"

"Father, it's simple really," chimed Toby. "Jeffrey Barstow is our Jeffrey Bartholomew."

"Please, Mr. Worthington, give me a little credit for figuring that out."

"I believe," said Sydney, "that you were Jeffrey's closest connection to a church. He could trust you to keep things confidential to put a point on it. After all, you are our club chaplain."

Toby could not contain his curiosity. "Anything perhaps we should know? Like things we don't know already."

Father Michael blanched but pressed on. "The letter is really in two parts. The first part is a confessional more or less. He's remorseful for a number of crimes he committed, and they're all itemized. As you can imagine, Jeffrey came to the realization that he'd taken a wrong turn in the road a long time ago. Now then, perhaps you fellows can shed some light on why he asks forgiveness for a Waldo Crampton."

"It's like this, Father," said Toby. "Waldo was the instrument of Jeffrey's fishing accident that was mentioned in his obituary. That pretty much sums it up." Up to now, details concerning Jeffrey's demise were not public knowledge, and if Sydney and Toby had their way, Jeffrey's death would be a mystery for a long time.

"I see, or do I?" said Father O'Connor shaking his head. "Jeffrey apparently didn't have a will and didn't mention any family outside of his wife. Now we come to the second part. It states that all his personal effects and possessions will go to Harriet."

"Yes," said Sydney, "I felt that might be the case. Before we left the Stoney Creek Club, we made sure that his belongings would be forwarded to her. We had to have our things sent back to us as well. Oh, except that our motorcycle had to go on a trailer to Peach Hill, but that's another story."

"It is, isn't it?" Father Michael, reading to himself, worked his way further down the letter to note the oddity he sought. "Now this is the reason I wanted to talk to you two fine fellows today. The only possession he designated left to anyone other than Harriet was his steamer trunk. The beneficiary is the Brookside Caddy Fund with Mr. Wadsworth and Mr. Worthington as trustees. May I assume you'll take up matters from here?"

"Of course, of course, Father Michael," Sydney's voice cracked. He fanned himself with his boater. "It seems unusually hot for this time of year. I think Toby and I would like to have a little sit-down." His mind raced back to Jeffrey's cabin. "My god," he thought, "there's a small fortune in cash hidden in that trunk! In the ruckus, I forgot all about it. Toby must remember the trunk. Cripes, it's going to end up with Harriet if it hasn't already. Flashing back to his recent conversation with Harriet concerning Jeffrey's obit, he remembered that she was going to call a junk dealer and throw out everything that belonged to Jeffrey." Sydney whispered to Toby that they had to get their hands on that steamer trunk with no one else the wiser. "As trustees we owe it to Jeffrey and the caddies, don't you know."

After his initial shock wore off, Toby collected his thoughts and croaked, "Of course we do. No question about it."

Out of curiosity, Father Michael leaned in to join their conversation, "You gentlemen look a little wobbly. Something you'd like to share with me?"

Toby responded, "Only that Jeffrey always had a good heart when it came to the lads. Mentioned all the time how hard the caddies worked lugging our golf bags, how they needed a good education and a chance to grow up on the straight and narrow. I know my caddy, Oliver, could use a little shove in the right direction." Looking into Father Michael's eyes he said, "Don't you think this gesture of Jeffrey's was his way of making amends?"

"Perhaps, but it's only a trunk." Father O'Connor remained puzzled but satisfied that there was nothing more that he could do. "You don't suppose there's something of value in the trunk?"

Toby replied, "Father, we haven't looked, but it would seem likely, and we do have hope."

Father Michael lit a cigarette, folded the letter back into the envelope, and stuffed it into his back pocket. Walking off the course, he looked back, smiled, and shook his head at the two men jabbering their heads off as they returned to the clubhouse.

*   *   *

Still at the club hours later, Sydney and Toby were reclining comfortably in Adirondack chairs with their backs to the sun overlooking the empty pond upwind from its decomposing crusty bed. The bell in the village church steeple chimed at four o'clock that all was well between heaven and earth. They imagined their beloved pond being full again and recalled the imposing challenge it presented to hit a ball over it to the safety of the fairway beyond. Both were dreaming of days past and days to come, sipping the sweet and tart of lemonade. Toby didn't notice Sydney's right hand fall from his chair to touch the grass or his chin drop to be cradled in his ascot.

Simone, now an employee of Brookside, wriggled her way across the clubhouse lawn and whispered softly in Toby's ear, "There's a call for you, Mr. Worthington. It's Harriet Bartholomew."

THE END

Edwards Brothers, Inc.
Thorofare, NJ USA
October 18, 2011